STARS OVER ABUNDANCE

THE ABUNDANCE SERIES: BOOK 4

SHANNA SWENSON

SHANNA SWENSON

WITH A TOUCH OF Reality

Stars over Abundance
Shanna Swenson

Stars over Abundance is an original work of fiction. Names, characters, places, organizations and incidents either are the product of the author's imagination or are used fictitiously. Any resemblance to actual persons, living or dead, events, or locales is entirely coincidental.

www.shannaswenson.com

❀ Created with Vellum

FOREWORD

To my readers:

This book is the by-product of a scene—completely unplanned—that happened during Book 3, *Escape from Abundance*. I didn't even know it was going to happen until I'd already written it...and once I did, I **knew** that the series would have to continue because Buck and Vivian needed their very own book too.

What follows is their story—along with the stories of two other characters that needed a happily ever after too ;-)

Enjoy your trip back to Abundance and stay tuned for a sneak peek (at the back of this book) into the Abundance finale—Savannah's story—Book 5: *ABUNDANCE LEGACY.*

PROLOGUE

$\mathcal{V}$ ivian Alexander sighed heavily and looked out onto the crowded dance floor of the luxurious Austere Hotel, one of Dallas's finest. She stood at the bar sipping a dirty martini with extra olives, wearing only a ridiculously expensive black lace Dolce and Gabbana dress, silver heels that were far more uncomfortable than the outrageous price tag claimed, and a matching silver comb that had been used to sweep her long sandy blonde hair up into a French twist.

She'd been dreading this charity ball all week, but her manager had *insisted* she go. Jill Bradley had been her manager for the last twelve years. And she'd been a good one, so when she told Vivian to do something, she did it— even if she grumbled incessantly about it along the way. But Vivian had actually been right this time. This "charity ball" was nothing more than a stuffy charade for a bunch of pompous jerks. It was all about appearances...and money. That's why she'd wanted to avoid it. Helping Heroes had received a rather large donation from her and all the hundreds of other celebrities in attendance. Vivian felt her contribution was more than enough of a bargaining chip, but no, Jill asserted that Viv absolutely *had* to make an appearance, albeit it be a short one. Jill was accurate of course. After all, it was good exposure and showed Vivian's commitment to the cause of donating and volunteering her time with underprivileged children. Plus, Vivian *had* been super engrossed in her work lately—what with multiple films and projects—and she'd not graced a gala or event in quite some time, so of course she'd found it prudent to acquiesce.

The Ponderosa Ballroom was indeed a lovely one with its fifty-foot ceilings and sparkling, cascading hand-cut crystal chandeliers. There were ice sculptures and bubbling marble fountains, cocktails were overflowing, and hors d'oeuvres were being passed around by waiters in white suits and black bowties. The ballroom was dimly lit with circling blue and gold disco balls and music streamed out of the speakers—poppy classical from the quartet playing nearby. It wasn't unlike any other charity ball Viv had ever attended.

Although she looked like a million bucks, Vivian felt as out of place here as a vegan at a Texas BBQ, but she plastered on that perfect smile that had made her famous, nodded to the stars she knew, and tried to keep to herself as much as possible. She wanted to quickly ride this façade out and go up to her room within the hour. Maybe she'd settle into the oversized, jetted jacuzzi tub with a glass of wine and simply enjoy the quiet for a change, or cuddle up and read the spicy romance novel Jill had thrown into her bag to relax her.

Vivian Alexander was an extrovert through and through. She'd always enjoyed being the center of attention and absolutely loved being an actress. Over the last fifteen years, she'd gotten used to being photographed, interviewed, stalked—followed by the media for every little move she made—and never getting an ounce of privacy to herself. She literally lived in the spotlight almost every single second of every single day. But one thing she couldn't stand was phoniness, faking it for appearance's sake. The founders of Helping Heroes were nothing but a gang of high and mighty corporate bigots, and Viv couldn't stomach them!

Vivian remembered that she was there for the kids and forced herself to move back into the crowd. It wouldn't help for the photographers to come around and see her standing off to herself, appearing to be sulking. She could just see the headline now:

Hollywood starlet found pouting at charity ball- Is it a new beau or is she simply feeling the effects of* middle-age*?

Vivian had seen a similar tabloid already. She was thirty-five years old now and felt her biological clock ticking ever louder as each day passed. Leave it to every media outlet to capitalize on the one short-coming Vivian had so far; her lack of a husband and children.

It had been an embarrassing lull in the interview with Naomi Wiley, one of the top talk show hosts on prime-time TV, as she'd asked Vivian when she planned to finally settle down. Viv hadn't expected the random question; it was completely off topic for one thing and highly personal for another.

Vivian had been so busy with her career she hadn't had time to think about settling down. She'd absorbed herself in the Kinsen children since she had none of her own and was too busy spoiling them and trying to keep up with their goings-ons. She hadn't really been looking for love; not to mention the last two men she'd dated had been *total* ass-hats.

She waved to Leonard Parker, a well-known director and former producer for one of her movies- *Destiny of Promise*, and greeted Trent Mooney, her former co-star. They talked for a bit as he introduced his wife, Jennifer, and she began to tell Vivian about their new baby. Vivian groaned internally. It wasn't that she didn't love babies, but it seemed the entire universe was trying to tell her something right now she wasn't quite ready to hear.

When she could finally pull herself away from the conversation that seemed to last ten years, she moved towards the frame of the French door and grabbed a glass of champagne from one of the passing trays, replacing her empty martini glass in its place. She downed it, the bubbles burning in her throat. That wasn't gonna do it!

She headed back to the bar.

"Martini, extra dirty," Vivian murmured to the handsome young bartender clad in a black button-down shirt who'd served her the same thing not just ten minutes prior. He nodded and gave her a grin. He had beautiful ebony skin and blonde hair with big chocolate brown eyes not unlike Vivian's.

"Rough night?"

"You could say that," Vivian flirted and winked.

Once he handed the martini over, she sipped it and immediately turned to avoid his eyes. He was giving her a look she was all too familiar with; not that she wouldn't enjoy a hot night with a young stud such as himself; it had been a four-month "dry spell" for her after all. But he was genuinely *far* too young for her and God forbid, that was the last thing she needed for the media to see at this moment in her life— A young college-aged kid leaving her hotel room in the walk of shame. Especially, after she'd been called out for being *middle-aged*.

She thanked him, handed over a generous cash tip from her black Michael Kors wristlet, smiled at him, and walked forward.

She froze in her tracks at the sight of a face she knew well but had surprisingly never been formally introduced to. It was the black cowboy hat that sat on his head—his trademark—that made him immediately recognizable.

"Howdy, ma'am."

Vivian shivered at the deep Texas drawl. "Howdy yourself, cowboy," Vivian murmured back and grinned playfully at the blond-haired, blue-eyed sex god before her. She felt the mind-numbing effects of the alcohol start to move through her system as she extended her hand to him.

"I don't reckon you and I have ever *officially* met. I'm Buck Jenkins."

"Vivian Alexander," her sultry voice rasped out.

He took her hand and brought it up to his lips, rubbing her knuckles ever so lightly with their full softness before tenderly kissing her prickling flesh. She gasped internally and bit into her bottom lip. Her pulse quickened, and she almost moaned aloud.

Her night had just gotten *exciting*.

"I see you're enjoying this shindig about as much as I am." He kept her hand as he brought it down in front of them.

"Glad to see I'm not the *only* one who's bored."

"Yeah, this is about as much fun as a sex-less frat party."

Vivian laughed, genuinely, for the first time all night as she gazed back into his ruggedly handsome face with his square jaw and dazzling baby blue eyes. She took in his black Versace suit and bowtie. His muscular body filled it out so nicely.

Buck Jenkins had been a defensive end in the NFL for almost twenty years. He'd played for the San Antonio Stallions his entire career and finally retired about a year ago. He'd headed home to Abundance not long after he'd announced his retirement and started a foundation, Buck's Buckaroos, for both disabled children and cancer research. He'd been out of the spotlight as of the last couple months even though he'd started to dabble in the movie business. She suddenly wondered where he'd gone and what he'd been up to.

"Well... I've always wanted my very own damsel in distress." The promise in his words made her center throb. In that moment, she wanted to know what this gorgeous cowboy tasted and felt like pressed naked against her.

"Hmm, I didn't realize the auditions were open," she cooed.

"They certainly are *now*." His eyebrows went up. "Wanna dance?"

"Absolutely."

He turned and pulled her away from her hiding spot at the bar area and into the crowd of rich and famous people. He led them onto a hard-wood dance floor where the gold, blue, and white lights shimmered across his broad back and all around them like stars bursting in the night sky.

Vivian smiled as he spun her around and into his hard-muscled chest, one of his big arms encircling her waist, his hand taking the one of hers that didn't hold the martini. Her free hand clasped his and she admired the size of his palm and length of his long fingers. She'd always been a sucker for big-muscled men. Her young and fleeting infatuation with Jack Kinsen all those years ago probably had everything to do with that.

Buck's head leaned down to look into her face, and she gulped suddenly at the intensity reflecting in his eyes.

"How is that we're best friends with the same exact people, yet I've never had the *pleasure* of meeting you until now?"

Vivian shrugged. *Good question.*

She'd been to Abundance, Buck's hometown, many times to see the Kinsens for the kid's birthdays, holidays, and get-togethers. Yet never once had she ever seen this man face to face. They, of course, lived different kinds of lives. He was a pro football player, and she was a movie star. She never got an off-season, whereas Buck had gotten to spend about half of his year off the field as on. She traveled constantly and was always on the go, and the few opportunities she'd gotten to spend time in Abundance, were short and sweet—just a few days—then it was back to the grindstone.

"Well, I deeply regret now that I didn't make it a point to seek you out," he murmured.

Vivian deeply regretted that herself as his big smile took her breath away.

She scolded herself slightly as her hips swayed with his to the harmonic sounds of violin, cello, and piano that beckoned to them from the subwoofers overhead; never had classical music sounded or felt quite so good as it did in this moment.

She was well aware of the type of reputation Buck Jenkins had. Everyone was… Hell, this was showbusiness! Being in the limelight assured that the entire world knew as much as possible about every star there was to know. He was a womanizer and as much as her brain tried to remind herself of that fact, her heart was floating on a puffy pink cloud that hovered just in view of his sexy self.

"You're a graceful dancer for a man of your size," she purred as she looked up into his gorgeous eyes.

"Sit that empty glass down and I'll *show* you graceful." Maybe it was those perfectly shaped eyebrows that raised in challenge, but again, Vivian found herself biting into her lip at the power of his eyes and his words…and his hands.

God, he was *so* hot! No wonder women dropped their panties in his presence. He was one handsome—and charming—devil! She was going to get a ride on this wild cowboy before the night was through, she knew beyond the shadow of a doubt. She'd gotten a little taste of one before—a real one—Tad Walters, but they'd only made out and it had been somewhat clumsy. Well, of course it had, they'd both been young and amateurish.

Vivian could see there wasn't one ounce of clumsiness in the man before her. He was older than her, more experienced, and a keen sexual prowess oozed from every pore of his skin. Every move he made was deliberate and planned; he knew exactly what he was doing, to her…and her body.

He steered them ever closer to the edge of the dance floor with slow, easy movements until Buck plucked the glass from her fingers and dropped it easily onto a passing tray. He gave her a crooked grin that made her insides quiver.

"You know the tango, Viv?"

"Do I?" she stated with confidence, and his sexy smile turned down right naughty. Her skin bristled with anticipation.

Buck cued up the string quartet next to them, and before Vivian knew it, they were in the middle of the classic Latin American dance.

He moved lithely and with intent, and she kept sync with him as he led her into a heart-pounding, mind-blowing show for all to see. Their audience had moved aside, eager to see the dance probably few of them knew and even fewer had ever seen performed live. It was graceful and beautiful and intensely sensual as he spun her and dipped her and carried her away, her legs wrapping around him and lunging out at the appropriate times in the style and rhythm of the music. His hands moved expertly over her, caressing her as a lover would, as their feet flew swiftly in cadence to the rhythm. They ended with an erotic dip, her extended back splayed over his big thigh, one hand cupping her neck, the other gripping her extended leg, his nose pressed to hers.

It was one of the most sexual experiences she'd ever had outside of a bedroom, and her entire body was tingling and fully aroused as she breathlessly gazed into the sky-blue eyes burning deep lust into hers. She gave him a sultry smile as he brought them upright then flung her arm out as they both bent into a bow. For all their pretentious audience knew, it had all been well-rehearsed and acted out just for their amusement, but Vivian comprehended Buck's intentions all too well. They were both performers after all, and she'd just auditioned, passed his test, and been given the part- a part in a very carnal game. A test of wills and dominance. Buck was a player, after all. And he played to win.

He pulled her back into his arms for a slow dance as the shock and awe of their explicit dance wore off from the onlookers. He gave her a big hearty laugh that made Vivian giddy.

"Now *that* was fun! We'll be the talk of the ball for sure. Hope you don't mind..." he trailed off as his eyes slid over her.

"I live for the spotlight as I'm sure you do!"

It wasn't a lie. Vivian was used to it. And Buck had apparently not gotten enough of it in the prime of his stardom.

"Someone needed to give these people something to talk about tomorrow." He winked. "They see *I'm* not leaving here empty-handed tonight."

"Is that so?" His arrogance amused her even if it *was* true- he knew he had her now: line, hook, and sinker.

"Well, now that you've seen what I can do on the dancefloor... just wait 'til you see what I can do in the bedroom," he whispered provocatively into her ear as his long fingers toyed with the shape of her collarbone. She fought the urge to moan aloud as her heart pounded in her ears, as much from his touch as from the dance they'd just performed.

"What makes you think I'm that type of girl, Buck? You only just met me!"

"Don't kid yourself, Viv." His mouth lowered to replace his fingers, and she almost whimpered. "We've known each other a long time."

It was somewhat true. After all, they'd heard all about one another over the expanse of so many years, but that didn't change the fact that she didn't know him like she should before hauling herself to bed with him.

She tried to come to her senses then even as his tongue lapped at her pulse point, drowning her in overwhelming and all-encompassing desire.

"Buck," she cried breathlessly and pulled away suddenly.

His eyes were dark as they flew up to hers. He was a physical warrior, used to getting what he wanted with aggression and strength, and he didn't like not having dominance over her. She smiled as much to herself as to him and cocked an eyebrow.

"I have to go bid on a painting for the auction first."

"Well, in that case, I'll accompany you."

They moved from the dance floor then, her arm through Buck's. One of their ostentatious hosts began a speech as they entered a separate room off to the west of the massive ballroom. It was set up gallery style with paintings on the walls illuminated with tubular lights shining down on them. Buck stopped at one of the more colorful paintings and he grimaced at it.

"They call *this* art?" he scoffed and shook his head.

"Well, *some* people call it that," Vivian corrected, indicating she wasn't one of them.

"Not all people can be as amazing as our little Savannah, I reckon."

"She *is* quite talented, isn't she?" Vivian smiled, thinking about the sweet thirteen-year-old girl that was more like a blood relative than not and how her landscapes put the viewer right into the action.

They walked slowly, deliberately, as their eyes skirted over each painting, other couples passed by, whispering quietly in the alcove-like room as if they were in a library instead of a charity gala.

Buck stopped at one particular scene, and Vivian almost laughed.

It was a sexually primed painting of a knight—set for battle—with a helmet in his hand, clinging to his lover; a woman scantily clad, one breast exposed with her head thrown back in the throes of both passion and anguish as his lips descended to her throat. Tears flowed down her face, and the knight's brows were drawn in a profound sadness.

The painting made Vivian uncomfortable. The sorrow emanating from it tore through her, but Buck smiled provocatively as he only saw the sexuality that the scene drew forth. "Now this one is worth the price tag."

"One hundred thousand, huh?"

"Chump change," he murmured and grabbed the pen from the stand in front of the painting, writing down his bid and placing it in the wooden box in front of them.

"Your reputation precedes you, Buck Jenkins."

"I'll take that as a compliment, Ms. Alexander. It *is* Miss, isn't it?"

Vivian laughed. *Indeed.* "I have yet to have a man who's *worthy* of the title, so yes, it's Miss."

She didn't miss the challenge on his face as he cocked his brow and his eyes descended down her body, stopping to lick at her most private parts tightly wrapped in the form-fitting gown of hers.

"Well, it would appear that tonight's your lucky night then." He looked around quickly, seeing if anyone was watching, before pulling her roughly into his arms and backing her against the wall. She gasped as his head tilted. His beautiful eyes focused on her mouth, and she gulped as the sexuality of it made her melt. "And when I say night, I mean *all* night."

She shivered at that, but tried not to let him see it.

"What you really mean is *one* night, and we both know it." Someone had to say it.

His eyes drifted back to hers and lingered there for what felt like ages before he responded. "I don't put labels on anything, Viv. Not until I know what it is, anyway."

That was fair, she surmised. After all, he hadn't said, "Yes, this will be a one-night stand." It made her feel a little better, but her heart had been split in two too many times before.

She'd dated many celebrities over the years and had let a few get close only to suffer the heartbreak when they'd told her she was too career-driven and work obsessed. As if she didn't have time for love in her life and that simply wasn't true. She guessed it hadn't really been love if she could simply let them walk away without a fight. Love, now there was a word that was an enigma to her...but looking up into the handsome face of Bobby "Buck" Jenkins, she suddenly wanted to take the risk, no matter the consequences. Chances of a life-time only came around once.

She licked the lips Buck's eyes seemed so riveted on and sighed. "Let's go find my painting." He stepped back then, looking down almost regretfully as if he were disappointed, his cowboy hat shielding his eyes. Her hand moved to his chest as she angled her head up to his, her breath mere inches from his face. "Then we can see whether your bedroom tricks are worth all your bragging."

She walked over to a seascape scene then as she heard him clear his throat and follow, and she tried not to laugh. An angry wave crashed against a cliff where a red and white lighthouse sat glowing brilliantly against a storm-darkened sky.

"Now that's depressing," Buck grumbled and wrapped a bulky arm around her waist, pulling her easily into his side. She balked and looked up at him, but he was dead serious.

"I completely disagree," she asserted. "It represents the beacon of hope in a dismal obscurity."

"Poetic words for a thespian."

"Big words for a dumb jock!"

Buck just laughed in response, and she nudged her hip against his.

"You really don't like it?"

"Nope! Look. That poor sailboat is about to sink into the abyss." He pointed into the obsidian darkness of the sea at the sailboat that indeed teetered on the very edge of fate.

Vivian shrugged.

"Oh, you don't care, huh?"

"A small price to pay for the beauty of light... Besides, you don't know if it's gonna sink or *not*. It's called hope."

"Ah, the perpetual dreamer. I admire that!" His generous smile proved his words.

Vivian tilted her head, appraising the painting with her eyes. "It's rather poignant and symbolic, and I'm sorry, but far less depressing than yours." Vivian moved to submit her bid.

"Depressing? My painting is *sexy*."

"Not if you look beyond the bare breast of its protagonist," she countered and looked up at him.

Buck belted out a big laugh then. "I sincerely apologize, ma'am. I'm just a bit distracted at the moment." His eyes came back to her breasts and she felt her nipples harden beneath the sheer fabric of her gown.

She gulped as he turned to face her, his hand rising from her waist to the top of her ribcage, just beneath her left breast, close enough to tease but without touching. Vivian felt electricity spike through her center as his eyes came back to hers, now dark again with desire.

"I've seen enough. I'm ready to appraise something besides artwork. How 'bout you?"

CHAPTER 1

*V*ivian used her keycard to unlock the penthouse suite and
open the door. Buck followed diligently, closing the door
behind him.

"Hot damn!" he called out, then whistled. "This is fancy."

Vivian laughed heartily as she moved over to the bar to set her
wristlet down. "We both know you've stayed in a penthouse before.
Don't be so gauche," she teased.

"There you go again using them big words on me." He sighed in
feigned exasperation, getting another laugh out of her as she
grabbed the chilling bottle of champagne that had been delivered
just a few moments ago upon Buck's request in the lobby.

"Wanna do the honors?" She cocked her eyebrow at him as he
approached.

"Mmm, this is the good stuff right here," he clarified and
removed the wire, aimed the bottle in the opposite direction and
popped the cork. Champagne spewed from the bottle and ran onto
the plush white carpet. "What are we celebrating again?" He winked.

"I dunno." She turned, looking seductively up at his big frame and the dusting of blonde chest hair peeking out at her where he'd unbuttoned his top two buttons on the elevator. "How about fame? Fortune? Or even us? How about to your hometown and the family we both love so much? How about the single life? Middle age? Now there's a word you and I have come to know *well*," she remarked as she grabbed up two champagne flutes and handed them over.

"Ah, Vivian Alexander. Hollywood starlet slash closet cynic."

"Sorry." She frowned, hoping she hadn't ruined the mood.

Buck just shook his head and smiled, filling the flutes halfway. He sat the bottle aside, and Vivian handed him his champagne. He clinked his glass against hers. "Here's to new paths."

Vivian smiled brightly at that. "I like that." She brought her glass to her lips, watching him as he did the same. She swallowed the bubbly semi-sweet and not too tart champagne.

"It's my favorite one and, I'm not a big fan of champagne."

"Me either, but this one is the exception."

"Here's to the heads we turned tonight." He brought his glass back to hers.

"And here's to the news coverage of it in the morning." She took another sip of her champagne as Buck downed his.

Buck chuckled- a deep booming laugh. "Oh Viv. You worry too much. What do you care anyway?"

"I don't! It was gonna be the young bartender before you came along, I'm certain of it."

"Robbing the cradle now, huh?" Buck teased and followed her into the spacious den. "I'm sure we could make room for him too if you're into ménage—"

"Nope! I only want *one* man at a time, thank you very much." Vivian smirked at him as she sat on the big couch, and he moved to sit right next to her.

"I'm enough man for you anyway, Viv. Trust me." He winked a dazzling blue eye at her. "I'm not sorry I interrupted you and Junior though."

"You shouldn't be. He was so young…"

"I doubt he could even *fathom* all the things I plan to do with you." He placed their flutes on the coffee table before them.

"Oh? Pray tell." She felt her tummy flutter and her body began to hum from her center.

"Why tell when I can *show?*"

Buck moved ever closer, his broad chest brushed hers as she turned into him. His smoothly shaven face moved in toward hers; his gorgeous baby blue eyes drank her in. Viv gulped, for she'd never been this aroused by a simple look before. She could only imagine the pleasure coming her way as he gave her a crooked grin. She licked the lips he was intent on and inhaled the scent of him- sweet and earthy, masculine and spicy, clean and soapy, leather and whiskey. His muscular presence oozed mind-blowing sex and all things carnal, and Vivian knew she was about to be in for the ride of her life.

His moves were calculated, like that of a cougar stalking out his prey, as his big palm cupped her cheek and his face tilted, his plump lips but a breath away. She thought she would die from anticipation as his sweet breath hit her face and his other hand came to her waist. Her eyelids fluttered shut as he closed the distance between them, and she felt his soft lips move gently over hers, brushing feather light, barely touching. She whimpered, wanting more. A strong hand gripped her hip then and lifted her, pulling her onto his lap. Her legs splayed instinctively as she straddled him, her tight dress inching up her naked thighs. Buck's hard chest bumped her breasts as his mouth covered hers, and she got the kiss she'd been waiting for. A passionate, sexy kiss that promised incredible things as his lips opened and a strong, curious tongue expertly invaded her mouth. The eager muscle curled and stroked her own and within minutes had her panting and arching her hips against his as his hands moved to her bare thighs. Rising swirls of hot desire licked at her center and she ached to have him, then and there.

"Vivian," he practically growled as he thrust his erection against her and his mouth moved to her neck. His big palm cupped her breast then and he squeezed her there, testing the firmness as he sucked at her throat, using his teeth and tongue in such an erotic way that she thought she might orgasm before he was ever inside her. She felt his hands come to the latch behind her neck and she realized just how much she wanted Buck's big hands on her breasts, her body, all of her.

"Yes, Buck, yes," Vivian cried as she began unbuttoning his shirt, peeling his big arms from his jacket. She wanted to see his battle worn body, feel those hard muscles of his bare beneath her palms.

The clasp on her halter dress gave, and he jerked it down, displaying her breasts for his eyes to see.

He must have liked what he saw for he moaned and his head bent as he took one of her puckered nipples into his hot mouth.

"Mmm," she murmured as pleasure spiked through her and she felt her center dampen as his hand moved to grip her bottom. His tongue and mouth almost became her undoing as he suckled her and teased her aching flesh. His hand moved then and as he loved one breast with his mouth, he loved the other with his deft thumb and fingers, then he switched.

Vivian was panting, her orgasm building, and her cries grew more desperate as she ground her hips against his, wanting to feel his naked sex against her own.

Suddenly, she was being turned and felt her back hit the couch as his hips moved along with hers. She was suddenly positioned beneath him, his thighs hitting the back of hers as he settled between her legs.

Buck grinned at her like a shit-eating possum and said, "My feast has only just begun, darlin'."

Her response was stymied as he inched the tight dress up to her waist and his head fell once again.

"Oh God, Buck," she cried out as his mouth delicately nibbled at her inner thigh, his big palms splaying her naked thighs apart. His teeth grazed her flesh and he kissed her tenderly there before nipping at her again. She practically whimpered as his fingers parted her.

"Mmm, let's see *just* how sweet Vivian Alexander really is," he grated then his tongue licked at her wet center as his hands moved beneath her to grip her bottom, pulling her sex closer to his sucking mouth. He began to kiss and lick and suck at her tender flesh, as if it were her mouth he was making out with, and she found herself gasping and shuddering and letting herself be carried away. He would give a little then pull away just before she could get too worked up, planting little soft kisses on the insides of her thighs before his hot mouth returned to her hungry sex. It was erotic and frustrating, and just as his thick fingers slowly entered her and she felt so close to oblivion, he pulled them quickly out before she could climax.

Buck's eyes were drunk with desire as he sat back on his haunches, looking her over, a man satisfied with his work. Vivian's breathing was erratic as her hands moved to his chest, tearing the last of his buttons open on his shirt before falling to the hard, restrained sex extending before her and he gasped. He shivered as she squeezed and pulled on his clothed erection for a moment before looking back up into his sparkling blue eyes.

"Take me, Buck," she breathed out.

In an instant, she was easily scooped up into his arms as he stood and she straddled him once again, her legs clinging to his hips. Her arms wrapped around his neck and her mouth sought his. He moaned as her tongue plunged in and he walked them blindly to the bed.

Vivian gave an, "umph," as she landed, back to the mattress, and felt bereft as he left her side to quickly remove his pants and rip the shirt off his arms. She peeled the dress from her waist and threw it across the room as she turned to appreciate his gloriously naked body.

Each hard muscle rippled as he breathed in and out. She admired the broadness of his chest and shoulders, the scattering light fan of blond hair that covered his chest and down his belly, his tapering hips, and the impressive thick rock-hard sex jutting out at her.

Vivian moaned as she took Buck's presence in. He was big. Bigger than any man she'd ever been with before. Of course she'd been with muscular celebrities prior to Buck Jenkins, and ones who were more cut than him, but never quite as broad in stature. Buck was a defensive player after all. His job was to take down the quarterback. He was a physical warrior. And she was about to go into sexual warfare with him.

He gave her that panties-shucking grin of his before putting his knee up on the bed. He crawled over to her, slowly, deliberately building up the mind-blowing sexual tension between them as his hands reached her ankles. He jerked her down into his embrace as she gasped and he chuckled. His plump lips found hers again as he positioned his giant body gently over hers. She felt his erection push into her thigh and her hands went to his sexy chest as she fiercely kissed him back, her palms tracing the indention of muscles there. She could have gotten off just by touching him as her hands moved lower down his massive, manly torso.

He groaned and winced as her hands found his sex again, and his big palm cupped her breast, squeezing it.

She cried out and her head flew back wantonly when his mouth sought the tender flesh of her neck and his thumb grazed her nipple. Buck growled; he'd had enough torture as he gripped her hips and positioned himself between her legs then, sitting back on his haunches.

"Mmm, yes, I want you so much, Buck. Please," Vivian murmured as she began pulling at his bulging cock, his fingers opening her.

Suddenly, Buck's body went rigid. "Fuck," he yelled, and Vivian's eyes jerked up to his. He sighed heavily and pulled the cowboy hat off, throwing a hand through his dark blond locks before once again replacing the hat.

"What is it?" she asked.

"I don't have a rubber," he said regretfully, "But, God, I need to bury myself inside you, Viv," he grumbled then swore again, frowning as his eyes moved over her body as if she were some delicious treat for him to devour.

Vivian bit into her bottom lip. How could she have been so careless? Her hand shifted from his member to his muscular thigh and she looked down, thoughtfully, then back up at him. "I'm on birth control," she offered but knew it wasn't the only reason he required a condom.

Buck hesitated only a moment more before he said, "Fuck it."

Suddenly, he was guiding himself into her and she was crying out as his girthy sex filled her. Her back arched and she gripped his broad shoulders as he stretched her, inch by tormenting inch.

Vivian hadn't realized just how aroused he'd made her until she was screaming his name in orgasm just moments after he'd started thrusting inside her. She basked in the slap of his large, muscular thighs against her own as his hips plunged and withdrew, ever so slowly, riding the wave of her orgasm.

He chuckled and pulled back to look at her, restraining his natural instincts for a moment. "Been a while for you, huh, darlin'?"

She narrowed her eyes at him as she squeezed her internal muscles around his steely erection. He moaned and his eyes darkened. "Shut up and ride me, cowboy," she smirked. He returned it then lunged hard, making her cry out again.

His body became a rigid missile, seeking nothing but rapture as he stroked her with his sex and hands and mouth. His thrusts were perfectly paced, giving much and taking nothing as he loved her body unlike it'd ever been loved before. Soon, she was falling apart in his arms again, this time intense spasms racked her as she gripped his back and her head fell to his shoulder, where she lightly bit into his bulky bicep, whimpering as her orgasm took her. Buck continued his deep, caressing thrusts as she came back to earth, his groans becoming more frequent, and she could tell he was close to climax himself.

Before he was there though, he pulled out and flipped her over onto her belly, roughly pulling her thighs against his own as he shoved a pillow beneath her.

"Fuck yes…ride me hard, baby," Vivian called to him as he moaned aloud and gripped her hips tightly in his oversized palms.

"Oh damn, Viv," he groaned as he drove deep. He winced and his head flew back as he began to pump hard and fast into her, a man on the brink of erotic torment. She took his weight and pushed her bottom back against him in a beautiful harmonious rhythm. Her hand fell between her legs and she stroked herself where they were joined. "Oh, God," he cried as she moaned again in orgasm, and this time he came with her, practically roaring as he tumbled too, his entire body jerking as he continued to thrust into her and withdraw until finally he slowed to a halt. He rested his heavy body against her for a moment before pulling out and coming to lay down beside her.

Buck grinned that big sexy grin of his as he pulled her into his chest. She stroked at the spattering of hair there and timidly looked down as he moved a stray strand of hair from her cheek.

"You're amazing, in case you didn't already know," he stated.

"You're just saying that," Viv chided him.

"Buck Jenkins don't just say *anything*. Besides, I already made my way into your bed, what more could I gain from blowing smoke up your ass?"

She threw her head back and laughed at his use of words. "Touché." She started to say something else but couldn't as his lips crushed hers. She moaned as his tongue moved across her own, and he deepened the kiss then as his hand fell down her arm to her waist. His hand gently cupped her breast and he kneaded it hungrily.

"Oh, Buck," she murmured as his lips moved to her jaw, then her neck.

"God, you're so damn gorgeous. Especially when you fall apart."

She felt her cheeks flame, even as his hand moved between her legs and she gasped.

"Mmm, yes," she breathed out as his fingers moved into her wetness once again and she instinctively opened her thighs for him, wrapping one leg around his hip. He began thrusting two thick fingers into her as she whimpered again and gripped his large shoulder.

"What you want me to do to you, baby?"

"I want to ride *you*," she said, reaching for his manhood.

He chuckled, then gasped as she gripped his generous member tightly in her hand. His hands moved to her waist and he shifted, pulling her atop him. She settled her thighs over his hips and gave his shaft a couple pumps with a tight fist, loving that she was in control for the time being.

He moaned and gasped as she tormented his rock-hard flesh with her hands and eyes. Soon, she was guiding the velvety soft tip of him inside her, and he was the one whimpering this time.

"Ooh, your cock feels so good inside me," she cooed to him. His eyes found hers as she impaled herself on him slowly, taking her time to torment him. He growled, and her eyebrow arched as her thighs moved.

They both moaned together as she came down hard on him. He took the hat off his head then and plopped it down on hers as her hands splayed across his broad, hard chest and chiseled abs.

"Might as well have a hat if you're gonna ride, sexy lady," he said as his hands moved to her hips, guiding her up and down on him.

Soon, she was panting as pleasure began to swirl through her center where his big sex filled her and her head was thrown back as she moved herself on him, unabashedly.

"Yeah, baby girl," Buck said, spurring her on as his massive hands sought her breasts once again. "Give it to me. Show your cowboy how crazy he makes you."

Vivian arched her hips as she climbed higher and higher, seeking oblivion. His lips found her nipple and pulled it back into his hot mouth as his hips thrust hard against hers. She felt herself edging closer and closer to climax, cries tearing forth from her lips as she rode him for all she was worth. She whimpered again and again as their rhythm propelled them onward.

Suddenly, Buck flipped her once again, easily picking her up and putting her down beside him, her back against his hard chest. His knee moved her legs apart, and she felt him thrust into her in one smooth motion as one of his hands moved underneath her. His palm moved across her chest, to hold her to him as he cupped her breast, his other hand coming down her waist, her belly, her thigh and in between, settling on her sensitive bud.

"Oh Buck," she gasped as she tucked her knee behind his and his mouth fell to her neck to tenderly kiss her pulse point as he withdrew.

"Oh, baby," he murmured against her throat as he lunged harder and deeper inside her. She cried out as hot spasms licked through her center, and he fondled her breast like his life depended on it. "God, I just can't get *enough* of your sweetness." He arched his hips sharply, slamming into her, and she pressed herself down onto him, gripping his large thighs with her fingernails. "You're so fuckin' sexy," he moaned. "Shit, Viv, I'm gonna come again."

"Yes, come for me, handsome."

"You first, darlin'."

She whimpered as his fingers strummed across her aching flesh with amazing accuracy and she fell into oblivion again, screaming out his name once more.

"God baby, you feel *so* damned good wrapped around my cock," he murmured. He bit gently into her shoulder and slammed his hips violently into hers over and over. His big body jarred hers as he spilled himself inside her once again. "Oh, oh, baby...oh, fuck yeah," he cried as his body jerked and his ragged breath grunted in her ear.

She grinned, pleased she had him in such a stupor.

His hands moved over her thigh then, her waist, lovingly

stroking her as he gently continued to fuck her, his orgasm slowly subsiding.

"Damn, Viv. You're sexy as hell," he murmured as he kissed her shoulder and up her neck. She moved her head to rest her face against his as her womanhood continued to clench around his sex. He gasped in response and kissed her jaw. "You probably hear that a lot, I'm sure."

Vivian wouldn't correct him and tell him she'd never had mind-blowing sex quite like this before...not ever. But there were things he just didn't need to know. His ego was already swelled to bursting as it was.

"Grab me some more champagne...then I'll show you sexy."

His brow arched at the words, and she giggled at how curious he became by her unknown promise. "Anything my naughty cowgirl wants, with an attitude like that."

Buck took his time letting his sex soften as he continued to stroke her naked flesh then he pulled away and refilled their glasses as she propped herself on her side to watch him.

Her eyes fell over his massive build, his sexy, muscled back and firm butt cheeks as he faced away from her, and she could feel the stirrings of arousal return as he moved back to the bed and took a seat, facing her.

Buck handed her a half full flute of champagne as she sat up and her eyes roved over his shaggy, thick blonde hair and down his face, stopping at his lips before falling down his chest then back to dazzling sky blue eyes.

She grinned as he appeared suddenly unnerved by her appraising eyes, sipping from his glass. She reached out and stroked his forearm, up his big bicep, gripping the massive muscle, her insides swirling in pleasure again.

He guzzled his drink down and looked at her as he pulled the glass down, waiting for her to say something. She threw the champagne back and downed it in one swallow, tossing the glass aside.

"Now you're *mine*, cowboy," she murmured as she moved next to him on the bed. He chuckled as he watched her come in front of him and move her body over his. Her mouth started at his, her lips sipping at his, then moved down his broad chest, licking and sucking and kissing until he was shivering. She giggled as her tongue teased at the hard plane of muscles on his belly and he gasped.

"Viv," he whimpered as her hands moved down his hips and over his cock, hard once again. "I don't know if I—"

"We're about to find out, aren't we?" she murmured as she reached up to pull the silver comb from her hair. Her blonde hair fell, framing her face as she looked up at him.

"Fuck, you're gorgeous."

"I thought I was *sexy*. Make up your mind, Mr. Gridiron legend." She puckered her lips at him as she came to her knees, and he practically growled. She grinned.

"You're both, for damn sure."

She chortled. "We'll see about that." Her head fell then and she heard Buck gasp.

"Viv…"

"Tell me how sexy I am now," she murmured as her lips fell on the head of his member and kissed the velvety tip lightly.

"Oh shit," Buck swore and moaned as his fingers fell gently into her hair and his head flew back.

"How sexy am I now…with my mouth around you?"

Buck swore even as her mouth encompassed the head of his thick, hard sex and moved all the way down to the base of him. "Oh, God. That feels fuckin' amazing," he breathed out as his hands gripped her hair at the roots.

She took nothing as she pleasured him, rewarding his moans with more passion, gaining speed and gripping firmer with both her mouth and her fist as she loved his girthy member with raw abandon.

Soon, his grip tightened in her hair and he was moving her head into him as he thrust into her stroking mouth and hand.

"Oh God, oh baby," he cried and she quickly moved back, leaving only her hand to work him as she stuck her chest out and he spilled himself onto her breasts, her eyes looking up into his as he did so. When he was done thrashing hard against her ample bosom and had come down from his sexual high, his smirk was back and he laughed on a sigh. "Jesus, Viv. That was about the hottest fuckin' thing I've ever had done to me."

She arched a brow and continued to stroke him, loving how he shivered and jerked when her fingertips traced the head of him. "Hmm," she stated simply.

Vivian moved away then to go clean herself off and when she returned to the bed, Buck had the champagne glasses full again. She smiled at his gorgeousness propped up against the overstuffed down pillows. He was the very definition of sexy himself, laying there with his naked, larger than life athlete's body sprawled out, beyond comfortable in his own skin.

She took the glass extended before her.

"I've realized what we need to toast to. To a night of un-fucking-believable sex." He clinked his glass against hers and drank deeply. "Now, I don't know about you," he stated, grinning as if he had some secret, "but I've worked up quite an appetite. Wanna order some room service?"

Vivian nodded and went over to find the menu as Buck refilled his glass.

"I reckon we need another bottle of this stuff too." He scowled as he poured the last of it into his flute.

Vivian laughed.

For the next hour they talked and laughed and dined on scrumptious crab cakes and shrimp cocktail, chicken cordon bleu, and truffle mac and cheese while they drank another bottle of the delicious champagne they both loved. Vivian told Buck about the movies she was working on and how excited she was for the roles she'd fought hard for, and Buck told her about his work with disabled children, the foundation he'd set up for cancer research, and how he'd moved back home in the last year. They talked about

Natalie and Jack and the Kinsen kids they both adored. Then Buck's eyes took on a sadness to them that stilled Vivian's breath, and he looked away.

"Buck? Where'd you go?" Vivian took his square jaw in her palm and moved his head back towards her, his blue eyes sparkling like diamonds in the dimly lit room amid the gold tasseled throw pillows and comforter. He gave her a quivering grin and before he could respond, she was pressing her lips softly to his.

Vivian deepened the kiss and moved closer, aligning her body to his. "Hey, if I forget to tell you, thank you. For making my night much better than I ever thought it could be," she murmured. She wrapped her arms around his neck, and he made love to her then.

It was different than even the first time...and definitely different than the second time. He held her tight in his arms as he laid her back and pushed himself deeply inside her, looking into her eyes as his sex and hands loved her body once again, claiming her for his taking. They climaxed together and when they finished, he stayed inside her. He moved slightly, just enough to take his weight off of her, but still held her snug within his embrace, and they fell asleep that way.

***

*B*uck awoke to the sound of his phone vibrating on the nightstand. He kissed Vivian's bicep, the one thrown over his own, as he moved her ever so slightly to grab his phone.

"Hello," he whispered so as not to wake the gorgeous sleeping beauty sprawled out across him.

"Bubba!" Beth's voice was frantic as she called to him.

"What's wrong?" he stated a little louder as he moved out from under Vivian and quickly shot up, panic seizing his heart. "Is it Momma? Is she?" He couldn't finish the statement. He wasn't ready for his momma to be dead. Not yet. They'd fought so hard in the last several months. He couldn't lose her just yet.

"Bobby, she's septic. It's...it's not good. It started with a minor infection in her leg and... They've put her into a medically induced coma."

No! he screamed inside his head.

He wasn't a medical professional by any means whatsoever, but he knew what that meant. Sepsis was blood poisoning... And she already had so many cards stacked against her with the terminal cancer diagnosis three months ago.

What the hell had happened so quickly as to move her down this path? She'd been fighting so hard and every treatment had seemed to help...and the pain had gotten better. She had been strong when he'd left just days before. What had caused this sudden infection? Deep inside his heart, Buck had known all the specialists and all the medicine and all the prayers would never be enough. She'd been diagnosed with stage IV metastatic ovarian cancer. Her doctor had said it was just a matter of time, less than six months, a year at most. It had just progressed too far. Even at this stage in the game, if they took it all out it was simply too late. He'd known it. It was everywhere. Buck had seen the conviction in the man's face when his mother had been given her prognosis. Her PET scan had lit her body up like a Christmas tree. And Buck had seen firsthand what cancer could do to a soul. Now his sweet momma would be its next victim.

"I'm on my way," Buck stated and steeled himself. He had to remain strong for his sisters, his mom and his dad. He could fall apart later; now wasn't the time.

"How soon can you be here?" his oldest sister asked.

"Less than an hour. I'm leaving right now."

"Alright. Be careful. I love you."

"And I love you. I'll see you soon."

He sighed heavily and pulled the phone from his ear, bringing it down to his thigh as his heart fell and his chest filled with dread.

Sepsis. A medically induced coma. Jeez. This was bad. She couldn't die. It was too soon. He had too many things he wanted to do with her. Too many conversations. Too many hugs to give...

He turned and looked at the gorgeous vixen laying on the bed, swirls of her golden, sandy, and honey blonde ringlets covering her slender back. He wanted to go to her, bury himself inside her once more, and thrust away all his anguish until he didn't ache with agony anymore. But Buck knew his desire for Vivian wouldn't mend his breaking heart. Not right this second anyway. He had to go and quickly.

He moved to the side of the bed where his boxers and pants lay and scooped them up, pulling his legs in one by one. Next, he pulled on his shirt, buttoned it up and found his suit jacket on the bar, thrusting his arms through the sleeves. He walked over to his shoes, sat down, put them on and tied them up.

He came back to the bed, looking down regretfully at Vivian Alexander once more. He should tell her where he was going. He should explain what had happened. But for the life of him, her blissfully ignorant slumber held the last trace of harmony in a world where chaos reigned, and he dare not break it. It was fragile, like glass. The calm before the storm. The cusp of the end of the innocence.

With a heavy heart, Buck blew her a silent kiss and walked out of her suite.

**

*V*ivian awoke to the sound of rain hitting the window of the high-rise hotel and stretched languidly. With a squealing groan, she extended her sore arms and legs. She smiled to herself, remembering the night of scorching hot sex she'd had with Buck Jenkins.

When she opened her eyes, she was aware of the darkness of the room and the emptiness of the bed.

"Oh no," she admonished, regretfully. She shot upright in the bed and looked around, listening for any sign of life within the hotel room she'd rented. "Buck?" she called out. When no answer came, she panicked, her heart lurching violently in her chest.

She jerked the covers from her naked waist and shot up out of the oversized bed, searching the dark den and bathroom. When she produced no Buck, she covered her eyes with her hands. "Oh my God! What have I done?" She moved them quickly away and scolded herself "Dammit, Vivian. You fool! How could you have been so freakin' stupid?" Hot tears of guilt hit her eyes, and she kicked at the loose comforter hanging off the end of the bed, slamming her toe into the frame as she did so.

With a cry of anguish, she fell to the ground, grabbing her throbbing appendage, her body racked with tremors as wave after wave of shame hit her full force.

She'd known Buck Jenkins was a player. She'd known his reputation as a playboy. And now she'd been just another mark on his bedpost. Vivian shouldn't be surprised or upset, but she couldn't control the tears or the self-reproach she felt in those moments. How could she have just let him use her that way?

But dammit, he had felt so good, so solid, so right. She'd never had a man love her body like Buck had last night. There had been no hesitations, no reservations, no holding back. Their passion had been untamed, undeniable, and unstoppable as they made love over and over again without abandon.

But that's who he was, wasn't it? Womanizing, charming, smooth-talking Buck Jenkins. He had the worst reputation for doing *just* that... Now Vivian was the next victim in his game of hearts. And she'd known she was susceptible already under the circumstances, but her body hadn't cared. It had been too long for her, four damn long ass months, and he'd been just too damn sexy for his own good.

He'd been everything a woman could want in a lover: giving, zealous, eager, unrelenting in the force of his presence and lust for her sex. Only now, he had slipped out as quickly as he'd slipped in.

Like a smooth criminal. Now she understood what that song of Michael Jackson's meant.

She picked her battered soul up off the floor and forced herself into the shower, washing the smell of him and remnants of his love-making from her body with sudden disgust and renewed anger at her carelessness. Once she was clean, on the outside anyway, she began to fume at the audacity of the man who'd taken advantage of her. How could he not have seen the bleeding heart she'd worn on her shoulder last night? He had to know she was in a vulnerably precarious state. After all, Vivian didn't drink like that often. She drank, of course and often, but not quite so much at one time. Of course, he hadn't known her, not at all really, so he might not have known how belittled she'd been by the talk show host's comments on her "middle-age" nor how despondent she'd felt for weeks now following that appearance. Perhaps it hadn't been as obvious to him that Vivian Alexander wasn't as sure of herself as she'd once been in her twenties.

"Ah, who are you kidding? Get over yourself!" she told her reflection in the mirror as she combed through her blonde hair. "He didn't give a fuck about you! You were just another one of his blonde *bimbos*. Used and discarded...like a condom."

Only he hadn't even used a condom with her.

"Shit!" she swore as she looked down at herself in the silk robe she'd donned because she was too ashamed by her nakedness and needed to cover herself once out of the shower; as if the robe could somehow take back the sins she'd committed against herself.

Buck hadn't used a condom, she reminded herself. Now she would need to go to the doctor and have tests ran just in case. After all, he'd been with a football field full of women— *pun intended*—she was certain, over the years. He'd gone through them like underwear, it seemed.

Vivian sighed and began dressing to clear her mind as much to put layers on top of the guilt that ate at her like a cancer. She smoothed some lotion on her face and body and applied some tinted moisturizer, mascara and lip gloss then scrunched her hair and did a quick blow dry of her long locks, leaving them looking like beach waves. Her stylist could deal with it later, she didn't even care. She was just going to be getting on a plane soon anyway, what did it matter?

Her phone rang at that moment, and Jill's frantic voice reverberated in her ears.

"Dammit Viv, do you know what time it is?"

No, was Vivian's first thought, then she looked at her phone and swore. A quarter past 10 AM. She would be lucky to even make her flight at this rate, but praised God she was a celebrity and the jet would leave at her own discretion.

"I've been trying to call you for hours now. Do you have any idea the buzz you've created? What on *earth* were you thinking?"

Oh God, Vivian suddenly recalled the sexually explicit dance she and Buck had performed last night and all the wandering eyes that had followed. People had witnessed her and Buck leave the gala together too...and get on the elevator. As if she could even attempt to hide the knowledge of their affair now.

She let Jill fuss at her— for she knew she needed to hear it anyway. Jill was more like an older sister to her than her manager and always had been.

"Are you even *listening* to me, Vivian Lisette?" Jill screeched. Vivian could only imagine how red her face was. Jill came from Irish roots and her face tended to get red at the drop of a hat anyway. Especially when she was flustered.

"Yes. I am," Vivian retorted back and grabbed up her toiletries, shoving them into her oversized bag. She moved into the bedroom then and began throwing her clothes haphazardly into her suitcase.

"How could you have been so careless?" Jill continued her verbal assault. "And with BOBBY 'BUCK' JENKINS!" she yelled. "Of *all* the people you could have gone upstairs with..." Jill huffed. "Have you *lost* your mind?"

Vivian closed her eyes, feeling tears come into them. But she held them back, refusing to give into her self-loathing again.

"Please tell me he used protection! I swear to God, Vivian. I don't wanna have to..."

Something caught Vivian's eye as she moved to the side of the bed and her breath caught in her throat when she saw what it was.

"What?" Jill asked, gasping.

"That son of a bitch!" Vivian exclaimed and reached for the black Stetson on the ground. Touching the smooth felt hat, she shivered as much from the memory of last night as from the touch of it that seemed to scorch her skin like fire. A punishment for eating the forbidden fruit.

"What did he do? Do I need to call Tony? I swear to God, I'll have his head on a *spike*," Jill hissed. Vivian would have laughed if her heart hadn't leapt into her throat then. Tony was her lawyer. Jill wasn't only the best manager ever, she was also fiercely protective of Vivian. As much as Viv hated what Buck had done to her, he hadn't physically harmed her—nothing that warranted calling a lawyer anyway, for the only damage was heartache after all—and she wouldn't have Jill believe for an instant he had.

"No, no, nothing like that," she stated calmly and then began to bristle with renewed anger at the symbolism of his hat being the only evidence to indicate he'd ever been there at all. His calling card... "He left me a souvenir, is all," she smirked and didn't let Jill respond as she abruptly said, "I'm on my way, Jill. Call my driver. I'm headed down."

Vivian hung up the phone and yelled out at the top of her lungs. The tears that stung her eyes were now angry, not sad. All self-loathing was gone. Now she was determined to pay Buck Jenkins back if it were the last thing she did.

She threw her toiletry bag into her suitcase and zipped it shut, extending out the handle and pulling it to the ground with a thud. She grabbed her wristlet from the bar, threw it into her brand-new leather Coach purse and hauled the heavy bag up her shoulder, throwing in her phone. She left the keycard on the coffee table in the den and saw her way out.

Thank God she didn't have to even stop at the desk to "check out", not that she would have anyway. Her mood was atrocious as she pulled her sunglasses from their case and threw them on. She didn't even speak to the bellhop as she got onto elevator, he was the same one who'd seen her up with Buck, and avoided the gazing eyes in the lobby that scrutinized her.

It wasn't until she was walking out the chiseled glass doors, thanking the doorman as she exited, that she noticed the paparazzi rushing at her from the street.

She was enveloped in raucous murmuring, flashes and banter as they called to her and gibbered without mercy. She was momentarily taken off guard as she heard their chatter.

"Ms. Alexander, tell us about last night."

"That was one stunning tango."

"Where'd Mr. Jenkins run off to this morning, Viv?"

"So how long have you been seeing Buck Jenkins?"

"Did you two spend the entire night together?"

Vivian was completely bombarded, her heart slamming into her ribs as she searched for an exit but couldn't find one. She was starting to panic and felt lightheaded until she heard a rough voice behind her and a firm hand pushing her through the crowd to her limo.

The doorman had stepped in and told them they weren't allowed there in front of the hotel and needed to disperse.

Viv saw her driver, Samuel, and reached for him, feeling as if she were about to pass out.

"I got you, Miss Vivian. Don't you worry now, I got you, baby girl," he murmured as his strong arms gripped her shoulders and assisted her into the back seat.

She'd never been happier to see his beautiful ebony face and grayish white hair.

She couldn't respond as he shut the door, scolded the crowd, and scooted into the driver's seat. She watched as the reporters continued to snap pictures through the heavily tinted windows, her heart filling with dread even though she knew they couldn't see her.

"You alright, Miss Vivian?" Samuel's smooth voice asked with concern.

It took her a moment to attempt to answer him as they pulled away from the commotion. She just nodded and settled into her seat. She sighed heavily and tried to calm her banging heart.

Buck Jenkins would pay for what he'd done to her. If that was the last thing he ever did, he would pay!

CHAPTER 2

$\mathcal{B}$uck sighed in contentment as Natalie Kinsen's soothing voice cooed to him over the phone.

"So, if she's doing alright, stop by. We'd love to see you."

"Will do, Nat. Thanks so much for the invitation."

"You know you're *always* welcome here, Bucko."

He smiled into the receiver, knowing she was telling the truth. He and Nat had been close friends for over thirty years.

"Seriously, even if you need to just eat and run. We'll have plenty. Dallie's headed off to college next month, I know she'd enjoy seeing you. And you sound like you need the break, Buck."

"I do." He looked over at his mom and smiled. God, she was beautiful. Even if her hair and eyebrows were gone now. Her frailty gave him pause as he turned and whispered. "You're right, Nat. I do." He squeezed his eyes shut.

This last month had been touch and go as she'd slowly healed from the septicemia. She'd been in and out of medically-induced comas since the morning he'd awoken in Vivian Alexander's penthouse suite to his sister's desperate phone call. His mom almost died twice during that time, and Buck had been afraid he'd never get to hear her sweet voice again. But miraculously, the infection had gradually started to subside and the doctors slowly withdrew the drugs. Three days ago, she'd awoken and Buck's prayers had been answered as she'd scolded him.

"You don't look so good, son," she'd said. "You need a good hot meal and a shower."

He'd laughed heartily and hugged her to him as gently as he could.

She'd been up and around since then and was hopefully going to get to go home soon.

The toll had been taken on Buck though. He and his sisters had been taking shifts the entire time, not leaving their mother's side for more than a few hours at a time for fear that it might be the last time they'd see her.

And it had been this way for months now, after her cancer diagnosis, and Buck needed a chance to get away from the stench of death and antibacterial cleaner and to eat a meal that wasn't from either a hospital cafeteria or some greasy fast food joint.

"I'll be there, Nat. What time should I come?"

"Six?"

"Sounds great. I'll see you tomorrow night then."

"Alright. See you then, Bucko. Love you."

"Love you too, Nat."

He hung up the phone and walked back over to where his mom sat, feet up in the recliner, an IV pole next to her with a tube running into her arm. She was covered in several thin, knitted blue blankets and her bald head was encased with a crocheted yellow beanie cap. She looked years older than her six plus decades and she didn't weigh more than an adolescent child. She looked like a strong gust of wind would blow her away.

Buck sat his big frame in the chair next to hers and took her hand as she extended it to him.

"Was that Natalie?"

"Yup. She was inviting me over to her and Jack's for dinner

tomorrow night. She's having Nate and Jordan over too and extended the invitation to me as well."

"Well, that's mighty sweet of her. Y'all always got on so well, you and Natalie Butler. It was Jordan you had the hots for though, huh?" He just smiled into her sunken face, wishing he had more time with her. "Bobby, please don't look at me like that."

"Like what, Momma?"

"Like you're looking at a corpse."

"I ain't."

"You are! Honey, I've made my peace with the good Lord. When He's ready, it's my time to go, son. Ain't nothing can change that."

"I know," he growled as tears hit his eyes. "That don't mean I got to like it though."

"The only regret I have is that I'm gonna miss out on my kids and grandkids. And your father. Y'all are gonna have to take good care of him, Bubba. He's gonna be lost without me. Billy is a strong man, but..."

Buck wiped at the tears that suddenly started to flow down his cheeks.

His parents had been together for over forty years, his father *was* going to be lost without her. His mom and dad had always been best friends as well as husband and wife; inseparable since they'd met at the age of twenty after his father hired her on at his insurance firm as a secretary... then married her just six months later. Buck knew just how much they meant to one another, how much they loved one another.

"Bobby, honey, look at me," her voice was weak and it scared him as he raised his eyes to meet ones almost identical to his in their shape and color. "Baby, promise me you'll find a good girl and settle down. Please? It's my dying wish for you."

"Momma..." he grumbled, not wanting to hear the word 'dying' come from her lips or have this awkward discussion either.

"I'm completely serious." At least she hadn't said 'dead' serious. "Baby, you gotta stop living life so fast. It's time, honey. Find a place to hang that hat for good." She touched the brim of the cowboy hat on his head for good measure.

He gulped, remembering he'd left his black one in Vivian's suite. He hadn't meant to, but in a way, it was fitting... Leaving his hat with Vivian was a profound symbolism that wasn't lost on him following his mother's words, for Viv had not only his hat but even more it would seem, as Buck hadn't stopped thinking about her since their incredible night together.

He'd been trying to call her over and over again and hadn't gotten an answer—not that he'd expected one in the first place. He never left a message, just listened to her sultry voice telling him she was unavailable and the caller knew what to do after the beep. Besides, what would he say that would ever make his leaving without a word justifiable? Especially when he was notorious for doing exactly that. He was practically the *king* of one-night stands at this point.

Buck knew Vivian must hate him now. If she didn't, she should.

As if reading his mind, his mother blurted out, "Blair told me about Vivian Alexander."

"Oh jeez, Mom. She believes *everything* she reads in the tabloids."

"That was a heated embrace, I must say."

"It was all for the cameras," he dismissed, pulling his hat off, swiping his hand through his unruly hair and planting his hat back down on his head, not meeting her eyes.

"Sure it was!" Blair called from the doorframe then, blue eyes burning. Her blonde hair was pulled into a ponytail, and she was clad in yoga pants, a tank top and sneakers. "I don't believe that for *one* second, baby brother. Chandler sit down and let me tie your shoe," she called to her eight-year-old son, who ran over to Buck then, smiling, as she sat two big bags of Chick-fil-A down on the bedside tray.

"I got it," Buck said and took the task of tying his nephew's shoe as much to avoid his sister's eyes as to help the boy.

"If that's the case," Blair continued, "then how come you haven't gone to the press and said so, instead of leaving the world to wonder why neither of you have *bothered* to enlighten them? Funny how every other *false* affair in the past has been acknowledged but not this one."

Ever the drama queen, Blair was never one to let her brother's short-comings go unnoticed. This wouldn't fall by the wayside either. She'd been pressing him for information for a whole month, but he hadn't budged on the matter. What happened between him and Vivian that night wasn't going to leave his mouth, not if he had any say in the matter. It had been too special, too personal. To hear anyone throwing Vivian's name in the mud like she was trash was unthinkable, so Buck had just gone and allowed the press to make their assumptions rather than add more fuel to the fire. It had died down some since they'd not been seen together since, and they were both scarce in the limelight as of late. Buck had come home to be with his dying mother, and Vivian was shooting out in Seattle; neither of them had acknowledged anything had ever happened.

That night with Vivian had been unbelievable. The fire that raged between them had been all-consuming, and he'd not been able to quench it, no matter how many times he'd claimed her. He'd bragged that he could last all night long, but he'd genuinely worried that he wouldn't entirely meet those expectations when the time came to ante up. At forty-one years old, Buck Jenkins was no longer quite the stud he'd been back in his twenties, so he'd been surprised at his stamina that night, despite that Vivian had been forewarned down in the art gallery. There was no reason for alarm though, as his endurance and libido fulfilled his overdramatized promise. Although with a woman as gorgeous as Vivian Alexander, he shouldn't be one bit shocked at his body's virile response to her. Everything about that stunning blonde starlet screamed sex kitten. Just thinking about how sensual and sweet she'd been beneath him got his blood to surging once more.

"I got you two things of tenders, hope that's enough," Buck's dad,

Bill, called to him as he came through the door with a carrier of drinks.

"Jeez, Dad. I don't play football anymore. My metabolism isn't soaring through the roof like it used to be." Buck patted his stomach and stood.

"Ah, well, someone will eat them," Bill stated and looked over at Chandler, who gave him a high five and came over to where his mom was laying waffle fries on the table.

As good as it all smelled, Buck was eager for some home-cooked food. He was excited to eat with the Kinsens and see the girls who also called him uncle.

He adored his family but being cooped up in this hospital room was starting to wear him down. A break would do him good and hopefully within a few days, they could get his mom home and she'd be more comfortable there.

✦✳✦

"*B*uck!" Jack smiled and extended his hand as he opened the door to him. "Come on in, man."

Buck took Jack's hand and shook it firmly, giving Natalie's husband a big grin as he pulled him in for a half hug.

"Glad you could make it."

"Yeah, me too. Believe me."

"How's your mom?" Jack pulled back, looking forlorn. He stepped aside as Buck came through the door.

"Today's been a little better, Jack. Thanks for asking."

He sized Jack Kinsen up, realizing suddenly they were around the same size now that Buck wasn't training to crush quarterbacks in the NFL anymore. Buck had lost some of his muscle tone and girth in the last year since he'd come home, seeing as his diet and workout routine were more flexible now. Not that Jack hadn't always been a broad and muscular dude himself—he worked out as much or more than Buck did—but Buck was surprised to say the least.

He followed his host into the spacious kitchen and smiled into Natalie Kinsen's gorgeous face as he took the hands she extended to him. God, she was a sight for sore eyes. His emotions got the best of him as she asked how he was doing and he was taken back all those years ago, when they'd been so close and life had been so sure. He hugged her tightly and shuddered as he shook his head against her shoulder.

She cupped his face. "Buck?" Apprehension hit her eyes.

"She's home now, but she's so damn weak," he trailed off, afraid he might crack under Natalie's concerned blue eyes.

She pulled him aside, into the doorframe of her office. "You look like shit, Buck."

She'd always been the one he could talk to about anything and everything. It was so good to have that.

"I needed to get away, Natalie. I needed this."

She pulled him into her embrace, and he steeled himself against the tears that threatened to come as he took a deep breath in. God, how wonderful it was to have friends like her. People who genuinely cared for him. He'd met many people in the world of fame and competition, but there were only a handful that had been there for him like Natalie and Jordan.

He felt another feminine hand come to his back and he turned to Jordan Butler, who hugged him next. He inhaled her scent and recalled when they'd once been more than friends. It was so long ago, and he'd been close to falling for her, but they'd never been right for one another. He knew it then and he knew it now.

"Buck, honey, are you sure you're alright?" The sweet and sassy redhead beckoned.

"I'm really glad to have friends like y'all," he stated truthfully. He'd known them both since they were just kids, they'd grown up together, gotten into all kinds of trouble together… Now they were adults with adult issues and just trying to get through life. "It's been rough."

They all held a brief look before walking back into the kitchen.

That's when Buck froze.

It was as if his dreams had materialized suddenly in front of him. Vivian Alexander stood at the kitchen island looking as gorgeous as ever in a purple silk blouse and grey slacks, her blonde locks curled to perfection and her deep brown eyes piercing into his soul.

"Viv?" he breathed on a sigh, her name the answer to his prayers. He couldn't stop the smile that spread out on his face. God, he'd missed her. He had no idea how much until that instant. He longed to run to her, sweep her up in his arms, kiss her, have his cock sheathed inside her once again.

But her haughty look stilled his blood. She was cursing him with every breath she took, he knew. He'd fucked her mindless, left her, shamed her, and if the news coverage wasn't exaggerating, humiliated her beyond belief. She had every right to look at him the way she was.

He was aware that Jordan said something in response, but it was Savannah's sweet little voice calling to him that broke his reverie.

He hugged Nat and Jack's young teenage daughter tightly, elaborating about her subtle beauty. For she was such a shy, sweet thing, he didn't wanna embarrass her too much. She was gonna be a knock-out. In fact, both the Kinsen girls were, Buck saw, as Dallie was next to embrace him. He teasingly said, "Dallas Kinsen, you're getting to be as gorgeous as your Momma, girl!" He looked over to Jack then. "I bet your daddy don't enjoy keeping those boys off a' you." He laughed big, eyeing the young man next to her he assumed to be her boyfriend.

"No, he certainly does *not*," Jack stated with a laugh and grabbed his wife, kissing her passionately.

Dallie intertwined her arm through Buck's and brought him over to the only person Buck didn't recognize in the Kinsen's kitchen—a brown-headed young adult with green eyes, who just gawked at him. "Uncle Buck, I want you to meet Cole," Dallie said as Buck extended his hand, and Cole gingerly shook it.

"You're...you're," the kid had a hard time speaking, and it amused

Buck, for it'd been a while since he'd encountered a star-struck fan in his hometown, seeing as most everyone already knew who he was.

"Buck Jenkins, pleasure to meet you," Buck said and tipped his hat at Cole after he got his hand back.

"Holy crap! I can't believe it. You're one of the best defensive ends to play football." Cole stood shell-shocked, basking in the glory of being in Buck's presence. All at once, he didn't feel like the old washed-up former football player. It was true after all, Buck had been a force to be reckoned with on the gridiron. He put many a quarterback down and prevented quite a few touchdowns in his time.

"Ah, don't be goin' and givin' him an even bigger head than he's already got, kid," Nathan Butler stated then and roughly patted Buck on the back. Everyone laughed.

Suddenly Natalie gasped, and they all turned to look at her as she cupped her hand over her mouth, blushing.

"Baby, are you alright?" Jack asked.

"Oh, of course," she waved him off. "I just remembered the potatoes."

Buck heard a little squeal then and turned to see baby Jackson, Nat and Jack's youngest, pumping his chubby little arms and legs, in his aunt Jordan's arms, smiling with his little chompers. "Where's my little buddy?" Buck said and tickled the little tyke, showing him how to do a fist pump. This adorable bundle of joy had been a big surprise for Jack and Nat, and Buck's heart swelled in that moment.

For the longest time, he'd never imagined having a child of his own, the thought just hadn't been appealing, but each time he saw Jackson now, he felt a longing cut deep into him. This sweet baby boy with curly blond locks like his sister, Dallie, and eyes like his sister, Savannah—a mix somewhere between his mom's azure blue ones and his dad's jade green ones—his chubby cheeks, and perfectly sculpted lips like Natalie's made Buck rethink fatherhood. His mother's words echoed back to him then.

Buck suddenly had an epiphany of what a baby comprised of his own DNA would look like, he imagined it wouldn't be far from what baby Jax looked like. After all, Buck was blond headed and blue-eyed himself.

Buck's eyes fell back to Vivian then. A baby of their making might have amber eyes, not quite as deep as her chocolate brown ones but not as bright as his sky blue, and would definitely be blonde.

Jack and Nate moved away, out to the back porch, and Buck longed to say something to the beautiful starlet scowling over at him; apologize, acknowledge the wrongness of what he'd done. The heat from those deep brown eyes scorched him like lasers, and he hesitated another moment before turning to head out the door to join Nate, Cole, and Jack at the grill.

Cole started rambling about Buck's many accomplishments with the Stallions and in the NFL, and Buck welcomed the distraction from his thoughts and anguish. It was nice to have another male he could talk football, highlights, stats and records with. Not that he couldn't do that with Jack and Nate—hell they watched football games also—but their ranches kept them too busy to watch much television as it was. Even Buck's pal, Scottie Warden, didn't recall all the players like Cole did as he prattled out numbers like an accountant. Buck was impressed, to say the least, and enjoyed their conversation while he watched Jack flip the steaks over on the scorching hot grill grates.

"I sure hate that your Momma ain't doing too good, Buck," Nate stated and patted Buck's back in comfort.

The pain that tore through Buck's heart at the mention of his mother nearly caused him to choke on the beer Jack had handed him just moments prior.

He faltered but gave Nathan a weak smile and nodded his head, his throat too tight to speak.

Jack saved him the awkwardness as he said, "So, y'all heard from Scottie lately?"

Buck took another swig of beer and propped his hips on the rail, adjacent to Jack. "Nope. Actually, I've been meaning to call him. Rick too. Damn it's been a while since I talked to him…" Buck trailed off.

Rick Singleton had moved to California—Silicon Valley—about five years after Jack and Natalie had gotten married. The poor bastard had held on as long as he could, waiting for Natalie Kinsen to return Rick's unrequited love for her. When she hadn't, he'd decided he couldn't take anymore. Being in her hometown, reading her weekly column in the local magazine, and hearing about her and her happiness with Jack Kinsen from every friend they'd had eventually just been too much for him, and he'd up and decided one day that he was moving. He was an insurance broker and pretty darn good at it too. They'd all given him a going-away party and wished him well. That had been eight years ago, and Rick had not been back since. Not even to see his family. *Poor Rick*, Buck thought. He'd had the guts to ask Buck about Natalie a few times over the years, as recently as just two years ago, and Buck had told him then that Nat and Jack had a baby boy on the way. His heart went out to the heartbroken fool at that time, for Buck could hear the bitter disappointment in Rick Singleton's voice as Buck updated him on the Kinsens and their brood. Rick was truly never going to get over Natalie.

"Son of a bitch is still in love with her, ain't he?" It was Nathan who asked.

Buck just shook his head and laughed humorlessly, his eyes shooting up to Jack's. "I don't know what it's gonna take; a mighty incredible woman, I reckon," Buck offered.

"I must say, my wife *is* rather unforgettable…" Jack trailed off, looking away, the love for his wife evident in every fiber of his being. "I really do feel sorry for the bastard though. Hell Buck, I reckon you're one of the only men in this town who *wasn't* in love with my wife." Jack laughed, his attempt to lighten the mood.

Buck smiled. "The love I have for Nat was always that of a friend…I was too busy chasing that gorgeous redhead of Nathan's around."

"Hey! Watch out, big guy. I may be old and not as big as you are, but I can still throw a mean punch," Nate bantered and jabbed at Buck's ribs, playfully.

Buck chuckled and batted him away.

He and Nathan had had a heart-to-heart before Nate's marriage to Jordan over a decade ago. Buck wanted no hard feelings between him and his friends of many years—not that there had ever been bad blood between him and Nate where Jordan was concerned. After all, she dated Nate long after Buck and Jordan had called it quits, but Buck had wanted Nate to know he was happy for them both and wished them all the best...and that his feelings for Jordan were completely platonic in the event that he questioned where Buck stood on the matter.

Jack guffawed at their banter and turned back to the steaks as Cole moved towards the grill to ask if he could assist. Jack just gave the young man a smile and told him he was good.

"How's your organization doing, Buck?" Jack asked as he turned to face him.

"Buck's Buckaroos is doing well. I'm gonna be hosting and sponsoring a celebrity golf event this fall. I figure it will be the biggest event to come to our town since well...*ever.*" Buck laughed.

He started telling them all about his ideas for the charity golf tournament in October that he'd started to plan and how exciting it was going to be. There was also gonna be a car show to go along with it, in an attempt to bring in more tourists and donations. It had all been his agent's idea to raise money for the company Buck had founded and become fully immersed in since his retirement.

Talking about all that he'd achieved and planned to accomplish seemed to ease his mind and heart some, and Buck was grateful he'd come to the Kinsens for dinner- even if it was only a short respite from the hell he'd been through for the last month.

Soon, Jack was pulling the steaks off the grill, Nate was handing Buck another cold beer and they were headed back inside, Buck's belly growling at the smell of the char-grilled steak he was following into the house.

They all were seated in the dining room, Buck painstakingly aware that Vivian was ignoring him completely, even despite them both being pulled into separate conversations. Cole once again commended him for his football feats and recalled his many stellar sacks and tackles over the years. Buck got to laughing again, appreciating the light-hearted atmosphere despite Vivian's cold glare at him when they were brought into conversation together or when he made a remark that she didn't seem to like.

He understood, he'd hurt her pride—a lot—but he was quite unprepared for what happened next after Jack asked how the ball went.

Buck responded with, "Quite eventful," just as Vivian smarted off with, "Typical."

All hands stilled on the silverware and all was quiet as Buck's eyes shot up to Vivian's.

Typical? What the *hell* kind of response was that? Their evening together had been magical, incredible, earth-fucking-shattering. It had been *anything* but typical.

Insulted, Buck scoffed, "It was most certainly anything but typical, Vivian."

"Ha! Apparently, it depends on who you ask," she remarked with that haughty look he'd first encountered her with earlier that night. Man, she could sure make someone feel small, despite that Buck was twice her size.

"What *exactly* about it was typical, I'd like to know?" he asked, crossing his arms over his chest as he cut his eyes right back at her, daring her to deny their night was spectacular.

"Wait," Buck heard Dallie say, stymying his next response. "*Both* of you attended the ball?"

Buck felt his heart leap in his throat, realizing just how much they'd given away to their surprised audience amidst their angry tirade.

Vivian recovered quickly, actress that she was. "Yes, and it was downright drab if you ask me."

Buck couldn't believe what he was hearing- first it was typical now it was *drab*? She was utterly audacious to say the least. His anger got the best of him. "Yeah, easy for *you* to say since you're constantly surrounded by the finer things in life! Talk about letting fame go to your head." He thought of his dying mother in that moment and how she would give anything to know the many luxuries Vivian Alexander had been privileged with over the years.

"That's not even what I meant, Buck Jenkins, so why don't you stop assuming that you *know* people you barely just met." Vivian practically shouted at him.

Nat cleared her throat then, and Buck realized the drama he and Vivian had just created. As if the media coverage of that night hadn't been bad enough. Hadn't Natalie and Jack had their fair share of drama over the years? He felt incredibly guilty for how he'd acted as he looked over to Dallie, Savannah and baby Jackson, seated by a smirking Jordan, who just eyed him as if to say, "We'll talk later." *Great!* So much for discretion.

Nat and Vivian went into the kitchen, and once Buck heard Viv exit the back door, he took his opportunity to take his leave. He walked in, apologized to Natalie, and thanked her for the delicious meal and the distraction.

He then ambled back into the dining room to hug the girls, shake Nate and Jack's hands, and kiss Jordan on the cheek, who handed baby Jax over to Nate then as she pulled Buck out the front door, her arm looped through his.

"Buck, what in the *hell* did you do? I guess the press wasn't full of shit like I originally thought, huh?"

"I really don't wanna talk about it right now, Jor, ok?" he pleaded with those all-knowing whiskey eyes of hers, feeling the fatigue of a thousand lifetimes hit him all at once.

She seemed to recognize the look on his face. After all, she probably knew him better than even Nat did. He and Jordan had been intimate after all—many times. He'd seen a whole other side to her, she'd fallen apart in his arms, over and over again.

It all started back in high school with flirting, making-out, curious touches, then by their senior year they were full out messing around. Neither had asked for more, they'd known it was just for fun but damn, he couldn't get enough of that sweet little firecracker in the bedroom. Her passion had been unquenchable, and they'd just kept falling into bed together when he'd come home to visit during college, and even after he was years into the league. He loved his fellow blondes—blondes had more fun or so the saying went—but Jordan Tate had his number, and he hadn't quite been able to scratch that itch he'd had for her.

Perhaps it had been her elusiveness that drew him to her. She'd been one of the few women in his life that hadn't wanted a ring on her finger or a chance at all his money. Perhaps it was her sassy mouth and quick wit, whatever it was, he'd finally asked for more, but she'd been adamant that their relationship stay just as friends, so he'd acquiesced much to his chagrin and disappointment. That had been over fifteen years ago.

Looking at his beautiful friend now, Buck was ever grateful for it too. After all, he was a Leo and she a Scorpio, it never would have worked. For as hot as they burned in the bedroom, it hadn't been written in the stars. He was too stubborn and full of pride, and she was far too rational for all his B.S. Buck knew she and Nate were meant to be. For Jordan and Nathan complemented each other so very well.

"Call me if you need me." Jordan sighed and pulled him in for a hug then. He took comfort in her embrace for a moment then pulled back, kissed her cheek and thanked her.

She and Nat had always been there for him, and he knew deep down in his heart that they always would be—and vice versa. They were more like his family than his friends.

On the ride back to his mom and dad's, Buck started to feel even worse about what he'd done to Vivian. He was a player, that was true; even *he* knew it. He'd broken many women's hearts over the years and spread many a pair of legs, too. Despite a Christian upbringing and a strong moral fiber that ran bone deep, Buck had more lovers than he could count on both hands...and well both feet too, if he were being honest. His mother had been begging him to settle down for years and his father disapproved of his lifestyle and reputation, but Buck had never intended to go through women "like underwear" as the tabloids stated. It had just kinda happened that way.

Buck was a gentle giant after all. Despite his size and aggression on the football field, he'd always been easy-going, soft-spoken, and charming...and women tended to flock to him. He'd never felt sorry for the ones he'd left behind once the deed was done, not really. They'd asked for it, hadn't they? He hadn't promised them anything, after all, and most were too dumb to realize he'd coaxed them right out of their panties until they were screaming in climax in his arms. The few "relationships" he'd had over the years hadn't truly satisfied him and hadn't lasted long enough to matter once he lost interest, which seemed more often than not.

What Buck hadn't realized was that the more he'd passed up stable, respectful women—and relationships—the more it had hurt him in the long run. He was starting to get lonely now. He was starting to see the error of his ways. He was starting to see that his mom had been right all along.

The problem wasn't that Buck was afraid of commitment, hell he wanted to settle down. Commitment didn't scare him like it had Jordan. No, commitment wasn't the issue. It had been the women he'd attracted. They'd just not been right, as cliché as that sounded. Yes, they'd been beautiful, leggy, attractive, and many even more famous than he was. But he tended to attract the needy ones, the clingy ones, the ones who didn't really shine so much without him. Buck craved a strong, independent woman who didn't need him or his money to sparkle. A woman with a light all her own. Jordan had it and Vivian did too. Only now, he'd treated Vivian as badly as he had every other woman before her, when in reality, she'd far surpassed all of them in her intrigue and magnificence. After all, they'd had a connection that night that went far deeper than sex ever had for Buck.

He pulled into the driveway, cut the engine of his silver Chevy Silverado and headed inside to spend some time with his mom, noting his sister's cars were gone.

He opened the door, moving quietly through the house as they had become accustomed to doing when his mom was home. Buck opened the master bedroom door and silently waved to his dad, who hushed him with a finger to his lips, indicating that his mom was sleeping. His old man patted his back and headed out to the living room as Buck replaced his father in the bulky recliner pulled up next to the hospital bed that sat in the center of the room.

Buck looked lovingly at his beautiful mother, clad in one of his old college hoodies, a white bandana wrapped around her head, the covers pulled up to her breasts. He smiled as tears hit his eyes and scooted the chair forward, wanting to be close enough to touch her, smell her, kiss her soft hand. He came close, but didn't touch her as he didn't want to wake her, and settled for watching her sleep and breathe.

He was running out of time, he knew. Soon, she would be gone, and he would be wishing for more time. Would he ever get over her death? As much as he didn't want to regret the last days and as hard as he prayed for her to live, he sensed her pending demise, as if it weren't evident enough in her weakened state and fragile bones. It was a burning deep in his gut, a knowledge that overwhelmed him even as he attempted to prepare his mind and soul for the blow that he knew would soon come. It was a blow that couldn't be anticipated, unlike a tackle or sack. One could usually stand after a hit from a lineman, usually, but this blow was going to hit him harder than any he'd ever had in his life. Losing his mother was going to literally destroy Buck Jenkins.

His mom must have sensed his anguish, for in that instant, she awoke from her slumber, smiling at him as hot tears ran down his face. He hadn't even noticed he was crying until he hiccupped and grimaced, angry with himself for both waking her and letting her see him cry. She was dying, she didn't need his tears right now, she needed his strength.

"Oh, my baby boy, what is it?" Buck's mom asked and reached for his hand. He gripped her little hand in his as if it were his lifeline, not realizing until then how much he needed his momma and her advice, despite that he was a grown-ass, forty-one-year-old man.

"I've done something bad, Momma," he confessed and bowed his head, ashamed at what he was about to tell her.

"Oh, Bobby. You're a good boy, you've always been a good boy. Surely you haven't done something quite as bad as you think."

"I hurt her. I humiliated her. And I feel terrible about it."

He proceeded to tell her all about meeting Vivian Alexander at the Helping Heroes Ball, how he'd been overcome by her beauty and allure, how they'd danced together...and how they'd tore up the sheets of her penthouse suite. He left out some of the juicier details —after all, he was speaking to his mother. He told her about how easy it had been to talk to Vivian, how funny she was, how he'd been eager to get to know more about her, take her out on a date... When he got to the part about walking out of her hotel room without so much as a word, his mother grunted.

"Bobby! Why on earth—"

"I know. I've beat myself up about it ever since. I should've told her, but she was so peaceful in that moment and..." he trailed off.

"Son, you have to apologize, explain to her why you left. No wonder she was as mad as a wet settin' hen," she scolded him, and he couldn't help but grin at her words and her sass, despite her delicate state.

"She was at Nat and Jack's tonight." Buck's blush deepened then as he remembered her words at the dinner table.

"She's *here*? In Abundance?" The excitement in his mother's voice amused him.

"Yeah, you know she and Nat are like BFFs."

"That's right... Well, now's your chance." When he looked at her confused, she continued, "Your chance to do the right thing. To take her aside and apologize. Explain what happened."

Buck hadn't really thought about that, but his mother was right. Vivian was here after all, barely ten miles away. This was his chance to do what he should have done the morning after their amazing night together—tell her what was going on in his life and why no one had seen much of him before the ball or since.

This was his opportunity to tell the one female he'd been unable to get off his mind since that magical night a month ago that the woman he loved more than anything in the world was on her death bed.

CHAPTER 3

"Natalie, you know it's been so long since I've been on one of these blasted things," Vivian scolded even as her horse followed Nat's into a canter.

"Oh, come now. It's like riding a bike, you never forget," Nat responded and looked over at her. "And you had a good teacher. I should know." Natalie winked and laughed.

Vivian was so grateful that she'd come to Kinsen Ranch when she had. This past month, following the morning that Buck had ditched her, had been difficult as she'd fought off the paparazzi, her family's and friend's questions, Hollywood's speculation, and her own misgivings. She'd felt overwhelmed with all the emotions that had come with Buck's duplicity and when she'd finally needed a break, she'd called one of her dearest friends, Natalie Kinsen to come to her house and get away from the city, media and chaos.

She and Nat had hit it off years ago after Vivian came to Starlight Valley to train for her role in the movie *Saddlebred* when Vivian was barely twenty-two and just starting out in Hollywood.

Her success had come fast and easily after her first big movie break in *Paradise Unknown,* where she'd won the lead role playing

Katie Baxter, the young daughter of a business tycoon stranded in the Amazon with a hunky pilot while they battled the elements, the treacherous river, creatures of the darkness, and a burning desire for one another. Her stellar audition had won her the starring role. It was the first of many parts to come that year and had paved her way to stardom.

But Vivian had been ill-prepared when she'd gotten the role of the English rider turned Western all those years ago. She'd craved the part in order to broaden her horizons even though she'd been terrified of horses at the time. She never let something so trivial as fear jeopardize her ambition and drive, so she'd auditioned, gotten the lead, and prayed for a miracle.

Natalie had come through, shown her the ropes and the way of horsemanship, as Natalie was the true definition of a female equestrian. Nat could ride both English and Western eloquently; she'd excelled in her teens, winning ribbons atop her gelding, Cheshire. She'd been a champion and forerunner in many equestrian events since her childhood including racing, jumping, and barrel-racing before moving away to Chicago to become editor-in-chief of one of the leading women's magazines, *Edge*.

Vivian had been grateful to have a woman of Nat's caliber teaching her how women rode horses—as her lead role depicted—and she'd felt an instant connection with Natalie that first day. Viv always thought their bond was due in part to their unwavering perseverance and burning passion for what they loved to do. For Nat it was writing and horse-back riding and for Vivian it was acting—portraying her characters with ardent perfection—and winning Oscars.

Vivian thanked God for his divine intervention that day she'd met Natalie. Not that Jack hadn't been a great teacher, but she'd been far too distracted with his strong sex appeal and charm. Looking back now, Vivian almost laughed at how taken she'd been with the broad-chested cowboy of Natalie's, Jack Kinsen, in those first days. He had the definition of cowboy perfected to a T—rugged, handsome, muscular, and sexy as hell with that ever-present tan Stetson on his head. As a young woman, she'd been instantly infatuated with him—and the other good-looking wranglers on the ranch—including Tad Walters. It hadn't taken Viv long to see though that despite her stardom and youthful radiance, Jack wasn't looking at her the same way, for he was far too head over heels for the gorgeous dark-headed beauty Vivian now rode beside. Viv hadn't a hope in the world. She and Nat had joked about it many times over the years.

She smiled over at Nat, admiring her beautiful friend who'd bore Jack Kinsen two equally as beautiful children. They'd been so happy here on their successful horse ranch for the last decade plus. No one would ever even suspect the sheer hell they'd been put through before she and Jack had gotten married at the hands of Natalie's evil ex-husband, Troy Cameron. Natalie Kinsen was one of the strongest women that Viv had ever known, and she was proud to call her one of her best friend's. But Vivian also envied Nat's life now, her swoon-worthy husband, her beautiful children and the peace she seemed to emit from her like a solar flare.

Vivian realized immediately that her melancholy over the last few months had been due to her own short-comings as a woman. She comprehended that she wanted the same thing her friend had—a husband who loved her like Jack loved Natalie—and she wanted to know what it was like to be a mother before she was too old to conceive one.

Vivian had confessed to Natalie what had happened between her and Buck last night after everyone had left:

"Oh, thank you. I really needed this," Vivian said as she took the wine Nat handed her, although another glass of wine was probably the last thing she "needed".

"Alright, Viv, spill!" she prompted.

"God, I knew you'd notice as soon as he got here."

Nat had always been able to see into people after all.

"You slept with him, didn't you?"

"Is it **that** obvious?" Vivian whined.

"Well," Nat proclaimed, "if it wasn't after your cold reunion, it was even more so at the insults you threw at him at dinner."

"Dammit, I'm sorry," Viv scowled and sipped at her wine.

"What the hell happened?"

"Well, we met at the Helping Heroes Ball—obviously. I knew who he was right away, despite his introduction, and I did my best not to be the least bit deterred by his good ol' boy charm, handsome swag and egotistical attitude, but by then I'd had several drinks," she indicated the wine, "and with his persistence, we danced and talked. We had a great time, really, and it was truly a beautiful evening. Yet, in spite of what I knew about his reputation with bimbos, I invited him back to my hotel room." Viv covered her face with the hand then, consumed with shame and remorse.

"You didn't?" Nat hissed.

"I did!" Viv confirmed and sulked. "But, oh my God, it was fucking amazing, Nat. Seriously, the best sex I've had, ever! We did it so many times... I know you can appreciate amazing sex."

"Of course I can," Natalie chortled. **Of course** she could, her husband was sexy cowboy extraordinaire.

"But then..." Viv sighed heavily. "I woke up and he was gone."

"Gone?"

"Yes. No note, no text, no phone call—no Buck. I was just another one of his one-night stands."

"Oh wow."

"I feel like such a fool, Nat. I was so completely mortified. Buck Jenkins made me do the walk of shame from my own hotel room....and the swarming paparazzi the next morning was my thanks for the night of hot sex he gave me. Dammit! I should've known better."

"Oh, Viv. I'm so sorry." Nat reached out and squeezed Vivian's hand then.

"Yeah, not half as sorry as I'm gonna make him," she brooded.

As if sensing her ongoing distress, Nat had woken Vivian early for a sunrise ride. It had still been dark outside as Natalie came in, grabbed her up, and told her she had thirty minutes to get ready as she'd rifled through Vivian's luggage and threw a pair of jeans, a button-up shirt, and a hat onto the foot of her bed. Vivian had learned long ago that if she was going to be visiting her friends on their ranch, she would need the proper clothing for the occasion. So now, each time she visited, she was well prepared.

Vivian had pinned her hair up, showered, sprayed her long locks with the best smelling dry shampoo on the market and covered her face in her favorite light-coverage tinted moisturizer along with a touch of mascara and a smear of lip gloss, her go-to for when she wasn't caked in heavy makeup for a Hollywood role. She'd dressed quickly, tip-toed out, and followed Natalie down to the barn. She'd been shocked at how fast Nat had tacked up their horses. She assisted some but couldn't remember all the exact steps, and they'd headed out toward the biggest hill on the property just in time to see the sun peeking over the horizon. The way the bright ball of celestial light subtly peered up at them made Vivian feel all gooey inside. It swiftly spread its warmth out like a paper fan, touching the trees, sky and earth with various vibrant hues of pink and purple against the azure blue sky before quickly swirling into magnificent shades of crimson red, brilliant orange and bright yellow.

Vivian wasn't sure when she'd even watched her last sunrise *or* that she'd not been distracted with her work when she did so, for she needed this break from her chaotic life, this peaceful sunrise with one of the dearest friend's she'd ever had. When the sun had cleared the trees, Vivian looked over at Natalie and realized with embarrassment that she'd been crying. She quickly wiped her tears away and waited for the emotions to dampen down some before she spoke, afraid her voice would crack.

"I'm starting to feel it, Nat," she'd confessed. Natalie hadn't responded, just guided their restless horses into a soft walk as she listened. "That damn biological clock ticking in my head...like some damn insistent unwelcome visitor pounding on the door!" Viv had huffed and looked down at her delicate hands on the saddle horn, hating that she was still crying, but grateful that her mascara was waterproof. "I was shamed by that catty talk show host and it stung —God, it stung—to hear the words 'middle-aged' like I was some dried-up old prune! Then Buck fucking Jenkins did what he did, and I was left to pick up the pieces in full sight of the media and the Hollywood gossip pool. I feel like I'm on the verge of a breakdown." She'd hiccupped and tried to rein in her emotions. "Have I really squandered my life away? Am I too career-driven that I haven't focused on anything else? Was Manney right?"

"Oh, Viv," Natalie had murmured and reached her hand out to squeeze Vivian's. "No, honey, you're still young."

"Young? No! I'm *not*! At thirty-five, I'm now considered high risk to have a baby and even if I wanted one, it's not like I have a man to get me pregnant."

"Vivian, sweetheart, calm down," Nat had cooed. Viv hadn't realized she was suddenly hysterical until she'd attempted to take deep breaths in to calm herself down. "First off, women are having babies now *well* into their forties with no serious issues. Heck, I was thirty-eight when Jackson was conceived, and no, you don't *need* a man to have a baby." When Vivian had given her a withered look, Nat chuckled. "Alright well, you need sperm, but not technically a *man* in order to do so." With that, Vivian had laughed. "If I wasn't so possessive of my own man, I would offer to let you borrow him for a round or two, but—"

Vivian laughed then, appreciating Natalie's attempt to lighten the mood. "I could never sleep with Jack, no matter how gorgeous he is. I could never do that to you." Vivian had shaken her head. She might not be the most moral person in the world, but there was one thing she prided herself on, beyond all measure—she refused to mess around with married men. "Plus, I wouldn't be surprised if he turned me down. He has before." She'd winked over at Nat, who laughed big.

"Did I miss this story?"

"Jack never told you?" Vivian had asked, surprised that Jack and Nat hadn't had a big laugh about it at Viv's expense.

Nat had pulled her horse to a stop and looked over at her, brows drawn in curiosity.

"I asked him out while we were training for that movie of mine. It was after you hurt your hands, and Jack was the one teaching me to ride." Nat's eyes had grown more intense as Vivian spoke. "We were out in the corral one morning, and I asked what he was doing later on that evening, if he wanted to go out for coffee or drinks or something and he grinned, chuckled, and blushed. You happened to be walking by at that exact moment, and he looked over at you with such longing that it took my breath away. I knew then—before he respectfully declined, told me he was flattered, but that his heart belonged to someone else—that he was speaking of you. Remember, I apologized for flirting with him later that day?" Viv was certain she'd told Natalie all this years ago.

Natalie had looked away into the distance and gulped, a wistful look on her face. "Wow! What on earth did I ever do to deserve him? I really *do* have the most wonderful husband ever."

Viv had smiled, her heart happy for the two of them. "Yes, you do, Natalie. You truly do."

"I mean, he turned you down...over *me*. Imagine that!"

Viv laughed along with her, although she didn't see what about that was so funny. After all, Natalie Kinsen was equally as gorgeous and worthy of Jack Kinsen in every way possible, far more worthy than Vivian could ever be.

They'd trotted out into the distance at a faster pace, and Vivian's grip tightened on her horse, Ladybird's reins. She wasn't alien to horse-back riding, but it had been some time and she wasn't ready for a jog or gallop quite yet, but relaxed as Nat didn't seem hurried to take them into one. They'd enjoyed the sounds of the birds and the breeze of the peaceful morning as the sun rose higher in the sky.

Nat had packed up an easy breakfast of homemade banana bread, yogurt, fruit and granola and they parked their horses near the creek and ate in a grove of trees as the sun peeked through the leaves of the treetops.

Nat had reassured Vivian again as she'd talked about Buck, her uncertain future, her upcoming movies, and the travel that would be coming with it. Nat spoke of her pride in her three amazing children and how difficult letting Dallie go away to college was becoming for both her and Jack. Their conversation had been light and easy with no more emotional outbursts or confessions from Vivian. Then they began laughing about old times: holidays, birthdays, and get-togethers Vivian had attended with the Kinsens over the years.

Vivian had loved the much needed quiet yet lively ride as they now headed back toward the house, Natalie finally taking them into a canter.

"You don't wanna race, do ya?" Nat asked

"No!" Viv cried even as she laughed at Natalie's free spirit coming out. "Race with your husband or Dallie. You know I don't like galloping."

It was true. Vivian wasn't the adrenaline junkie her cowboy family counterparts were. It was a miracle she was even *on* the horse, she didn't need to race it to feel the power of the half-ton animal beneath her.

She noted Dallie riding her horse off in the distance as she and Nat approached the back gate, and Jack ambled up then and opened it for them, as if anticipating their arrival.

The look on his face as he glanced at her gave Viv pause, and she knew before he spoke that she didn't want to hear what he was about to say, for she knew she wasn't going to like it.

Nat could sense it too as she brought their horses to a halt after they were through the gate and looked down at her husband, who grabbed for Vivian's reins.

"Buck called," Jack began and frowned at Vivian.

Vivian's heart began to hammer in her chest as she said, "And?"

"And he's on his way here." Jack's green eyes pierced hers.

"Why?" Vivian couldn't contain the annoyance in her tone. The nerve!

"He says he needs to see you."

Vivian scoffed and looked over at Nat, who scowled back at her. "Jack! Why did you—"

"Viv, you need to hear what he has to say," Nat interrupted.

Vivian huffed and crossed her arms over her chest, looking between the two of them. "Whose side are you guys on anyway?" She couldn't contain the pout that suddenly popped up on her face.

It was Jack who broke the awkward silence between them all. "Viv, hon, just hear him out at least?" He reached for her hand then and helped her down off the horse, and she frowned up into his face as she jerked her hand back.

"You could have told him I was out riding with your wife and would call him later."

"I did," Jack insisted. "He said you wouldn't call him back, so that's why he's on his way to you."

"Uh." Viv looked over at Nat then, frantically. "I'm not prepared for this. I look terrible. We've been riding all morning; I'm sweaty, my hair is flat, and I smell like a horse." The look she got from both Nat and Jack was nonplussed. "You guys!" She needed to get to a mirror and to doll herself back up. Her hair got frizzy when she got sweaty.

"Viv, you look beautiful," Nat offered. But Viv wasn't convinced.

She looked to Jack then and evaluated his honest eyes.

He nodded and gave her that crooked, laconic smile that had drawn her to cowboys in the very beginning. "You always look beautiful, Vivian. I've never seen you look terrible. Not once. I don't think you could even if you tried." He winked. Finally, she was somewhat swayed, but still wanted a glimpse in the mirror just to be certain.

She wouldn't get it. For at that moment, a brand spanking new silver Chevy Silverado 1500 pulled up in front of the barn, and Buck Jenkins stepped out of it with all the pride of a peacock. He was larger than life in a brown Stetson, white Baylor University t-shirt that looked a size too small on his big frame as it stretched taut against his muscular arms and chest, a pair of well-worn jeans that looked like he'd been melted and poured into them and a pair of tan cowboy boots. Vivian gulped audibly and tried to ignore the flush that hit her cheeks as her body tingled appropriately in response to the walking sex god that was Bobby Buck Jenkins.

She looked uncertainly over at Jack, who seemed amused by her shaken confidence as he was the first to step up and greet Buck, extending his hand as he left her with the horse. She licked her lips then and straightened her spine. She fluffed her hair and raised her chin high as she walked up beside Jack then attempting to calm her frayed nerves. Nat had dismounted by that point and was pulling Buck into her for a tight hug.

Vivian took a slow deep breath in before raising an eyebrow and acknowledging Buck with a curt and simple, "Buck," drawing on her natural talent so as not to swoon all over him.

"Viv, you look—" If the grin on his face wasn't indication enough, his wandering eyes gave him away as they slithered slowly down her body. She shivered again as much from the heat of his gaze as the reignition of her confidence. "Like a sexy little cowgirl I'd like to take for a ride. I rather like it when you hang out with Natalie, I must say." His blonde eyebrow raised.

Eww, he was infuriating. Despite that she knew she looked like a million bucks in her designer jeans, top, and boots that she was sure Jill paid more than two thousand dollars for—the Re/Done jeans alone were over $300 a pair—the audacity of him talking to her so nonchalantly, like he shouldn't be groveling at her feet, had her outraged. She practically stared him down as he blushed and shuffled his feet. Good, she'd made him uncomfortable. He deserved it.

"Well, Nat, uh, let's get these horses brushed down. We'll leave y'all to it," Jack said and turned to grab Ladybird's reigns as one hand went to his wife's lower back.

Nat glanced uncertainly at Vivian then, as if to say, "Are you ok?"

Viv just nodded and looked back up at Buck then. A sadness took over him at that moment, one she'd seen before, the night of the ball before he'd made love to her—well if that's what one wanted to call what round number three had been. Some of Vivian's edge dropped, and she took in the subtle dark circles beneath his eyes, the paleness of his face, the weariness that suddenly emanated from him. She frowned, but he smiled, putting on a good front as if she'd not noticed; she'd noticed.

"I was, uh, gonna see if you wanted to…go to lunch," Buck said, his tone had changed.

Vivian couldn't dare say no to the tenderness in his face at that moment, but she wouldn't be so quick to acquiesce before making him grovel a little.

"And if I weren't hungry?" She arched a brow at him.

"Beer? Coffee? Ice cream?" he asked. She answered with only a withered look and crossed her arms over her chest. "C'mon, Viv, just give me a chance to talk to you, please?" He gulped, looking far older than his forty-one years, as if whatever burden he had on his shoulders had aged him.

Vivian balked for a second. What on earth did he have to tell her? Dread seized her heart as she suddenly felt uneasy about whatever it might be.

She looked at her watch, as if absent-mindedly, and noted the time. "It's close enough to lunch time, I *suppose* I could accompany you."

Buck smiled big then and extended his elbow, nodding his hat to her for her to take his arm. She huffed, but approached and allowed him to escort her to his truck. He opened the passenger door and saw her in, making sure she was settled and buckled in before he shut the door and came around to the other side. She cleared her throat as he got in and cranked the truck, shifting into reverse.

Viv looked around the spacious new truck with its leather seats and wood grain interior; it was a beauty. She tried not to feel rattled by the overpowering presence of his massive frame as it seemed to fill the big truck. His smile took over his whole face as he looked over at her beside him.

"What?" she asked, feeling self-conscious.

"You look really good in cowgirl gear." His eyes slid over her body once again as they drove down the black top, and she felt herself flush.

"Thank you. My uh, my designer...she picked it out." Vivian dismissed and tried to focus her eyes ahead and away from his tempting gaze.

"You looked amazing in that dress at the ball too, but that hat- it suits you."

At the mention of the word "hat", a barrage of emotions hit her as she remembered that he'd left his own cowboy hat in her room as a slap in the face. She closed her eyes against the anger as she scowled and asked, "Buck! What are you doing?"

"I'm taking you to lunch," he surmised as if the answer was quite clear.

"No, you *know* what I mean." She dared a glance over at him.

"You're not gonna make this easy on me, are you?" he asked, regretfully. *Why would I?* she wanted to scream at him. But before she could actually respond, he said, "You know I haven't stopped thinking about you since that night."

She couldn't hide the sarcasm she felt in that moment, "And what makes *me* any different than all the other blondes of your past?" She crossed her arms over her chest once again, trying to hide her breaking heart from him.

"Viv," Buck said and sighed heavily. "I'm truly sorry. I swear I *never* had any intentions of leaving you alone in that bed."

"Oh?" her voice trembled as she clamped her lips closed, blinking back the tears that hit her eyes.

"I wanted more."

"More? More *sex*?" she asked incredulously. God, the man was insatiable! They'd had enough sex to make her sore as shit the next day.

"No, Vivian," he scoffed and turned towards her. "Well, yes... but...well, more *everything*."

Vivian hadn't realized he'd parked the truck until she looked over at the old gas station that looked to be long abandoned decades ago.

She looked back at him. The cowboy hat shielded his face as his head fell, and she heard him take a deep breath in. She felt the tears fall then as the bitter regret and anger of the situation hit her full force and she loudly said, "Do you *know* how humiliating it is to be labeled as yet another one of Buck Jenkin's *bimbos?*"

"I know," he stated gravely and slowly brought his head up to look at her. "But I swear to you, I never meant for that to happen." He sighed again, looking away, his own eyes cloudy with unshed tears. "Viv, there's somethin' I need to tell you." He looked back at her with such intensity that her heart leapt up into her throat. What was he about to tell her? Was he married? She quickly looked to his left hand on the steering wheel—no ring, thank God! "My sister Beth called me early that morning and told me that my mother was septic and had been put into a medically-induced coma." Vivian gasped and covered her hand over her mouth. "All I could think about in those moments was getting to her." Buck's voice was thick with emotion but soft as he spoke. "You see, there's a reason that no one has heard much from Buck Jenkins over the last four months...that's because my mother was diagnosed with metastatic cancer and we've been fighting like hell since that day to try and battle it. But about a month ago, things started to go downhill. Vivian." Buck swallowed hard. "My mother's dyin'. Her time is comin' to an end. She's home now and she's alright for the time being, but she grows weaker by the day. There's nothing more that can be done. It's all palliative care now."

Vivian just let the tears fall as her eyes took him in. How horrible that must be, to know that his mother was dying and there was nothing all his fame or fortune could do to stop it. Vivian gulped as she reached out her hand to take his then, feeling such sorrow for him and the trials and tribulations his family had been through.

"I'm so sorry, Buck. I had no idea," she stated truthfully. "No one told me, not Nat or—"

"It wasn't their story to tell," he admonished. She just nodded. That much was true. "That morning, you were so peaceful, so beautiful laying there. So sweet. The purity of your ignorance held me captive, and I couldn't wake you if I'd wanted to. I couldn't interrupt your slumber, so I left. You don't know how much I regret it; it's eaten me alive all this time. That I made you feel like you were nothing more than a one-night stand, just another 'bimbo' in my line of past lovers... It's the farthest thing from the truth, I swear it." He kissed the back of her hand, and she gulped against the fresh wave of tears that coursed down her cheeks.

She couldn't let it go at that though. He had to know what he'd done to her. "You left me to deal with an overwhelming band of paparazzi when I left the hotel; they ambushed me. I've been harassed by them mercilessly for weeks now."

"I know. I saw. I'm truly sorry. Please understand." He bowed his head again, and Vivian's fight left her. It wasn't in her to hold grudges, not when this man had been through his own personal hell during that time frame too.

They sat there for long moments, taking in the silence of the truck, Buck absent-mindedly stroking the back of her hand with his thumb. She rested it on his left pectoral muscle and felt electricity spike through her, remembering their night together a month ago. Finally, her tears ceased, and she tried to make light of the situation, for despite that drama was her life, she didn't do so well when she was facing it head on.

"So where on earth can we go in this town where the media won't be ogling us like the celebrities that we are?" she asked.

"Oh, don't you worry none about that; home is where I come to get away from them." He smiled big as his head came up then.

He held her hand as he cranked the truck again and headed back down the road. She tried to calm her frantic heart as holding his hand made her entire body tingle and the stroking of his finger in her palm made her center throb.

They didn't speak until he pulled up in front of a quiet downtown restaurant with the title, Bob's Burger Bar. Vivian couldn't help but laugh at the name.

"Bob's Burger Bar?"

"Yup! Best burgers and shakes in town."

"I take it Bob is your dad?" she asked, looking over at him in curiosity.

"No," he said with a laugh. "My dad's name is Bill actually. I'm not sure that Bob knows he has a burger bar or, furthermore, who Bob even is since the lady who owns the place is Doris."

Vivian laughed at his pun. "Perhaps, it's a late husband? "she offered.

"I dunno, Doris isn't married. Her boyfriend's name is Earl." Buck shrugged.

He got out of the truck and came around to escort her, seeing her unease at the crowded street before them. "Don't worry. No one's gonna harass you here. Not while I'm around," he whispered and winked.

They entered the little burger joint with an array of red leather booths and tables and checkered black and white tile floors. It was a fairly casual place that resembled any other chain burger restaurant, save for the wooden counter ahead of them and the handwritten chalkboard menu above a large galley window that gave the patrons a peek into the grill.

"Bobby!" an old-lady's voice called from behind the counter. Vivian presumed it must be Doris, as she looked over at the old white-headed woman, who laughed as she saw Buck. "It's about time you came to see us. It's been a while, kiddo. And who's this lovely cowgirl you got with you?"

The old woman, who looked to be in her late fifties, came around the counter with two menus and approached them, kissing Buck's cheek. She wore a dirty white apron and floral dress that was tighter around her pot belly than the rest of her. She couldn't have been more than five feet tall, but her caring nature was evident as she hugged Buck and extended her hand to Vivian.

"I'm Doris Patterson, and you are?"

"Doris, this is Vivian," Buck said quietly, looking around quickly, seeing if they'd been noticed. Vivian shook the older woman's hand before doing the same and noticed the murmuring that had taken place among the lunch crowd. Her unease grew.

Doris must have sensed it too, for she said, "Your usual table, I reckon?" She winked and escorted them toward the back of the restaurant as Vivian tried to keep her head down.

We'll be bombarded by the press come tomorrow, she thought. Thank goodness Jack owned land that was private property, and she wouldn't see them on the Kinsens' lawn come morning at least.

Once sat, Doris took their drink orders and told them she would give them a few minutes to peruse the menu.

"I know they don't have organic salad and...stuff here, but I figured most places wouldn't, so this was as good as any." Buck shrugged, blushing.

"This is perfect." Vivian smiled back at him and debated on whether she wanted onion rings or French fries as she looked over the grease laden menu that listed everything from meatloaf sandwiches to foot-long chili slaw dogs. Well, she was in a burger joint after all, and judging from the size of the one that just came out of the kitchen, they looked delicious.

Doris came to take their order after several minutes had passed.

"What'll it be, hon?" Doris looked to Vivian, but she motioned for Buck to go first, not sure what to order. He hesitated momentarily but soon obliged. He ordered a burger royale, which was a traditional cheeseburger topped with bacon and a fried egg, he added a side of fries.

"Oh, that sounds delicious. I want the same, only with onion rings. Those look fantastic." Vivian nodded over to the heaping plate of onion rings at the table adjacent to them.

"Oh, they are. Beer battered." Doris winked.

"Even better," Viv said with a smile and licked her lips.

After Doris walked off with their orders, Buck smiled slyly at Vivian.

"I'm pretty surprised that you ordered like that. I was expecting you to get a salad with tofu or something."

"Tofu? Yuck!" Viv stuck out her tongue in disgust. "No. When I'm on vacation, I actually eat how I want. I'll probably regret it later, but after the steak last night, I figured what the hell?"

Buck grinned again, "Yeah, I've been eating a lot of junk lately myself with Momma being in the hospital and all. I've gotten soft." He patted his belly then and looked up at her regretfully.

Vivian couldn't help but scoff. Considering his chiseled biceps, veined forearms, and broad chest, she had no idea what he was talking about, he looked like he'd just left the gym. "If that's your version of 'soft' I'd *love* to see your version of 'hard'." Her brow cocked as her eyes fell over him once more.

"You already have, lover," he admonished and winked. Viv gulped as heat engulfed her at the look in his eyes. She remembered his hard-muscled body loving her, his big hands touching every part of her, and she felt a longing for him so deep it startled her. She wanted to feel his naked body against her again so badly that she ached with it. She wanted to lose herself to his kiss and his passion.

He must have recognized it himself for his eyes burned hard into hers. "I want you to know how amazing that night was."

She looked down then, blushing. It truly *had* been amazing. Every single minute of it. She wanted to tell him so, but her chest seared at the heartache he'd already caused her and she hesitated.

About that time, she heard a deep voice call out, "Buck fuckin' Jenkins! What the hell, dude?" They both turned to see a man with cropped brown hair and a goatee approach them, Vivian steeled herself, hoping this man didn't recognize her and start a frenzy; there were so many people around already.

"Scottie Warden! Damn, I ain't seen you in a month of Sundays. How are ya, brother?" Buck stood and quickly embraced the man whose arm was tattooed with a half-naked cheerleader that winked at Vivian, who just looked up from the booth at the two of them. They patted one another's backs as they pulled back and smiled. He was obviously a friend of Buck's, she surmised.

"I'm fine. I'm fine. How the hell are you, man? Patty said your Momma finally got to go home the other night. I'm glad to hear it. How is she?"

Buck's demeanor changed then and he frowned as his voice lowered, "Not good, friend. Not good. I've been meaning to call you."

The man named Scottie cursed and patted Buck's big shoulder, shaking his head. Suddenly, Scottie's gray eyes fell on Vivian. "Damn, dude, I ain't interrupting, am I?" Scottie murmured, and Buck turned to look at her, smiling.

"Scottie, I want you to meet Vivian Alexander. Vivian meet Scottie Warden, one of my oldest friends. Scottie went to high school with me and Nat."

Scottie gaped as he extended his hand to her, and she took it politely. "Nice to meet you, Mr. Warden."

Vivian beheld a ruggedly handsome face as Scottie's open mouth slowly pulled up into a broad smile. He looked every bit of his forty-one years as his laugh lines and crow's feet were far more pronounced than Buck's. He was deeply tanned and the hair on his chin and around his ears had some grey in it. Instead of making him look old, it made him look distinguished. She liked him immediately as he took her hand, turned it over and kissed the back of it.

"Vivian Alexander! Wow. You're even more beautiful in person. It's truly a pleasure." His eyes returned to Buck's as he gently dropped Vivian's hand. "How on earth do ya get so damn lucky?" Scottie shook his head. "If I didn't love ya so much, I'd freakin' hate ya." Scottie punched his arm. He looked back at Vivian then. "So, you know Natalie?"

She nodded as Buck answered with, "Yeah, her and Nat go way back. You know, she and Jack trained Vivian for that movie all those years ago. They've been close ever since."

"That's right, that's right," Scottie recalled, rubbing his chin. "I remember now. You staying with Nat then I reckon?" Vivian just nodded again and smiled. "Wait a minute." Scottie frowned and pointed at Vivian then. "Is this the one that you *left* at the hotel after the ball?"

As if cutting open an already gaping wound, Vivian visibly shuddered. Her chest burned once again, and she swallowed hard at the reminder.

Buck growled with a curse, "Thanks for bringing that up, Scottie. Who needs enemies…"

"Hey, *you* did it, not me!" Scottie laughed big then and looked back at Vivian, who couldn't contain her frown. "If it's any consolation, Miss Alexander, he don't ever take his girls out on dates. They're usually just taken to the bar." Scottie winked.

"Jesus Christ, you get more ornery as you age, you asshole." Buck punched at Scottie's arm.

"Well, I might just need a Vivian Alexander in my life." Scottie winked at her again. "You let me know if this old man does you wrong again. I'll give you my number; Scottie Warden'll take *good* care of you." Vivian couldn't help but laugh at his conviction. Buck just rolled his eyes and told him to shove it. "Yeah, I know. Still the same ol' charmin' S.O.B. I've always been." Scottie shrugged then, and Viv giggled at his earnestness. He certainly was funny, she'd give him that. He seemed genuine enough; she didn't think he'd intended to hurt her feelings mentioning Buck's jilting at the hotel. "Well, I reckon I'll let y'all eat in peace. Buck, take care and let's get together soon, huh?"

Buck shook his hand again and nodded as Scottie took his leave.

"I'm really sorry about that," Buck murmured. Viv's hand went up, signaling that an apology wasn't needed as she closed her eyes. "Honestly though, Viv." He grabbed her hand, suddenly and firmly, commanding her attention, and her eyes jerked up to his. "Somehow, some *way*, I'm going to make that up to you. I swear it before God." The intensity in his clear blue eyes held her captive.

About that time, Doris approached with their food, and Buck pulled his hand back as she sat the heaping plates down.

Vivian looked to the giant burger, knowing she'd be lucky to finish half of it as Buck laughed at her expression.

"Big burger for a little thing like you," he whispered as Doris walked away.

"Believe it or not, Mr. Jenkins, this girl can put away some meat." Viv winked, realizing her double entendre just as Buck bit into his burger. His eye shot up to hers, and she practically cackled then covered her mouth and looked around to see what attention she'd drawn to herself as Buck attempted to swallow down his bite without choking on it.

After he did so, he balked, his eyebrows shooting up. "Oh, I remember...very well, in fact." His gorgeous blue eyes pierced hers and she had to look down to tear her eyes away from the scorching lust that licked at her from his gaze.

She remembered their night all too well herself, her center suddenly aching to have him filling her once again. She cut her burger in two and grabbed one half up, bringing the gooey, juicy mess to her mouth. She bit into it and savored the taste of flavorful beef, smoky bacon and tangy mayo and moaned aloud as she chewed. She didn't indulge her appetite often and felt this was a treat knowing she wouldn't have it again for God only knew how long.

"Good, right?" Buck asked in between bites.

"I'll pay for it later," Viv murmured, taking another bite as she reached for a big onion ring that was almost the size of a dinner plate. "Where do they *get* onions this size?"

Buck just shrugged and took another bite of his burger, yolk from the fried egg leaking out of the corner of his mouth. Viv laughed and grabbed her napkin, reaching up to wipe it off his lips. His eyes softened then as he swallowed his bite and took her hand again.

"Thanks for giving me another chance, Viv," he said softly, just loud enough for her to hear him. She shivered at the intensity in his eyes and simply nodded. "I know that I don't deserve it, but truly I swear..."

Vivian shook her head and shushed him. He'd already apologized enough for one day. He didn't need to continue to grovel. "Let's enjoy our meal, ok?"

And they did. Viv was able to finish half her burger and almost half her portion of onion rings, while Buck finished the entire plate, licking his fingers as he did so.

Doris came by then and grabbed their dirty dishes, asking if they wanted dessert, to which Viv shook her head. "Oh, come on now. I just made a fresh peach pie this morning... it comes a-la-mode," she insisted, sing-songy. Viv smiled and looked to Buck, whose eyebrows went up.

"Sure. We can split it, Viv," Buck stated, confidently.

"Good deal. You need a box, hon?" Doris asked and looked to Vivian.

"No... I—"

"Yeah, bring us a box, Dory. Dad'll eat that," Buck stated and nodded to the leftovers. Viv just smiled at Doris as she walked away, and Buck's hesitant gaze fell on her once again. "He doesn't eat much lately, so that'll be perfect for him," Buck trailed off and looked down suddenly. "I honestly don't know what he's gonna do without her."

Vivian said nothing as she steeled her nerves. She couldn't imagine losing either of her parents, despite that she and her mother didn't get along well at all. Her parents had divorced when Vivian was only sixteen years old and things had been tense between them ever since. Vivian didn't see them often as she and her mother hadn't been close—even since before the divorce; she'd caught her mother cheating on her father. Viv had gone to live with her father afterwards, not far from her childhood home, in Burbank, California. He hadn't remarried until Vivian was an actress; he now had two daughters, ages eight and twelve.

Viv felt like the outsider in her family. Her maternal grandmother blamed her father for not giving her mother, Gwenyth, the attention she'd deserved which she claimed had led to the affair. Gwen was quite the drama queen, it was where Viv got her acting skills, but she'd married the man she'd cheated on Vivian's father with. His name was Carl. They'd moved to Atlanta when Viv was eighteen where Gwen had become the wife and mother—to two teen boys—with her new family that she'd never been with her old.

Vivian's father, Jacob, in turn had been a devoted father to Viv and spoiled her, giving her anything and everything she'd wanted, perhaps to do whatever it took to keep Vivian from leaving as her mother had. He'd only remarried once she'd found stardom and even then, it had seemed to be just to have someone to dote on. His wife, Liz, had always seemed jealous of Vivian and had told her once that she thought Jacob was still in love with Gwen, despite that he'd been a loving husband and father over the last thirteen years. Their marriage wasn't a match made in heaven, by any means, but they'd stayed together and appeared happy regardless of their various differences.

In lieu of her family's obvious dysfunction, Vivian loved them, even if they all didn't see eye to eye. Her mother and father had not been in the same room together in almost two decades and probably never would again. Viv's holidays always consisted of duplicates, reunions were chaotic, and she'd never felt a true connection to any of her four siblings not only due to the generation gaps but because her parents tended to favor them over her. Perhaps it was because they were younger and needed the attention, either way Viv felt like she was on a different planet when she was in their midst. Which was why it was seldom that she was.

Suddenly, Buck looked up at her uncomfortably.

"What is it?" Viv asked.

"Would you come and meet my mother?"

Viv gasped softly and hesitated.

"I know that may seem off-putting, but she would be thrilled. She's one of your biggest fans, and I don't know if she'll be—" He let the rest hang in the air as he looked away and gulped. He didn't need to finish the sentence for her to know what he meant.

She hesitated only a moment before saying, "Of course I will."

"Are you sure? I didn't mean to be presumptuous. You don't owe me anything, after all, but it would mean the world to her."

"Buck." She smiled and reached for his big hand. "I would be honored to meet your mother."

CHAPTER 4

*V*ivian was actually nervous about meeting Buck's mom. She'd met many fans over the years and even dying ones, but this was the woman who'd birthed the legendary defensive end, Buck Jenkins, the man with whom Vivian had had raw, unadulterated, gratuitous sex with just a month ago and truth be told, wanted to have it again. What was she going to say? *"Hi, Mrs. Jenkins. I'm Buck's current bimbo?"*

She tried to act nonchalant as Buck parked the truck. She glanced at her reflection in the side view mirror as he came around to open her door and escort her in.

The red brick ranch-style house looked to be in an older but well-kept neighborhood with mature oaks and sycamore trees. The houses were spaced a good distance apart and the drives were private and long, which Vivian appreciated.

The door was unlocked as Buck went in first and held the door open for Vivian to enter.

The house was quiet save for the soft drone of a television and an overhead ceiling fan. The kitchen was off to the left of the small foyer with a living room to the right.

An older man, presumably Buck's father, approached from a dark hallway then and waved at them. He had flaxen blonde—nearly white—hair, was clean shaven and had eyes similar to Buck's. He was tall, like Buck, but he was nowhere near as broad or muscular. He wore khaki slacks and a polo shirt.

"Hey, Dad," Buck spoke first as the older man closed the distance between them. "I want you to meet Vivian Alexander."

Buck's father balked for a moment before recovering and extending his hand. "Miss Alexander. Boy, Laurel's gonna be stunned. Welcome to our home. I'm Bill Jenkins."

"Mr. Jenkins." Vivian shook the older man's hand. "You have a lovely home; I love all the pineapples."

She pointed to the gold pineapples on the fireplace mantle, the kitchen towels, and the sign over the hallway door that said "Imi Ola."

Bill laughed. "Laurel has always loved Hawaii and pineapples. I took her there before Bobby here came along…he, uh, he was actually conceived on that trip come to think of it."

Vivian laughed heartily, Bill joined her, but Buck just blushed and stared at his dad in shock.

"Hawaii *is* a romantic place after all." Viv shrugged as she looked back at Buck.

Buck cleared his throat then. "I brought you half a burger. We went to Doris's for lunch."

"Thank you," Bill stated and took the to-go container Buck handed him. "But Doris's? Really, son? Of all the places in town to take a Hollywood star to, you choose a greasy burger joint?" Bill scoffed and shook his head, entering the kitchen. He mumbled something that sounded like, "No wonder you don't have a girl-friend." Vivian couldn't help but stymy a laugh.

"Is Mom up?" Buck asked and moved towards the kitchen bar where two barstools sat, his big hands gripping the back of one of them.

"Yeah, your sister's here talking to her."

"Which one?" Buck grumbled.

"Beth."

"Oh, good." Buck seemed relieved.

"You know you'll have to call Blair. She'll make you live to regret it if you let Miss Alexander leave before she gets to meet her."

Buck swore under his breath before saying, "Alright." He rolled his eyes and grabbed his phone from his back pocket. Vivian heard the clicking as his thumbs texted and in less than ten seconds his phone was ringing. He looked to Vivian apologetically and motioned that he was going to take the call. She nodded, and he walked into the living room, out of ear shot.

"I apologize. My spawn, as you can see, isn't the most couth of us." Bill shook his head as he sat the container down on the counter top. "I'll blame all the hits he took to the head while playing football." Bill winked, and Viv could see where Buck got his charm from. "Please, have a seat." He beckoned to the bar stool. "Can I get you anything—coffee, tea?" Viv shook her head and smiled.

She wouldn't correct Bill and tell him that up until Buck had left the morning following their fling, he'd been more of a gentleman to her than any man she'd ever met before in her life...well, save for Jack Kinsen.

"So, what brings you into town, Miss Alexander? You filming a new movie?"

Vivian laughed as she sat herself down on the bar stool, and Bill turned and opened a cabinet, grabbing a plate. "I am, but it's not here in town. It's out in the Vancouver/Seattle area. I needed a break though, so I called Natalie up. I'm staying with them."

"Ah, the Kinsens. Such great people."

"Indeed. Some of the best."

"Well, I'm glad you're getting a break," Bill said and placed the half burger and onion rings on the plate, tossed the container and took the plate over to the microwave. "How long you in town for?"

"Just a couple days. They're holding filming until I get back, so unfortunately—"

"Wow, that's nice. But I guess when you're a big star, you get to call the shots, huh?"

Actually, Vince Vogner had been livid with her for taking off as abruptly and inconveniently as she had. He'd cussed, threatened, and showed his ass when she'd told him she was taking a few days off with or without his permission. He'd said he'd never work with her again, and for good reason; they'd literally started shooting barely three weeks prior, but she'd not backed down, for her nerves were shot and she simply *had* to get away. She realized she'd probably bit off more than she could chew doing back to back movies in various locations, but once she was done with this one, she was taking some time in between.

Buck came back in about that time, frowning.

"What'd she say?" Bill asked before biting into the reheated burger.

"She's on her way," Buck huffed. "I'm not to *think* about taking one foot out the door before she gets to meet Vivian. You see what I have to put up with?" Buck rolled his eyes, and Vivian just grinned big. "You sure you're up for this?" He arched a blond eyebrow at her. She just shrugged. "Come on. Let's go see my mom."

Buck led her through the dark wide hallway to the very back of the house which opened to a large master suite. He knocked briefly before entering, and Vivian heard a soothing voice call out, "Bubba," followed by an excited, "Uncle Bobby!"

Buck embraced an attractive blonde and a little girl ran at him and wrapped her arms around his leg. Vivian smiled at her; she was a cute little thing, scrawny with scraped knees, wearing mint green shorts and a paisley purple top. She looked up at Vivian after giving Buck's thigh a squeeze and stepped back.

"Uncle Bobby?" the little blonde asked.

"Yeah, babe?"

"Who's that?" the little girl pointed up to Vivian, and the woman stepped out of Buck's embrace; they both turned simultaneously toward Vivian. Viv took a deep breath as the woman gasped and covered her face.

"Oh my God! It's her! It's...it's..."

"Beth, Heather, I want you to meet Vivian Alexander."

It took Beth a moment to gather herself before she finally stepped forth and took Vivian's outstretched hand. Beth was gorgeous with lavender eyes, dimples, and thick platinum blonde hair with golden highlights. She was dressed in a lovely peach-colored dress suit—that complemented her porcelain complexion—with a silk white collared shirt underneath it.

"It's great meeting you, Miss Alexander. I'm Beth Harwick, Buck's oldest sister." She gave Viv a firm handshake.

"It's nice meeting you too, Beth." Vivian returned her smile.

"And I'm Hea-thw," the little blonde doll beside her spoke out with a lisp.

"Well, it's nice to meet you, Heather." Vivian squatted down to shake her hand and Heather took it, giving her a toothless grin. "How old are you?" Heather held up seven fingers and Vivian gaped. "Wow! You're such a big girl." Viv tickled at the little girl's belly, and she gave a little giggle. "You know. When I was seven, I met my first actress too."

"Really?" Heather's eyes got really big.

"Yes. You're probably too little to remember her, but I met the stunning Kat Khan. My dad took me on a studio tour, and she just happened to be on set, walking by. My star on the Hollywood Walk of Fame isn't far from hers, can you believe that?"

Heather just shook her head in awe. She probably wasn't even aware of what the Hollywood Walk of Fame was, but Viv would let her be, for the look she was giving Vivian now was why she wanted to become an actress in the first place; she'd given Kat Khan the same stare. She stood then, and Buck's hand went to her lower back, she smiled up at him.

"We stopped by after my showing. Heather wanted to give

Momma what she made her in art class yesterday," Beth stated and smiled down at her daughter.

"Nana's gonna hang it up right there." She pointed to the wall beside a large hospital bed near the back of the room, where a small older woman lay.

Despite her weakened state, she gave Vivian a massive grin, and Vivian immediately moved toward her without hesitation.

Her small frame was cloaked in a giant hoodie that literally swallowed her—it had to be one of Buck's—and her head was hugged by a lovely knitted beanie cap that accentuated her crystal-clear blue eyes. She wore a necklace made of elbow macaroni and was propped up by several large pillows behind her back. Vivian could immediately see where Buck and Beth got their looks, for their father was handsome, but their mother was a true looker, well, at least before cancer had taken her health from her. Viv saw what Buck had been talking about though; his mother was so pale and fragile-looking. Her tiny arms appeared to struggle with the effort as she lifted them up to embrace Vivian. Vivian leaned as gently into Buck's mother as she could, her arms hugging the frail older woman's tiny frame, feeling bones as she did so.

When Viv pulled back, Buck's mom grasped her hand and a tear slid down her sunken cheek. Viv couldn't help but return her exuberance.

"Vivian Alexander. In my home. I can't believe it! I'm Laurel Jenkins. I'm so happy to meet you."

"Laurel, the pleasure is all mine, I can assure you."

"Ha! Nonsense," Laurel waved her off. "Meeting a dying woman on her death bed is no pleasure at all. But I appreciate you coming here anyway. I see my son made amends. I'm so proud of him." Laurel looked over at Buck with such pride that it burned a hole in Vivian's stomach. Buck didn't seem to be one to admit his faults much, Viv assumed. This must be a big deal for his family.

She wouldn't admit to the older woman that things still weren't entirely smoothed over, for Viv's heart still burned with anguish at what he'd done, but Buck's mother didn't need to know that. Vivian just nodded.

Buck whispered to his sister then and kissed her cheek, patted the little girl's head, and ambled over as Beth and Heather took their leave. He scuffled his feet as he stopped at the foot of the bed and appeared to be nervous as he looked down at Vivian, who had sat down next to his mother.

"Uh, Beth's gonna bring you some dinner from Annie's, she said you like their chicken and dressin.'"

"Oh, that sounds good, something different. Tell her I want peas and mashed potatoes to go with it too."

Buck gave her a crooked grin and nodded. "I'll tell her. Sounds like your appetite is back."

"Yeah, it tends to wax and wane. Today is a good day. Billy made me a sandwich earlier. I ate about half of it."

"That's good, Momma. I'm glad." He came to the other side of the bed and sat, taking her hand in his. Her little hand could have been a child's as he held it in his own massive one.

"I'm so glad to see the two of you made up," Laurel said, her eyes scrutinizing them both. "Vivian, you're even more beautiful in person. Bobby's lucky to have met you. He's a good boy, my son, even if his moral compass has been spinning round and round all these years. I'm glad it led him to you." Vivian just blushed. His moral compass hadn't even been in the picture on the night they'd met, for their union had been anything but moral. "And Bobby, you take care of this girl, you hear me. You don't be going and doin' her no such a way as you did. I don't care *what* happens in the future, that don't give you no right to go breaking hearts like you have."

"Momma," Buck mumbled, indignantly.

"I know, I know. But I'm a wise old woman and I'm *dying* and it's important for you to find someone to share your lives with. That's all I'm sayin'. Can I ask you somethin'? And answer me truthfully now, both of you." She gripped their hands in her own, squeezing tighter than Vivian thought could be possible. "For all your fame and fortune, all your success, all the Oscars, all the Super Bowl rings, all the fans... Are you happy? Was all of it even worth it if you don't have someone to go home to, someone to love, someone to lay down next to at night and share your stories with?"

Vivian was taken off guard as she looked down into the frail woman's candid gaze. Then she glanced over to Buck, whose head had turned to look at her at the same time. The clarity in his sky-blue eyes held her captive, and she gulped as her nerve endings tingled with electricity. She was aware of his breathing, his warmth, his presence, his focus on her; it was as if time stood still and held them suspended for a moment. The subtle smile that lifted the corner of his mouth took her breath away; her entire body hummed, not just from desire, but with a certainty she'd never felt before. As if Buck had sent out an indiscernible pulse of sonar and she was the ping back to him.

She started as the door swung open without warning, and Bill said, "Bobby, phone for you."

Buck turned and grimaced, unhappy with the interruption. He excused himself and jerked up off the bed.

When the door was shut, Viv looked to Laurel and gave her a weak smile.

"My son has feelings for you, you know?" Wouldn't any dying mother say that, in hopes that their child had someone to hold on to when they were gone? "I know you don't believe that, but it's the truth."

"Buck and I barely know each other." Vivian blushed. She didn't want to give Laurel false hope despite that she was on her death bed. She didn't deserve to be lied to; she deserved the truth.

"When the heart knows, it knows, honey." Laurel gave an easy shrug.

Yeah, well, hearts were complicated, that much Vivian knew, but she just nodded at the older woman. "You have a lovely home, Mrs. Jenkins." Viv wanted to pull the attention off herself.

"Don't change the subject!" Laurel huffed and looked her dead in the eyes. "I know he did you wrong. He ain't the best when it comes to his feelings; never has been. But don't give up on him just yet. He cares for you. I feel it in every ounce of my being."

Then why did he **treat** *me like he did?* Vivian wanted to ask, her heart still trying to mend its broken pieces back together. He'd known she was in a vulnerable state that night. And it didn't stop him from walking out the door without a word. It would have taken him two seconds to tell her good-bye. But he hadn't even had the decency to do *that.* She couldn't build a relationship on a faulty foundation. She'd done that far too many times already. She was too old for the games that Buck liked to play. She wouldn't be had by him or any other man, not ever again.

As if sensing her resolve, Laurel said, "He's *never* brought a woman to meet me before, you know?"

Vivian frowned at her, surprised. "Never?"

"If you wanna count Jordan Tate then yes, but she was his friend back in grade school, long before they were ever lovers."

Buck and Jordan had been lovers? When the heck had that happened? Of course, Vivian hadn't been around Jordan as much as she had Nat and Jack, so she wouldn't have known either way. Jordan and Nate had gotten together not too long after Viv had grown close to the Butlers and Kinsens, so Jordan and Buck must have been together when Buck was much younger. Either way, Buck had really *never* brought a woman home to meet his family? Viv found that rather difficult to understand.

"Vivian, he's in love with you. A mother knows her child. He's never looked at a woman the way he looks at you, and when he talks about you…" she trailed off as Viv looked down. *He'd talked about me?* To his mother? Wow! "Child." Laurel lifted Vivian's chin then. "He was a wreck knowing what he did to you. It was eating him up inside. I've never seen him so distraught." Was that true? Could he have been as miserable as she was? This whole time?

Their conversation was interrupted as the door was thrust open once again and a vivacious blonde burst through it, beaming as brightly as a Christmas tree. This must be Buck's other sister.

"Oh *my* God!" the lovely woman stopped upon entry and covered her mouth with her hands as her eyes fell on Vivian. She had on sporty gear, her sandy blonde hair was curled and hung to her shoulders. She had an athletic build and favored Buck more than Beth had.

Buck stepped up behind her and grumbled, again looking embarrassed. Vivian couldn't help but smile. His family seemed so great. He mumbled something to his sister, and she pushed at him and scoffed then moved forward toward Vivian.

"Wow. You are simply stunning. I can't believe it."

Vivian moved from Laurel's side and approached Buck's beautiful sister, who threw her arms around Viv in a tight embrace.

Buck huffed as he said, "Viv, meet Blair. Blair… obviously, this is Vivian."

"Oh my *God!*" Blair said again as she pulled back. "Wow!" She was utterly star-struck as she looked Vivian over from head to toe and gripped Vivian's shoulders. "I just *love* you. You're such a great actress. I have *all* of your movies." She squealed, covering her mouth once more.

"Yeah, yeah, go grab a piece of paper so she can sign something for you and you can leave her alone."

"Oh, would you stop it?" Blair turned and swatted at her brother's big bicep then, frowning at him. "Let me have my moment! You never bring women home for us to meet, let alone movie stars, so shove off." She kicked at him as he walked away griping, and Vivian laughed at their playful banter. She didn't have that kind of relationship with her siblings; they were too young. She'd been seventeen when her first sibling was born, and they lived on the other side of the country from her.

"Now, tell me how awesome it was to kiss and touch the abs of that stud, Paul Whittaker in *Paradise Unknown*," Beth pleaded. Vivian laughed heartily. She'd only just turned twenty-two and had been so nervous to kiss the famous and ridiculously handsome Hollywood star, but he'd made it super nonchalant as their steamy love scenes had turned ever hotter. It had been both awkward and sexy, but all in all, he was a sloppy kisser despite their on-screen performance. She didn't want Blair to know that though for her bubble would probably burst. So, she just blushed, and Blair squealed in delight. "Gosh, you're so lucky!"

She *was* lucky and she knew it. She'd literally stumbled upon that role and had soared to new heights after that, from one action-filled romance adventure to another, until she'd been swept up in the spotlight, where she couldn't get enough. Now, here she was at thirty-five years old, childless, husbandless...but with six Oscars.

"Blair! That's enough," Buck's mother scolded. "Give the poor girl some breathing room. You're squishin' her." Viv looked down at Blair's hold on her waist and laughed out loud. Blair's grip had been tight, but Vivian enjoyed the fandom. It wasn't often she got a face to face reception with her fans, most the time it was from a distance, and she was surrounded by far too many of them.

"Jeez, I'm sorry." Blair pulled away and bit at her bottom lip.

"Jesus, Blair!" Buck grabbed Viv then and pulled her away from his sister's grasp. "I didn't know I was gonna have to play bodyguard with my date today from my own sister. Most stars would sue you for shit like that."

Vivian balked at Buck as Blair's mouth dropped in horror. Viv waved the statement off and looked at Blair as if to say, "Don't listen to him."

"Bobby Joe Jenkins, what did I tell you about taking the Lord's name in vain in my presence?" Laurel scolded. With that, Buck sighed and looked down at Viv, who tried to hide a giggle. Blair stuck her tongue out at her brother before crossing her arms over her chest. "Eadie Blair Parks, you get your tail over here and kiss your Momma. Bobby you too."

They moved simultaneously together to their mother's bedside, coming to either side and sitting down, taking their mother's hands.

Blair leaned in to hug Laurel first and kissed her cheek then Buck took his turn. Vivian's throat grew tight as she turned to give them some privacy. She could hear Laurel softly scolding the two of them on their manners and smiled to herself. Laurel told them to get along, although the banter between seemed to be playful in nature and not malicious.

Vivian was drawn to a group of pictures that sat on a dresser adjacent from the bed. She smiled as she picked one up of a very young Buck, playing out in the yard with a water hose, clad only in a diaper. His almost white blonde hair was curly and his little chompers shown as the water sprayed around him. He had a broad frame even then, she noted. He couldn't have been more than two years old in the picture.

She felt a solid frame against her back then as he stepped in behind her, his chest hitting the back brim of her hat. Her skin hummed at the closeness of his body to her own.

"Man, I liked to be half naked even then," he teased into her ear.

She couldn't help but grin, remembering his beautiful nakedness in that moment. "You were a big baby," Viv stated, noting his stockiness.

"Still is!" Blair joked and shoved at his big frame, not moving him an inch. She then leaned in and kissed his cheek. "He was my first best friend though and still is." Buck threw his arm around her then and chucked her chin.

"I love to tangle with you, sis."

"And you love that I badger you back and ya darn well know it."

He laughed and their familiarity stirred Vivian in amazing ways. The love simply oozed from this family, like it did with the Kinsens, and Vivian felt drawn to their warmth, like a moth to a flame. She turned around and faced Buck then, smiling as she remembered the Kinsens.

"I should be getting back."

Buck practically frowned then as if he'd forgotten his time with her would be short. He gave a stiff nod.

"Aww," Blair pouted. "I was gonna have y'all over for dinner. I wanted to spend some time with you, Vivian. It isn't every day my brother brings a girl home, let alone my favorite movie star. Please? I'll make anything you like, you name it."

Vivian smiled at her sincerity. "It isn't that." She looked to Buck for help.

"She's Natalie's company this weekend, Blair. I promised to bring her back after a couple hours."

"Ohh," Blair whined again. "Please? I know Nat will understand…"

Buck's eyebrows went up and he shrugged, giving the floor over to Viv. Great, now she was on the spot. "Well, I'm sure Natalie won't mind. We've been gone for several hours now as it is. What's a few more?" Blair nodded in encouragement. "Alright. Let me just give her a quick call, so she knows not to expect me for dinner then. And thank you for the invitation. It's very kind of you."

Vivian moved towards the door to step out and call Natalie. She couldn't believe she'd even gone to lunch with the man who'd jilted and jaded her…now she'd agreed to stay for dinner with him and his family. *My how the winds have changed!*

٭٭٭

*B*uck laughed as Greg Parks' mouth hit the floor at seeing Vivian Alexander seated in his living room.

"Honey, look who's our dinner guest tonight!" Blair practically shrieked.

It took Greg a moment to regain his composure, and Buck stood and gave his brother-in-law a half hug. He returned it, sat his briefcase down and grabbed his niece as she launched herself into his arms.

"Uncle Greg, Vivian is a movie star!" Heather stated with conviction.

91

Greg laughed. "I know! Your Aunt Blair is like her biggest fan. Where's your cousin?"

Heather shrugged and kissed her uncle's cheek then squirmed out of his embrace to run back over to Vivian.

Buck's heart swelled at how welcoming his family had been with his date. His mother had taken the visit well and after Blair left, he and Vivian had stayed for another couple hours chatting with her and Buck's father before Buck and Viv left to come to Blair's house. It had been an amicable conversation between the four of them. They'd talked about Buck's family, the weather, sports, movies, current events and life in general. Vivian had talked about her movies, but not much else, until Buck's mom flat out asked her about her family. Buck could tell her relationship with them must be strained for all she said was that her parents had divorced when she was sixteen, were both remarried and had other families now. She'd quickly changed the subject. They'd gotten to laughing then about her skit on *Saturday Night Live* a couple years ago and time passed easily. It was as if everything was right in the world, as if Buck's mother wasn't dying, as if he hadn't treated Vivian so poorly by leaving her that morning.

"Thanks for doing this," Buck had said once they were on the way to Blair's house.

Vivian had just smiled at him, her expression unreadable.

Now, they were all seated in the living room of his older sister's while something delicious baked in the oven, and Vivian chatted it up with Blair and Heather, leaving Beth to talk with their mother back at his folk's house.

"Buck," Greg whispered as he came to sit next to him in an arm chair beside his. "This is the one from that ball in Dallas, right?"

Dammit! Buck would be glad when his wrong-doing had blown over some. He just nodded to his brother-in-law, who shook his head. "She's amazing," was all Buck could say as he took her beauty in.

Vivian Lisette Alexander was the most beautiful woman he'd ever seen. Her blonde locks came to the middle of her back, curling in waves beneath her tan cowboy hat. Her jeans and shirt fit her just right, tight enough to be flattering without being too revealing. But he remembered all too well what lay beneath her clothes. Perky, round breasts and a long, slender torso, legs that went on for days and a firm, plump rear-end. He longed to have her naked beneath him once again, crying his name as she had so many times that night. Her deep brown eyes glanced over at him then and she gave him a stunning smile that took his breath away. It lit up her face and accentuated those gorgeous high cheekbones of hers.

"I can see she left quite an impression," Greg murmured back, seeing the exchange between them as he moved to greet his wife, who graciously introduced him to Vivian.

Vivian took it all in stride; she really *was* amazing! She'd had a long and trying day; she'd swallowed her pride, went to lunch with him, met his dying mother, now she was entertaining his fan-girling sister as they gave his mother and sister, Beth, time to talk.

Buck scowled, remembering the conversation he'd had earlier with his oldest sibling.

"Buck, she needs to know!" Beth had argued.

"No. She's dying. She deserves to believe that you're happily married and that everything is going to work out fine," he'd contended.

"But I'm not and it's *not*," Beth had said tearfully. "I can't keep it from her, she knows something is up. It's going to be fine. I promise you. She knows how strong her children are, she raised us." She'd taken his hands, pleading with him to understand. He'd finally agreed. But made her swear not to get into gritty details. Buck had done enough to stress their mother out; she didn't need to hear anything else that was going to weaken her health any more than it already was.

"I won't, but that doesn't mean she won't hear about it from someone else, Bubba." Buck knew that to be true. "If she asks me, I'm going to tell her."

Stanley Harwick had been cheating on Beth for a time now, and she'd only recently found out about it. She'd been crushed. They'd been married since Buck was in college. And had tried to have a child for so long; Beth had taken infertility treatments for years before Heather was finally conceived. Even then, Beth's pregnancy had been unstable and she'd had to be on bed rest for the last three months of it.

Buck wanted to beat Stan to a bloody freakin' pulp. He meant to have words with the man before all was said and done. There were perks to Buck's size, money, and stardom, and he meant to use that to his advantage in this situation. No one ran over his family and got away with it.

"Bubba, you got your hands full with this girl; she's a wild one. Is there anything she can't do?" Blair said, getting Buck's attention.

Buck just smiled at the beautiful vixen before him as her eyebrow went up and he shook his head in awe.

Vivian Alexander really was somethin' alright; with six Oscars, over two dozen movies and multiple appearances on various prime time talk shows, cameo appearances on TV series, and commercials, and her just peaking thirty-five years of age; Vivian was a force to be reckoned with. He couldn't wait to get to know her more and was grateful for this unexpected time with her.

When dinner was ready, they all sat around the table, Chandler finally making an appearance as he shyly glanced over at Vivian in wonderment.

"Wow, this looks delicious," Viv said as Greg sat a large Dutch oven full of beef bourguignon on the table and lifted the heavy lid, setting it aside. Blair began scooping out portions of fresh whipped potatoes onto plates and passing them to Greg, who served helpings of the hearty beef stew atop them and handed them out.

"Blair's the gourmet chef of the family," Buck stated with pride, winking at his older sister.

"What is that?" Heather asked, pointing to a pearl onion in disgust.

"It looks like a teardrop, doesn't it?" Viv said. Heather just wrinkled her nose. "You should taste it, you might like it."

"Mommy, I don't like onions," Chandler whined.

"And this is why we don't cook gourmet often." Blair shrugged, getting a laugh out of Vivian.

"You know what, son? If you don't like onions then don't eat them, but you *will* try a bite of what your mother cooked or you'll go to bed hungry," Greg insisted and cut his eyes at his son.

Heather's eyes widened and she quickly looked down, fearful she would be scolded next. She grabbed up her fork and hesitantly took a bite of beef and potatoes, looking up at Buck, who winked at her.

"Mmm," Heather said. "Aunt Blair, this is *so* good."

"'At a girl," Buck smiled and took a bite of his food.

"A girl after my own heart," Vivian said and elbowed Heather gently, who grinned brightly up at her.

After dinner, they all played a board game, even Chandler, who seemed to perk up at dinner as Vivian entered him into conversation. It took her several attempts to get him out of his shell, but once he was out, he was like a different child. Buck had gotten to know his family better since he'd come home full-time following his retirement and he'd enjoyed this time he got with them. Chandler was a shy child, but enjoyed baseball and playing video games. Heather was all girl and loved dressing up and Barbie dolls. Blair was a trainer and yoga instructor at the gym she owned, Parks Place, in downtown Abundance. Her husband, Greg was in advertising. They'd been married a little over fifteen years and seemed content, unlike Beth and Stan, whose marriage had been rocky from the beginning it would seem. Beth was a real estate agent and Stan, a CEO of a telecommunications company in Denton.

After the game, the kids went into Chandler's room to play, leaving the adults in the living room. Blair sat down beside her husband and kissed him softly on the lips. When she pulled back, she smiled up at him, and Buck grinned, grateful that at least one of his sister's was happy for the time being.

"You have a lovely family," Viv said, as if her thinking had been in line with Buck's.

"Thank you. We're very happy... you know, we lost our first child?"

Buck's hand stilled midway as he was bringing his glass to his mouth. Why was she telling Vivian this? "Blair?" Buck frowned and shook his head.

"It's ok, Bubba." Blair's eyes penetrated his for but a moment before darting back to Vivian, who looked as if she'd been slapped.

"Oh, Blair. I'm so very sorry," Vivian murmured.

"Thank you. Her name was Abby. She was just two years old when she drowned."

Buck's heart ripped open suddenly as he was taken back to that horrible day. It had started out so good and ended in such tragedy. It had been a beautiful day on the lake in Conroe; they'd taken one of his boats out. It had been the beginning of Beth and Stan's problems, for Stan had been the one nearest Abby when she'd disappeared in the water and Beth had blamed him for her death. Blair and Greg had to have years of counseling before they'd started trying to conceive again, Blair especially, after she'd attempted suicide not long after Abby had been buried.

All the flashbacks hit Buck at once, and he swallowed the lump that had grown in his throat as he watched Vivian's eyes blink back tears as Blair handed her a photo of the angelic little girl they'd all lost that fateful day.

He could see Vivian struggling as she looked down at the photo of his niece. He could almost see Abby alive again in his mind. Young, innocent, little older than a baby. She'd been the first born in their family and had stolen his heart the first day he'd held her. She would be eleven years old now if she'd lived.

Vivian handed the photo back to Blair then and looked down, trying to hold onto her composure.

Buck watched as Greg's hand settled over Blair's then and he kissed her cheek as they looked at the picture together. Buck had to look away as tears came to his own eyes in that moment. He'd seen that picture a million times at least; here, at his mother's, at Beth's, in his own house and burned forever more into his brain. It had been taken just a month before her death. She looked like a little model; posed on a pink blanket on the grass, her elbows planted, hands beneath her chubby cheeks, blonde hair curled and seafoam green eyes shining, a wide-mouthed grin on her face.

Buck got up and walked back into the kitchen then, placing his glass in the sink as he pushed the air out of his lungs, trying to calm his breathing. He held onto the countertop then as his mind reeled. He lowered his head and closed his eyes against her giggling voice reverberating in his ears.

"Bubba," a quiet voice called to him, and he turned to see his teary-faced sister approaching him.

"Blair, why—?"

"We never talk about her anymore. None of us do. It's like she didn't exist."

"It's not—"

"It's painful, I know. But we need to honor her memory. She deserves at least that, doesn't she?"

Why was she doing this now, of all times? "Blair."

"Is this how it's gonna be when Momma passes too, Bobby? Are we just gonna stop talking about her? Let her memory die along with her?" Blair's voice echoed loudly.

"Blair, please?" Buck shook his head, feeling hot, wet tears fighting at the corners of his eyes.

"It wasn't Stan's fault, Bubba. It wasn't *mine* and it sure as hell wasn't *yours*."

How had she known he blamed himself? It was his boat after all that Abby had fallen from. It had been his idea to go to the lake.

"I don't blame you, brother. I never have. I don't blame anyone. Not myself. Not Greg. Not even Stan." Buck's eyes burned into hers. "It's taken me years to see that it was just an accident. Accidents happen. We can't change the past. We can only move forward. Little brother, why haven't you moved forward? Is Abby's death why you haven't?"

Buck couldn't give her a truthful answer as he didn't really know himself. Maybe. Her death had torn them all in two and none of them had really ever been the same after. He just shrugged.

"Vivian is amazing. I can see you two together. I believe that she'll make you happy, Bubba." Blair's hands came to his biceps then and squeezed. He leaned down and let her embrace him. She kissed his cheek. "I love you. Please, don't mess this one up, ok?" When she pulled back, she winked and elbowed his belly, lightening the mood. "She's feisty, huh?" Buck just smiled and nodded. "Good. She'll need to be to put you in your place." She laughed as she took his arm and they walked back into the living room.

Greg had placed the photo back in its spot and smiled weakly up at them. Buck frowned, wondering where Vivian had gone, but his unspoken question was quickly answered as she stepped forward from the bathroom, her cheeks red.

"You ready?" he asked.

She only nodded and smiled big at Blair beside him, moving forward to hug her as she gave her a, "Thank you." They said their goodbyes to his sister, brother-in-law, and the kids.

Once they were back in his truck, Buck sighed deeply. He wanted to apologize for Blair's spontaneous confessions but held his tongue as they headed down the road.

"You have a lovely family, Buck," Vivian said, breaking the silence.

"Thank you. I apologize for the drama."

"No need to apologize," she said as she looked absent-mindedly out the window, clearly disturbed by his sister's revelation.

Buck sighed again. There was a coldness in the air that he hadn't felt prior, and he started to become anxious the longer the silence stretched out between them.

When he pulled into Jack and Natalie's driveway, he shut the engine off and turned to her. "Viv, thank you for today. I know that wasn't comfortable for you and I'm truly sorry." She said nothing as she looked over at him, her eyes moving over him, and he longed to reach out and pull her against him and kiss her beautiful lips. Instead, he extended an open palm to her and she took it. "I would really like to see you again before you have to leave town." He leaned in closer.

"I don't think that's a good idea, Buck." A flicker of doubt hit her eyes, and he scowled.

"Why not?"

"Buck, you need to be with your mom right now." He sighed again, feeling so torn in that moment. "Look, we had a great time together. But we both knew what that night was gonna be before we went upstairs to my room." Why was she saying this? It might have started out as a one night stand but clearly hadn't been!

"Viv—"

"We're just too different. We have separate lives. I'm an actress. I live in Malibu, Buck. And you live here."

Buck swallowed the hurt her words caused him. Was this her way of saying she thought she was too good for him? Or just that she wasn't willing to fit him into her busy life? He analyzed her face then, seeking out answers, but could find none as her lips drew firm.

"Vivian, I don't want it to end like this. We owe it to ourselves to see where this is leading."

Viv shook her head. "It's just poor timing."

"Poor timing for you or poor timing for me? Have you ever considered that there are things in life that aren't mere coincidence?"

"Buck, I can't do this right now," she whispered, swallowing hard.

"Please, Viv. Don't make me pull you into this back seat and *show* you just how wrong you are. Do you have any idea how much I want you right now?" He cupped her face then.

"Don't." She jerked his hand away. "Please, don't." Her eyes closed as if his touch was painful to her. "You're just vulnerable right now. And so am I. But sex isn't the answer to everything."

How could she not see that sex wasn't all he wanted from her?

Had he not been showing her that all day long? How had she misinterpreted him so?

"I wish you well, Buck. But I need to go now." She turned and leaned into him, bringing her face ever closer to his. Just when he thought she was going to kiss him, she turned her head and kissed his cheek instead, softly, regretfully, then said, "Take care of yourself, big guy." Her hand came to his chest and her eyes sought his. He saw something in their chocolate depths that he couldn't quite place, and he swallowed his pride, for she'd wounded it terribly. She turned and got out of the truck, leaving him to ponder his thoughts as he watched her head up the porch and into the house.

"So," he told himself, "*this* is what it feels like to be rejected."

CHAPTER 5

Scottie Warden was brooding as he took his usual seat at the bar of The Rusty Spur. He ordered his usual Miller Lite and glanced up at the television screen that was showing an old rerun of *Green Acres*. He was in an extra melancholy mood tonight after seeing his high school buddy, Buck Jenkins, out with the stunning Vivian Alexander. It appeared Scottie was the last single one of the bunch. It had all started when Jack stole the heart of the recently divorced Natalie Cameron, Abundance's favorite sweetheart, then it had progressed from there. Not too long after, Luther and Bella had gotten together then Nathan and Jordan, now it appeared Buck was next in line. All his guy friends were either hitched or with some stunner, well except Rick Singleton, and no one had heard from him in at least a year, so who knew *what* he was up to.

Scottie had dated several women in town, but he'd never gotten serious enough to settle down. He wasn't really sure why. It wasn't that he didn't want what all his friends had: companionship, love, families. He'd had a couple serious relationships over the last fifteen years, but they'd not worked out. Scottie considered himself a fair and generous lover, a decent boyfriend and a charming partner, but he wasn't sure that he was husband material. He worried about having only one woman for the rest of his life and he wasn't good at confrontation, it wasn't the fights he minded, it was being wrong. He wasn't really one to admit his wrongs. He was a simple man with simple needs; he hated drama and hysterics and he enjoyed quiet... which was probably why he was still single. If the going had ever gotten tough, he'd wanted out. No arguments, no fights, just goodbye.

Women had always been easy to love, for Scottie was a lady's man, but women had always been an enigma to him too. Women were beautiful, wonderful creatures that he couldn't quite get enough of... but they puzzled the hell out of him. Just when he thought he'd figured out what they wanted, they threw him for a loop. Nat and Jordan had been friends of his since high school and he could flirt like crazy with them, dance with them, and throw back some drinks with them, but as charming as he was, he'd never gotten either one of them to go to bed with him before they'd off and gotten married.

Just as Scottie began to ponder just what Jack and Nathan and Buck had that he didn't, Louise interrupted his thoughts.

"What's the matter, Scottie?" the old woman inquired as she sat another beer down in front of him.

Scottie couldn't help but smirk; she was the last person he wanted to discuss his lack of a girlfriend with. What did Louise know about relationships? She hadn't had one since he'd known her.

"Ah, it's nothin', Louise."

"Rough day at work?"

Scottie shook his head. No, work hadn't been too bad.

Scottie had managed a hardware store since high school. He hadn't gone to college like Buck, Natalie, Jack or Rick had; he didn't have a degree, which was probably another reason he was moping. Abundance was the only place he'd ever call home. He'd never seen exotic places or owned a ranch or moved away.

As if sensing his distress, Louise said. "Aw, hell, Scottie, is this about Buck?"

He looked up into the old bartender's tan and wrinkled face, taking in her bright red lipstick, her sparkly blue eye shadow, the brown eyebrows she'd drawn on her face as her real ones were starting to fade away, and he saw his own grim future; he actually gulped.

It was if his life flashed before him, and he saw himself sitting in this bar as an old man, grey and lonely, as a stooping, ancient Louise struggled to put his drink on the bar counter. He felt as if he were suffocating. Louise was one of the closest friends he had, as he was a regular at The Rusty Spur and had been for a long time now. She saw him at least 4 times a week, for hours at a time, where they talked town politics, the weather, and the latest on the gossip train.

And suddenly, Scottie hated that he'd allowed his life to fall into such a routine and mundane pit of nothingness. Time had marched on...and left Scottie sitting in its wake. He snuffed out his cigarette and as he was turning to grab his wallet, he heard a female yelling as she entered the old, squeaky door.

"Momma, your daughter's about to be sent to jail!" Scottie turned at the voice and stopped dead in his tracks. A short, petite little thing in daisy dukes and a yellow tube top, big breasts bouncing into view was headed his way. Her freckled face was blushing red and her strawberry blonde curls flew back as she approached the bar and stopped beside him. "I'm gonna kill that son of a bitch!" the sexy ginger stated loudly.

"Dammit Ginger, I told you to let the courts handle this."

"I tried and I'm fed up. Bart's just gone too far now. I mean it. If my child comes home *one* more time cryin', I'm killin' his ass, dead as four o'clock," she said and slammed a paper down on the countertop.

"Honey, I'm sorry but this is my place a' work and you can't just come in—"

"This is what his bitch of a wife told my daughter." The woman scooted the paper over to Louise then and Louise begrudgingly took it and skimmed it over as Scottie's eyes did some skimming of his own.

Louise's daughter was *hot*. Her breasts were the biggest thing on her small frame, at least a C or D cup, he surmised, with a trim waist and muscular legs. His eyes shot back up to her face as she looked over at him then and said, "What the fuck are *you* lookin' at?"

Ooh…and a redhead's temper to go with it!

"Sorry, I—"

"Ginger! Don't talk to my patrons like that," Louise interrupted. "Now you apologize for your smart mouth. Right now."

Ginger frowned, pursing her big lips, and Scottie felt as if he'd just died and gone to heaven.

"Sorry, I ain't havin' a good day is all. I didn't mean to take it out on you." The redhead blushed again, and Scottie smiled for the first time all night.

"I understand. My day hasn't been so good either."

"Yeah, well did your ex-husband's wife call your daughter a slut like her momma?" A perfectly arched eyebrow went up and the apology Ginger had made went up in flames.

Scottie almost laughed; she was something. Scottie just shook his head, knowing no response from him was actually needed. "Then I'd say your day was better than mine." Both eyebrows came up then and she turned to her mother. "Give me a shot of Patrón."

"No!" Louise smarted. "I ain't doin' no such thing. You'll get plastered and end up making a fool out of yourself once you get your drink on. You need to cool off, girl."

"I'll buy you a shot," Scottie said and motioned his head to Louise, who balked.

"You ain't buyin' her shit. She's goin' home to cool off. I mean it. You ain't seen this girl drunk." Louise turned from Scottie to her daughter. "Your kids don't need your temper; they need stability," Louise replied and handed the paper back to Ginger. "Don't stoop to their level, hon. Besides, what you're wearing ain't exactly what a mom should be wearing any way."

"Like you're one to talk, Momma." Ginger motioned to the mini-skirt and tight-fitting top of her mother's. Louise had always dressed that way; apparently, her daughter had modeled after her. Ginger jumped up onto the barstool then and sighed heavily. "I don't know what to do anymore." Ginger's face dropped into her hands, looking so lost that Scottie felt bad for her. He looked to Louise, who frowned at him across the bar.

"Ginger, you gotta get a good lawyer. Take him back to court. It's not good for Valerie and Rhett to have that kind of influence. This is on paper. Now you have proof that they're unfit."

"I can't afford to take him back to court." When Ginger looked back up, she had tears in her hazel eyes. "They cry every time they have to go over there. He's constantly throwing my shortcomings in their faces, as if he can punish me through them. What am I supposed to do?"

Louise stretched her arm out to her daughter, and Scottie felt a punch to his gut as he watched the scene play out before him.

Ginger echoed misery. He didn't have any children, so he could empathize but couldn't entirely understand her pain. He couldn't imagine being in the predicament she was in or having no legal recourse for such harassment.

Then a thought came to him.

"Uh, Ginger?" Ginger's head slowly turned toward him then and she scowled up at him, a cautious look on her face. "I'm sorry. You don't know me and I don't know you, but I'm Scottie Warden, a friend of your mom's." Ginger looked at her mom, who nodded, before looking back to Scottie. "I didn't mean to eavesdrop, but I have a brother who's in law enforcement. He might be able to help you."

Scottie's younger brother, Mark, dealt with domestic cases all the time and had some connections in their community in social services. Surely, Mark knew someone who Ginger could talk to about these kinds of things. If not, Scottie could make certain Ginger got the money she needed to take her ex back to court; after all, he'd saved enough of it the last twenty plus years, what with not having a wife or kids to spend it on.

Ginger smiled apologetically over at him. "Thanks, Scottie." She extended her dainty little hand, and he took it and shook it firmly. "Sorry to have met you this way. I'm Ginger Fortner, Louise's eldest child. It's nice to meet you."

He took her in in that moment. How had he missed that Louise had a daughter? Surely, since he'd been coming to this bar, she'd mentioned her child, but Scottie couldn't recall. The sexy little vixen before him couldn't be a day over twenty-five, which would explain why he didn't know who she was; he was at least fifteen years her senior.

"Pleasure's all mine, Ms. Fortner." Scottie tipped his ball cap at her and hesitated in giving her hand back, which brought forth a throaty laugh that made his dick jump in his pants.

"Want that shot?"

"I do. Momma, come on, just one shot, with my new friend, Scottie, here."

Louise gave Scottie the mother of all looks then. She'd seen him walk out of The Rusty Spur *far* too many times with far too many women… and drunk to boot. That wouldn't be happening tonight, he could see. Under no circumstance. "Like hell," she said and put her palm out, indicating for him to pay his tab. "Scottie, here was just leavin.'"

Touché, ol' girl. "That's right, I gotta head out, but I'll take a raincheck though. Here's my card." With that, Scottie pulled out a card from his billfold and a twenty, handing the card to Ginger and the money to Louise. "Keep the change, Louise. Ginger, give me a call and we'll see what my brother can do about that ex of yours. Ladies." He stated, winking at Ginger before he turned and ambled away.

⁎

"*I* can't, Lucian, my love. For the tables are against us and have been from the very beginning." *Oh, no.* "Please. Don't look at me like that!"

Jeremy grabbed Vivian's arm, spinning her around, the mint green crinoline scrunching against him as he pulled her taut to his chest. Viv's stomach lurched again as her head turned dramatically away from him.

"Please, Victoria. We mustn't give up hope. I can't live without you." His tart breath brought forth a faint gag as he leaned in for a kiss, and she felt the bile rise in her throat. When his lips touched hers, her gag reflex took over, and she pushed him forcibly away, running toward the exit door of the set, hearing Vince yell, "Cut!"

Her bulky dress and hoop skirt were forgotten as she hurled that morning's breakfast over the railing of the stairs. When she'd emptied her stomach, she turned, hand to her forehead as she tried to calm her breathing. She wiped the edge of her mouth with her hand as Jill ran to her.

"Jesus, Viv. Are you alright?"

"Yes. I am now. It must have been something I ate."

She chalked it up to her nerves. The last three weeks had been awful. First, upon her return, she had gotten her ass chewed up one side and spit out the other by her director and one of the movie producers, and she'd had to do a bit of groveling—as if she wasn't still reeling from how she'd left things with Buck. Then, not soon after leaving Abundance, she'd seen on a morning newscast where Dallie had been kidnapped and she'd frantically called Jack only to be told that Dallie was home safe, much to Vivian's relief. Apparently, Cole had been a fugitive of the law during his stay with the Kinsens and had taken Dallie hostage at gun point. According to the last conversation Viv'd had with Natalie and Dallie just days ago, Cole was no longer a suspect in the murder case he'd been accused of, he'd actually been framed, but was looking at jail time for the kidnapping, despite that the gun hadn't been loaded. Vivian told them she'd help in any way she could. After all, anyone could see that Cole and Dallie cared deeply for one another. Even Jack, who'd been ready to murder the young man himself, had gone to talk to him and had gotten one of the best defense attorneys available to plead his case, so who was Viv to judge? Desperate times and all.

Filming had been an utter nightmare in horrible storms and weather conditions, her co-star was a total drama queen, she hadn't had a decent night's sleep since returning from Texas, and now her stomach was uber sensitive to whatever she ate...and apparently smelt.

"I think this set is cursed," Jill said, looking up at the ceiling.

"Don't say things like that. It *is* Hollywood, we take our curses seriously around here." Vivian grabbed at her stomach as Jeremy approached and she heard Vince scoff as she rounded the corner.

"Are you alright, dahling?" Jeremy's British accent filled her ears.

She covered her nose with her hand, praying the smell of his breath didn't elicit more vomiting from her. "I'm okay." She motioned for Jill to give him a peppermint candy from a nearby tray. She did and he took it, much to Viv's relief.

"Vivian, can we *please* finish this scene? Are we not far enough behind schedule to suit you?" Vince's dark eyebrows raised as he crossed his arms over his small chest.

Vivian simply counted to ten and took in a deep breath. If she didn't kill him before this movie was a wrap, it would be a miracle.

In a matter of minutes, she and Jeremy were in their places, the take was rolling, and she was back in her element, acting away her part of the lovestruck Victorian couple whose elicit love affair would be their undoing.

When their sex scene started, Vivian performed with profession-alism and expertise as always, but noticed her nipples were more sensitive than normal as Jeremy cupped her naked breast in his hand, her gasp as real as the scene called for. She was contemplating that perhaps it was that time of the month as his mouth came to her neck and they rocked their bodies together, faking their love-making to perfection. As his hands came to grip her thighs, she cried out in frustration, realizing she hadn't had a period, as the time came for her to perform her "climax", making the sound even more realistic than she'd intended.

Before Jeremy could finish their scene, Vince was yelling, "Cut!" again, and they were made to do seven more takes before the take was done. By then, Vivian stomach was rolling again and her body was literally aching with unquenched desire.

How strange, she thought as she headed out to her trailer. *I usually don't get that turned on with sex scenes*. After all, Jeremy was gay, she wasn't attracted to him, and most times, sex scenes were far more awkward than they appeared to be onscreen. *Well, it* has *been almost two months since I've had any*, she deduced.

"Oh my God," she said to herself in the mirror of her trailer as she was changing into jeans, noticing they were a little tighter than they had been.

She grabbed her phone and called Jill, who'd gone to grab them some takeout for dinner.

"Jill, I need you to get me something…"

"What?" Jill asked, nonchalantly.

"I need a pregnancy test."

"Are you *kidding* me?"

"I wish I was."

"Alright, hang tight. I'll be there shortly."

Vivian waited impatiently for her assistant and felt both anxiety and elation at the fact that she could be pregnant. The thought hadn't occurred to her until right then, and she didn't want to get her hopes up, but the thoughts of having a baby made her want to squeal with delight. Perhaps since her biological clock had been loud enough for the entire world to hear it, divine intervention had interceded and threw her for a much-needed loop. How wonderful it would be to have a sweet child of her own. A baby like little Jackson, one who would have her heart and her looks. She'd been so far removed from her family for a good many years and now there was a possible that she might be able to have one of her own.

She tried to tap down her anticipation long enough to find out, but when Jill came pounding on the door, Viv was pulling her in and taking the bag from her.

She ran to the bathroom and did what she needed to then sat with Jill—with bated breath—as they waited for the time to be up. It was Jill who went to retrieve the test as Vivian sat biting her finger-nails, saying, "You look. I can't. If it's negative, I'm gonna be crushed."

Jill gave her a look of incredulity and hurried off to the bathroom.

When she came back, cheeks blushing, Viv's heart felt like it was going to explode in her chest. "Well?" she asked, impatiently.

"Well, it looks like we need to go see a doctor. It's positive...but... here, take another one, just to be sure." Jill's frown made Vivian tremble. "Dang it, Viv. What are you going to do? And how the hell are you planning on telling Buck Jenkins that you're pregnant with his baby? I mean, it *is* Buck's right?"

Vivian hadn't thought that far ahead, for she'd not heard a word beyond, "it's positive."

About that time, Jill's phone rang and she handed the test off to Vivian before answering it with a terse, "Hello."

Vivian looked at the lines on the test, the positive indication that she was going to be a mother. She felt like she was on cloud nine, transported to a place of utter happiness at the prospect of new life growing inside her. She even reached down and touched her lower abdomen, willing this baby to know how very much she loved him already. A tear came to her eyes, and she smiled brightly.

"Wait! Say again." Viv heard Jill say into the phone. "Oh no. Alright. Ok. I'll tell her. Yes. I'll call and get her on the first plane right away. Don't worry about Vince. I'll handle him." Jill hung up the phone. "Shit!" she cried and looked to Vivian. "Well, looks like you'll be telling your baby daddy sooner than you thought." Viv just looked at her, confused. "Buck's mom just passed away."

**

*B*uck looked down at the dirt falling onto the silver coffin and wished he were going into the earth with it. He felt cold and numb and just stood in the pouring rain as the crane lowered his mother to her final resting place. Why was it so hard to say goodbye? She'd been ready to go, but he hadn't been ready to *let* her go. The last five plus months hadn't prepared him even when he knew his time with her was short.

Their family had already lost a loved one who'd been taken from them too soon. His mother had been far older than Abby and yet her death had been just as jarring. Death was unmerciful, relentless and at many times, unjustified.

The graveside service had been short and to the point as Buck and his family mourned for their loss. His father was inconsolable as Buck had known he would be. His sisters, Beth and Blair, had held up far better than what he'd expected; they'd all been a united front for his dad. But once his family left, followed by Nathan and Jordan then finally Natalie Jack, Buck had fallen apart. His hard exterior had crumbled, and he'd began to let the tears flow like the rain around him as he watched the hole being filled with dirt. With each layer that covered the coffin, another piece of his heart was ripped away, until finally nothing was left. The funeral director came up to him then as all the flowers were laid upon the bulky dirt mound. He patted Buck's thick arm and gave him a solemn smile.

"Take all the time you need, son. Your momma was a jewel. She'll be sorely missed," he stated and walked away, leaving Buck fully alone at the graveside.

The rain was merely a mist now, but the emotions inside him could have been likened to a hurricane for all he felt was angry pain.

He balled his fists up and roared at the sky as fresh, hot tears burned his eyes.

When he finally turned away from the interment, he froze at the sight before him.

A gorgeous Vivian Alexander looked sadly up at him from a big red umbrella. Relief soared through his entire body, and he rushed to her, pulling her into his arms as his head went to her shoulder, his nose burying into her blonde curls. He was overcome with her scent, an intoxicating sweet floral fragrance that pulled him in and made his already emotional heart overflow with equal parts need and elation.

"You came," he exclaimed. "I wasn't sure you would...or that you *could*. God, I've missed you," he confessed with no remorse, for it was true. She was all he could think about these last few weeks as his mother grew weaker and weaker.

"I'm sorry. I got here as soon as I could," she said, breathlessly.

He held her for a few moments, reveling in the feel of her soft body against him, then realized that he was soaking wet, he pulled back, looking regretfully down at her now damp black dress.

"Damn, sorry. I—"

"It's alright. Let's get you home, shall we?" Viv grabbed for his arm and looped her arm through his as they walked towards a black limo on the gravel road ahead of them.

An older black man opened the car door and took the umbrella from Vivian as she moved into the seat; Buck followed and shivered as the vents blew cold air at him.

"Oh, let me turn that off." Vivian reached up to shut the A/C off then took his hand and smiled weakly at him. "Why don't you take that jacket off and I'll grab a blanket for you."

Buck obliged and shucked his wet jacket from his big shoulders as Viv pulled a soft microfleece blanket around him. He couldn't help but feel warmth spread through him at the tenderness in her eyes. She'd seemed so detached and distant the last time they'd seen each other; he enjoyed this softer side of her.

"Miss Vivian, where we headed?" The older man asked as the partition opened.

"145 Winchester Drive," Buck answered. "It's unlisted."

The old man just nodded to him and closed the partition, leaving them in silence as the car began to move.

"How are you holding up, Buck?" Viv asked, shyly.

"Better now that you're here." His eyes gazed deeply into hers. He'd made the statement on absolute truth. He was overjoyed to see her beautiful face, to be in her presence once more.

"I have champagne. Would you like some?"

Buck nodded, and she began pouring the already opened and chilled bottle into a flute. He noted it was the same one they'd ordered in Dallas and he couldn't help but smile at the memory.

"None for you?" Buck asked, observing she wasn't partaking in the libations.

"Uh," her eyes shot up to his and she balked, "no, um, I—I'm cutting back." She looked away quickly, and Buck just shrugged as he shot the glass back and downed it in one gulp.

After a few minutes, Vivian gingerly took his empty glass and refilled it, handing it back to him.

"So, how'd you manage to get away *this* time?

"Oh, uh, Jill handled it all. Vince wants to replace me. I told him to go ahead and do so, because I wasn't sure when I would be back." Wow! So, she was potentially giving up the job to come and be with him. The sentiment touched him, but he didn't want her to know just how much.

"I'm sure he's not used to working with someone who's such a rebel like you." Buck couldn't help but make humor of the situation. He winked at her.

"I hadn't intended to be so difficult. It's just...well, shit happens."

"You can say that again!" Buck toasted her bottle of San Pellegrino and downed the champagne.

They sat in companionable silence as the rain and the ride lulled them into an easy stillness. Vivian filled his glass up once again, and he sat sipping it easily this time, trying not to drown his sorrows with alcohol, even if it would be an easy thing to do at this moment in time.

But Buck had Vivian now. He could bury his cares away inside her and planned to do so the very minute his feet hit the marble floors of his foyer. He looked over at her smooth, shapely legs peeking out beneath the slit of a long black dress that fit her well enough to define her curves. The straps hung off her trim shoulders which were covered by a thin paisley shawl. Her makeup was thicker than last time he'd seen her; her gorgeous brown eyes were smoky in shades of copper and mocha and her mascara was heavy. Her lips were painted a pretty coral color and he longed to see it staining the white collared shirt he wore, for he wanted her as passionately as he had in that penthouse suite not two months ago.

He could barely contain his enthusiasm as the limo pulled out front of his black wrought-iron gates and he gave her driver the code. When they pulled up front, he got out and took Vivian's outstretched hand, pulling her gently out of the back seat. She waved to her driver, and Buck took the key out of his back pocket as they ran up the long, curved concrete steps out of the rain.

Vivian looked up at the massive wooden front door as Buck unlocked it and pushed it ajar then her mouth fell open as she took in the vast and elegant foyer before them. Her beautifully made-up eyes widened as they moved over the curving double staircases, the white marble floors, and the vaulted ceiling with its cascading chandelier.

"You might wanna close your mouth before bugs fly into it." Buck couldn't help but laugh.

She closed her mouth then, attempting to recover her composure. "I'm sorry, I just wasn't expecting this."

"Not all cowboys live on ranches, darlin'," he drawled and laughed again.

"If I remember correctly, you aren't a *real* cowboy." She swatted at him, and he grabbed her hand and hauled her roughly against him, getting an, "Oof," out of her as her chest hit his.

"And if *I* remember correctly, that certainly didn't stop you from riding me like I was."

With that, he laid a perfectly timed kiss on her soft lips, killing whatever smart response he knew was coming. Her moan only heightened the sexual sparks flying from his mouth to his cock as his hand fell into her hair and his arm wrapped around her waist. His big hand moved to her jaw then tilting her head as his tongue plunged deeply into her hot compliant mouth, and he answered her whimper with a growl. His hands moved down her sides to her thighs as her hands wrestled with the buttons on his shirt. Suddenly, he gripped her hips and picked her up, her legs going around his waist as he began climbing the stairs two at a time, needing to be inside her more than he'd ever needed anything in his life.

When Buck got to his bedroom, he brought them both down onto the large sleigh bed, his hands going to his wet slacks as she ripped the last of the buttons away on his shirt, exposing his chest. He unzipped himself and freed his raging erection then shucked his shirt from his shoulders and launched himself at her. His hands moved up her thighs as he pulled the thin lacy thongs from her hips. Vivian whimpered again as his mouth found hers and his hands sought out her breasts. He kneaded and squeezed at the firm mounds, his fingers seeking out her nipples, bringing them to hard peaks as he lowered his mouth to torture her through the thin gown. Her head flew back and she cried out, making his sex jump in response.

"Mmm, you like that, sweetheart? So sensitive," He positioned himself between her thighs and guided his hard sex to her wet center, and they both moaned as the tip of him entered her. "Oh, baby, how I've missed your sweetness."

"Oh, Buck, please, please..." she whimpered, grabbing for his hips.

He chuckled and stroked the little triangle of hair at the delta of her thighs then, as if he were stroking the fur of a cat with an arched back. "My little starlet," he murmured as he slid further into her. "Mmm, damn, you feel so fuckin' good." He stretched her slowly, feeling her silkiness fully engulf him, more delicious than any hot bath he'd ever slipped into.

He let her adjust to his thickness for just a moment then he began to move, with purpose and intent as his mouth returned to hers. Her hands gripped his shoulders and her legs wrapped tighter around his hips as he thrust in and out of her, bringing exquisite sounds from her beautiful lips.

"Oh yeah, darlin'. You missed my cock, didn't you? It missed you too, can you tell?"

Vivian answered with a cry as his fingers moved to torment her wet folds the way that thoughts of her exactly like this had tormented him for weeks now. His other hand moved to the strap of her gown, pulling it down to reveal her full breast with its light brown tip. His head lowered to it and pulled it into his mouth, tugging gently as his hips arched harder and faster. Her violent climax came as his tongue began to swipe at her nipple, darting back and forth, and she cried out, her sex clenching him in beautiful bittersweet agony. Buck rode the wave of her orgasm, loving the feel of her body spasming and falling apart to his touch. His pace quickened and he couldn't hold out for long as her hands moved to his ass and squeezed. When the earth split, she came again with him. They tumbled together, groaning their release as wave after wave of pleasure arced through them both as if bouncing from one to the other.

As his breathing slowed and his body stopped trembling, he looked down at the gorgeous sex goddess beneath him and smiled. "Fuck, Viv, you got me all wrapped up in you, beautiful. How'd you do that?"

She just grinned back, almost bashfully, and it took his breath. He continued to stroke her thighs as his erection waned and slowly he moved off her and fell to her side. She rolled to face him and just watched him for the longest time, propping herself on her elbow and resting her head on her fist.

His big hand cupped her cheek then and he leaned in to kiss her. "Thank you for coming," he said when he finally pulled back. "I'm really glad you're here. It was an awful day, but your presence has made it much more bearable." She smiled again as his hand fell down her hips. He looked down at her wet thighs and swore, "Dammit, Viv, I'm sorry. I did it again… Fuck, I forgot to use a fuckin' condom." Vivian gulped and looked away, uncomfortably. "Sweetheart, I'm really sorry. I swear, the minute I lay eyes on you I forget everything else. I promise you that I'm clean. I don't—"

"It's ok, Buck, really." She sighed.

"But it's not. I can see that you're upset."

She straightened her dress then, pulling the straps up to cover her breasts and the fabric down over her thighs.

"Viv, please, I haven't been with anyone since you. I swear it on a Bible." Buck reached for her as she turned away from him, facing the wall.

"Buck," she stated tersely, "there's something that I need to tell you and I don't know how to say this, so I'm just going to come out and say it, okay?" Buck felt dread slide over him as he watched her jump up from the bed and turn towards him, hands on her hips. "I— We—we're…pregnant."

Buck felt his eyebrows shoot up to his forehead. *She's pregnant?*

"That's why it doesn't really matter whether you were wearing a condom or not, I'm already knocked up, so you don't have to beat yourself up about it now. The damage is already done." She laughed nervously.

"It's—it's *mine*?" he asked, but already knew the answer by the look on her face.

"Yes," Viv confirmed, not offended as he'd expected she would be by the question. "I hadn't slept with anyone in four months when you and I—Look! I know I am *literally* springing this on you, like two seconds after sexual euphoria, and like barely an hour after your mother's funeral…but you needed to know. And I don't know how you feel about all this and how you feel about illegitimate children and all, but I intend to keep this baby. No amount of begging from you is going to convince me to terminate this pregnancy, so let's get that straight right now." She cupped her lower abdomen for emphasis even though he was already shaking his head. He would never have asked her to do a thing like that!

"And I don't expect anything from you. We both have a lot of money, so we don't have to worry about this child ever wanting or needing for anything, and I want you to know that I won't keep him from you. I plan to let you visit him whenever you want to."

"It's a boy?" Was all Buck could say as he tried to absorb all the information being thrown at him at once.

"What?" Vivian asked as she crossed her arms over her chest.

"You keep saying *him.*" Buck swallowed hard as he sat up in the bed. "How do you know it's a boy?" Wasn't that something that wasn't detected this early in the game?

"Oh, well…I don't. I just—I keep calling it a him. I don't know why." She looked down then, scuffling her feet. "I want him to have your last name though, if you're ok with that, of course."

Wow! He was gonna be a father. Buck Jenkins was going to have a child. He couldn't stop the joy that spread through him suddenly as realization started to dawn on him. He beamed brightly as Vivian's eyes came back to his. He stood and moved towards her, pulling her stiff frame into him. "Vivian," he murmured as he cupped her face. "This is wonderful news. I can't believe this. But I'm really happy about it."

"You are?" Vivian's big brown eyes searched his. He nodded. "I thought you'd be angry."

"Why the *hell* would I be angry? I'm the one who 'knocked you up'. I reckon I could be mad at myself, but where would anger play out in all this?" When she looked at him incredulously, he stated again, "No. I'm not angry. Not in the least. I'm elated. And I'm so very glad that my mom got to meet her grandchild's mother before she died. She would've been tickled pink that her son was gonna be a father."

With that, he pulled Viv into his arms and she rested her head on his shoulder. He breathed her in, feeling like the luckiest man alive, despite that he'd just buried his mother. Vivian Alexander, the most beautiful starlet in Hollywood, was going to have his baby and love would have another soul to live on in.

CHAPTER 6

*S*cottie was surprised to hear the knock on his door as he ran from the kitchen to grab it. He'd just gotten home from the store with a six-pack of Bud and a large frozen pizza. It was Friday night and he was once again alone and having a typical night of reruns and crap food.

He pulled the front door open and felt his jaw drop as his eyes fell on Ginger Fortner. To say that he was shocked to see her there would've been an understatement. She'd called him several weeks ago at work and he'd given her his brother Mark's information, but the conversation had been terse and to the point. He'd been wanting to call her to ask her out on a date, but he kept chickening out and he didn't want to seem like a weirdo since he didn't even know her. He'd not been expecting to hear from her again, let alone see her standing on his front porch steps.

"Ginger?"

"Hey, Scottie." She gave him a weak smile and motioned to the door. "Can I come in?"

"Of course. Please do?" He stuttered and pulled the screen door in and stepped back, motioning for her to have a seat on the couch.

"Can I get you something to drink?" He headed over to the kitchen, and she followed, wringing her hands as she stopped at the kitchen counter opposite him. He opened the fridge to assess what he had. "I got milk, tea, beer. Slim pickin's."

"I'll take a beer."

He grabbed a bottle of beer, popped the top with the keyring on his belt, and handed it over to her, giving her the once over as he pulled his hand back.

She looked good tonight, dressed in a pair of fitted worn denim jeans, a low-cut pink tank top, and matching flip flops. Her hair was down and framed her heart-shaped face which adorned a decent amount of makeup. His eyes lingered at her big breasts which teased him, peeking out from a lacy black bra beneath the thin shirt. He gulped as his eyes came back to hers.

"I'm sure you're wondering what I'm doing here," she began.

"Well, yeah," he confessed.

"I just wanted to thank you for helping me. It was mighty kind of you. Your brother has been a God-send. My kids are going to be staying with me full time now. And it's all because of you."

Scottie smiled big, glad to hear things were going to work out. "I'm glad to hear it."

"I'm not used to people being nice to me, so I was a bit surprised when Mark gave me the information of this Denise lady. She's wonderful. I really can't thank you enough. She's proven my kids are better off with me than my ex and—Dammit, I'm sorry, I'm ramblin' now."

"It's alright. I'm happy for you. Honest, I am."

Ginger stood there, looking him over, and Scottie was suddenly aware of the blast of heat he felt from her presence. His jaw and cheeks were scruffy from not shaving, his shirt was probably wrinkled from working all day, and he was somewhat sweaty since his old truck's A/C had crapped out on him a few days ago. Her hazel eyes seemed to evaluate him thoroughly and moved slowly over him only to return to his face. She scowled.

"I'm not gonna sleep with you, if that's why you did it."

"What?" Scottie couldn't help but laugh at that statement. Did she really think him so shallow?

"You heard me!" she exclaimed, pointing her beer at him before taking a swig. "Momma told me what kinda man you are, and I'm just here to tell you that I've been with enough of your kind and I won't be had like that again. Hell, it's why I got two kids. I'm done with men like you."

She didn't even know him. How could she say something like that? The statement angered him. Then again, she wasn't far off the mark. Scottie had been a hell-raiser most of his life. His face dropped then and he turned to the fridge to grab his own beer. When he turned around, Ginger was right behind him, and he almost gasped.

"I've been hurt a lot. But I'm anything but weak. You should know that." Her hand reached up to his cheek then. "You owe me a shot of tequila, if I remember correctly."

He grinned smugly, his hand going to her waist. Hazel eyes scorched his as she gazed up at him, and he sat his beer down on the counter before running his fingers up her ribs.

"You didn't come here for a shot of tequila and you damn well know it." He felt his sex start to pulse to life as her body moved closer to his and her hand went to his chest, unbuttoning the first two buttons. He practically growled as his face lowered to hers. "Why don't you tell me why you're really here?" he whispered as his lips hovered inches from hers.

She chewed on her plump bottom lips and practically whimpered, "Just don't hurt me, Scottie." She moaned as she popped up on her tiptoes, closing the distance between them and pressing her lips to his.

It was as if sparks flew, and Scottie's mind reeled as his senses were assaulted by her feel and touch and taste. She was like electric fire as her body pressed hot against him, her sweet and spicy scent invaded his nostrils, her lips feeling like flames scorching his as he kissed her. He moaned as one hand gripped her back, the other plowed into her strawberry blonde locks, and his mouth slanted over hers. Ginger opened up for his tongue to claim her and melted against him as he deepened the kiss, his tongue tangling with hers in a fight for control. He pressed her back into the fridge as his palm moved to cup one of the enticing breasts pressed against his chest. He squeezed it hard and heard her breathy moan, his cock jumping in response.

"Mmm, you taste like fire," he grumbled as his mouth moved to her neck and sucked at the tender skin there as she cried out. His other hand moved to the thigh she brought up to wrap around his hip and he squeezed her ass, loving the sounds that came from her throat as he kneaded her plump flesh.

"Bedroom," Ginger whimpered, and Scottie picked her up and blindly walked them back to the master bedroom as her lips sucked at his.

Her hands were all over him as they stripped, not able to get naked quick enough, ripping at his shirt as he peeled the tight jeans from her hips. She threw her shirt off as he moved to the nightstand, pulling a rubber from the drawer as her hands went to his fly. He turned and crashed against her naked frame, covering her as they hit the bed simultaneously. She panted as she tore at his pants, and he couldn't help but chuckle at her eagerness to have him.

"Easy, baby," Scottie groaned as her palm tightened around his hard sex, pumping him with her fist. "Or it'll all be over too quick." He ripped the package open and moved her hand, sheathing his cock before guiding the tip of it into her dripping, wet center. "Oh, fuck," he cried as he filled her slowly and gripped her hips as she bit into his shoulder. "Damn, darlin'," he moaned and huffed out as his lips came back to hers and he began to pump inside her. Ginger's head flew back as his mouth lowered to a puckered nipple and drew the hard pebble into his mouth, suckling her.

She cried out and cupped his head as her hips bucked up to meet his. He plunged deeper, his hand moving between her thighs.

"Oh, yes, Scottie. Right there," she whimpered again, and he realized it had probably been as long for her as it had for him. "Harder," she begged and he grinned into her beautiful face.

"You got it, spitfire," he groaned as his hips slammed into her and his pace quickened.

His body began a stiff and steady rhythm as his hands moved over the gorgeous woman he barely knew, but all that mattered in those moments was pleasing her and watching her face crumble as his rock-hard member became her undoing. When Ginger came, her sex squeezing his tightly, he almost lost himself but held back as he kissed her freckled face and chest and big, bouncing breasts, waiting as she came back to earth before picking back up and hammering into her with a fierceness that frightened him. Suddenly, he was exploding as her tightness clenched his cock again and he groaned out his release as his body shook and his hips hit hers again and again. Finally, he slowed, aware of their simultaneous panting and intermittent moaning as his hands returned to her face. He smiled at her and she returned it, blushing.

"God, you're beautiful," Scottie said, his eyes moving over her peachy skin dotted with thousands of brown spots, his fingertips playing 'Connect the Dots'. "Feel free to come back and thank me anytime you like." He laughed as he lowered his body further down over hers and kissed her lips.

She kissed him back as her thighs tightened around him and her hands went around his neck. He pulled her into his embrace, wrapping his arms tightly around her and felt a tenderness he hadn't before. "I'm glad you came," he whispered into her ear then pulled back to look into her hazel eyes. "In more ways than one." He chuckled, a low, deep rumble in his chest.

She gave him an uncertain smile and looked away. "I should be going." She began to peel herself from him, and he felt bereft as he released her.

"You don't have to go, Ginger. I want you to stay. Please?" He reached for her hand as she shot up from the bed and turned to look at him.

"I shouldn't have come. I knew I was gonna do that. Dammit!" She turned and covered her face with her hands. "God, I'm so fuckin' weak."

Scottie flew to her side and wrapped an arm around her waist as his other hand pulled hers down. She had tears in her eyes as she looked up at him. "Hey...you just said that you *weren't* weak. Make up your mind, darlin'," his voice softened as she gulped. "Please don't be upset. You got nothin' to be ashamed of, alright? I've wanted you since that night I met you at your Momma's bar. It was just a matter of time." His eyebrows shot up and he shrugged.

Ginger frowned and began to pull away from him again.

"Wait! That was the wrong thing to say. I'm sorry. Ginger, please?" he pleaded as she turned from him and started gathering her clothes from the floor. "Ginger?" he grabbed for her hand as she started to walk away and whipped her around and into his chest.

She was fully crying now, and Scottie felt his heart rip in two. "Shh..." He cupped her head and brought it to his shoulder. He laughed humorlessly then. "I'm kinda shitty at this, you should know. Relationships. I ain't had many, but I—" he paused, pondering how he should word what he was trying to say so that he didn't fuck it up even further than what he already had. "Sweetheart, I can try...I *wanna* try. Can we—Can we go out and let me buy you that shot I owe you?"

Ginger looked up at him then and smiled weakly, her green-flecked brown eyes rimmed with red. "I have to pick the kids up from practice here in a few minutes."

He cupped her face and kissed her swiftly then pulled back. "Well, I can come pick you up later on. And we'll get to know each other. How 'bout it?"

She nodded in response. "I can get my neighbor Cheryl to babysit for a little while."

"Alright then. It's a date."

⁎⁎⁎

*R*ick Singleton cursed as he looked at the mound of paperwork on his desk. His mood was atrocious as a knock came at his door. He knew who it would be before the dark-headed beauty opened it, saw her way in, and shut the door behind her.

Rick sighed and tore his eyes from her enticingly long legs that ran all the way up to her armpits. He closed his eyes and mentally counted to ten. It had been like this since he'd hired her two weeks ago. She was fucking gorgeous and looked far too much like Natalie Kinsen to suit him, but he was a lonely man, and because of that likeness, he'd hired her the minute she'd opened her beautiful mouth.

Her name was Carmella Lopez, she appeared to be Latin-American and save for a sultry hint of a Spanish accent and her deep olive skin tone, she could have been Natalie's twin sister. She had flowing long raven-colored hair, dazzling blue eyes and lips that could entice even the most celibate man alive. The way she continued to look at him had his mind whirling and his heart pounding.

"Sir, you have a message from a Mr. Garland, and this came in the mail for you," she purred and leaned over, giving him a clear shot of her perfectly-rounded cleavage, and Rick's dick hopped in his pants as her eyes licked him from behind her black-framed glasses.

Fuck, he swore in his head. How much longer was he gonna be able to take this? What had he been thinking? Every single time he saw her, it got worse; his desire to take her, pull her on top of his lap, and love every inch of her flawless skin. All he could think about was burying himself inside her. For two weeks now, he'd fought the need...and the flashbacks of Natalie's gorgeous body writhing beneath him some nineteen plus years ago that weekend he'd shown up on her doorstep in Chicago.

God, he was pathetic! He'd been in love with Natalie Butler Kinsen since high school and no matter the number of women he'd pulled into bed or the distance he'd put between them had eased the pain of not having her for his own. He'd moved to Sunnyvale years ago and yet his heart still broke into a million pieces at the thought of her being with another man… it didn't matter that the man was her husband. Rick hated Jack Kinsen. Cursed his name. Prayed for his death.

He knew how ridiculous it was. But that hadn't changed how much he wanted the wrangler's blood. Even still, if Jack died tomorrow, Natalie wouldn't have Rick back, he knew. Buck had told him long ago that Natalie didn't care for him, not like he did her.

Well, she wasn't opposed to me ramming myself inside her for a whole weekend! Rick thought and tried to calm his anger as Carmella tilted her head at him.

"Sir, can I be so bold to suggest a massage?"

"A massage?" Rick smarted off then tried to ease his tone. "Why?"

"You're *so* tense," she pouted and moved to the back of his chair. She pulled at the wool blazer on his shoulders, and he hesitantly shucked it off, practically jumping as her dainty hands cupped his deltoids. "Just relax," she cooed, and he groaned as she dug in with her long fingernails. "Close your eyes and just breathe. Relajarse."

Rick hesitated again but finally did as she'd asked and let her touch and accent pull him away.

He was slightly aware that they were probably violating company policy, but slowly his mind sailed away and settled back to the familiar place it always went—Natalie.

Her beautiful smile as he kissed her soft plump lips, her sultry moan as he kneaded her full breasts, her breathy gasps as he loved her with all his might, her hips arching up to meet his as he buried himself deep inside her, her firm bottom as he gripped it tight in his—

Dammit, I'm doing it again, Rick sighed heavily and huffed his breath out quickly.

"Shh, listen to my voice," he heard Carmella tell him as he frowned, eyes still tightly shut. "Relax your face. Relax your mind.

Relax your whole body. Concentrate only on your breathing." *Man*, that sexy accent of hers made his insides shiver.

He'd thought moving away from Abundance would be the answer he sought after his heartbreak had only amplified once Natalie and Jack had gotten married and he'd tried unsuccessfully to move on. He'd see them from time to time in town and Dallie too and the wound would rip back open as fresh as it had been that day he'd first called her—after the affair they'd had when she was still married to Troy was over, hoping for a love that would never come. Years of reading her column and hearing about her and Jack from Scottie, Buck, Keith and Luther had kept his emotions bubbling on the surface. Then Natalie had Jack's first child and the permanence of his one-sided love for her had almost ripped Rick apart. Savannah was as beautiful as her mother and all Rick could do was wish how much she could be *his* child. He'd thought Dallie might have been at one time, but after doing the math, there was no way for it to be possible, no matter how much he'd desired it to be so. Besides, Dallie looked too much like the Camerons to be a Singleton.

After fighting it for far too long, Rick realized that his unhealthy obsession with Natalie needed to be remedied, and when his firm called him with the opportunity for expansion on the west coast, he'd taken the prospect to run away from her and the life they could never have together.

Rick had worked very hard to extinguish his feelings, dampen them down, and he'd done a good job of it, or so he'd thought. He'd buried himself in work, women, and exploring different hobbies: cooking, hiking, running, even sailing. Yet everything he did, reminded him of the life that another man was living in his place. In the back of his mind, he kept to the hope that maybe one day, *somehow*, he could be with the woman he loved. Then Buck had called to tell him about his retirement, and Rick had been stupid enough to ask how Natalie was doing. When Buck had told him about her being pregnant again with Jack's baby boy, Rick had lost it. He'd gotten drunk and cursed his life and his fate. Why? Why couldn't he be the one she loved? And why couldn't he get over her? Why was his life a total shit-show? He'd pulled woman after woman into his bed since then but nothing and *no one* seemed to be able to quench the thirst he had.

It was hopeless. *He* was hopeless. He would be pining for his gorgeous and untouchable Natalie until he was dead. At this point it had been almost twenty years- twenty prolonged damn miserable years. He felt his shoulders fall and a tear escape his eye even as he steadied his breathing and lost himself to the kneading of his shoulder muscles.

"Who's Natalie?" he heard a soft voice whisper into his ear.

At the sound of her name being spoken aloud, pain ripped into his chest so fast and hard that he grimaced. "What?" Rick tensed.

"Relax. I asked you *who* Natalie was?"

"How did you—?"

"You were saying her name as you were supposed to be relaxing."

"Oh. She's..." Rick trailed off, not knowing how to describe to Carmella exactly who Natalie was. The woman of his dreams. His long-lost love. His life. His heart. His torment.

"It's alright, I understand."

"You do?" he scoffed. "Stop!" he commanded. His hands went to hers as he noticed his raging boner. He dejectedly tried to cover it, but it was too late; she'd seen it.

"Oh," she gasped.

"Jesus," Rick swore and leaned forward, scooting his chair up.

"It's alright. I can fix it."

Fix it? Rick almost groaned aloud. "No, you've done enough. Thank you," he grumbled.

"Please? Regard me?" Carmella leaned across him then and rolled his chair back, squatting down to her knees in front of him.

"Carmella, *what* are you doing?" he growled, even as his sex suddenly tingled with anticipation.

"Mr. Singleton. I did this to you. It's only right for me to unburden you." Her hands went to the button of his slacks, even as his hands moved to block her.

"No, I can't allow you to—"

"It's alright, Rick. I *want* to."

Rick stilled as he gazed into the sultry blue eyes that looked up at him and gulped. He felt the fly of his slacks come undone and his sex was suddenly freed. He groaned aloud as Carmella's hand gripped his rock-hard erection and gasped as her head lowered.

"Carmella, you can't—" His protests died on his lips as he felt her tongue lick the length of him.

"I think you just need a woman who's strong enough to make you forget *all* about Natalie."

"Holy fuck," he whimpered as her lips kissed the head of his cock and her hand cupped his scrotum. He shuddered, his hands tightly gripping the arms of his executive chair as his head flew back.

Carmella moaned as her mouth encased him, and he almost blew his load right then and there. He shivered as inch by inch, she moved her mouth moved down lower on him, taking his sex deeper. His hands fell into her thick, wavy hair as she pulled back, her sky-blue eyes watching him, then suddenly she began rocking her whole body, her mouth pumping his erection in the most exquisite way; he stared down at her, watching her mouth around his throbbing manhood, going in and out, in and out... Her red-nailed fist moved over him and squeezed him each time her mouth pulled back, and he thought he'd died and gone to Heaven. Her mouth and hands and eyes began to unravel him as his grip tightened in her hair and her hot mouth sucked him into mind-blowing oblivion. Rick practically roared as his sudden release came and her grip on his cock and scrotum tightened. He spilled himself into her throat and watched as she licked him clean, all the while her eyes burned a scorching hot heat signature into his, his sex pulsing as he shuddered, coming down from his sexual high.

When he caught his breath, she smiled up at him. "See. I told you that you simply needed to relax, Mr. Singleton. How do you feel now?"

"Carmella," he began, grabbing for his fly as she stood and sat her plump bottom on his desk, crossing her arms across her ample bosom. He gulped again, feeling the stirrings of desire return to his flaccid penis.

With one finger to his lips, she leaned down and whispered, "Don't worry, boss. My lips are sealed." Who the hell *was* this lady? Rick's eyebrows went up and he started, even as that long, pink tongue of hers slowly licked his chin and lips, he stifled a groan. "Dinner at my place tomorrow night?" A dark brown eyebrow arched at him. "Does eight work for you?" She kissed his lips, a quick but soft, sensual kiss then she winked at him as she pulled back. Rick could do nothing but nod as Carmella turned and left his office, sashaying that curvy, round bottom of hers before eye-fucking him and closing the door.

"What the *fuck* just happened?" he asked himself as he tried to calm his nerves.

If anyone had heard that or knew about it, they would both lose their jobs.

Just as Rick was contemplating the consequences of his end of the day, impromptu blow-job, his phone rang from his back pocket, forcing him to dampen down his apprehension.

He smiled into the phone as he answered, "Buck!"

"Rick! Hey, buddy! How the *hell* are you?"

Rick couldn't help but brag; hell, it wasn't every day he got sucked off by his secretary. "Well, considering I just got blown by my gorgeous new assistant, I'd say I'm pretty damn good right now."

Buck gave a rich laugh before he answered, "Wait! You're being serious?"

Rick couldn't help but laugh himself. "Swear to God! You should see her, Buck. She is fuckin' *smokin'* hot." Of all his friends, Buck would be the one to understand.

"Wow. I have to say, Rick, I never pegged you to let your guard down like that. I'm proud of you, man. Congrats. Let that freak flag fly!" Buck laughed again. He seemed fairly jovial, and in addition to his release, Rick felt his spirits lift for the first time in a while.

"So, what do I owe the pleasure, Bucko?"

"Well, I actually called to give you some good news, although you might not find it quite as exciting as what you just had done… Guess who's gonna be a father?"

Rick sighed and pinched the bridge of his nose, anger shooting through him as an image of a pregnant Natalie flashed through his head. "If you say Jack Kinsen again, I swear to *God*, I'm gonna go cut my wrists in a bathtub somewhere!"

"Jesus, dude, don't even joke like that!" Buck roared into the phone. The line was silent as Buck sighed then he said, "Me, Rick. Me! *I'm* gonna be a father."

"You?" Rick was stunned to say the least. Had Buck married and somehow Rick had missed it? He tried to think back. It had been a while since he'd talked to any of his old friends back home. Buck had never even had a steady girlfriend but once or twice in the entire time Rick had known him. When had he settled down with a woman? And furthermore, if he *hadn't* then why in God's name was he so damn excited about being a father? Then Rick remembered seeing the tabloids where Buck had jaded the Hollywood actress Vivian Alexander. Could it be her? "Who'd you get pregnant?" Rick couldn't hide his curiosity.

"I'm sure you've heard of her- Vivian Alexander."

"The actress you left at the hotel after the Helping Heroes Ball?"

"Sonova—" Buck swore and grumbled. "It wasn't *like* that, first of all, and yes, it's her. We're gonna have a baby. Can you freakin' believe it?"

No. No, he couldn't believe it. How could it be that Buck Jenkins, of all Rick's friends, would have a child before he did? He couldn't hide the envy or sullenness that suddenly washed over him. "Wow, Buck. That's great, man. I'm happy for you." It wasn't true, but he tried to make it so. He even gave a slight chuckle. "I'm shocked."

Rick heard a female voice then, "Buck Jenkins, who did you tell *now*?" A chirpy little giggle tittered on the other end of the line, and Rick felt his heart stiffen. He was jealous...of Buck. Damn, did his selfishness *ever* end? "You shouldn't tell people before the first trimester. It's bad luck."

"Oh, c'mon now, Viv. I'm excited. I can't hold it in. This is one of my oldest friends. He knows Nat—" Buck stopped, but it was too late, her name was already in Rick's ears, her image already in his head—again. "Dammit, Rick, buddy. I'm sorry."

"It's alright," he stated, feeling his veins burn with pain. "How—how is she by the way?"

"Well, you saw where Dallie was kidnapped, right?"

"What?" Rick gripped the phone tighter. "No. When?"

"It's alright now. She wasn't harmed. It was apparently a big misunderstandin'." A misunderstanding? What the hell? "Everyone's fine now. I shouldn't have even said anything. I apologize. Rick. Uh, I wanted to ask if you would come be a part of the golf tournament in October."

The thoughts of returning to Abundance made him physically sick to his stomach. He couldn't return to his hometown without seeing her everywhere he looked, and she would most likely attend this particular shindig for certain. It was for Buck after all, and she was Abundance's local journalist. There was simply no way he'd be able to avoid her if he went.

"Can I think about it, Buck?" he asked through a clenched jaw.

"Of course. It would mean a lot to me, and I know some of our buddies wouldn't mind seeing ya." Of course they wouldn't, but again, he would see Natalie, even seeing them. It was yet another reason why he'd left. She'd touched every aspect of his entire life.

"I'll give it some thought, okay?"

"Ok." Buck agreed, leaving it at that.

"Hey, I should have called you before now. I'm really sorry about your mom, Bucko. I hate it for you. She was a wonderful lady." Laurel had been like a second mom to Rick, well and Corrine Butler,

Marnie Tate, and Martha Boyd too, so her death had hit him pretty hard. He'd wanted to call Buck the day he'd found out, but he was afraid Buck would ask him to come to the funeral, and Rick couldn't bear seeing Natalie and Jack, even if he should be there for one of his oldest friends in his time of need. Again, proof of Rick's self-loathing and never-ending selfishness. He didn't deserve his friends.

"Thank you, Rick. I appreciate it. Those flowers were beautiful by the way. She would've loved them." Buck's gruff voice trembled. And Rick once again regretted not being there for one of his best friends. "Think about October, alright? It would be great to see you."

"I promise that I will," Rick answered earnestly, knowing he owed it to Buck to be there.

"Alright. Call me soon."

"Will do, Buck. Good night."

"Bye, buddy."

The silence on the other end of the phone had never felt so deafening as Rick ended the call and sighed.

He was going to Carmella's tomorrow night and dammit, he was getting the hell over Natalie Kinsen, if his life depended on it.

CHAPTER 7

"*W*ow, so we're gonna get to see the baby today, on my birthday, huh?" Buck asked. Viv just nodded in response. "Oh, boy. I can't wait!" Buck smiled over at her and grabbed for her hand.

They'd flown into LAX an hour earlier and headed to Malibu, long enough for Vivian to stop by home for clothes and grab her mail before they headed to see her doctor for her first pregnancy visit. She'd tried to read up about what to expect and saw that she'd be getting bloodwork, a pelvic exam and usually the doctor wanted an ultrasound done too. She'd just informed Buck of all this when he'd asked.

The last week had been relaxing and easy as she and Buck basked in her pregnancy. They'd spent their days unhurried, cooking—although Viv still battled her morning sickness— watching old black and white movies, swimming in Buck's pool and taking long naps during the hot summer days. They'd work out in the basement before finding recipes to cook for dinner. Vivian had started reading pregnancy books in the evenings as Buck worked in his office. Then each night they devoured each other with a heat that wouldn't be squelched. Vivian's sexual drive had never been higher and she found herself waking in the middle of the night reaching for the sexy, brawny man who was not only her lover, but the father of the child growing inside her, in hopes of scratching the itch her throbbing hormones elicited deep within her.

If she didn't know any better, she'd think she'd worn him out. The bags were dark under his eyes this morning, and he'd fallen asleep during their movie on the plane. She couldn't help but grin over at him as they rode silently in the limo.

Buck looked as handsome as ever in his white linen button-down shirt, khaki slacks and a pair of Sperry's. He was clean-shaven and donned a pair of dark Oakley's that had been shoved into his unruly thick blonde hair. He looked like he could've been a California boy instead of a Texan, but his deep drawl squashed whatever doubt anyone would have.

When the limo pulled to a stop, Buck opened the door and got out then stuck his hand out to help Vivian onto the sidewalk.

"Welp, here we are, darlin'."

"Thank you kindly, sir." Vivian did a fake curtsy and grinned shyly at him.

She'd dressed in light and flowy olive-green palazzo pants, a black halter-neck tank top and a denim blue jean jacket. They'd attempted to be inconspicuous, so as not to draw too much attention — Ha! She'd be kidding herself. Buck Jenkins and Vivian Alexander were gonna be seen going into her doctor's office together. The secret would be out any second now about their secret love child.

She'd known this as soon as she gotten back to Abundance. The media was already in an uproar on her prompt departure from the set she'd been on a little over a week ago. Jill hadn't even called to tell her how pissed Vince had been. Come to think of it, Viv needed to call her and let her know they were in town. She could only imagine; Jill had probably gotten Viv's lawyer involved to break the contract she'd written to Bernard-Hartley Productions. She was bound to lose a lot of money on this—oh well, it was a done deal now.

Buck took her hand and looped her arm through his as they walked down the busy street and up some concrete steps into the quiet and discreet office of her obstetrician, Dr. Namita Anjani. Jill had found the lovely Indian doctor through some references and had assured Vivian she had impeccable reviews. It had been a while since Vivian had even been to a doctor, aside from annual check-ups, eye visits, and routine teeth cleanings, so in addition to her unexpected pregnancy, she felt anxious too at the thought of being naked beneath a thin cotton gown in front of both a complete stranger and a man she'd known for just two months.

They were taken right from the reception desk, upon Viv's announcement of who she was, and into a private room that looked to be the size of the penthouse suite she and Buck had spent their first night together in.

"Wow," Viv couldn't hide her surprise as she looked at the 'exam table' —which more resembled a large bed— a changing area, a bathroom, a television screen and a couch adjacent to a sizable desk and executive chair.

"Dr. Ajani likes for our patients to feel as comfortable as possible," the young medical assistant cooed as she motioned for them to have a seat on the couch, clipboard in hand. They obliged.

"Now, Miss Alexander. I'm going to get a full medical history from you as well as from Mr. Jenkins before Dr. Ajani joins us. I'll also be getting your blood pressure, drawing some blood and getting a urine sample. Can I get you some refreshments before we get started? A water or tea perhaps?"

"Y'all don't got any whiskey back there, do ya?" Buck chuckled nervously.

The medical assistant just gave him a polite smile, knowing he was only kidding.

"I'll take water, please?" Vivian asked.

"Cucumber mint, lemon, bottled or sparkling?"

"Damn, Viv. They *do* have a full bar back there. I knew it!" Buck joked.

Vivian laughed, feeling some of her nervousness melting away. He was good at doing that, she'd noticed. Buck was not only handsome, he was also easy to talk to, funny and gentle. He might be full of himself, but he was a giving man with a heart of gold. She'd seen that in just the last several days she'd spent with him as he'd practically catered to her every whim, making sure she wasn't lifting anything too heavy, feeding her healthy foods and even assisting her as the morning sickness had taken her.

The assistant, Marta, excused herself to get the waters Viv and Buck requested.

"Are you nervous?" Buck asked as he threw his big arm around her.

She would be lying if she said no. She nodded, avoiding his eyes. "A little."

Buck cupped her face and moved a stray strand of hair back with his index finger. "Me too," he admitted, much to her surprise, and gave her a grin as she looked up at him.

She took in his ruggedly handsome face, square jaw, eyes as blue as the sky and kissable lips. Their child was going to be gorgeous, she knew. Just as she was about to tell him so, he leaned in to kiss her, and she took comfort from the warmth of his lips on hers. Her body was greedy though, and she felt the stirrings of desire fill her core as his mouth opened. Her tongue reacting involuntarily, and a strangled moan escaped her lips as it stroked across Buck's. God, how could she be so aroused again? They'd just made love merely eight hours before. He pulled her closer, slanting his mouth across hers, his tongue fighting for control as his big palm slid up her back. She was the first to come up for air and realized her hand was gripping his bicep, she gulped and pulled back some, her insides tingling.

"Mmm, we'll have to play doctor later, my little starlet," he murmured, his mouth moving to her neck, and she gasped as the intensity of her desire overtook her. She felt the hair on her arms raise and her nipples pebble as he licked at her pulse, his lips planting messy kisses on her quivering flesh. She gripped his shirt and moaned breathlessly, pressing her palms into the hard muscles of his chest and felt her sex clench in response. *Holy crap!* She could've let him take her right then and there. What was wrong with her? They'd been like this since they'd reunited. "I don't know if I can wait 'til later," he whispered, and his hand moved up her ribcage. "How long do you think we got 'til—"

He was interrupted by the sound of the door opening, and they shot apart like two teens caught making out in the living room by a little brother.

Vivian cleared her throat and turned, adjusting her shirt as Buck pulled at his khakis. The assistant just set their glasses down and eyed Viv, blushing.

"I'm sorry, I—"

"It's alright. It happens frequently. It's those pregnancy hormones."

"Pregnancy hormones?" She hadn't gotten very far in those books she'd bought; she kept falling asleep after two minutes of reading. First her sex drive, now her sleep patterns.

"Oh, yes. You've probably noticed an increase in your libido?"

Buck coughed as if he'd suddenly swallowed gum, and Viv felt her blush deepen.

"It's perfectly normal." The assistant winked. "Now, let's begin, if that's alright."

They both nodded, and Buck took Viv's hand as Marta began asking her numerous personal questions regarding her medical and family history then it was Buck's turn to be interrogated. After about fifteen minutes of intense questioning, another young woman entered and took a blood sample as Marta laid a gown and blanket down on the exam table. Once the blood was drawn, Marta took Vivian's blood pressure then handed her a plastic cup.

"Ok, now I need your urine sample. Just fill it up to the line." She motioned to the line on the cup. "The instructions are in the restroom. Once you're finished, change into the gown. Everything off. Gown open to the front. And Dr. Anjani will be in shortly."

Vivian just nodded. This was all stuff she was used to doing at her annual check-ups. No surprises. She took the cup with her to the restroom, did as instructed, and came out to see Buck sitting in the chair beside the exam table, elbows on his knees. He looked at her and gave a small smile as she grabbed the gown up and moved behind the changing curtain. After she'd disrobed and hung her clothes up on the hangers provided, arranging her bra and panties neatly on the table, she put the thin, cotton gown on, open in front and stepped out.

Buck grinned as she quickly peeled the front of the gown open and just as rapidly closed it, flashing him. His deep, throaty laugh was laced with sexual promise as he said, "Oh baby, now I *really* wanna play doctor. I can't wait to examine my patient." He winked as she sat down on the exam table and pulled the sheet over her thighs. He took her hand then and brought it to his lips, her insides fluttering as he did so. At least he was helping eradicate the nervousness of being naked, waiting for her body to be examined both externally and internally.

"Now, Dr. Jenkins, you'll have to be sure and do a thorough job," she purred.

"Oh, I intend to inspect every inch of your gorgeous skin, darlin'." God, the way the man said the word "darlin'" made her literally shiver with desire. She could imagine his hands and tongue all over her as his fingertips moved up her arm and he stood, his big palm cupping her cheek as his sweet breath fell over her face. "Now, you just lay back here and get comfy, my sweet lil' star. Rest your head and my baby." She did as instructed and rested her head down on the thick pillow. His hand moved to rest on her lower abdomen, his touch ever light on the skin covering her womb. "Once all this is over, Daddy's gonna have some birthday fun." Viv giggled as Buck's hand lowered between her thighs, tickling at the stubble there. Her bent legs parted slightly and she moaned as his fingertips flirted at the folds of skin. "Who knew a doctor visit would be so arousing?" he whispered in her ear, bringing goosebumps to her exposed flesh. He pulled her hand—the one resting on the table—towards his crotch and let her feel the erection that her impromptu teasing had elicited. She gripped at his firm flesh through his khakis and turned her head to look at him as he moaned, feeling his fingertip dip into the opening of her body. "Mmm," he growled, arching his hips against her palm. "This damn doctor needs to hurry before I violate doctor/patient confidentiality."

Vivian practically cackled and took his hand from between her legs, realizing that they should probably put a lid on this before it got too far out of hand; after all, the doctor would be in the room any moment now. She moved his hand up to her lips, pulling the finger he'd entered her with into her mouth, sucking gently and swirling her tongue around it.

"Fuck, Viv," Buck growled, breathlessly. "I swear to God I'm gonna—"

He didn't finish before the door opened and he planted his bottom quickly in the seat beside her, pulling his finger from her mouth and taking her hand again. All the while, Viv couldn't hide the childish grin at her lips as she watched Buck guiltily glance at the doctor. Finally, she turned her head and looked at her new obstetrician.

"Ms. Alexander. Mr. Jenkins. It's a pleasure to meet you both. I'm a big fan, I must admit." The lovely, slender, Indian doctor extended her hand and Viv sat up slightly to take it. "I'm Dr. Ajani." Vivian noted her beautiful espresso-colored skin, deep brown eyes and gorgeous red lips. She had matching red framed glasses which she shoved into her wavy, thick dark hair. Once she'd shaken Vivian's hand with her ungodly cold one, she took Buck's hand, which seemed to swallow her small one whole. "Congratulations are in order I see." The doctor giggled, and Vivian knew immediately that she was going to love her. Dr. Anjani pulled her hand away, glanced down at the chart in her hands, and pulled a rolling stool over to the end of the bed, looking up at them both.

"All your bloodwork came back good. All your numbers look great. So, at this point, keep doing what you're doing, diet and exercise wise. Obviously, no heavy-lifting or strenuous activities. I'm gonna start you on some prenatal vitamins and give you a list of foods and products to avoid. Did you have a question, Mr. Jenkins?" She giggled again and looked past Vivian to Buck.

"Oh, darlin', it's Buck, and yeah, I sure did."

Vivian smirked and looked over at her handsome baby daddy.

He grinned slyly over at Viv before taking her hand in his again and kissing the back of it before turning his attention back to the doctor. "Now, as far as 'strenuous' activity goes…"

"You can still have copious amounts of sex, if that's what you were gonna ask?" Dr. Anjani stated boldly.

Buck's response was stymied slightly as his eyebrows went up in surprise at the doctor's answer.

"I don't expect much to change in the bedroom department for most couples, but I do ask that you refrain from anything that would cause abdominal 'trauma'. Oh, and no sex swings or hot tubs." When Viv and Buck raised their eyebrows the doctor's hand went up and she said, "You know what, don't ask, just—" She laughed again. "No funky, kinky circus sex. Try and have sex like normal people until the baby's here, ok?"

"Fair enough, doc," Buck stated first, and Viv looked over at him, stifling a laugh. "I mean. I just wanted to make sure I could still have my way with my woman here, that's all."

"Understood. Yup, you have the green light there, as far as I'm concerned. Unless you are having pain, fluid leakage or excessive bleeding after sex, you two are good to go." She smiled at them both. "Now, I want to give you a quick pelvic exam then we'll take a quick look at the baby." She motioned to the ultrasound machine as the door opened, and Marta walked back in with a kit.

The doctor listened to her heart and lungs and examined her

breasts, which was uncomfortable to say the least with her lover looking on. Dr. Anjani's gloved hands moved down Vivian's belly to her lower abdomen, gently pressing.

Vivian sighed heavily, and Buck gave her a weak grin when the doctor moved the stool down to the end of the bed. She tried hard to relax as the doctor performed her pelvic exam. Buck was an angel; taking her hand and coaxing her to look at him, while her insides were assaulted by gloved fingers and a speculum.

"You're so strong," he mouthed and puckered his lips at her. She couldn't help but smile as his sweetness. She was glad he was there with her after all. She would have felt even more awkward without him.

"Alright, everything looks great. Now let's take a look at this little peanut, shall we?" Dr. Ajani said and slid the machine over. She pulled Vivian's gown apart, away from her belly, making sure the sheet still covered her nether-regions and placed the gel-covered probe on her lower abdomen. She moved it around a little before settling on a spot. "Ah, there we are. There's your baby." She pointed to the screen monitor, to a little white blob floating within a big black circle.

"There's the yolk sac. The brain. Oh and—" the doctor moved a trackball on the machine and a line appeared. She hit a button and spectral waves appeared on the screen. "Hear that? It's the heartbeat." They could hear a thumping, swishing sound over the speakers.

Vivian gasped, amazed at both the sight and sounds of life within her.

"That…that's the heartbeat?" Buck asked. "Wow, it's so fast."

"Yes, it's supposed to be." The doctor gave a little giggle. She pressed more buttons and the image of the floating blob in blackness reappeared. "See the flash? That's the heart." She pointed.

"Oh my God! That's incredible," Buck exclaimed, his excitement uncontainable. "Baby, that's our *baby*." Vivian felt his lips kiss her cheek then as tears fell, unbidden from her eyes. "Viv. We made that. You and me, darlin'. Holy shit!" She looked over at Buck then and the incredible happiness on his face made her cry even harder. He was mesmerized by the image on the screen, and if she wasn't mistaken, his eyes were glistening as the doctor measured the fetus and pointed to the "arm and leg buds" forming.

Vivian was blown away at how amazing fetal development was as the doctor continued to spew forth information on their baby and the process of conception. When Buck looked over at Vivian after the doctor put the probe away and stepped out, she swore he'd never been as tender as he planted his lips softly on hers. He cupped her cheek, gazing into her eyes.

"Thank you, Buck," she stated, trying to ease the seriousness of the moment. "For coming with me."

"No. Thank *you*. I wouldn't have missed that for anything in the world. We got to see our baby. And on my birthday to boot." He smoothed the back of his hand over her cheek and helped her sit up. "We'll get to meet her come March."

"Her, huh? You think it's a girl?"

"Well, I dunno. Honestly, so long as the baby's healthy, I don't mind either way."

Vivian felt the exact same way herself and smiled.

"Wanna get dressed? I want to take you out to dinner and celebrate."

"Oh? I thought we were gonna play doctor." Viv pouted up at her handsome lover.

"Oh? I apologize. Is your sexual appetite stronger than your craving for food now?" His voice lowered as his hands opened her gown and slid it down her shoulders. "Mmm, you know, my craving for you is never quite satisfied." His eyes appraised her naked skin, and he grinned as his head lowered to her breast. He kissed the top of the plump mound and nestled his nose against her. She moaned as his hand came up and he cupped it, pushing it up and bringing her rigid nipple to his lips. He gently kissed the swollen peak then pulled it into his hot mouth, striking it with his tongue. Her head flew back as her center reacted to his suckling, and she whimpered. Buck stepped closer to the side of the bed, and Viv extended her legs, encircling the back of his thighs and bringing him even closer to her, her hands going to his waist. "Mmm, Viv," he murmured as his hand cupped her head and his lips took hers in a sizzling kiss that made her hips buck up against his. "Fuck, baby, I wanna take you right here on this damn exam table."

"Then do it, birthday boy," she challenged, arching a brow, even as her hands moved to the button of his pants.

"Don't tempt me, little mama. You're such a non-compliant patient right now. I oughta bend you over my knee and spank you." He chuckled as he picked her up and off the table, pulling her tight against his big frame. His head came to her neck and he breathed in deeply, inhaling her as his nose fell into her hair. "God, I could lose myself to you, Vivian Lisette Alexander." Her hands came around his neck then as she slid down his broad chest and she reveled in the feel of him, so strong and solid against her. Her heart did a little flop that had nothing to do with the desire coursing through her center and when she pulled back, she stared up into his dancing blue eyes. He grinned at her with the same intense gaze that he'd given her just moments before and time seemed to stand still as they stood there simply looking at one another. She took in the hard lines of his face, the arch of his brow, the faint scar that ran from the edge of his right eye to his temple, the curve of his lips, his hairline…and she was sure he was doing the exact same thing, memorizing her face.

A knock came at the door, and Viv bolted for the changing curtain—as she was buck naked at that point—before it opened, and Marta stepped in carrying a bag.

"Miss Alexander. Here's some vitamins, pamphlets, and information for you. I've already scheduled you for your next appointment. Feel free to call if we need to reschedule. Dr. Ajani's cell phone number is in here as well. Do you have any questions?" Viv changed quickly as Marta talked and stepped out just a moment after she asked.

"Uh, no, I think we're good. I can call if I think of anything."

"Of course. I'll see you two out."

Buck took her hand and they were escorted out of the office, his hand patting her bottom as he whispered. "You look flushed, lil' mama." She scoffed and smacked his big arm.

**

One week had passed since Rick had been literally ravished by his new assistant…and one week since he'd avoided eye contact with her…and one week since he'd stood her up for the dinner he had failed to attend at her house.

But how could he after what she'd done? He'd been completely blindsided by her taking possession of him—well, his dick— and his desires. He'd been embarrassed, ashamed, and taken off guard by her advances. He could only take so much, and she'd been able to see right through him. How had she done that? His love for Natalie Kinsen had ultimately been his downfall, but it had been his security blanket too. It had been the one constant in Rick Singleton's life, the one thing that hadn't changed in over twenty years. His job and his home had been uprooted, but his memories of Natalie were rock-solid; something he could hold on to when all else in the world was unknown. Being with her had been a small glimpse into a life he'd wanted so very badly…one he'd painstakingly had to let go of. And Carmella had rattled that unshakable blanket; she'd ripped that fucker right the hell off!

Carmella was equally as mysterious, intriguing and beautiful as Natalie, but was she any different than the other women Rick had tried to bury his memories in to? That fear had been what had stopped him from acting.

Rick had called out that very next morning, the morning following the afternoon that Carmella had gone down on him in his office. He'd felt inadequate, hesitant to see her again, and knew that he couldn't go to her home that night, no matter how much he wanted to fuck his unrequited feelings for Natalie away with yet another woman. His cover had been blown after all, his secret out, the last of his resolve had faded. Natalie was his weakness and his weakness had been exposed for Carmella to see and wound that afternoon. Rick was a troubled soul, but it wasn't her place to "fix" him as she'd said she needed to do.

No, he'd bailed. He couldn't do it. He'd avoided her eyes and being alone with her since. He'd purposely left his door open, refused to be at work after hours and was practically dismissive to her. It was for her own good, right? After all, how many women had Rick had over the years that couldn't live up to Natalie in his eyes? He'd slept with them, attempted to move on, and when they hadn't been able to hold a candle to his "perfect Natalie" he'd gotten rid of them. No explanations. No call backs. Just radio silence. It was enough that his own life had been destroyed by his love for Natalie; no one else needed to be ruined in his path to achieve freedom from the bonds of his everlasting feelings for the woman he'd fallen for in his teen years. Carmella deserved better, hell, *any* woman deserved better. No one wanted to play second fiddle to the ghost of the lover that remained forever in his heart and mind.

Rick knew it was fucked up! And he wanted to abolish it. It was why he'd bailed. Not because Carmella wasn't drop dead gorgeous and worthy of his affections, but just the opposite…she absolutely was!

And now he felt like absolute shit, for she looked as if he'd ripped her very heart from her chest as she blushed and brought him his messages for the morning.

"Mr. Garland called again. Oh, and this came in the mail for you," she murmured sullenly and sat a manila envelope down on the desk. The return address was from Abundance, Texas, and Rick felt his heart literally jump into his throat.

"Dammit!" he swore and sighed heavily. "I forgot about this. Fuck!" He planted his head into his hands and felt a rush of emotion fill his chest as an image of Natalie overtook his mind. The pain and fury and violation of it caused him to squint his eyes. God, would he ever stop wanting her? Would he ever be able to move on?

He gasped as a soft hand gripped his shoulder. "Rick?" He looked up to see Carmella staring down at him, a concerned look on her pouty-lipped face. Dammit, if he wasn't pulling those plump lips back to his cock and fucking his frustrations into that sexy, enticing mouth of hers. He only flinched from her touch, as these thoughts filled his head, as if she'd scalded him, and she lowered her head, pulling her offended hand from his arm. Before she could walk away though he grabbed for her hand and pulled her back to the side of his desk, taking her off guard.

Her uneasy eyes took in his as he stood, unsure at first what to say, for an apology would be too commonplace. She gulped and looked down to the envelope. "What *is* that?"

Rick had to force himself to look back at it; for just the name of his hometown brought far too many painful memories back to him.

"It's nothing. It's—"

"What is it?" she asked again and held his eyes for long moments. He felt himself being pulled into her dazzling blue orbs. They weren't quite sapphire like Nat's. They weren't sky blue either, but deeper with small flecks of a very light green. Beautiful. Unique. The color of the ocean they were mere blocks from, but...not.

When she cupped his cheek, he felt a stirring within him. A desire that surpassed need. A tingling that left him wanting more. It was refreshing, fulfilling, and unexpected.

"It's from my friend, Buck. He wants me to attend a charity golf tournament in my hometown of Abundance, Texas," he finally answered her. Carmella studied him, gauging his own reaction to his words. He hadn't been able to keep from flinching when he'd said the word "Abundance". As if it were an abhorrent word instead of the fulfilling one the founders had been going for when they'd picked it over two hundred years ago.

"Will she be there?" No need in asking who *she* was...but damn, how did Carmella know? Rick only nodded, a lump growing in his throat. She looked down then, past her own plump breasts, displayed so beautifully in the low-cut lacy silk top of hers, to the floor. "You didn't come over for dinner..." Mel trailed off, swallowing hard like it was difficult for her to say that.

Rick sighed. "Carmella...I—"

"You don't want me."

"That's not why." His hand cupped her bicep gently, clothed in the dark cotton blazer. "You deserve better. You deserve the attention of a man who's not a slave to his past. You deserve to be adored. I can't give you that. I wish I could, but—"

"But you won't try," she admonished and sharply looked up at him, her perfectly arched eyebrows shooting up.

He had no recourse—it was true. He didn't have any intentions of trying. It was a moot point, wasn't it? Natalie would never leave his mind...would she? She was embedded in his soul. The day she'd finally given in to his advances had been the day she'd engulfed his heart, marked him, ruined him to any other woman. It would be cruel of him to think for one second that there was hope with Carmella. Why would this time be any different when the other times hadn't been?

"Why me, Carmella?"

"Why *not?*"

He could think of at least a dozen reasons why not, including that he was her boss. Besides, he didn't consider himself an incredibly handsome man—average maybe—with an average build, muscular but nowhere near as ripped as Jack Kinsen. Yeah, Rick worked out and routinely, as he used the gym as one of his many stress outlets and he'd gained a decent amount of muscle in doing so, but he wasn't an athlete or a cowboy. He didn't do hard labor; he sat behind a desk all day. He wasn't ruggedly handsome or even overtly "manly". He tried to be. He wanted to be. But he wasn't. He liked martinis and yoga and shopping...and watching sports bored him.

"I like you, Rick. A lot." She gave him a sultry smile, but it did nothing to strengthen Rick's deflated ego.

"Why?" For truthfully, she didn't even know him.

"I think you're sexy. And smart. And well...elusive." *Elusive?* What did that even mean? He wasn't elusive. Was he? No, he knew that he wasn't elusive, or anything even close to it...or sexy for that matter.

Carmella seemed to pick up on this and murmured, "You don't think much of yourself, do you, Rick Singleton?"

She cupped his jaw and the feel of her soft hand took him aback. All this time, Rick had been too busy comparing himself with the men Natalie had chosen for herself; Luther Boyd, rugged- check, handsome- check, muscular- check... Troy Cameron, rugged...hmm, yeah maybe, handsome- definitely, muscular...yup! Jack Kinsen, hell, he was by far all three and then Captain America to boot. But what about himself? And one point, she'd thought Rick was good enough for her. Or at least good enough for her to sleep with. But why had she chosen him? He'd once believed it was because she loved him too? Deep down. Secretly. But then after years of avoidance, he'd seen that he'd merely been an outlet, an escape, a fling. He'd been there and he'd been convenient for her. She'd used him. He was only a puppet, and she'd been pulling the strings. But he'd been good enough—at one point in time—like her other manly conquests. He'd been deemed worthy of her affections- handsome, rugged, and muscular.

"Rick. I want—I want you to come to dinner at my house. Give me a chance. Please? I promise I won't push you. But at least give me a chance?"

With that, Rick nodded. He would. He would give this a chance, for he wanted to get over Natalie. He wanted to move on, finally and truly, and as he looked at the stunning dark-headed beauty in front of him, he thought with her it might just be possible...just maybe.

CHAPTER 8

*T*hey barely made it back to her house before Vivian was grabbing for Buck.

"Oh, baby. You just can't get enough of me, huh?" Buck asked as Vivian grunted and struggled to pull him atop of her, practically ripping her panties off to vanquish the barrier between them. "Alright. One second, darlin'. I'm gonna give it to you." He pulled his boxers down, freeing his hips.

"Buck, please? I'm *aching*. I need you. Please," she'd begged as she guided his thick member into her soaking wet center, and he gasped at the sensation of his sex kissing hers.

"Fuck, Viv. You're so wet," he groaned as his mouth covered her nipple and he arched his hips, sliding so easily into her. After just two deep thrusts, she was climaxing, screaming his name like a mad woman and crying out as her sex violently contracted around him. He thrust harder and deeper, stoking the fire that continued to rage even as she orgasmed a second time and he came himself not long after. But she was still arching her hips up to meet his, almost desperate to still that never-ending yearning to have him there deep within her. "Baby doll," he groaned, stilling her hips. "I'm spent. You drained me." He chuckled but her gasps were choppy even as she felt his sex deflating and withdrawing from her. She felt like a sniveling child as her desires remained unquenched and she whimpered. He looked up at her and gave a slight grin. "I won't leave you hanging, sweetheart," he whispered as his head moved down her body and he pulled her nipple back into his mouth and pulled on it, darting the peaked point with his tongue and electricity spiked wildly through Vivian's center.

She whimpered again as his big hand moved from the breast he was suckling at, down her belly, and in between her legs, parting her and sliding two fingers in. Her head flew back and she moaned, feeling swirls of pleasure lick deep within her.

"My insatiable lil' sex kitten can't get enough," Buck growled in her ear and nibbled at the flesh of her neck, drawing her skin up in gooseflesh and sending shivers running all over her body. Her gasps of stimulation were sexy even to her own ears. "Oh baby, you're so fuckin' hot when you're putty in my hands like this." He gave a breathy laugh, his mouth moving to the other nipple that he'd not tormented yet and loving it like he had the other one. His fingers pushed deeper inside her, hooking with every other thrust, and Vivian cried out as she felt her pleasure accelerating. "Let's see if this can take you where you need to be."

With that, his mouth moved down her chest, her belly, to the delta of her thighs. His mouth lowered over her center, and she felt his fingers slide out and his tongue slide inside her. Her cry was loud as he began to love her with his mouth like he had that first night, sucking and licking and caressing her with a frenzied tongue as if he were eating his favorite dessert. Using his fingers to thrust hard and deep, his free hand came up to knead and caress a breast and nipple as his persistence paid off and he pushed her over the edge. She came with violent spasms and cries, tears falling from her eyes.

"Wow," Buck said and kissed her inner thigh after several moments had passed and her orgasm had waned, his fingers still inside her. "I got you *all* worked up back there, huh?" He gave her a wink. "I mean, I *am* Buck Jenkins after all...sooner or later, all the ladies bow to Buck."

She couldn't help the laugh that crept out of her throat at his overconfidence. He really *was* a stud...and he damn well knew it too.

Vivian should feel bad for her sudden desperation, but God, the lust that had filled her back in the doctor's office had refused to be put off. Especially once she'd seen the product of their desire on that monitor. She'd wanted the virile man who'd fathered her baby so fiercely at seeing his awe of the little human that they'd made together. He'd been dumbfounded and happy, and she'd wanted nothing more than to pull him inside her and love him for the gift he'd given her.

But her body had never responded to any man like it did to Buck, whether that was the pregnancy hormones or Buck's ridiculously irresistible sex appeal, she wasn't sure, and the intensity of it suddenly overwhelmed her. She bashfully began to extricate herself from his embrace and started grabbing for her clothes.

"Darlin', I was only kiddin'. That was damn sexy as hell." He pulled her against his big-muscled chest and began stroking her face, pulling her chin up to look at him. "I don't know that I've ever had a woman want me quite as much as you do, honestly. It's rather humbling." Those dazzling baby blue eyes held her captive in that moment, and she finally relinquished a smile into his achingly handsome face.

Later, they dined at a ridiculously expensive French restaurant to celebrate both Buck's birthday and their baby. They'd only needed an hour's notice before because...well, they were who they were, and Buck toasted to their "sweet angel growing inside her hot momma." They enjoyed their dinner, as if they *always* spent over a grand for one meal. But they were celebrating the life they'd created that magical June evening. Buck was good company and kept her laughing. She was falling for him, she realized with painstaking clarity as they rode back to her beachfront home on the Pacific Ocean, his hand interlaced with hers as he drove her Audi. He buried his face at the crook of her neck and nibbled lightly on the shivering flesh there when he came to a stop sign. How could he get her so turned on so quickly? She felt like a quivering bundle of nerves at his mere touch. She'd never been so out of control of herself when she was in a man's presence, but his sheer sexuality—his big, muscular body, the handsomeness of his face, the magnitude of his bigger than life personality—had her heart pounding and her sex pulsing. To the point that when they pulled into the garage and got into the house, she was tearing his clothes off and he was putty in *her* hands this time.

**

"*T*his was a mistake," Rick said aloud as he rang the doorbell and waited for Carmella to open it. He could hear heels clicking on the tile of the foyer beyond the wooden door and attempted to still his pounding heart and frayed nerves.

But nothing could prepare him for the absolute lust that ran through him at the sight of her. She was dressed in a tight, dark red dress with a plunging neckline that hugged her curves in all the right places. Her voluptuous breasts threatened to spill out of the V of it, the slit up her thigh left way too little to his imagination and her muscled arms were more bare than he'd ever seen them. The dress could have been poured on.

As amazing as she looked in the dress, her face and hair were his undoing. Her plump lips were painted a red the same shade as the dress and her dark hair had been curled into ribbons. Her shimmering blue eyes held him captive as he said, "I—I can't do this."

He turned, ashamed and filled with anger and desire so fierce that it overwhelmed him.

She grabbed his arm. "Rick, wait," she murmured and turned him gently. He closed his eyes so that he couldn't see Natalie standing before him. He'd been tortured enough and this simply wasn't fair. He flashed back to that afternoon almost nineteen years ago when he'd been on a doorstep not unlike this one and a woman who looked almost identical to the one before him now stood with a look of surprise on her beautiful face.

"Rick," he heard her voice in his head or was that Carmella? "What—? What a pleasant surprise. Please, come in. Won't you?" Natalie's ghost took over. Then Rick was pulled into the door and felt a warm hand on his shoulder. He opened his eyes. Dammit. He was going to enjoy himself tonight, memories be damned. He focused his eyes on Carmella and said her name three times like a chant in his head.

"Are you alright?" Carmella asked. He could lie, or he could tell the truth, either way it wouldn't matter. She just stared back at him, trying to understand. But how could she? "Rick, I—" she began, only to stop. "I want to do something. It's completely unconventional, but I—" Again, she stopped, huffing and grasping his shoulders as her eyes bore into his. "There's something I should go ahead and tell you." She dropped her arms and extended her hand, motioning for him to enter what he assumed was the kitchen.

He just followed obligingly and walked to the bar where two stools sat adjacent to a dark green granite island. The kitchen was spacious—by California standards—and was vibrantly painted in blue hues, not unlike the ocean. He smiled for the first time since he'd come. There were mermaid accents; signs, figures, even salt and pepper shakers. He hadn't been expecting that.

"Can I get you something to drink?" she asked and moved to the fridge. "I have beer, wine...or liquor. Pick your poison." She grinned over at him and his lips pulled up too.

"Uh, do you have gin?"

"Martini?" she asked, almost knowingly. He nodded. "Ah, a martini kinda guy. I dig." She laughed and it was a musical sound that warmed him. She moved away into another room and brought back a bottle of his favorite liquor, some vermouth, and a martini glass. She set them down in front of him and moved to a cabinet on the back wall, grabbed a shaker, and began mixing his drink. "Dirty?"

she said the word so erotically that he couldn't help but lick his lips. He gulped as he nodded and glanced at her backside as she opened the fridge, pulling out a jar of green olives. God, how he wanted to slide his hand down the curve of her ass cheek and squeeze. It looked so plump and round and delicious. Suddenly, his glass was set before him and her eyebrow cocked almost as if she could've read his mind, a knowing grin playing at her red lips. "Dirty martini for the gentleman in the grey suit." Again, with the damn word "dirty". His cock jumped in excitement.

"What about you?" he asked, awaiting to try his drink until she had one herself.

"Oh, me? I don't drink."

"What? Really?" He'd never met anyone who didn't drink.

"Yes, really." She giggled, amusing at his bewilderment. "I never have. I was a bartender for a long time." She looked down as if the memory caused her pain.

"Seen too many drunks hauled out of the bar, huh?"

She smiled big. "Well, yeah, but I didn't drink before that even."

"So, how come you're not a bartender anymore?"

"Well, after my husband died, I didn't need to do that kinda work anymore. I had more money and wanted a better life for myself than slapping men's hands off of my ass."

Rick blushed, slightly embarrassed now by his own thoughts of grabbing her ass.

Carmella just laughed big, as if sensing his distress. "Don't worry. I'll admit, my ass is quite grab-able." She winked when his wide eyes met her own. He just blushed. "Rick. You remind me of my husband." He couldn't hide his surprise at that statement. "Yes. It's why I 'chose' you. You asked me the other day, remember? It's why you have nothing to be ashamed of. I remind you of Natalie. You remind me of Tommy." She looked away, her eyes misting over for a moment before the glistening blue orbs settled back on him. "Tommy was murdered. Right in front of me, by a hulking giant named Tio. All because he was defending his wife's honor against some horny, drunk biker in a hole in the wall bar. He was stabbed to death...for me." Silent tears were streaming down her cheeks now. "It's why I quit. It's why I sought secretarial work. *Any* work beyond bartending. I would have nightmares about him. About Tommy. About Tio coming after me. I moved from New Mexico to here. For a better life. For a life where I could block out those memories. But then I met you and the memories I've tried so hard to bury have come back."

Rick was shocked—beyond belief—that her life had been so terribly skewed. And that he reminded her of her dead husband, Tommy. He didn't even know how to respond to that. Any of it. The most tragedy he'd ever known was at the hands of Troy Cameron and it wasn't as if he'd even seen it firsthand. He'd heard about it on the news. He hadn't been directly affected by it, even though he'd wanted to destroy the man for the pain he'd inflicted on the woman Rick loved. Saying sorry to Carmella for all she'd been through seemed superfluous. He just reached out his hand to her and gave a sympathetic smile. She took his hand and squeezed it, understanding his lack of words.

"I'm sorry. I hope I haven't shocked you. I didn't mean to unload on you like that. It's just— You're so much like him that it terrifies me. And my attraction to you in turn...it takes my breath away. If I didn't know any better I would think you were his twin."

Holy shit! It was the exact same thing he thought of her, and he said so.

"Carmella—"

"Call me Mel." She gave him a sexy grin.

"Mel, I feel the same way about you and Natalie."

"Tell me about her."

Oh, God. What in God's name would she think of him if she knew that Natalie was not his wife, or even his ex-girlfriend, but just some sporadic fling of his past? That Natalie was happily married to another man with three children that weren't his, that Nat had never really even been *his* in any sense of the word but one? That he was pining over a woman he'd slept with almost twenty years ago and hadn't been able to get over her to this day? How could he explain Natalie to Carmella without sounding like a total lunatic? She seemed to sense his hesitancy and gave him a slow grin.

"Please? Tell me about her," she insisted once again.

Why? was Rick's first thought. Why would she want to hear the sordid details of his story? But she'd told him hers, so it was only fitting.

He took in a deep breath and sighed, looking down at the soft, feminine hand in his own. "Natalie was my first love. I didn't even realize how I felt about her until it was practically too late. She was married when I—when we slept together. I was the other man." There he'd admitted it. He'd been in the wrong. The fling. The affair. "I was in love with her long before that though. And I've been in love with her ever since. She—she's since remarried." And to the only other person who knew the story he was now telling Carmella, Rick realized, much to his chagrin. He'd never even told Scottie, Keith or Buck about the affair with Natalie. They'd known something had transpired, and Rick was sure that Nat had told Buck at some point in the last nineteen years, although he'd never come right out and said she had; Rick knew that Buck knew. But it had never been uttered from Rick's lips and until he'd gotten shit-faced drunk that night at the Spur, he'd never intended for anyone to know. But Jack had been there when he'd confessed it for the first time. *Of course he had!* Irony in its truest form. Dammit! He told Mel this. About Natalie and Jack and their children. About Rick's hopeless love for her. How she'd avoided him after the affair. Everything. His conscience was clear, and his heart was hurting as he finally looked back up into her face, feeling tears running down his cheeks. He wiped them away but the stain of them lingered on, as if scalding his face.

Carmella gave him a faint grin as he said, "I'm pathetic. I know this. It's utterly *ridiculous* that I can't move on. What kind of man yearns for a married woman who was never his to begin with?"

"Oh, Rick. No, you aren't. You can't help who you love."

Rick shrugged. It didn't matter; his life was a joke either way. "I want it to stop. You don't know how much I want that." It was true. He didn't want to be in love with Natalie Kinsen. He wanted his life back. To be free of the bonds she'd placed on him the minute he'd claimed her.

"Rick, I want to do something. To help us both move on."

Rick just gave her an incredulous look. "Carmella, a blow job isn't gonna help me move on. No offense. It was amazing and all but—"

She laughed. "That's not what I had in mind."

"Sex? Not gonna help either. Trust me. I know…" he trailed off, blushing. He thought of the countless women he'd slept with over the years. He could barely remember their faces, let alone their names. Only one face burned bright in his memory's eye, a face so similar to the one before him that it scorched his heart.

"Now just hear me out before you freak out, ok?" *Freak out?* Why would he freak out? "It's more of a psychological experiment than a physical one… well, technically, anyway." She sighed big and took his hands in her own. "Let's go into the living room."

Rick followed diligently, drink in hand, as Carmella grabbed a big glass sitting on the back countertop and headed from the kitchen into another spacious living space—presumably the living room/great room. She sat her glass down on a coaster that had been strategically placed on a dark mahogany coffee table and motioned for him to sit on a leather couch. He obliged and set his own drink on the coaster adjacent to hers. She sat too, and he watched as her body seamlessly adjusted to the tight confines of the dress. God, how he wanted to see her naked. He could only imagine how beautiful her flawless olive-toned skin was, how smooth. His groin started to respond as his eyes moved up to her face and he swallowed the lump of sheer lust hitting the back of his mouth. He was salivating, like a damn dog. She smiled, almost knowingly.

"I turn you on." Rick only gulped and gave her a soft nod. "Good. You turn me on too."

She gave him a sultry smile and moved again, this time cutting the dim lighting down even further than it already was, plunging them into shadowy darkness. It took a moment for his eyes to adjust and when they did, his gaze focused on her hands which were coming to the sleeve of her dress. *Oh, God!* But he couldn't see her, only her silhouette. He wanted to see her big, full breasts spill out as she pulled her arms from the fabric. See their color, strike those dark brown nipples that he knew resided there with his tongue. He wanted to watch her come apart to his touch and his mouth. But he could barely make out her features as she moved toward him and the top portion of her dress was peeled down to her waist. He could see the outline of her nakedness, her bare arms and breasts glimmering in the light spilling in from the windows, the kitchen. He moaned aloud and reached for her, but she took his hands in her own. She pulled their hands up above their heads as she came to straddle him, her almost bare thighs resting on top of his. He hadn't been this excited in a long time. He loved this mysteriousness, this sultry sex goddess's temptation. It was thrilling and different, and he wanted more of whatever she was offering him.

Her hands moved to his shoulders as his rested on her bare waist, and he looked down at the shadowy torso in front of him, wishing he could see it fully lit. She leaned forward, and he felt her warm center graze his manhood; he groaned as she rubbed against it, moving her hips in a steamy, provocative way. His hands fell to her hips as he pulled her even closer. Suddenly, he was engulfed in her scent and the heat that radiated from that amazing part of her. He moaned again and tried to pull his face up to see her. It was pointless, he couldn't see her expression, couldn't make out whether she was smiling, frowning or...

"Rick?"

"Yeah," he ground out as her fingertips touched his collar, and she began unbuttoning his shirt. He just rested his head back against the couch and let her do what she wanted. At this point, his erection was full throttle and all he wanted was to bury it as deep inside her as their flesh would allow.

"I want to pretend." *Pretend?* Weren't they a little old for children's games? But hell, this lady was smokin' hot—as he'd told Buck just last week—and her hands were all over him, now moving across his pecs and his belly and tickling at his belt-line. If she wanted to play…then by all means! "I want to play." *Play! Yes!*

"I wanna play too, baby. With your ass, your tits…" he grabbed them in his hands then and squeezed hard, feeling his cock jump. The breathy moan that sounded in her throat blocked all rationale from his mind and his mouth moved to the crook of her neck. He nipped her with his teeth, letting his fingers bring her nipples to rigid peaks. He kissed and sucked at the sensitive flesh of her throat until she was grinding on his cock and rocking those amazing hips on his again. He feared he would blow his load right then and there. She was so fuckin' hot. Her moans, her firm breasts in his hands, her tight abs. His hand moved to cup her sex, his finger grazing a thin line of pubic hair. He gasped. "Oh, baby, you aren't wearing any panties," he stated, surprised, as his finger moved into the wet folds of her skin. "Fuck. I want you." He slid a finger into her silky wetness and heard her cry out. Lust swept his vision then and he was overcome by it. Nothing mattered now. Nothing at all. He wanted this gorgeous woman with a heat that hadn't consumed him in a long time. He wanted to fuck her so hard that she wouldn't be able to stand up straight come tomorrow. He wanted to mark her. Claim her. Take her. And as he began thrusting his finger inside her, his mouth found her nipple and suckled. She cried out again and he groaned. Needing more. Needing to be inside her. Right then.

He flipped them over, her back hitting the couch with a thud as his hands moved to his pants and he quickly relieved himself of them and his boxers, shucking them off and kicking them away as his knee hit the couch and he positioned himself between her muscular thighs. He gripped them in his palms, his cock throbbing in anticipation.

"You're so sexy, sweetheart. You make me so hard."

"I do?"

"Fuck, yeah! Feel for yourself." He grabbed blindly for her hand and pulled it down to his rock-hard sex.

"Mmm," she moaned as she gripped it and began pumping it in her fist. "Just like the first time, Rick." *What?*

"Come again?" he grunted as her other hand cupped his scrotum and began to stroke him. He moaned.

"You know what I'm talking about. The first time we made love, at my house. So long ago."

He furrowed his brow, grimacing, as he looked down at her, although he knew full well they couldn't see each other's facial expressions in the dark. What he could see was dark hair spilled over the cushion, big breasts, and legs splayed open on either side of him. "Carmella?"

"*Carmella*? No. You know my name very well, so why don't you go ahead and say it out loud?" *Natalie!* It was out before he could take it back and he grunted, uncomfortably. "Yes. That's it. It's me, Rick. Natalie."

For a moment he was taken back to that time, so very long ago. The memory was forever burned into his skull, and he couldn't destroy it no matter the times he'd tried. He'd held fast to the visions, kept them just within reach as he comforted himself at night by whatever means necessary.

He looked down...and saw Natalie, as she'd been that day, as he was seeing her now. Her beautiful dark hair spread out on the pillow, trim torso beneath him, sex wet and ready for him, hands gripping him, head thrown back as he drove inside her... But this wasn't Natalie! This was Carmella, his mind screamed.

And he was inside her now, thrusting with all his might. Oh God, she felt so good, as good as she'd felt in the past. So silky, so sweet... Her legs tightened around his waist and his hand grabbed her breast as his other hand moved into her hair. "Natalie?" But it wasn't her. *Or was it?* What had Mel put in that drink? He tried to look into her face, but all he could see were glistening orbs staring back at him. She sure the hell looked like Natalie. He felt full lips on his own. Full, plump lips. Natalie's lips?

It **was** her! He moaned, reveling in the feel of them on his for the first time in what felt like an eternity. He drove deep, and she pulled her mouth from his, throwing her head back once more, moaning loudly, exposing her throat, and his lips moved to her slender neck. He licked and sucked. It was how she liked it, he told himself.

"Oh, Natalie, baby." His breath was choppy as he withdrew and thrust again, moving his hands to her hips. He wanted to separate every barrier that had ever been between them. Make her regret ever leaving him. Make her regret Jack...

He stilled then and looked down into the face before him. His eyes were playing tricks on him. His mind was clouded. Natalie would *never* leave Jack. Would she? His senses began to adjust and he began to remember where he was. She didn't smell like Natalie. She smelled like cinnamon and cloves and lavender. Natalie had smelled like... What the hell had she smelled like? He couldn't remember. Dammit! He was forgetting. What the fuck? He felt panicky all the sudden, as if he were stuck in limbo somehow. What was happening here?

"Natalie?" he ground out, confused, trying to search the eyes below him. They gave nothing away.

"You need closure, Rick. This is how you're going to get it. You need to tell me goodbye." That voice. Was it Natalie's? He couldn't remember what her voice sounded like!

Oh, God! *I'm losing my mind!* He felt a panic attack coming on as his heart pounded in his chest and his breathing grew ragged. He grabbed for her arms, and she pulled him down to her bosom. He took comfort in her embrace as her legs tightened around his hips and his sex screamed at him to be inside her. He needed to finish this. It was the last time. She'd said it herself. He had to let her go. And this was the way...

He moved back atop of her, aligning his body with hers and

thrust inside her again. His hand moved to her face and he cupped her jaw as he pulled out and drove deep once again. She moaned. His other hand gripped her hip, pulling her closer to him. Her hands moved to his face, and she kissed him. He lost himself to the moment. To her lips, her tongue, her breasts against his chest, her hot silkiness wrapped around his steel-hard member, her cries of pleasure as she came apart to him. He moved back to his haunches and gripped her plump bottom in his palms. He was thrusting hard and fast, pounding into her as his passion superseded everything else. Sweat poured from his head as he grunted and gasped and arched his hips, seeking his climax. And finally, it came. With mind-blowing clarity. He roared out as his body and mind soared into a blast of stars and pleasure he hadn't felt in far too long. He gasped and sputtered and arched his hips as his orgasm waned. He continued his slow, gentle thrusts until he was spent and he attempted to catch his breath, looking down at the woman who'd freed him.

For it hadn't been Natalie's name he cried out when he came undone, it had been Carmella's.

CHAPTER 9

*B*uck Jenkins grunted as his phone rang obnoxiously and vibrated incessantly on the nightstand beside him. He grumbled and reached out blindly to grab it as he looked over to Vivian, sleeping soundly, curled up beside him.

God, she was beautiful. And perhaps even more beautiful now that the reality of her being pregnant with his baby felt more tangible. He'd actually seen the tiny speck of life growing inside her yesterday, the miracle of life with a flashing heartbeat; the one he'd planted inside her womb just two months ago. His heart filled with joy, and he couldn't help but grin over at her as she breathed deeply in.

The buzzing phone brought him back to reality then and he wondered if it might be his father. Buck had spoken with him just two days prior, making plans to see him in the next few days when they got back from L.A. Bill was doing better than Buck had expected, despite that he'd not been back home since Buck's mother's death and he wasn't getting a lot of sleep. Buck looked at the bedside clock, the red numbers indicated that it was five fifty-nine in the morning, he huffed as he answered it in a rough tone.

"Hello?" *This better be someone important, otherwise they're gonna get an ear full.*

"Is this Buck Jenkins?" A soft feminine voice asked.

"Yup," he answered sarcastically, as he didn't recognize it, "and just who is *this*?" He smarted off. How the hell was it that solicitors managed to be able to harass an unlisted number in the first place? Wouldn't be the first time.

"This is Gwenyth Stanfield. I'm Vivian's mother." What did the caller just say? She was Vivian's mother? What the hell! Buck sat up and touched the lamp beside him, flooding the room in light.

"Oh, uh...hi, Mrs. Stanfield?"

With that name, Vivian's eyes shot open and she looked at Buck, startled, coming to a sitting position beside him.

"Is my daughter available? I apologize, but I've been trying to call her for hours and hours and I desperately need to speak with her on a matter that is dire for both of us." If Buck had ever wondered where Vivian got her theatrics, the answer was immediately apparent to him then. He boldly laughed.

"Actually, Mrs. Stanfield. She's layin' right here. Give me a second to get 'er up."

Vivian looked as if he'd just slapped her. Her palm smacked her forehead and she pursed her lips, swearing under her breath.

Buck muted the phone before attempting to pass it over to her. "It's your momma," he murmured, amused.

"Buck Jenkins, what the *hell*?" she hissed angrily as she grabbed for the phone.

"What? It's not like you ain't pregnant with my baby and all," he countered, stating the obvious. "She might be glad you're shacking up with your baby daddy. That's what happy couples do, am I wrong?"

Vivian shook her head in frustration at him and dropped her palm, signaling for him to hand her the phone. "You aren't the one who'll get the lecture. It'll be me."

"Put it on speaker then. I'll take the lecture along with you."

Vivian smirked sassily and did just that, getting a snicker from Buck.

"Hello, Mother," Vivian said impersonally, which stymied Buck's response.

"Vivian Alexander! I am virtually fuming. What in God's name is going on?"

"What on earth do you mean?"

"Obviously you haven't turned the news on or checked the internet or—"

"Mother, it's barely six AM here on the west coast. It's still dark," Vivian interrupted and rolled her eyes.

"Well, you *might* want to turn the TV on and give Jill a call because your social life just took a major plummet. And I would personally appreciate hearing news like *this* straight from my daughter and not in some overexaggerated tabloid!" Gwenyth sighed heavily and ground out, "Is it true?"

Vivian looked like she was about to be sick as her eyes found Buck's and he frowned.

"What exactly have you heard, Mrs. Stanfield?" Buck asked.

"Well, it involves *you*. You 'knocked' my daughter up according to *Daily Stars* and Vivian gave her career up to be with you. Vince Vogner has some horrible things to say on the matter."

"*What?*" Vivian practically screamed into the phone then dropped it and scooted off the bed, reaching for the remote control.

She fumbled with the remote for a moment, aimed it at the television and gasped when she found a station that showed the two of them walking hand in hand into her ob/gyn's office. The headline read *"From Hollywood starlet to Buck Jenkin's harlot?"* Vivian whimpered and covered her mouth with her hands. Buck immediately grew angry.

"Oh my God," Vivian cried as she continued to stare at the next line that flashed across the screen. *"Oscar winner leaves big movie deal to chase former NFL playboy?"*

"Vivian!" her mother's voice called loudly over the speaker.

169

Vivian turned, numbly, to grab the phone back up. Her tearful eyes gazing into Buck's. Anger flowed through his veins, sharp and poignant as her pain ripped into him like a knife.

"I'm here," she stated weakly and her hand instinctively went to her lower abdomen. Buck moved to pull her next to him, but her hands went up in protest. He ceased his attempts to comfort her. "Mom. This. I—I don't know what to say—" She was at a loss for words then as she breathed in and out, attempting to rein in her frustrations.

"Is it true? Are you pregnant with his child?"

Vivian looked uncertainly up at Buck and he shrugged, unsure why she was so hesitant to tell her mom that she was pregnant. Her lips drew in and she closed her eyes.

"Vivian!" her mother cried again.

"Yes, she is," Buck answered for her once again.

"Uh," Vivian huffed out and shoved at him. Again, he merely shrugged. What was the big deal anyway? The entire world was obviously gonna know soon enough.

"We just found out yesterday," Vivian finally found her voice.

"I assume he plans to marry you?" her mother admonished.

Buck's brows drew. What *year* was this anyway? Hell, they'd only known each other for two months, why would he go and do a rash thing like marry her? Vivian's brows went up, as if to say, "Told you so."

Suddenly, Buck made his mind up. He'd been the one to get Vivian into this mess, now he was gonna be the one to get her out of it.

"Actually, Mrs. Stanfield, you're the first one to know…Vivian and I are getting married."

Vivian looked up at him, her brown eyes burning into his as if he'd just lost his mind, she covered the receiver with her palm and gaped. "Buck! What the hell are you *doing*?"

"Just go with it, I'll explain in a minute."

"Mrs. Stanfield," Buck stated. "We'll be making an announcement later this morning. So, be sure to turn the news on at noon your time."

"Well, the audacity! I haven't even met you yet...How—"

"Well, would you like for us to fly to Atlanta? I'm sure Viv would love to see you?"

Vivian's cheeks were red and she lowered her head, unsure what to say.

"Yes. I would like that very much," Gwen said.

"Great. We'll be to you by dinner time then. Can't wait to meet ya." With that, Buck said his goodbyes and closed the flip phone.

He looked hesitantly up at Vivian, whose eyes were red-rimmed like they were filling up with tears.

"What did you just *do*, Buck Jenkins?"

✦✳✦

*B*uck nervously took to the podium his PA had set up with every media outlet on the west coast. Cameras flashed continuously around him, blinding him, as he tapped the mic and made sure he was live. He smiled into the cameras, being sure to put on a good show for entertainment's sake.

Vivian's obvious distress had rattled him to the core, and he'd done the only thing he knew how to do when he'd been put under pressure—defend his star player. After all, he'd been the reason for all the slander. He'd left her that night at the hotel after seducing her, not spoken to her for an entire month as his mother lay dying, and been the one to knock her up, forcing her to leave the movie contract she'd signed. He was to blame for all of that and he couldn't stand the thoughts of the paparazzi throwing her name in the dirt like she was some two-bit, white trash whore. Now was the time to redeem her good name while he still could, and leave it up to the competitor in him to make this his best performance to date with the press conference he'd called merely two hours ago.

"Mr. Jenkins," they began before he could even speak.

171

"Buck is it true that—?"

"Is Vivian Alexander—?"

Buck held his hand up, silencing them all. "Thank y'all for coming today. I appreciate it," he interrupted and took his stance. "I know this was last minute and thrown together, but there's been some rumors going around about me and Vivian, and today, I'm setting the records straight." More flashes erupted and the roar of their voices came once again. He tipped his black cowboy hat and turned toward Vivian, who looked stunning in her khaki trousers and red silk wrap blouse. Her hair fell in ringlets, framing her face, and her makeup was thicker than usual but still natural looking in earthy shades. He gave her a big smile and beckoned her to join him. He saw the momentary hesitation in her eyes, a twinge of panic, but she quickly concealed it behind a radiant smile and waved to the crowd as she came up to the podium to join him.

She'd been furious with him as he'd closed the phone on the conversation between them and her mother.

"I have to make things right, Vivian. I'm the reason for all this after all," he'd insisted even as he'd called Shaun, his PA, to make the arrangements. In two hours, he'd delivered, and they'd arrived in the studio to make their announcements.

"Folks, you already know this gorgeous young starlet needs *no* introduction." He put his arm around her waist and pulled her into his side. "However, I want y'all to meet the future Mrs. Jenkins, my bride-to-be, Vivian Alexander." The roar was deafening as he took Vivian's face in his palm and leaned in to kiss her with raging passion that couldn't be faked even if he tried. All the lights from the flashing cameras were drowned out as nothing existed but her and her slender frame pressed softly into him. His fingers sunk into her thick hair as he angled his face to deepen the kiss and his arm wrapped tighter around her waist. When he finally pulled back, the look he gave her probably melted off all the panties in the room. He made sure to let his lips linger on her cheek as he hugged her tightly to him then emotionally took the podium again.

"Vivian."

"Buck."

"How long has this—?"

"When did you—?"

"Is she really *pregnant?*" One voice called above the others amid the crowd of mics and cameras.

"Yes. Yes, she is," Buck answered and grinned lovingly at his fake fiancée.

"When did y'all get engaged?"

Buck smiled big and took the hand of Viv's with the five-karat round cut diamond set into a diamond and garnet split shank. He brought her knuckles to his lips, making sure it sparkled brightly amid all the lights.

He turned to the crowd and beamed. "We were engaged about a month before the Helping Heroes Ball." Again, the intermingled voices were deafening. "We met up there that night, but I unfortunately had to leave my fiancée behind due to my mother's poor health." *God, and Momma, forgive me for bold-faced lying.* "Our baby was conceived that night." He grinned at Viv and kissed her forehead.

"Miss Alexander."

Vivian turned to look at the young lady who'd called her name and her eyebrows went up as she centered herself over the microphone; the spotlight becoming her. "Yes?"

"How long have you known Buck Jenkins?"

Viv turned to smile at him before saying, "A long time now. We are best friends with the same people and met each other through them."

"When's the wedding?" one journalist asked.

"We're planning a fall wedding after Buck's charity golf event in October. But we'll be holding it in his hometown of Abundance."

"This is ridiculous," Vivian scoffed when he'd told her the plan.

"It's the only way for us to redeem your name and your career, Vivian," Buck asserted.

There'd been no other way without them both looking like fools. Buck didn't give a shit about his career, it was over, but Vivian was in her prime, and he would be damned if that piece of shit, Vince Vogner, would throw Vivian to the wolves for simply being in the wrong place at the wrong time—or right place at the right time, depending on how one looked at it. Not when he could easily fake an engagement, make all of it look pre-arranged, and make Vince look like the fucking asshole that he was. Buck's lawyer was already on the warpath, demanding a retraction for Vince's statements. Buck would clear Vivian's name if it was the last thing he did. Then when the time was right they'd figure out the break-up, but for now, Buck was going to enjoy having a fiancée—soaking up every ounce of attention Vivian Alexander was giving him— be there for the woman who carried his baby, and play the devoted fiancé for Viv's mother.

Once their statements were made and questions answered-

Where would they live: For now, Abundance.

Was Vivian done with movies: Only until after the baby was born.

What were they planning on doing: For now, heading to Atlanta to see Viv's folks.

What were they naming the baby: When they found out the sex, they would decide.

They headed back to Vivian's to pack their bags and had a light lunch before heading to the airport and boarding Vivian's private jet by one PM.

The flight was smooth and Viv laid down to nap while Buck made some calls and watched a movie. It was 7:35 PM when they landed in Atlanta and 7:59 PM when they pulled into Gwenyth and Carl Stanfield's driveway.

They lived in an established neighborhood of large three-story, three-sided brick homes surrounded with large pines, magnolia trees, and long driveways. Whatever her mom and step-dad did for a living, they were fairly well-off, Buck noted, looking over the well-groomed lawn with its perfectly manicured gardens.

"Please let me do most of the talking and try not to be your usual self," Viv begged, looking up at him apprehensively as she straightened his tie.

He'd been shocked on the plane when she'd suggested they dress formally.

"Is that a joke?" he'd asked, eyebrow raised.

She'd given him a look that dared him to argue—she *was* pregnant after all—so he'd headed to the bathroom to change right before they landed at Hartsfield-Jackson International.

Now, he was opening the limo door, helping her out, and escorting her to the door. Viv's driver was attending to their luggage as Buck hit the doorbell and waited patiently, giving Viv an encouraging smile even as she looked like she might hurl.

The door swung open and a lovely middle-aged woman in a floor length black gown stood before them. She was unmistakably Vivian's mother, for she was an older version of the woman who carried his baby, with her blonde hair pinned up high on her head and dark hazel eyes. Buck could tell she'd had some plastic surgery done but despite that, her face looked like she wore a perpetual frown.

"Vivian, darling, I'm so glad you are punctual." *Punctual.* Who the hell was this woman?

"Mother. It's so good to see you." Viv entered and approached her mother but instead of hugging her, which was what Buck was expecting, they leaned in opposite one another and kissed at the space between them. What the fuck? Air kisses! Was that really a thing? Who *were* these people? Was Gwen a germ-a-phob or something? "I want you to meet Buck Jenkins...my fiancé," she added like an afterthought, not used to the accompanying title yet.

She gripped Buck's arm in a virtual vise grip as he approached and smiled at Gwen. He extended his hand and Gwenyth took it, giving him a limp noodle for a handshake. God, he hated when people didn't give a proper handshake.

"It's nice to meet you, ma'am," he stated as he pulled his hand back and tipped his hat at her. Viv had begged him to omit it, but it was his emblem after all, he rarely went without it. And at least he'd met her halfway, he'd caved and worn a suit.

Gwen gave him a look that let him know she was nonplussed by his southern charm. Well, she could kiss his ass. This good ol' boy had gotten more tail than he could count on both fingers and toes, millions of dollars, and had gone to three Super Bowls. He could care less if Gwenyth Stanfield was impressed in the least.

This Leo was undeterred and looked around at the gold embellishments, crystal chandeliers, and oil on canvas portraits that surrounded him, feeling the need to yawn at the superficial façade he was encompassed by. The mere appearance of luxury, not proof of it.

An impeccably dressed man with silver hair and beard approached then and smiled at Vivian, taking both her hands in his. "Vivian, you're looking beautiful as ever." He kissed her cheek, and Buck swallowed down the sheer possessiveness he felt in those moments. He knew the man had to be her step-dad, but it didn't matter because he didn't like having another man touching her with the familiarity that Buck did. This sudden knowledge nearly knocked him off his feet; so much so that when he extended his hand, Buck wanted to throat punch the older man.

What the hell is the matter with me? Buck thought, even as he took the man's hand and shook it firmly.

"My what a handshake," the older man winced as he pulled his hand back, and Buck realized he'd gripped it with more force than necessary. Well, what the hell did he expect from a guy who was six foot four and two hundred and sixty-five pounds?

"Buck, this is my step-dad, Carl," Viv said stiffly, looking back at her mother.

"Nice to meet you, Mr. Stanfield. Lovely home you have here," Buck stated before moving his arm back around Vivian and looking her over. She looked gorgeous tonight in a lacy black Giorgio Armani one-sleeved dress, her hair pinned over so it was all on one side. He longed to kiss her long, slender neck...and he would before the night was over.

"Shall we move into the den for some cocktails?" Gwen asked and extended her hand for Vivian to lead the way.

She did, not letting Buck out of her grasp, and they entered a high-ceilinged room surrounded by large glass windows with a stone fireplace on the back wall. Vivian guided them towards a leather loveseat while Gwen took one of the velvet King George style arm chairs across from them.

"What would you like to drink, Buck?" Carl asked from the bar to the right of them.

"Scotch on the rocks, please? Johnny Walker Black if you got it."

"Ah, a fellow scotch drinker." Carl winked and grabbed for some glasses above his head.

Gwen took the glass of wine that sat on the high side table next to her and practically smirked at Vivian. "None for you, I take it... since you're pregnant and all." The disgust in her voice was blatantly apparent, and Buck held his tongue, not understanding where the hostility came from.

Vivian just shook her head and looked down, her usually fun nature dejected by her mother's animosity.

"Tea then, Viv?" Carl asked as he handed Buck his glass. Buck fought hard not to throw it right into Viv's mother's face and immediately didn't want it but wouldn't be rude and thanked Carl.

Viv nodded and thanked Carl, and Buck felt like the room got hotter as Gwen's eyes assessed him.

"So...the Kinsens introduced the two of you?" Gwenyth asked as her eyes darted back to Viv. "I haven't heard you mention his name prior to now." Her lips pursed.

"Yes ma'am, Nat sure did. I took one look at this doll sitting next to me and knew I had to make her mine," Buck drawled, throwing his arm around Viv's shoulder. He could see her eyes squint and her lips drew in and knew she was mentally counting to ten. Now, he understood why she'd wanted him to let her do the talking…he was in for a long night with this pending interrogation.

"Mother, I've mentioned Buck before," Viv's voice finally took hold and she momentarily gave him the stink eye, warning him to shut up. He wouldn't be so easily swayed.

"Well, you could have given us some forewarning. I mean, why all the secrecy?"

"Well…you know that Buck's mother recently passed from cancer."

"No, I didn't. Buck, I'm so very sorry to hear that," Gwen said softly and her eyes were sincere as she pouted over at him. So, she *had* a softer side, she just preferred to be a hard-ass.

"Thank you. She fought like hell for months before…"

Gwen gasped and covered her mouth, and Buck looked to Vivian confused. She again looked like she was walking on egg shells, and Buck waited for Ashton Kutcher to walk out of the room some-where and tell him he was being "Punk'd".

"Buck, watch your mouth." Viv elbowed him in the ribs lightly, and he took the hint. Oh, so he was dealing with holy rollers. Ones who didn't cuss, but they drank…so hypocritical ones at that! Even fellow Baptists weren't quite *that* bad. They cussed, drank and swore, partied like hellions on Saturday nights…then went to church on Sundays. Wait, didn't Viv's mom have an affair with this guy in the first place? *Alright, Ashton, you can come out at any time now, buddy.*

Buck regrouped and gave Gwenyth his best panty-melting smile. "I apologize, ma'am. Forgive my manners. I ain't been right since Momma died."

"Oh, it's alright, Buck. I can call you Buck, right?" Carl didn't wait for a response as he smiled and moved in front of them, handing Vivian a cold iced tea. "No harm, no foul." He brought his glass up to the two of them and began a toast. "To your future. And to my new grandchild. May he or she be as lucky in love as we've all been." He hit their glasses with a "tink" and took a swig of his drink before moving to sit next to his wife.

Carl was growing on him; he seemed to be the one to balance out the coldness of the woman next to him, the house, the atmosphere. How had Vivian grown up with such an oppressive person?

The conversation turned from Vivian and Buck, much to his relief, to Carl and Gwen as Carl explained that he was a stockbroker and investor, which explained the nice house. He spoke about his sons, Jared and Miles, and their accomplishments. One was a baseball star with a scholarship to UGA, the other was a math whiz with aspirations of attending Georgia Tech next year. Talk about having a house divided. Then somehow, Gwen found a way to bring it back to Buck.

"So, I'm sure you're going to have the baby sprinkled when it's born."

"Well..." Viv swallowed down her tea, almost choking on it. "I'm sure Buck will be okay with that."

"Oh? Buck don't tell me...you're not a believer?" Gwen's face looked as if she'd seen a ghost.

"No, no...he is. He's...well...Buck is a Baptist." The way Viv gingerly said Baptist, she might as well have said he was a terrorist for Gwen's eyes flew to hers, her face still aghast.

"Oh," she finally said, recovering. "Well, I guess it's better than being Episcopalian."

Buck could have nearly fallen out. Who died and made this woman akin to the pope?

"And what religion are you?" He directed his question to Viv, to avoid the gaze of Gwenyth's scrutinous eyes, but Viv's wide mouth made him gravely regret the question.

Quickly, Vivian's acting skills took over and she laughed hysterically at him before saying, "You're funny, love." She kissed him swiftly on the cheek. "You know we're Methodist."

Methodist? That wasn't too far off from Baptist. Why was she so opposed to him being a Baptist? And Buck highly doubted that Vivian had set foot in a church recently either way.

"Dear, I think it's time we fed these two and saw them up to their rooms. I'm sure they've had a long day," Carl stated, seeming to be as done with this conversation as Buck was. Thank God there was another man around. Buck tipped his hat at Carl as he stood and escorted Vivian into the dining room.

This room was even more stuffy than the last with gold embellished wallpaper, a large hanging chandelier, an antique credenza and an oversized, mahogany dining room table with high-backed leather chairs that could seat twenty people. To be so religious, these people lived to try and impress others. Well, Buck Jenkins wasn't impressed. He set his hat down in one of the empty chairs next to him and knew Viv was cussing him ten ways to Sunday for his hat hair.

Carl brought in a large silver pot of what Buck assumed to be soup and when he took the lid off, it smelled heavenly.

"Crab bisque, it's my own recipe," Carl bragged and began ladling it into the bowls atop their china.

"It smells wonderful, Carl," Viv smiled up at him, and he seemed truly pleased.

Buck thanked him and once Carl was sat, they all dug in. Buck could have devoured the soup in one sip for he was starved, but he took his time relishing the sweet bisque of lump crab meat, sherry, tomatoes, shallots and onions and soon, Carl was bringing out the main course of lamb chops, saffron rice and creamed spinach. So, Carl was the breadwinner and bread baker it would seem. What was it that Gwen did besides dress up, drink wine, and complain about her daughter's short-comings?

As if reading his mind, Vivian said, "Carl loves to experiment in the kitchen."

"It's delicious, sir. Honestly. I'm not a big fan of lamb usually, but this is perfectly cooked," Buck said, cutting into his juicy chop and taking another bite.

"Thank you. Low and slow is how I like to roast it. I marinate it overnight in this savory turmeric rub from Williams-Sonoma."

"Well, it works. It's better than my chef's." It wasn't entirely true, but they didn't have to know that. Mora was amazing, and she always made the best chicken dishes. But he might just have to get the recipe for the chops from Carl after tonight.

"I had my time in the kitchen. Now that Carl's retired, it's his turn. I'd be happy eating salad all day, but Carl needs his meats." Gwen smiled lovingly over at her husband, and Buck began to wonder if her overbearing air was just a front for her own insecurities.

"I'm a bit of a meat-eater myself." Buck laughed and patted his belly. "My diet used to be much more strict until my retirement, but now, I eat more of what I like."

"Well, I eat what the baby likes and so far, so good." She gave Carl a thumbs-up.

Buck knew her pregnancy belly had reared its ugly head a lot as of late. She'd been plagued with bouts of morning sickness and poor appetite. It was good to see her eating a decent plate-size tonight. He grinned at her as he put an arm around her shoulder.

Once they'd finished dinner, Carl brought out coffee and a fresh peach pound cake.

"Man, I hope you didn't do all this on my account," Buck said, looking the lovely yellow cake with large chunks of peaches over with newfound interest.

"Oh, he's always one for wooing guests with his specialties." Again, Gwenyth was starting to soften...that or maybe the wine was kicking in, Buck couldn't be sure.

"Well, thank you kindly for having me. I'm glad to finally meet you guys."

"The boys are going to be shocked to make your acquaintance." Carl chuckled.

Buck stirred some cream and sugar into his coffee and took a bite of the generous slice of cake in front of him. It practically melted in his mouth; it had a crunchy, glazed top and the peaches were perfectly ripe as he bit into a large chunk of one. He moaned aloud. "Man. That's delicious. I love peaches."

"Me too," Carl admitted and laughed at Buck's reaction to his dessert. "We are in Georgia after all. Had to take advantage of the popular favorite."

"Believe it or not, most peaches come from California, I'll have you know." Viv winked at her step-dad and Buck.

"This is true," Gwen added.

"Well, those were grown just down the road, I'll have you know." Carl defended then chuckled again. "Frank the fruit man."

His relationship with Viv seemed to be warm. The coldness came from Gwenyth, not Carl. So, what had made her a holy roller after the affair they'd had together and why did she seem to be so critical of Vivian and her work?

"So, I assume you've taken care to demand a retraction from Vince, right?" Gwen asked out of the blue, sipping her coffee.

Before Viv could answer, Buck replied, "Oh yes, my lawyer is all over this."

"Well, if you hadn't *left* her at the hotel like you did that morning, none of this would have happened in the first place." The ice that shot out from her gaze stilled Buck; he had no comeback, none whatsoever. He lowered his head.

"Mother, I—"

"No, it's true, Viv," Buck stated softly and looked at her apologetically.

"Buck, it's alright." She took his hand and interlaced it with her own, her deep brown eyes tearing into his very soul. "Your mother needed you that morning, more than I did." She smiled so sweetly at him in that instant that he knew he was head over heels in love with her.

Buck Jenkins had finally found the woman who made him feel like mush on the inside when she looked at him. The woman he wanted to stand next to, spend his life with, and make love to forever, forsaking all others. The woman who made him feel alive and stimulated his mind as much as his body. Vivian Alexander hadn't just stolen his breath that night at the Austere hotel, she'd stolen his heart.

He pulled her to him even as she gasped, leery of their audience's reactions, and he kissed her lips with a tenderness that pulsed through him like a shockwave. Her soft, sweet lips pulled gently on his, on his heart-strings, bringing forth the love that spilled over from him, a fountain of bliss erupting from within.

When she pulled back, she touched her lips in surprise—as if she too felt it—the tale-tell sign in her eyes making him want to hit his knees and confess to love her with every breath in his body until the end of his days.

"Well, we can see you weren't just faking it for the cameras." Gwen's rough tone jolted Buck back to reality, and he fought the urge to tell her to go fuck herself.

"Sorry about that, we get carried away sometimes," Buck offered, giving a quick laugh.

"Yeah, I can see that," Gwenyth scoffed and gave her daughter the once over. "I can see now *why* you're in the condition you're in."

Vivian's cheeks flamed red, and Buck held in a growl, feeling it vibrate deep in his chest.

"Carl, see these two up to their rooms." Emphasizing the word 'rooms', Gwenyth waved her hand dismissively, sipping her wine. "They need a cold shower and to sleep it off. There's still a great deal of time before the wedding."

If that bitch honestly thought for one minute that Buck Jenkins was waiting until the wedding to make love to his gorgeous bride-to-be, she had another thing coming. As soon as he was in her room, he was going to hike that sexy as hell dress of Vivian's up to her waist and take her against the wall…and he prayed Gwenyth Stanfield heard every damn sinful second of it.

CHAPTER 10

Oh dear Lord, Vivian thought as she unzipped her suitcase and searched for her pajamas.

She'd known bringing Buck to meet her overbearing, overly religious mother had been a grave mistake, but this was even worse than she'd thought it was going to be. Buck was an alpha male, a powerful force to be reckoned with, and wasn't one to let things go at face value. But he didn't know Gwen Stanfield. She was conniving and when she wanted something, she made it happen. She'd never approved of Vivian's lifestyle since it was highly unorthodox and unscrupulous. "After all, what type of woman parades around half-naked, pretending to be someone else, kissing men *and* women and carousing with homosexuals?" her mother had asked her one day.

It didn't matter that Vivian had been the one to catch her mother and Carl in the throes of passion that day in her parents' bedroom of her childhood home, her mother had found some way to turn it around on Vivian's father. She'd been the innocent victim in all of it…yet now she was a practical saint.

Vivian had long since stopped trying to explain logic to her mother, stopped trying to reason with her, stopped trying to defend herself, and had just slowly distanced herself from the woman who'd become someone Vivian no longer knew—or cared to know —anymore.

It was easier to find excuses why she couldn't be at family gatherings than to actually be subjected to her. After all, this was how she acted each time Vivian was around. Like she hated the sight of her, like Vivian disgusted her, like Vivian reminded her of her own flaws...and frankly, Vivian was damn sick of it.

When Buck had suggested that they fake an engagement, she'd known it was risky, but it had made perfect sense and would be enough to salvage the damage that was done with Vince. Vivian couldn't say no. They were together, they were happy. So what if they were gonna fudge it a little? Vivian was an actress, she could pull this off...right? But after the way Buck had looked at her at the table, her heart had nearly exploded at the softness in his eyes and his loving kiss. It was as if it were all *real*, as if he weren't faking it, as if he—

A knock sounded on the door, and Viv started, realizing she'd been standing staring into her suitcase for far too long. She blushed, annoyed with herself for letting a man affect her so much as she walked to the door.

She opened it to see a sight for pregnant sore eyes and felt her ovaries explode at the walking, talking sex symbol before her.

Buck Jenkins's broad, muscular body was propped in her door frame, big arm resting on the door panel, leaned into her. His tan chiseled chest and abs were bare, and he wore only his boxers; her whole body lit up ablaze in hot, licking flames.

Her mouth immediately went dry at the crooked grin he gave her, and she gasped as he entered without invitation and shut the door behind himself.

She whisper-yelled, "Buck! What are you doing? My mom—"

"Is about to hear me fuck your gorgeous brains out," he murmured as his hands went to her waist and his face descended, his lips colliding with her bare neck. She moaned, his confident mouth *and* words touching every nerve-ending of her hot skin. Her eyes closed as his hands worked the dress up her hips.

"Mmm… Wait. No, we can't." Viv whimpered as his tongue licked at her quivering flesh and he lifted her, gently pressing her to the wall. The feel of his solid frame against her own, his powerful body, made her knees weak.

"We can and we *are*. I'm taking you. Right here and right now," he admonished as he peeled her panties off and slung them behind him. He took her lips as his hand fell between her legs and he began to softly caress the damp skin that ached for his touch.

"Oh Buck," Viv moaned as her hands stroked his shoulders, his biceps then gripped his forearms as his fingers entered her.

How was it that he could turn her to a pile of quivering desire so easily? They'd just had sex last night, not even twenty-four hours ago, yet she reveled in his touch, like it had been years since she'd felt it.

"Damn, always so wet for me, my sweet starlet. Is it my big body you like best or my big cock?" His lips moved to her jawline, and she felt her skin prickle as his fingers moved in and out of her.

"Ahh, both, God, I love them both." She rubbed her hands back up his sinewy arms, his shoulders and down to his chest, tracing the indention of hard muscle on his pecs and squeezing.

Buck gave a quick chuckle and lifted her. "Then both you shall have, darlin'."

Her legs naturally went around him, and she felt his hard sex pressing gently into the entrance of her body. His hips lunged, smooth and fluid, and he was suddenly filling her completely. He groaned as he held himself there, savoring the union of their sexes, the beautiful harmony of their joining before he began to pump in and out of her gently. Her arms wrapped around his neck and she held herself to him as he made her his with each thrust of his hips. She loved his strength, his confidence, his protectiveness—she loved *him*. All of him. Every inch of his big, bulky frame and cocky swagger. She wanted to tell him so, but she held back even as his thrusts drove harder and deeper, and she felt herself falling, not just into climactic oblivion but in love. In love with this charming, sweet, swoony lion of hers and when she came, she didn't care if her mother heard her for her heart swelled with joy as her mind exploded in beautiful shades of color, her insides basking in the pleasure of their connected bodies; sex, mind and soul.

"Buck, oh God, oh yes," she cried as her body succumbed to him.

Buck's roar would have made his zodiac sign proud as he growled his indulgence and satisfaction, filling her ears with groans and gasps as he rode his climax out. He took his time slowing his rhythm, savoring the after-effects of their worlds colliding together, before finally pulling out and setting her down.

He grasped her neck in his big palm as he kissed her lips with passion then moved his hand down to her breast and squeezed. He looked down at the nipple that stood at attention at his touch and gave her that sexy crooked grin of his. With his five o'clock shadow and desire-darkened eyes, she could have begged him to take her all over again like he hadn't just rocked her socks off.

"Mmm, you're an insatiable little banshee tonight, aren't ya?" he asked knowingly.

"Buck, you prey on my pregnancy weaknesses...you *know* she heard that. They're just down the hall," she scolded even as her hands fell to stroke his still erect manhood.

He groaned deeply and smiled big. "That was the whole point, darlin'." He stroked her cheek with his index finger before he kissed her. "Besides, my *cock*-i-ness is why you love me." He bounced his eyebrows at her.

Viv blushed at the word love then gave a quick laugh. She threw her hands on her hips then realizing she had a point to make. "I understand you're plight but that's just disrespectful."

Buck scoffed. "I'm your 'fiancé' remember? And you've already got my baby growing in your belly. The 'damage' is already done. The *sin* has been committed. What's the big damn deal anyway?" Buck scowled and crossed his arms over his chest. "If I want to make love to the mother of my child, I'll do so when and where I please, and I'll be damned if *any*body tells me I can't."

He was just as sexy when he was being possessive, and Vivian couldn't help but smile, even if he had made love to her as much out of defiance as out of lust. She wrapped her arms around his neck and brought her lips to his. They softened as her mouth moved over them then she deepened the kiss as his arms came around her and he moaned, a deep rumble in his chest. When she pulled back, the look he gave her made her all mushy inside. God, he really was gorgeous. And their child was going to be also. She couldn't wait to meet their little bundle of joy.

"Buck," she said softly and his big hand came to her lower abdomen then as he gently palmed her where their baby slept. She was suddenly speechless, her words lost, as the love she felt for him overflowed from her heart and spilled all the way down to her womb. God, how she wished she could be his real fiancée. He just stared back, his dazzling blue eyes dancing as they took her in. They both stood transfixed for a time before she finally remembered what she had been planning to say. "I'm sorry for this." She gestured around the room.

He shook his head. "No, sweetheart, don't you dare be sorry. Hell, we can't help who our parents are. And don't you worry none. I've handled worse adversaries than your mother. Believe me. Twenty-two men as big as me, some bigger, on the gridiron, out for blood. If I can handle that, I can handle Gwenyth Stanfield." His eyebrow cocked and Viv laughed. "You know, Nat once told me I could charm the habit off a nun." He rubbed his scruffy chin thoughtfully. "Well, I think it's time I put that theory to the test, cause darlin', your momma is about as tightly wound as the tail end of a nun's habit."

Again, Viv laughed and nodded. "I tend to agree, but she's been this way for years now, so as amazingly charming as you are, my great *studly* football star," she said and kissed his jaw, "she isn't going to be apt to change her ways just because you bat those sexy eyelashes of yours."

"Oh, now, don't be so sure, Miss Alexander." Buck gave a devilish chuckle as he began walking them backwards, peeling the dress from her waist. In less than three strides, he had the dress off her body, had tossed it to the ground, and was gently bringing his big body over the top of hers as they fell onto the bed together. *How the hell did he do that?* "I'm Buck Jenkins. And I'm not just sayin' it, but I'm pretty damn good at persuadin' the ladies as you well know."

She moaned as his large palms cupped her breasts and his mouth came down on hers. He deepened the kiss as her hands came to stroke his back. She was the first to come up for air as his mouth moved to her cheek, down her jaw, to her neck where he licked a trail all his own. All the while, her sex smoldered in want once again at his mere closeness. She whimpered as his mouth moved down her collarbone, to her breasts, bringing her desire full throttle as his mouth suckled her into a puddle of wanton desire and she cried out, needing him back inside her before she fell into that sultry void again.

"Buck." She reached for him but his head fell to her belly and down between her legs.

"Do you doubt my suave ways?" His naughty gaze held hers as his lips softly kissed her inner thigh, and she gasped and shook her head. But he had a point to prove and he made it once again as his tongue, fingers, and mouth became her undoing; her orgasm violently plowing into her before Buck was once again thrusting inside her and unraveling her very essence, peeling her apart from the fabric of her insecurities, short-comings and doubts. He was the shuddering mess of quivering flesh this time, and she grinned know-ingly as his melting gaze held hers. He spilled himself inside her crying her name a bit louder than what she would have liked with her mom and step-dad just doors down. When his climax was spent, he stayed inside her for a long time, stroking her cheek and gazing down at her. His sexy look brought forth emotions she couldn't explain nor understand. He was going to be her downfall—had already *been* her downfall—and she couldn't help continuing to plummet into the beautiful bliss beneath his deep blue gaze. He smiled big and kissed her so tenderly that she almost winced. When he pulled back he said, "We need to take a trip?"

"A trip? Why?"

"To get away from all this bullshit. The media. Your pompous mother. This shit-show that has been our lives since the morning after—" he paused, but she knew he had planned to say 'our one-night stand', for that's precisely what it had been. She gulped and he frowned. He sighed. "We need a vacation."

"And where will we go? Where can we get away from all this?" Vivian waved her hands around.

"I have a friend with a house in Cancun. He told me to call him any time I wanted to stay."

"Oh, Buck, that's really sweet, but—"

"But nothing. I'm taking you there." The sincerity in his eyes held her captive. "You, of all people I know, deserve a vacation."

"I think Nat and Jack deserve the vacation more than anyone we know." She laughed then Buck looked at her thoughtfully.

"You know, that's not a bad idea."

"What?" Viv balked, confused.

"Taking them with us. We could all use some time away. Besides, Linc's house is huge down there. I've gone once before. We wouldn't even know they were in the house with us."

"Buck, I—"

"It's settled. I'm calling my buddy, Lincoln, and getting his house. We're gonna have some salt, sun, and spicy nights down in Mexico."

Well, Buck's mind was made up. They were going to Mexico. But would Nat and Jack come too? There was only one way to find out.

⁕⁕⁕

"*N*ow this is the way to travel, right baby?" Jack said, looking over at Natalie as Buck handed him a flute of champagne.

They were seated in the luxurious and comfortable leather seats of Vivian's private jet at Dallas/Fort Worth International airport getting ready for takeoff.

They had boarded the plane just about ten minutes prior, now their luggage was being stowed and the airplane and gear were being checked before they would be airborne and heading to Mexico.

Vivian smiled over at Jack and Natalie seated across from her and Buck. They looked both eager and anxious. Baby Jax was strapped in on one of the loveseats to the right of them, covered in a blanket as he slept. This would be his first flight.

Natalie looked gorgeous as always in a blue sundress that brought out the color of her sapphire eyes. Jack looked like his handsome, rugged self in jeans, boots, a navy polo and his ever-present cowboy hat atop his head. Vivian smiled to herself— it was going to be funny seeing him in flip-flops and swim trunks. She was eager to see him shirtless though, see how he sized up to Buck in the muscle department. She silently scolded herself. Jack Kinsen was her best friend's husband, she needed to calm her hormones, but her pregnancy had her all amped up—besides, there was nothing wrong with simply admiring, was there?

Five days on the beach with these two studs, baby Jackson, and her BFF was gonna be like heaven. They would have an enormous house right on the Caribbean with a private beach, pool, gym, media and game rooms, personal chef and their own master suites. It didn't get much better than that in Vivian's book.

She and Buck had woken yesterday morning to find her mother in a worse disposition than the night prior, Viv had known her folks could hear their love-making, but perhaps it was that combined with all the alcohol her mother had drank, either way her mood was utterly atrocious. So, after a terse and awkward breakfast, Buck had announced their sudden departure. They had a plane to catch, he'd said, much to Vivian's surprise. He'd actually been serious about the vacation after all! Not that she hadn't taken him seriously, but she'd not been expecting it to be so soon. He'd made the arrangements with his friend Lincoln in the limo on the way out of Atlanta, and she'd called Natalie soon after. They'd boarded her plane, stayed in Dallas for the rest of the day, shopped for clothes, and spent the night.

And just minutes ago, met Jack and Nat on the runway.

Nat had been stunned when Vivian had called her; the surprise of the invitation had taken her completely off guard.

"Nat, did you hear me?" Viv had giggled into the phone.

"Uh, yeah, sorry. Umm, Mexico? You want us to go with you to Mexico?"

"Yeah! I mean, it's just for a few days and it's been so long since you guys took a vacation. We would love for you to join us. I know it's last minute, but all you need is some outfits and bathing suits. The rest is taken care of."

"Well, we'd have to take Jackson with us." Viv could practically see the wheels turning in Nat's head then. "I mean, he's been fussy with his teeth lately, and I couldn't possibly leave him for five days."

"Of course! I expected as much; he's more than welcome. I adore that baby boy. Buck and I just wanted a little getaway and knew you and Jack deserve it as much as we do."

It took a little more coercion from Vivian and for Jack to say, "Let's do it, honey," before Nat finally relented. Dallie was already settled in at college, Luther and Bella were going to keep Savannah, and Wyatt and Nate were going to take care of the ranch.

Now, Jack clinked his glass with Nat's before leaning forward to toast Buck's. Nat's eyes suddenly flew to Viv's and she noticed that Vivian didn't have a flute of champagne. Then her brows furrowed and her eyes widened. Suddenly, Natalie gasped and leaned forward, grabbing Vivian's left hand.

"Oh my God! Vivian. What—" Nat stumbled over her words as she took in the huge ring on Vivian's dainty ring finger. Vivian blushed.

"Viv and I have some things we want to tell y'all...especially since you *obviously* never turn a damn TV on." Buck scoffed and rolled his eyes.

"We've been so busy these last couple weeks, what with taking Dallie to College Station last week, and Jax not leaving my side for more than a second with his teething—"

"Nat, I'm messin' with ya. I'm glad you get to hear it straight from the horse's mouth," Buck said and grinned that sexy grin of his that made Viv's insides clench.

"So, you're engaged? When did *this* happen?" Natalie asked and shifted her gaze to Vivian, who's smile suddenly fell.

"It's a fake engagement," she cut Buck off before he could tell them. She then looked over at his face. He didn't look happy at the word fake, but it was true, and she wouldn't lie to Natalie and Jack about it. "Vince was trying to throw me under a bus. The headlines were horrible, Nat." She'd wanted to call Nat before now to tell her all that had happened, but there'd been such a whirlwind of things since she'd saw the first headline on the news just two days prior. But now she was glad she could tell her in person. "It was so embarrassing," Vivian felt tears sting her eyes suddenly, and Nat's sincere eyes stared back at her. She took her hand as the plane jerked and they began to move on the tarmac.

"This was all my fault," Buck intervened then and huffed. "I had to try and salvage the situation. So, Viv and I decided to fake an engagement."

"But why would you do that? Even if—"

"She's pregnant," Buck blurted out and Vivian frowned, wishing she'd been the one to tell her BFF instead of him. She looked over at him and the genuine concern in his sky-blue eyes swamped her with emotion. It took Nat's stroking thumb to bring her back to reality.

"Oh, Vivian. This is amazing news. You two are going to have a baby." Nat smiled, and Vivian saw the tears fill her friends' eyes. It was too much, and she too started to tear up. "I'm so happy for you." Nat pulled her hand away and wiped at her own eyes, beaming brightly at Buck. "Buck, you rascal. I can't believe you're gonna be a daddy."

"Yeah, that makes two of us." Buck laughed heartily. "We weren't keeping it from y'all or anything when we were back home. We just wanted to make sure everything was alright before we let the cat out of the bag."

"Of course!" Nat agreed.

"Congrats, Vivian and Buck," Jack said, smiling at them as he raised his glass and tipped his hat. "Now, I understand the trip...*and* the champagne." He winked at Buck then laughed. Viv had never seen Jack drink champagne before and assumed he'd wondered why he'd been given the flute instead of a beer or glass of whiskey.

Natalie laughed as well and Viv turned the conversation to Dallie as she asked about the sweet girl she'd always loved like a daughter.

"She's settled in her dorm. Already enjoying her classes. But, she's really anxious too." Viv's brows drew down, questioningly, and Nat waved her hand. "Oh, she's fine. Just worried about Cole—he's still incarcerated—and she's worried about what's going to happen with this trial," Nat replied.

"Wait, I thought the murder charges were dropped," Viv said.

"Yeah, they were. The wife and brother were the guilty parties. They had planned to frame him before the tables turned and the wife ended up confessing and implicating the brother," Jack explained. "It's the kidnapping charges. They denied Cole bail due to his priors. Our lawyer said that the state will continue indictment and he's probably going to serve time for it even though we've dropped the charges. A kidnapping is a serious offense. He's going to do his best but feels like even with our testimonies that it won't be enough to keep them from sustaining the sentencing. Dallie's tore up about it."

"Aww, I hate that. Poor Dallie." Vivian frowned.

"She's strong, and they love each other, so they can get through it." Jack's eyes drifted off into the distance; Dallie's pain affecting him too.

"Love can withstand it all," Nat's bright voice piped in and she interlaced her fingers in Jack's. He gave her a sweet smile and Viv melted.

Oh love. What a beautiful thing.

"Here's to a much-deserved vacation," Buck stated and lifted the champagne from its chiller in front of him, pouring more into his glass, then Nat's then Jack's. "Cancun here we come!"

CHAPTER 11

*N*atalie squealed as they entered the large wooden French doors of the two-story Mexican casa they would all be sharing for the next five days.

"Oh my goodness, this is paradise," she said as she moved the baby to her other hip and walked through the white-tiled foyer. It was as open as a house could possibly be, with large white stone columns holding up the high-ceilinged walls, an open kitchen, long granite island, and only a wall of floor-to-ceiling windows separating them from the beach outside. The sand was stark white and the gorgeous blue-green ocean waves crested and lapped just barely fifty yards away.

"Damn!" Jack stated and looked longingly out at the water. "This is luxury right here."

"Right?" Buck called back and sat the bags in his hands down at the foot of the staircase. "Aren't you glad you came now?" Buck asked as he patted Jack's back and moved to the bar adjacent to the kitchen island. "It's fully stocked and ready for a party." He pulled out two beers from the bar fridge and grabbed some lime slices, complements of their chef who'd been by earlier that morning. He twisted the lids off the beers and shoved a lime slice into each bottle before offering one over to Jack. He took it and clinked his bottle neck against Buck's.

"Thanks, buddy."

"Wa-wa," Jackson called as he moved toward the large window and planted his tiny palms on the glass.

"Oh, son, don't do that," Jack scolded softly. "Man, we're through the door just five seconds and there's already handprints on the glass." Jack's palm smacked his forehead.

Buck laughed heartily. "No worries, man. Let the kid enjoy himself. That's what they made Windex for. Linc don't mind for the place to be lived in. He bought it for his family; to be enjoyed." Buck shook his head, watching the baby in awe of the beach. "He drools over the ocean like I drool over Vivian." He winked playfully over at Viv, who rolled her eyes at him even as she covered a bashful grin.

"Lincoln? As in Lincoln Porter?" Nat asked and approached the men then.

"One and the same."

"The son of Alvin Porter?"

"Yes ma'am."

"Wow. Alvin played for Chicago. What a small world." Natalie tilted her head in thought.

"He did. Got to meet him when I first started in the league. Great guy. Him and Linc both. Hey, want some wine, Nat?" Buck started to peruse the stacked shelf of wines for a bottle of Malbec inside the cabinet, but Nat shook her head.

"No, I'm good for now. I'll save it for tonight after I put Jax down for bed." She winked.

"Well, I don't know about *you* guys, but I'm ready to hit the beach," Viv said as her eyebrows went up.

"I second that. Jax, baby, you wanna go swim?" Nat walked over to Jackson and picked him up.

"Sim," he cooed and pointed out to the water.

Jack laughed and walked over to their luggage. "Which room is ours, Buck?" He angled his head up, looking at the large open metal and glass staircase and landing.

"Pick one, there practically identical master suites, mirroring one another."

"Nat?" Jack asked.

"Umm," she shrugged, "I don't care."

"Y'all take the one closest to the stairs, in case you need to come down to the kitchen at night for the baby," Viv suggested, and Buck smiled at her thoughtfulness.

Vacationing with some of his favorite people was going to be fun. And being around the baby was going to be interesting, getting Buck ready for his and Viv's bundle of joy when she or he got here.

Buck would have preferred it be just the two of them, for the thoughts of making love to Vivian in various scattered places—on the beach, in the pool, on the couch, on the kitchen counter—filled his head. But he was glad Nat and Jack had come along. He could still make love to his woman where and when he wanted; they would just have to be more discreet and creative, which was gonna be just as fun as what he'd originally had in mind.

Jack moved up the stairs after Nat headed up with the baby, and they moved into the first room off of the landing. Buck motioned for Viv to go on ahead of him, set his beer down on the table next to the stairs and grabbed their two suitcases, following her. The view only got better as he watched her plump bottom round the landing on the opposite side of the house. She opened a set of large white French doors and gasped as she entered.

"Buck, this is gorgeous," she said as she moved forward and looked over the enormous suite with white carpet, a California king bed on the wall farthest from the door, a huge balcony overlooking the ocean to the left and an oversized bathroom to the right. She opened the French doors that led into the bathroom first and her eyes grazed over the heated marble tile floor, giant jacuzzi tub and stone shower, and the large mirrored vanities before opening the sliding glass doors to the outside. The sound of the gentle ocean waves lapping the shore greeted their ears along with the sounds of seagulls crying.

"I told you," Buck said smiling, dropping the luggage at the ottoman and jumping, belly first, onto the bed. "So, should we break the bed in first?" His eyebrow went up as he looked her over like she was a juicy piece of meat. She looked to be just as edible as one, dressed in a floppy beach hat, big tortoise shell sunglasses, yellow sleeveless silk dress and a pair of brown leather flip-flops.

"We," she smirked and turned, approaching him then, "have a beach calling our names right now. We'll break the bed in later tonight, I promise."

Buck whined. "But I want my dessert *now*." He pulled her dress up and tickled at her thighs, tracing up to her groin and the silky pair of panties beneath.

Her breath took and she stepped back. He grinned up at her.

"Fine." He acquiesced. "Then at least give me a good striptease, darlin'."

Her eyes moved over him so erotically that it took everything in him not to pull her down on the bed and claim her, right then and there.

"Mr. Jenkins. That would only increase your hunger for me. And I believe we have guests waiting for us, so as much as I love to torture you, you're going to have to wait." Her eyebrows went up.

"Hey, no fuckin' fair." Buck whined again as she unzipped her bag and took a yellow bikini out of it.

She threw her head back, looking at him as she walked away and sashayed her hips. "Patience is a virtue, baby." She moved into the bathroom and winked before closing the doors behind her.

Buck huffed and moved to his suitcase. He knew they'd done it just this morning, but he wanted her again. He wasn't sure if it was the fact that they were in paradise or that there was a couple next door that could hear them that turned him on more. When had he become such an exhibitionist? Perhaps it was simply because he'd recently realized how much he cared for her and being buried inside her as often as possible was simply where he wanted to be.

He rifled through his bag, grabbed his swim trunks and flip-flops, dropped his drawers and had just pulled his trunks up when the bathroom doors opened and he felt his cock stiffen in response.

Vivian looked like a beach lover's fantasy in her tight bikini that hugged her ample bosom and hips. Buck's mouth curled up in a grin as his eyes licked at her. He gave a cat call but suddenly realized she was frowning. He approached her then.

"Baby, what's wrong?" He forced her chin up to look at him, her sunglasses pinning her hair up,her hat in her hand.

"I look fat," she whined and her full lips quivered.

Buck shook his head with conviction and looked down at her beautifully curvy body. "Darlin', no, you look like pure sex on the beach." His hand moved to her hip and he growled as he pressed his growing erection into her lower belly. "See. My cock thinks you look fucking delicious and he wants to devour your succulent little California peach."

Vivian laughed, amused, and swatted at his chest. "My belly looks pudgy." She covered her belly with her palm, and he shook his head and pulled her hand to his lips, kissing her fingers.

"Would you dare argue with your lover's arousal?" he asked, once again pressing himself into her. He moaned, rubbing the head of his sex across her front.

She smiled up at him then and shook her head.

"Feel what you're doing to me?" He cocked his eyebrow at her.

She nodded. "I feel it." Her hand went to his member and she gripped him in her hand.

His head flew back. "Oh, baby." He growled as she stroked him. "Just five minutes. I need to be inside you." He was begging now, but he didn't care. She turned him on so much. "Please." He moved her backward toward the bathroom counter. Her restraint seemed momentarily thwarted as his head fell and his lips ravaged hers. His hand cupped her breast and he moved his fingers down the silk of her string bikini. "Fuck, Viv. I'm so damn hard for you. See what you do to me. That bikini is so sexy, darlin', but I wanna see it in a pile on the floor as I make you scream my name."

"No," she huffed out as she stopped his hand, and he furrowed his brows, confused. "You're gonna be patient, Buck Jenkins. I'm not done tormenting you just yet." Her eyes danced over him as her hands moved and she played with the top of his swim trunks, her fingers dipping in to tickle at the skin just beneath the elastic. He whimpered like a child. "I like seeing you beg for me, you bad boy."

"I'm about to show you bad boy," he growled as he reached for her again but she spun, giggling, and rubbed her firm bottom into his pelvis. "Oh fuck, Vivian. You're gonna make me come right here and now." He grabbed her breasts in his palms and shoved his hips hard against hers, pumping his cock against her tight ass, loving the torture and hating it all at the same time. She bounced her bottom back against him and grinned seductively back at him in the mirror of the vanity. His eyes narrowed and his fingers tweaked at her nipples. She gasped and scoffed, arching her back and moving her hair off her neck. Damn, if he wasn't tugging her bikini bottoms off right that second and slapping his dick across her sweet little plump ass before blowing his load all over it. But suddenly, she moved and straightened her back against his chest as his breathing came out in raspy huffs. His heart hammered against his ribs and he held her tightly against him, looking her curvy body over in the mirror. "You think you've had the final say, huh?" He wasn't entirely kidding. "You'll pay for that little tease, darlin', I assure you. Your sweet little *peach* is gonna pay." He growled in her ear and his cock jumped as she whimpered. His hand moved into her bottoms and stroked at the fuzzy little peach he'd just mentioned. Two fingers moved into the wet folds and caressed ever so lightly. He watched her eyes darken in the mirror as his mouth moved to her neck and licked at her pulse point. She gasped loudly, her lips pouty as he grinned against her throat. "Remember, two can play your sexy little game." He continued to stroke as her moans intensified, rubbing his cock against her bottom, and licking and sucking at her long neck until the hair stood up on her arms and his body was roaring for release. Then he stepped back and dropped his hands.

The eyes in the mirror assessed him, and he looked arrogantly back in challenge. It was a battle of wills, of wits, of possession. And he wasn't sure who had won. For she turned and licked her lips at him before dropping her hat on her head and walking away.

Buck took a few moments to regain himself and let his erection deflate before grabbing some beach towels from the closet and joining the trio downstairs.

He heard Vivian laugh and tried to lighten his mood as he came down the stairs. He was so fucking horny and frustrated that Vivian was tormenting him like she was. Since when had she played so unfairly? His balls were as blue as the ocean in front of them. *Tonight*, he told himself. Tonight, he was going to show her not to tangle with a lion.

* * *

The smell of the ocean and the feel of the warm gulf breeze against her skin hit Vivian before she felt the heat of the sun on that gorgeous late August afternoon. She felt incredible as her morning sickness had been tolerable that day and her torment of Buck had put her on cloud nine. She smiled over at Natalie and baby Jackson on her hip as they turned towards the guys, who hauled all the beach gear- bags, an umbrella, chairs and a cooler.

"This looks like a good spot, huh?" Nat asked as she sat the baby down.

Jack and Buck dropped the bags and began to open the chairs as Viv looked out over the beautiful emerald waters of the Caribbean Sea. It was a perfect day, ninety degrees with a good breeze and enough cloud coverage to give them ample sunshine without scorching them.

"Wa-wa," baby Jackson said and pointed out to the ocean.

"You wanna swim, sweet boy?" Viv asked and shucked her cover-up, tossing it into her beach chair before bending over to pick up the baby. She turned to Nat, who tickled at her son's belly before shucking her own cover-up, revealing a black bikini that flattered her curvy figure, flat belly, and porcelain skin tone. Vivian only prayed that after her pregnancy, she could get her figure back as Nat had, even after three babies.

Viv heard a whistle and turned to see Buck assessing them. "Man, I don't know which view is better, do you, Jack? The beach or the ladies on it." His eyes did wonderful things to her insides and boosted her confidence. She smiled to herself as he removed his white shirt, admiring his muscular torso. He sat his bottom down in the chair, grabbed a beer from the cooler, and eye-fucked her until she had to tear her eyes from his big, enticing frame. Her gaze unconsciously moved to Jack, whose hard-muscled body was equally as impressive, shirtless, in a pair of dark blue trunks that hung low on his hips, cowboy hat still on his head. She admired the chiseled arms, pecs, and six-pack abs that practically matched the man beside him as he folded his frame into his own chair and took the beer Buck handed him.

"You guys gonna swim?" Nat asked Jack and Buck.

Buck shrugged, "For now, I'm just admiring the view." His eyes moved back over to Viv, and she gulped. Needing to cool off from the blast of overpowering male pheromones affronting her, she turned to the ocean and began walking into the surf. The baby in her arms squealed and she laughed as she sat him down to let his feet touch the waves hitting the shore. He giggled as the water hit his shins, getting a laugh out of his mother, who moved ahead of them into the water.

"Ma-ma," he called to her and reached up to Viv, who took him and walked into the ocean.

The warm, salty water felt good; not too hot and not too cold. It was refreshing and exhilarating as she moved in little by little, jumping the waves, turning the baby away from the spray, and letting the water move up her legs as she moved forward. She was in at her hips before she came to where the waves stopped breaking. She stopped not far from Natalie and held Jackson in front of her. He giggled and splashed, cooing up to her as he dowsed them in water. Viv laughed heartily and let him play. Natalie smiled over at them.

"What?" Viv asked, knowing where Nat's mind was.

"I'm just so happy for you guys."

"Thanks, Nat."

"I mean, it doesn't even seem like so long ago that you were afraid of being a washed-up old maid."

Viv laughed, "I did practically say that, didn't I?"

"Yeah, you did!" Nat reached for the baby and he went to her, kicking his little legs and laughing. "But now you don't have to worry about that, do ya?" Nat gave her a wink. Viv looked back at Buck and Jack talking. They both looked content and sexy as hell.

"I hadn't realized just how ripped your husband was," Vivian said, admiring the muscles on Jack's arms and torso.

"No?" Nat asked, as if surprised by her comment.

"I mean, I knew he was muscular but…" she trailed off, not meaning to ogle her best friend's husband. She blushed apologetically. Nat just laughed. Viv joined her.

"He *is* mouth-watering, I have to say." Nat eyed Vivian, knowingly. "Buck is too." Her eyebrows went up. "He's in love with you, you know?"

How could she possibly know that? Viv's glaze flew to Buck. He was watching her, his eyes taking her in. She lowered her eyes then looked back at Nat. "Oh, Nat, I don't know…"

"*I* do. I've known Buck Jenkins a long time, Viv. He's never looked at anyone the way he does you. Not even Jordan."

Jordan. He'd been with Jordan. He'd not really discussed that with Vivian. Was it because he couldn't? Didn't want to? Or simply that it was too painful? Viv tried not to let the uncertainty bother her. They'd not discussed her past either, so why was it a big deal? As much as she liked Jordan, Viv felt a jealous twinge knowing that she and Buck had slept together. Multiple times, she was sure. But it had been years ago. And Jordan was now a happily married woman. Buck had mentioned how great it would have been if Luth and Bella and Jordan and Nate could have joined them too. But now Vivian was glad that they hadn't. Viv didn't really understand where her jealousy came from. She'd never been a jealous person...but when it came to Buck, the thoughts of him and another woman turned her ravenous for blood.

"Viv," Nat asked, sensing her discomfort. "I'm sorry. I didn't mean to touch on a sensitive subject." The baby jumped in Nat's arms, splashing again.

Viv shook her head and smiled at her best friend.

"I just think it's great to see you two together. Y'all make a great couple."

"Our engagement is fake though, Nat, and I'm pretty sure that Buck likes it that way."

"Don't be so sure." Nat's eyebrow cocked and she tilted her head confidently at Viv. "You forget that at one time, I was closer to Buck than anyone else was and I can tell you with certainty that there's *nothing* fake about his feelings for you. You're carrying his child after all."

As reassuring as that should be, it didn't take away the pain of him leaving her that day at the hotel or that he'd had so many women in his past... What made Vivian so special? And if she *wasn't* carrying his child right now, would he even be with her at all? The sting of the answer to that question cut into her, and she shivered.

Nat came closer then, grabbing for her arm. "Hey."

Vivian started as she gazed up into Natalie's face. She smiled trying to take the attention off herself, this was far too personal and painful, and they were on vacation after all. She looked back over to Jack then and giggled. "Does he go anywhere without that cowboy hat?"

Nat looked to her husband, her eyebrows going up. "Not if I can help it," she scoffed.

They both burst out into laughter at that.

Soon, the guys stood and came into the water to join them. Buck pulled Viv into his arms, and her heart overfilled with the power of his masculine presence. He had her all wrapped up in him—body, heart and soul—and she was smitten. She couldn't find another word to describe how he made her feel. He kissed her forehead and picked her up just as a wave broke and crashed into him. She laughed as water came over him and he spit and sputtered.

"Hey, I was blindsided," he stated and held her close, kissing her lips.

They heard Jax cackle as his father threw him up and skirted him over the waves and the sound of that sweet little voice hit Viv's heart and shimmied all the way down to her womb. Their baby and Jackson would grow up together. They would know each other. And who knew, they might be best friends. That thought made Vivian smile brightly as she looked up into the handsome face of the man who had planted that seed inside her. The man who had given her such a precious gift. A gift that had changed both of their lives. A gift that had brought them together unlike anything else could. He smiled back equally as radiantly, as if knowing what she was thinking, and she reached up, wrapped her arms around his neck and kissed him. She kissed him with gratuity, with lust, with passion, with honesty. Their kiss grew hotter and the fire smoldered within her as his big arms wrapped around her waist. It wasn't until a giant wave crashed over them that she pulled back, coughing and choking on salt water.

Buck was laughing when the water poured from her ears and mouth, freeing her from its salty grasp, as he righted her in the water. Viv wiped at her eyes and pushed her wet hair back on her head, looking at him, unamused. He laughed again, and she couldn't help but smile at his handsome face.

They all stayed in the water for a time until their fingers were pruney before heading back to the beach to enjoy their lunch and grab some rays of sun. Jackson fell asleep beneath the little tent they'd brought with them as Viv and Nat caught up on their reading. Buck and Jack made a sandcastle, and when Jackson awoke, he helped cover his Uncle Buck in sand, giggling in happiness as Buck pretended to be sucked down into a pit.

It was a beautiful, fun day and as the sun sank low into the water and the sky lit up in stunning colors of orange, pink and crimson, Viv's heart swelled as the man beside her kissed her cheek. His eyes were so warm that it took her breath.

"I'm so glad you brought me here, Buck."

"Me too, darlin'." God, his sexy drawl made her entire body shiver.

She kissed him gently on the lips. "Extra props for you tonight, lover," she murmured before deepening the kiss. His tongue plunged into her mouth and her insides literally melted beneath his grasp. Suddenly, she was falling onto the sand, and Buck's big body was atop hers, tickling her. She giggled and cried, "No, no, stop it." Her laughter brought baby Jackson over, who cackled as he took his little shovel and began scooping up sand to cover her.

"San," he said as he patted the shovel on her belly.

"Oh no, is it my turn to be buried in sand?"

"Aunt Viv has been a bad girl, Jax," Buck cooed as his big hands scooped sand up and over her hips. She swatted at him even as his gaze did her in.

"Bad," Jax cooed. "No, no."

Buck laughed as he encouraged Jackson on, and Viv shook her head, claiming defeat. Her eyes fell on Jack and Nat, who sat between her husband's legs admiring the sunset over the water before turning her head to Viv and smiling big. Jack kissed the top of Nat's head, and Viv sighed, content even as Buck and Jackson continued covering her in sand.

An hour later, everyone had showered as their chef, Marcel, had prepared an incredible dinner of fresh carne asada and grilled shrimp tacos, rice, and charro beans with fresh guacamole, pico de gallo, and crema fresca. They all sat outside on the large patio table just feet from the pool that was lit with moonlight and tiki torches. The meal was delicious, and they all dug in, working up an appetite after their day at the beach.

"Man, I'll never be able to eat regular Tex-Mex again after this," Jack said, licking his fingers. "God, it's heavenly."

"Mo, mo," Jackson pleaded for "more" as his mom gave him another bite of the cheese-covered beans.

"That's it," Buck replied. "I'm never leaving Mexico." He laughed.

"This guacamole is the best I've ever had," Nat agreed, nodding before dipping another tortilla chip into the green condiment that tasted so much better than it looked. "Buck, if you've meant to spoil us, you've outdone yourself, my friend. This is amazing." She closed her eyes and she bit into the guacamole-laden chip. Vivian laughed.

"It really is all so delicious. This pico is to die for." She moaned as she took another bite of her freshly made taco.

"Fresh sopapillas," Marcel said in his sexy Spanish accent, sitting a huge plate of gorgeous brown tortillas covered in cinnamon, sugar, whipped cream and strawberries.

"Marcel, seriously, I'm already married," Nat whined, and they all laughed at her.

"The food alone might be enough to make a man turn," Jack joked.

Buck and Nat busted out in laughter at that one, and Viv shook her head at poor Marcel, who gaped at Jack in horror.

"He's kidding, amigo," Viv said. "Jack is strictly heterosexual. Trust me, you have *nothing* to worry about on that end," Viv stated with a laugh.

Marcel smiled sweetly before looking Jack over from head to toe and back again. "You may be kidding, but don't knock it until you try it, vaquero." His brows went up, and Jack's face paled as he gripped his bottle of beer.

Buck almost fell on the floor, he was chuckling so hard. Jack turned beet red, looking like he'd been slapped as Marcel puckered his lips and winked before walking away. Natalie and Vivian joined in on the laughter, and Jack looked incredibly disturbed by what had just taken place.

"See what you started, Jack," Nat said after catching her breath, gripping Jack's bicep.

"Man, that was the funniest damn thing I've ever seen," Buck said, wiping the tears from his eyes.

"Looks like Montezuma's revenge isn't the only thing I gotta worry about down here in Mexico," Jack grumbled, and the entire table cracked up again.

Later that night, after Nat had put the baby to bed and they'd played a few rounds of cards, the guys poured night caps and they sat outside, enjoying the crashing of the waves on the shore mere yards in front of them beyond the pool.

Buck and Viv were curled up on one long chaise and Nat and Jack were on the other. Viv could hear Nat giggle as they whispered behind her. She was tucked up against Buck across his lap, her chest touching his, as silver moonlight spilled over them. His finger moved a stray strand of blonde hair off her cheek, and she heard Jack moan behind them.

"I don't wanna know what they're doing, do I?" Viv whispered with a giggle.

"I can't see them," Buck whispered back, looking down at her. "All I see is you, my sweet star."

Viv gulped at the seriousness in his tone.

"Jack, you tiger!" Nat exclaimed and giggled again as Viv turned her head to see Jack stand, scoop Natalie up, and nod to them.

"'Night, y'all." He winked before turning to go through the screen door and into the house.

Buck chuckled lightly and smiled back down at Viv, his eyes shimmering in the moonlight. "Have I told you how beautiful you are?"

"Perhaps, but you can always tell me, I love hearing you say it," she divulged.

"You're the most gorgeous woman I've ever seen, Vivian Alexander." His eyes darkened.

"You're only saying that so you can get me naked, we both know the truth." She winked at him, but his smile faded, the intensity in his eyes amplifying.

"As much as I want you naked, it's the God's honest truth. The moment I saw you, I knew that I had to make you mine."

His words stirred her in ways that made her heart soar on wings of anticipation, hope and eagerness.

"Buck, I—"

"I need you, Viv. I want you, so very much. And not just right now. I want you tomorrow. And the next day. And—" Buck stumbled over his words as his big palm cupped her cheek.

"Oh Buck, make love to me. Make me yours," she murmured even as his lips came down to hers.

He moved atop her then positioning himself between her legs. He kissed her with such passion that it took her breath and not because of his long kisses either. Their hands moved frantically to undress one another as their moans and grunts and tongues tangled together. His big palm gripped her bottom as his hard sex slid into her hurriedly and his head flew back on a groan.

"Oh, fuck, baby, you feel so good. Each time. It's even better than the last. What are you doing to me?" He growled into her ear as his cock pumped into her and his mouth fell to her nipple; she cried out. She could ask him the same question for she'd never been as out of control beneath a man until him. Sure, sex had always been fun and passionate, but when it came to Buck Jenkins, he had her body all swooning and her mind soaring, feeling out of sorts with herself.

"Mmm," she whimpered as her insides clenched his sex. "I'm gonna come, baby, make me come."

"Yes, my darlin', anything my sexy starlet wants," he smirked and angled his hips, hitting a spot inside her that made her shudder. He bumped and stroked it with his sex over and over and over again as his thumbs brushed her nipples, watching as her brows furrowed, her mouth opened, and her orgasm finally took her over the edge.

She screamed out, her cries echoing in the concrete and stone patio, bouncing off the walls back at her, intensifying her pleasure. Once she came back to earth, he turned them over so that she was on top and let her ride him. And she did so with an incredible skill she'd not known she'd possessed, for in a matter of minutes, he was gripping her bottom and hammering into her so hard that it almost hurt as he too climaxed in a roar.

"Good God, woman," he huffed out as his orgasm subsided. "You have such power over me, if I didn't know any better I'd think you were a wicked enchantress." At that, Vivian laughed heartily, and Buck's brows drew as he moaned hungrily and clenched her bottom tightly in his hands. "Fuck *me*, Viv. Baby, that felt incredible. Do it again." She did, simply due to his words and as he whimpered, she felt his sex growing hard again inside her. "See, a fuckin' enchantress. I swear to God. You're hell-bent on destroying me, aren't ya?"

Viv smirked and raised an eyebrow at him. She moved her body off him and down his legs, gripping his sex in her hands and stroking softly. He moaned and propped his head up to watch her. Slowly, her head fell and her tongue licked the tip of him, tasting herself on him, and he gasped. She grinned again. "I knew it, tryin' to destroy me," he muttered. She began loving his hard flesh with her mouth and fist. Soon, he was groaning loudly and his palm was cupping her head as she went to town on him. "Oh yeah, baby. God, your mouth feels so incredible."

Vivian grinned even as she had him sputtering beneath her.

She loved the power she had over him in those moments, but in the back of her mind, she wondered just how long that would be.

.*.

*T*hree days on the Yucatan peninsula overlooking the Caribbean was enough to make Buck wanna stay forever; here with his beautiful Hollywood actress. They all toured the ruins of Tulum, dined at one of the best taco joints in downtown Cancun, and taken an incredible sunset sail on day two of their trip. On day three, he and Viv left Nat, Jack, and the baby home while they spent the day at Isla Mujeres and got to snorkel in the reef, swim with dolphins and eagle rays. Later that night, they'd headed to the Coco Bongo where they'd hung out for a couple hours, dancing so provocatively that they'd came back to the house and he'd taken his sexy starlet in a passionate rage under the spray of the showerhead, right against the stone wall, their fingers interlocking as he'd loved her with a fury he couldn't seem to satisfy no matter the times he buried himself inside her. His craving for her only grew the more time he spent with her and he was starting to think he might stretch this engagement out as long as he possibly could.

He was planning to ask Vivian to come back to Texas and stay with him for a while. He wished they could change doctors and she could find one there in Abundance. She wasn't due until March, so they had some time to figure things out. But the thoughts of having his child born in Abundance appealed to him far more than in L.A. Abundance was peaceful, quiet, less hectic, and he could have Viv there close to his family and to Natalie and the Kinsen brood.

Today, day four, was a washout as the rainy season was in full swing on the Yucatan peninsula on this early September day, so they were forced to stay in and watch movies, play games and nap. Buck wasn't complaining, he was tired after partying all night. He pulled Vivian into bed after lunch for more than just napping, and they'd spent the better part of that time having toe-curling sex. They didn't come out until around four PM to see Nat and Jack curled up, smooching on the couch. This trip had been good for them too, and Buck grinned big as he flipped Jack's hat and came to sit on the couch adjacent to them as *Jurassic Park* played on the television screen. Little Jackson napped in his play pen not far from them, and Nat laughed as she caught Buck's eyes, giving him a blush.

"Having fun, I see," Buck said and motioned down to their torsos covered in a blanket.

"I was having *more* fun before you showed up," Nat admitted and pouted a little as she pulled back from her husband just a smidge.

"Hey, three's a crowd, four's a party." Buck winked back.

"Don't tempt me, Bucko." Nat's blue eyes burned into his and he balked, surprised, before Nat threw a pillow at him and laughed at his expense.

"In your dreams, Jenkins," Jack threw over his shoulder before pulling Nat back to him in a smoldering kiss.

Viv hadn't been kidding when she'd said these two were still like honey-mooners...sheesh. They might just be worse than him and Vivian; but were far better at discretion.

Buck shook his head in amusement, yawned, and threw his arms behind his head, enjoying the sight of the water even in the squall that assaulted the windows. He waited for Viv to come out of the bathroom, so he could cuddle up with her and watch one of his favorite movies. His belly was starting to grumble, and he wondered when Marcel was coming to make dinner. He pondered what their meal would consist of tonight- enchiladas, tostadas, fajitas? He didn't much care, for he knew it was gonna be delicious no matter what, although he could really go for some tacos al pastor.

Viv came down the hallway then her face pale as she looked over at Buck, and he shot up, feeling anxious as she handed him his cell phone. "It's... it's Jordan. I'm sorry. I wouldn't normally answer it, but this makes three times now she's called you," Viv's cheeks went from white to red in an instant, and Buck's eyes caught Natalie's, who looked like she might be sick. He nodded and reached for the phone, pulling it to his ear, and Nat and Jack turned to face him.

He prepared his body for the hit and heard Jordan sobbing as he asked, "Hello?"

"Buck. Oh, thank goodness. I've been trying to call Natalie all damn day, but..."

"She's right here, Jor. Is everything alright?"

"Oh, God, I don't even know where to start. Hold on. I need—"

"Jordan?" Buck's voice grew louder, the fear inside his heart threatening to overtake him. Was something wrong with Savannah, Dallie, his family? Why was she so upset and furthermore, why the hell was she calling *him*? He looked up anxiously to Viv, who in turn took his free hand as she sat down beside him.

"Hang on, I'm putting Nate on too. Turn your phone on speaker. I need to tell all y'all this." Buck did as instructed, motioning for Natalie to approach. She did, and Jack followed, holding her to him as her hand fisted against her mouth. She looked like she might be on the verge of breaking down. They all heard the rustling of the phone being moved and held their breath before hearing Nathan come on the line. "Nat?"

"I'm here! Nathan, what's wrong?" her voice cracked and tears sprang to her eyes.

"Oh, wow. I don't even know how to tell you this. It's incredible! It's—Nat. I'm a *father*."

"What?" They all said in unison.

"I— Jeez. Do you—Do you remember Joanne Dean?"

Jack's head went up at the name. "The girl you were..." Jack faltered for the right words then, although at that point, they knew what he was trying to say, "the one you met...at one of the rodeos in San Antonio? The pretty blonde?"

"Yes. Exactly! Well, so after we...ya know. She had a son..."

"Natalie, he freaking looks *just* like him, I swear to God. It's uncanny! They could be *twins*," Jordan's happy voice interrupted, and Buck looked up to see Nat looking incredulously up at Jack.

"I mean, we don't know anything for sure yet, but she left a letter after she died claiming that *I'm* his father. I wouldn't have believed it, but the timing was just too perfect. We had dinner with him and his grandparents. He's a good boy, Nat. I—I—"

Natalie beamed then and smiled even as tears streamed down her cheeks.

"I'm sorry to interrupt your trip, but I couldn't wait to tell you, baby sister. You're an aunt. I don't have the test to prove it just yet. We're gonna do that tomorrow. But I *know* in my heart...You... You're an aunt!" Nate's excited, tearful voice had them all choking up then as he told them about his newfound son. Buck grinned over at Viv, whose eyes stared back into his so sweet and loving that he leaned in to kiss her. When he pulled back, he kissed the tear running down her cheek. He then grinned up at one of his oldest and dearest friends.

Natalie wiped at the tears on her face and took the phone Buck suddenly thrust up at her. "Nate," she said, pulling her lips in. "I'm so happy for you." She burst into tears, and Jack pulled her into his arms, stroking her hair. Both she and Nate cried into the phone for several minutes as Viv joined in, trying unsuccessfully to muffle hers, before Natalie cleared her throat and asked. "So, what's my nephew's name and how old is he?"

"Morgan and he'll be fifteen years old in two months."

"Oh wow!" Natalie smiled over at Buck and Viv. "When do we get to meet him?"

CHAPTER 12

*V*ivian smiled over at Buck and he beamed brightly back at her from the driver's side of his truck. They were headed to Nat and Jack's for a big barbecue to meet Nathan and Jordan's son, Morgan.

They'd spent their last day in Cancun with Jack, Natalie, and baby Jax enjoying a day of sun and sand on the Caribbean. They'd dined on fresh crab and fish and watched a beautiful sunset from their beach chairs before having a big beach bonfire and roasting marshmallows.

Their trip had been so wonderful and relaxing—so much so that Vivian hadn't wanted to hurry home. Buck told her they could go back any time they wanted, according to Lincoln. When they'd gotten back to Buck's home in Abundance, they'd went straight upstairs and made love in Buck's big king-size bed, tearing the sheets up like they'd not just made love hours prior to that.

They'd spend the last three days organizing everything for Buck's upcoming charity golf event next month and shopping for baby stuff, basking in their joy, when Nat had called and told them the paternity test had come back and Morgan was indeed a Butler. Viv had cried, and Buck had congratulated Nat on being an official aunt. Natalie had, in turn, cried—albeit it tears of joy—and said she was throwing a big BBQ to celebrate.

That had been four days ago.

As they headed to Nat's now, Vivian took Buck's outstretched hand and smoothed down her white eyelet cotton midi dress, noticing the baby bump and cupping it tenderly. As much as she wasn't enjoying the changes or morning sickness, it was the proof that their little peanut was growing, and she couldn't be happier.

As they pulled into the driveway, Viv noticed the abundance of cars and trucks there, wondering who all Nat had invited over for this big celebration of hers, as Buck's big palm moved her hand away and cupped her baby bump. He leaned down and kissed it tenderly, cooing to their baby. He'd been doing this same exact thing the last few days and as sweet as it was, it made her somewhat self-conscious, knowing that he too was noticing her no longer flat tummy.

He seemed to recognize her discontent as he looked up at her and straightened, bringing his lips to hers. "What is it, my sweet little star?" he asked as he pulled back, angling his cowboy hat-topped head at her, his palm moving mindlessly over her barely-rounded belly.

"Nothing," she tried to sound nonchalant, being thankful for the life growing inside her, knowing full well Jordan, who'd never been able to have a child, wouldn't bat an eyelash at stretch-marks, morning sickness, or a tiny—practically non-existent—baby bump. She gave him a big smile, and he returned it.

He looked so handsome today; wearing his tan Stetson, a baby pink polo shirt and his tight Wranglers. Man, he looked good in pink; it brought out the tan he'd gotten in Mexico. He kissed her knuckles before getting out and coming around to help her out of the truck. His arm went around her waist as they went up the stairs, and Buck rang the doorbell.

Vivian was anxious to meet Luther and Bella, their brood, and to see the Butlers again.

The house was loud as the door opened and Savannah greeted them, rolling her eyes at the girl behind her.

"Kelsey, seriously—Hey, Uncle Buck! Hey, Aunt Viv." Vanna's tone immediately changed and she threw herself into their arms, squeezing Viv, her gorgeous green/blue eyes glowing up at her. "You guys are gonna have a baby?" she whispered, mesmerized as she looked down at Vivian's belly.

Viv looked up at Buck in surprise, and he shrugged.

"News travels fast in a small town. Plus, we *were* on the news, remember?"

"Uncle Buck!" came the voice of the blonde girl behind Savannah as she practically shoved Vanna away to get to Buck. "I missed you."

"I missed you too, darlin'." He picked the little girl up and hugged her to him before turning her around to introduce Viv. "This is—"

"OMG, I already *know* who she is, Uncle Buck! Vivian Alexander. I can't believe it! My daddy said I was gonna get to meet you today, but I didn't believe him."

Buck set the pre-teen down as she took Vivian's outstretched hand, and Viv laughed, shaking the beautiful little girl's hand.

"Viv, this is Luth and Bella's eldest child, Kelsey Jean," Buck stated when the star-struck Kelsey didn't supply her name.

"I'm also the prettiest *and* smartest of the crew, I'll have you know," Kelsey corrected Buck, and he shook his head, laughing.

"Luth has his work cut out for himself with this one. I tell ya right now."

Buck took Viv's hand as the kids moved into the house and he followed, coming into the kitchen where the noise came to a head.

Dallie sat at the bar with Jackson in her arms, talking to Natalie, who was chopping vegetables. Vivian moved to hug Dallie and the baby then Natalie before being pulled into David Butler's arms and finally Corrine's. She embraced them lovingly and chatted with the couple for a little bit before Buck was pulling her over to meet a beautiful blonde woman by the name of Bella Boyd, Luther's wife, and their brand-new baby daughter, Cassidy. The barely one-month-old infant was tiny with white-blonde hair, and Viv just oohed and aahed over her. Soon enough, she and Buck would be holding their own darling infant. Viv couldn't wait for that day to come.

Buck was asked to grab Jack from the grill for something Nat needed in the kitchen and he dragged Viv with him to the back porch where the laughter and cries of children echoed from the backyard. Jack was wiping sweat from his brow, replacing his hat, and flipping beef brisket on a big smoker next to a man Vivian didn't recognize as they approached.

"Howdy guys," Jack said, wiping his sweaty face with his arm as he smiled over at them.

"Hey ya, Jack. Your wife sent me to fetch you. Want me to watch the grill?"

"And get that pretty pink shirt of yours all dirty? I think not." Jack laughed and pretended to slug at Buck's middle. "Hey, have you guys met my brother? Buck, Viv, this is Gavin."

The man who favored Jack a great deal, but was dressed in business casual, like he might be running to the country club later, stuck his hand out to shake Vivian's hand.

"Pleased to meet you, Ms. Alexander. My wife's a big fan." His handshake was warm and friendly, and brief, as he then turned to Buck. "Buck, I'm surprised to say, I can't believe we've never officially met."

"Likewise, Gavin. I've heard a lot about ya, man. Can't say all of it was good either." Buck chuckled and elbowed Gavin.

Jack patted Viv's shoulder then. "I would hug you, Vivian, but I'm all sweaty, so I'll save it." He winked, and Vivian blushed into his handsome face, thinking how unfortunate that really was. He shut the lid to the grill and motioned to the cooler next to it for them to grab some drinks before heading inside through the French doors.

Suddenly, a little head of brown hair peeked out from behind Gavin.

"And who's this handsome young man?" Viv asked and smiled at the little boy, who looked to be about five years old.

"Oh, this is my son, Elias. Elias, this young lady is a movie star. Do you recognize her?"

Elias nodded and gave Viv the sweetest small-toothed grin. "Hi." He waved, and her heart did a little flip-flop. What a cutie he was and favored Jackson, his first cousin, a good deal.

"Hi. It's good to meet you, I'm Vivian."

Elias gave her a little giggle, and Vivian squatted down and tickled at his belly. His cuteness was infectious, and she turned and looked up at Buck, whose burning eyes on her made her heart stop.

"Who's he?" Elias asked, looking up at Buck then. "Is he a cowboy?" Elias asked on a whisper.

"Well, he's wearing a cowboy hat, so that must mean he is, huh?" Viv winked at him and smirked up at Buck, who lifted his brow playfully.

"I wanna be a cowboy." The little boy stared mesmerized at Buck, and Viv couldn't help the next giggle escaping her throat.

"You wanna be a cowboy, huh?" Buck chuckled and squatted to his haunches.

"Oh, here we go again," Gavin smirked, his tone more playful than annoyed. "As if we don't have enough cowboys in the family *already*, Eli."

Eli just grinned sweetly up at his father then his eyes fell back to Buck.

"I tell ya what, little man. Here, have my hat. You can't be a cowboy without a hat, you know?" Buck pulled his Stetson off and placed it on the little boy's small head. The hat practically swallowed it, but the child looked as if Buck had reached right up and pulled down the stars, for his eyes went wide in wander.

"What do you say, son?" Gavin asked and patted Elias's shoulder, prompting him.

"Thank you. Oh, thank you." He held the oversized hat to his head proudly and tilted his chin up.

Buck gave a chuckle and popped back up, pulling Viv with him.

"You didn't have to do that, Buck. I'll be sure he gets it back to you—"

Buck held his hand up and was shaking his head. "Nah, man. I have plenty of them, trust me." He chuckled then his eyes settled back on Vivian. "Besides, my hat's already where it belongs."

Vivian gulped as her heart literally jumped out of her chest then, his meaning all too clear to her. She was legitimately gaping as Gavin said, "Well, that was a kind gesture. Thank you. I know you've made his day for sure. Eli, come on, let's go show Mommy what you have." He chuckled loudly then nodded at Viv before taking his child's hand and moving off.

Viv just stared into Buck's gorgeous eyes as her heart overpoured with love for this man whose gaze literally held her captive.

"Want somethin' to drink?" Buck finally asked, breaking the stare as he moved to the side of the grill, opened the cooler, and grabbed a beer for himself and a Sprite for her.

"Well, I'll be damned. I heard it through the grapevine, but I didn't know if it was true or not. Buck Jenkins, you're the luckiest sonovabitch I know!" A voice came from behind Vivian, and she turned to see a handsome man with a scruffy face, brown hair and eyes, and dimpled cheeks. He, too, wore a tan Stetson, jeans, and boots with a green shirt that said, "Got Beef?" on it.

Vivian smiled brightly as the man did a funny little handshake with Buck, and Buck laughed big before embracing him.

"Luth, I want you to meet my woman." His *woman* indeed; wow, how Viv liked the sound of that.

"Vivian Alexander. My dear, it's certainly a pleasure. I'm Luther Boyd. Father of these rowdy kids running around back here." He motioned to the boys chasing each other in the yard before taking his hat off, nodding his head, shaking her hand and replacing his hat. Viv curtsied and laughed as his brows raised at Buck. "Man, you got a live one, huh?" Luther joined in, chuckling. "Hell, I reckon, we all got pretty damn lucky in the lady department and damn proud of it too. I believe congrats are in order, Big Daddy." He patted Buck's shoulder and pulled a beer off the railing, toasting to them.

Buck nodded and raised his own beer, wrapping an arm around Vivian as he smiled down into her face. God, she was so in love with his big, bulky, blond self...and she was having a hard time suppressing it as of late.

When the back door opened, Savannah and Kelsey came out. They moved to the east of the porch, looking out over the railing and giggling at who knew what. Viv smiled over at them, they looked to be close, and she suddenly remembered her teenage years, the silliness and awkwardness of not being a kid anymore yet not being an adult quite yet either. She'd had a best friend named Sarah whom she'd shared everything with. Come to think of it, she needed to try and reconnect with her. It had been far too long, and watching Vanna and Kelsey banter and whisper warmed her heart. She smiled up at Buck as he chatted with Luther about their trip to Mexico, and Dallie and Jax, Bella and Cassidy, Gavin, a woman Viv assumed to be Gavin's wife, Corrine and David, Jack and Elias all came out onto the porch. Viv and Buck's baby would have Jackson and Luth and Bella's baby girl, Cassidy, to buddy up with. Viv could only hope for a friendship that was strong between them, like the rest of this family seemed to have.

Natalie came out with Jordan then, and Viv smiled big, pulling the gorgeous redhead into a hug, feeling her emotions rise as Jordan trembled against her. Viv was happy for her and Nathan and their new son, Morgan. Jordan patted her back and kissed her cheek before turning to Buck and pulling him into her embrace. The jealousy Viv felt for Jordan was starting to wane, for she knew Buck didn't love Jordan—maybe he never even had —but the familiarity was still there and probably always would be, for the way Jordan held onto him and kissed his cheek as if she'd done it dozens of times before had Vivian perturbed. She knew it had to be the pregnancy hormones or something because she'd never been jealous before. This was a new feeling for her, and she tried to calm the burning in her heart as Nathan stepped through the doors with a young man whom he could have birthed himself.

Morgan Butler was close to six feet tall already, his russet skin, sapphire eyes, and raven hair identical to Nathan's. Viv couldn't help but cover her mouth in surprise as she looked him over. Nate's arm went around the shy young man's shoulder as everyone hushed and turned to look at them.

"Everyone, I want you to meet my son, Morgan Dean Butler." There was such emotion in Nathan's voice that Viv felt her heart swell and tears sting her eyes. She moved her fingers up to swat the tears away and felt Buck's soft lips kissing her cheek. "He's almost fifteen. I had no idea he even existed, until his mother's recent demise, sadly. But I'm eager to have you know that he'll be staying with Jordan and I from now on and attending school at Abundance High starting this month."

Jordan took Nate's outstretched hand and beamed over at her husband, the love there unmistakable, and Viv felt a twinge of guilt that she'd ever been jealous of the woman staring back at Nate Butler so fondly. Jordan looped her arm around Morgan's waist and he grinned, dropping his head shyly. Jordan's hip bumped his, and he shuffled nervously on his feet, his eyes scanned the crowd, who began applauding and cheering.

Morgan's eyes stopped on Vivian and he gaped. Jordan laughed and patted his back as Vivian approached him then, shaking his hand. "It's very nice meeting you, Morgan. I'm Vivian."

The young man continued to stare at her as he robotically pumped her hand in his then Buck came up and he nearly fell back in shock. "You—you know *celebrities*?" he asked, looking to Jordan.

Jordan laughed and nodded. "Well, these are really the only two. Meet your Aunt Vivian and Uncle Buck." Jordan's eyes burned into Viv's then, and the love radiating from them dissolved anything but adoration in Vivian's heart for Jordan Tate Butler. It was as if a lock had been shorn off, opening the gate of fresh air.

"Welcome to the family, son," Buck said and patted his shoulder.

Luther came up then, introducing himself and his wife, Bella, and daughter, Cassidy. He shook Morgan's hand before moving to embrace Jordan and Nathan.

Buck and Viv stepped back and watched the interchange of hands and greetings.

"Think he'll remember all these names he's gonna hear today?" Buck asked joking before taking another swig of his beer. "Hopefully we're not overwhelming the poor kid."

"He does look a *bit* overwhelmed," Viv noted as Morgan's shy eyes fell once again.

"Now, he met Nat and her crew just a few days ago, right?" Buck asked.

"Yeah, on Thursday night. Nat and Jack went over there with the kids along with Corrine and David. Nat said it was amazing. He just took to the girls and baby Jax like he'd known them forever and of course, David and Corrine were over the moon." Viv smiled, recalling the conversation she'd had just yesterday with Natalie about the reunion.

"Over the moon, huh? I reckon you been down here in Tex-ass too long, California girl, you're starting to sound a little southern." Buck's arm around her waist tightened.

"Hmm, it could just be that you're starting to rub off on me." Her hip bumped his as she looked up at him.

Buck leaned down and whispered in her ear, "Mmm, I'd like to rub one off on you." She giggled and swatted at his chest. "Well, I'll be a sonovabitch, would you look at that?" Buck raised up and his gaze fell on Morgan, who was shaking Kelsey's hand in awe.

It wouldn't have been anything to note- just a simple handshake, introduction, two kids meeting for the first time...only...their eyes were focused solely on one another, burning into one another's as if nothing else in the world existed. Kelsey's face took on a look of admiration, acknowledgement, and wonder so profound that it almost stilled Vivian's heart. It was as if an electric pulse had gone out and shocked everyone, for the chatter had suddenly stopped and all their eyes moved to Kelsey and Morgan, whose dazed look mirrored Kelsey's. Time stood still as the two youngsters held each other's gaze for long moments before the back door opened once again and Kelsey pulled back, startled, as if she were just broken out of a trance.

Vivian smiled knowingly as Kelsey looked around, embarrassed, and took in Morgan's equally stunned expression. His head bashfully lowered and he walked off with his father through the French doors, as if eager to seek a reprieve.

"Uh oh, Luth," Jack was the first to say as Kelsey ran off, around the other side of the porch, pulling Vanna with her. "I think we all know what *that* means." He looked over at his friend, slightly amused.

"Motherfucker," Luth mumbled under his breath and scowled. "Kels ain't even old enough for that shit yet."

"Well, I think we all just witnessed who's gonna be chasin' after her when she is," Jack maintained.

"Ah hell, lighten up, Luth," Jordan offered. "It was only a matter of time before the Boyd and Butler clans collided. And I wouldn't be surprised to see the Kinsens joining the force either." Her eyebrows went up at Dallie who held baby Jax. He, in turn, looked over at Cassidy and cooed, "Baby," as he squealed and clapped his hands.

"Now, c'mon, Jordan. They're babies, let's not be trying to pair 'em up just yet," Luth scoffed and rolled his eyes.

"You just never know!" Jordan laughed and approached Buck and Viv then. "Or perhaps the Jenkins and Kinsens?" She shrugged, and Buck batted playfully at her as her finger pointed to him.

"Hey, you leave *my* kid out of this, you crazy redhead. She ain't even out of the womb yet," Buck defended and moved his hand down to Viv's lower abdomen.

They all laughed big, including Vivian, at Buck's facial expression. His hulking arms wrapped around her and her heart melted at the sheer protection she felt in his embrace. She knew he would be there to defend their child no matter what and it made her love him even more. She looked up at him then, smiling tenderly as her lips came to his in a steamy kiss. Soon, nothing existed but the two of them as Buck's tongue slid into her mouth and she moaned, moving her hand to his muscular pecs. He deepened the kiss and turned, pulling her stark against him, one hand splaying on her back, the other moving into her hair.

It took an elbow nudge to get Buck to pull away and suddenly, Vivian was completely embarrassed and aroused at the same time.

"Jeez, get a room, you two," Luth grumbled as he stood next to them with yet another couple.

She cleared her throat and smoothed her dress before hearing Buck say, "Viv, you remember meeting Scottie at the burger joint, right?"

"Ah, yes." Viv smiled up at Scottie and extended her hand to shake his. "Nice to see you again, Scottie."

"You as well, Miss Alexander. This here is Ginger Fortner, my girlfriend," Scottie said, introducing a lovely freckled, green-eyed, strawberry-blonde young woman.

Vivian didn't miss Buck's surprised look, but he quickly recovered and shook Ginger's hand, giving her his best smile. "Buck Jenkins. My fiancée, Vivian Alexander."

Vivian gave her a nod and took her hand.

"Oh my. I didn't know I was gonna be meeting *you* here. I would have worn more makeup," Ginger said bashfully to Vivian.

"Nonsense," Viv insisted. "You're lovely."

"Alright everyone, grab a plate," Nat shouted suddenly, ushering the kids inside first.

"Dinner time, sexy mama," Buck growled in her ear. "I'd much rather have your sweet California peach though," he whispered and smacked a kiss right in her ear.

"Behave yourself." She smirked up at him even though she wanted to devour him as much as he did her.

The line was long and the chatter was endless as they all moved into the kitchen to make their plates. There were rows of food, not unlike every other holiday at the Kinsens and once again, Viv was surprised that after all these years, she'd not met Buck Jenkins until the Helping Heroes Ball just months ago. It seemed uncanny. *Well, that's fate for you,* Viv thought, knowing that Buck had come into her life at just the right time and vice versa as she smiled at him joking with Scottie.

"Girlfriend, huh? Since when are you the steady relationship type, Scottie Warden?" Buck asked as Ginger moved off to make herself a drink.

"Since shut the fuck up." Scottie raised his fist. Viv wasn't sure if he was serious or teasing at first. "Every other one of you jerk-offs has steady pussy coming at you non-stop, well, dammit, *now* it's my freakin' turn."

"Whoa, dude." Buck raised his hands in defense. "Sorry I asked. But surely that's not the *only* reason you have a girlfriend." Buck winked at Viv as he turned his head back to look at Scottie.

"Nope. She gives good head too…if you must know."

Viv gaped up at Buck, appalled by Scottie's crude words regarding Ginger. Buck just rolled his eyes and shook his head. "Scottie, you're getting to be such a romantic in your old age, man, it's so fuckin' sweet." Buck swiped at an invisible tear in his eye, and Viv held back a laugh, realizing that he'd been simply baiting Scottie the whole time.

Scottie shoved at him and laughed, apologizing to Viv for her having to hear their banter. "I swear, I really don't think like that about her. She's pretty awesome, I must say. And her kids too," Scottie whispered as he leaned into Buck and Vivian. "I honestly don't even know how it all happened. We met one night, and I've been smitten ever since by that sassy little ginger."

Buck elbowed him. "Looks like I know the *next* couple gettin' hitched."

Once they'd grabbed their fair share of brisket, slaw, fries, corn, baked mac and cheese, green beans and rolls, Viv and Buck joined Nat, Jax, Dallie and Jack at the dining room table. Everyone was scattered around the dining room, living room and breakfast table. The house was louder than Viv had ever heard it, but it was good to see everyone smiling, laughing, and having a good time. The food was delicious as always and the company was jovial. Viv chatted with Nat about the baby and Nat's column and with Dallie, who seemed more distant than usual, about her classes and Viv encouraged her to be patient with Cole's trial and not to worry too much.

Morgan sat at the end of the table, chatting with Nate and David. He appeared shy and quiet, serious even, but perhaps it was simply because he didn't know anyone and didn't have much to say.

Viv could see that he'd already grown close to Jordan, following his own mother's untimely death from cancer, for she seemed to make his smile brighter with her presence. Who could blame him? Jordan was funny, witty, and flirty- a breath of fresh air.

Scottie and Ginger chatted with Luth and Bella, their boys bantering as Luth gave them a look. Gavin, his wife and son were seated at the bar; Elias playing peek-a-boo with baby Jackson, who gave out sweet little cackles. Viv wasn't sure where Vanna and Kels had gone to but there was no telling with those two. Wherever they were, they were probably avoiding Morgan like the plague—well Kelsey anyway. Viv smiled again, remembering the sparks that had flown from the two adolescents and wondered if fate would see fit to bring them together one day after all. She cupped at her belly and rubbed ever so lightly, contemplating fate's twisted sense of humor and how it had seen fit to bring her and Buck together. She smiled up into his scruffy handsome face, falling for him even more than she already was. He seemed to sense it too and gave a grin back before hopping up from his seat, grabbing a fork and his glass, and getting everyone's attention.

Buck hit the fork against his crystal goblet of water and the entire house began to quiet down. "Everyone. Sorry. Not tryin' to steal the show or nothin' here. But I mean, I *am* Buck Jenkins and all though, so that would only be typical of me." That statement got a few laughs and even Vivian couldn't help but smile as Buck's sexy brows raised and he shrugged. "Naw, seriously though, I just wanna commend Nate and Jordan on finding their son. I know that they're both stunned and excited. Kinda like me with my little peanut over here."

"Aww," surrounded them, coming from the ladies, and smiles greeted them as the crowd began to congratulate them on their baby. Viv blushed and looked up at her baby's father.

"Morgan, it sure is good to meet you, buddy. I recently lost my mother to cancer too, so I know what you're going through, and I just wanted you to know that I'm here any time you need to talk to someone...especially if it's about football." Buck winked, and Morgan gave him a sly grin and nodded. "Now, that gorgeous redhead to the right of you is also a good one to talk to, and she keeps your secrets too." Jordan's teary eyes met his and she puckered her lips and blew him a kiss. "Your Aunt Natalie and Uncle Jack are some of the best people I know. Their kids are gonna be your best friends, I'm certain of it. Your Grandma and Paw-Paw are simply amazing and this crazy group right here," Buck pointed to Luth's brood then and Scottie. "Well, they're all on your team too... What I'm tryin' to say is- you couldn't have hand-picked a better family to be a part of. We've all been here for one another through thick and thin. Good times and bad. We've all had each other's backs—well, that is until a couple of knuckleheads got to fightin' over—" Scottie shoved him, and Buck laughed.

"If I remember correctly, you weren't exactly innocent in all that crap either, you shit-starter," Scottie threw back, and Buck shook his head, amused.

"Like I said- good *and* bad...but here we are. Grown with kids of our own coming up. It seems like just yesterday we were their age."

He pointed over to Vanna and Kels, who'd poked their heads into the dining room doorframe, and Viv smiled at the two of them as they blushed at being called out. "Anyway, I just wanted to say welcome to this crazy family, son. Don't take it for granted." The seriousness in Buck's tone hit straight to Viv's gut, and when Buck sat down, she pulled him to her for a searing kiss. When she pulled back, there were tears streaming her face. "What was that for?" Buck asked softly, taking her hand.

"For being wonderful."

"*Wonder*ful, huh? Well, darlin', you just wait till—"

"Buck?" Nat was standing behind Buck's chair with her cell phone in hand, looking solemn. "It's Blair."

Buck's eyes went from Nat's to Viv's, and apprehension grew in Vivian's tummy as he stood and took the phone from Natalie. Viv went with him and proceeded out to the front porch, following him as he said, "Hello?"

They were the only two out there, much to Viv's relief as the conversation turned heated.

"Dammit, I'm sorry! I know…No. Blair! Alright. Where? Just calm the hell down. Fine! But— Alright. Yes. I'm goin' right now." Buck huffed and ended the call, looking anxiously over at her.

"What's the matter?" Viv asked as her palms went to his chest and his head lowered.

"Dad's drunk over at the Rusty Spur. I gotta go get him and take him home."

Viv thought about how early in the day it was; it wasn't even four PM yet. She simply nodded.

"Just stay here and I'll come back and get you."

"No," Viv said and shook her head. "I'll just go with you."

Buck gazed intently at her before nodding. "Alright. Let's go."

CHAPTER 13

*B*uck had never felt worse in his life following the butt-chewing he'd just received from his sister, Blair. She was livid with him. He'd not called them since before he and Viv had gone to L.A. to Viv's check-up, but things had happened in such a whirlwind, one after the other—the press conference, the trip to Atlanta, the impromptu vacation, getting the charity event situation organized, the barbecue with the Kinsens and Butlers. And when they were on the vacation, he hadn't wanted to call, he'd just wanted a break from everyone and everything. He had no excuses, he knew that. But being around his father right now wasn't easy for him. It reminded him of the loss, the anguish, the pain of not having his mother around. Vivian had helped some of that. Following the funeral, she'd breathed life back into him, and he'd held tight to the prospect of joy that the life growing inside her yielded. Seeing his father crying, upset, drunk, and emotional was going to be difficult.

He knew he'd been back from Mexico for four days now and could've made a five-minute phone call just to check up, could've made plans to go out on the lake fishing with his dad, but Buck just hadn't had the heart to hear the sadness in his father's voice, the permanence of his solitude, the finality of death that permeated every pore of his father's skin.

Viv's grip on his hand tightened, and he looked over at her, giving her a soft smile. God, he was so in love with her. She was gorgeous, everything about her, and radiant, and he wanted to feel her light shine into every dark corner of his being.

He pulled into the gravel parking lot of the dilapidated bar that had as many bad memories for all of them as good. He started to tell Viv to stay in the truck, but she opened the door before he had a chance. Buck simply prayed his father didn't cause any more of a scene than he probably already had.

He took Viv's hand as they approached the door, opened it for her, and let his eyes adjust to the darkness before them.

He spotted Louise behind the bar and waved at her, getting a reproachful smile, before he noticed his father seated on a barstool, leaning over the bar counter.

He cautiously approached and planted his big hand on his dad's back. "Hey, Pops. How are ya?"

"Why the hell would *you* care?" came a muffled voice as his father's head raised.

Here we go, Buck thought, waiting to be lashed out at for his negligence.

"You just go off and live your life, to hell with your family."

"C'mon Dad, don't be—"

"It's been two weeks, five days and twelve hours since she passed away, and I've heard from you once in that time frame. *Once!*" his dad yelled. "Do you know how upsetting it is to hear that I'm having a grandchild from the fuckin' news instead of from my son's own lips?"

"Dad, I know. I'm sorry."

"You're fuckin' sorry, alright. Selfish! You're fuckin' selfish is what you are, Bobby Joe Jenkins."

The infliction in his father's eyes hit him right where it hurt. Buck *had* been a bit selfish as of late. Blair had said the same thing.

After all, his father had been sleeping on her couch and Beth's too, so he didn't have to go home alone when Buck had a huge mansion his father could have stayed in, but he'd been too selfish to volunteer it…and he'd been too wrapped up in the sweet little starlet he was starting to fall head over heels for.

"C'mon, Dad. We're goin' home."

"I don't wanna go home," his father cried, shoving at Buck's reaching hands. "I'm not going home. It's not home without her." His tone softened, and he began to sob, ripping Buck's heart in two.

"I know. I'm taking you home with me."

"I don't wanna go home with you. I'm mad at you."

"Yeah, well, Blair and Beth need a break too, Dad," Buck whispered, sadly.

The eyes that sought his out were azure blue and filled with water. "I know, I'm a damn mess. I don't need any of you to say it."

"Dad, you're just drunk right now. You need to rest. It's gonna be alright."

"No. No, It's not. It's never gonna be alright. I don't know how to live without her." His father began to weep and laid his head back down on the bar, tearing a hole straight through Buck's chest. It hurt so much that he winced.

Buck suddenly felt a soft hand gripping his forearm and turned to see Vivian smiling compassionately at his dad. "Mr. Jenkins," she cooed and her hand moved to his father's shoulder. "Why don't you come home with Buck and I? We have plenty of room. In fact, we'd love the company, and I have some things I want to show you that we bought for the baby. We could really use some help setting up the nursery. Besides, I make some mean pancakes." Vivian's eyebrows went up and she got a smile out of Buck's old man. "Don't tell me you don't like peanut butter banana pancakes because if you say no, I'll have to make a believer out of you." Her smile deepened, and Buck's dad actually laughed.

"I would like that," Buck's father finally said and he turned toward them.

Buck had to assist him to the truck. He was staggering, and Buck shot a scowl back to Louise. How damn many drinks had the man had? And why in hell hadn't she cut him off?

"My truck," Bill said absent-mindedly as Viv jumped into the backseat and gave shotgun over to Buck's father.

"Don't worry, Dad. Let's just lock it up, and we'll deal with it tomorrow, alright?" Buck took the keys from him and hit the lock on the keypad before hauling his dad up into the passenger seat.

When Buck hopped into the driver's seat, he noticed that Vivian had leaned forward, taken his father's hand in her own, and was softly stroking it as Bill leaned his head over on the window, sobbing again.

Tears hit Buck's eyes, and he turned to face forward, not wanting Viv to see how affected he'd been by what had been said and what was happening.

The ride was silent save for his father's sobs that tore right through his heart and broke it into a million pieces. When they pulled up out front of his house, Buck parked close to the stairs and assisted Viv out before helping his father. Viv took the keys, unlocked the door, and opened the guest room door downstairs, helping Buck remove his dad's shoes as he moved him into the bed and under the covers. By then, his old man wasn't coherent, and Buck cut the lights off and shut the door. He turned to Viv whose eyes were red-rimmed and gave her a gentle nod; a silent thank you for simply being there.

She understood and cupped his cheek, her chocolate brown eyes burning deeply into his so intensely that he knew in that instant he wanted her to be his for all eternity. Vivian Alexander. His woman. His love. His life.

He was going to marry her, make her his wife, love, cherish, and worship her like his father had his mother, so that even in death, he'd be unable to live without her there beside him, giving him the breath he needed in order to do so.

*

*B*uck awoke to an empty bed, turning to see that Vivian wasn't there. Easing himself out of bed, he frowned, remembering that she'd come to bed alone last night.

"I need to make some phone calls. Including one to Blair. She's furious with me," he'd said after they'd put his father to bed in the downstairs guest room.

Viv's beautiful blonde head had simply nodded in understanding as she went into the kitchen.

He'd started to tell her he wouldn't be long, but he'd known that wasn't entirely true. He'd gone into his study to think—as much to run from the feelings consuming his heart at that moment as to make those phone calls he'd needed to make.

He'd began with his sister, Blair, whose phone went straight to voicemail; of course she was gonna make him grovel, typical Blair fashion. Then he'd called Beth, who *did* answer and they'd had a long and lengthy discussion about what they should do regarding their parent's house. Beth had hesitated when he'd said they should sell it, that their father wouldn't go back there, but she'd said to give it more time. Their father could continue to stay with one of the three of them until he was ready to go home, that they shouldn't push him, but Buck knew in his heart that Bill Jenkins wouldn't step foot back in that house now that their mother had passed away there.

Then Buck had called his lawyer to discuss the retractions, their suing Vince for slander, and finally a prenup, to which Stan had been taken aback.

"*Really*, Buck? I figured the engagement was all for show," he'd scoffed. Yeah, that's what Buck had originally thought too, but was quickly starting to love having Vivian around full-time. Stan said he would draw one up to have on hand when the time came, but for Buck not to do anything *rash*. Why in hell was everyone telling him how to run his fuckin' life? Like he wasn't smart enough to do things right!

After that phone call, Buck had made several more, including one to Lincoln Porter, one to Marty Palmer, his former coach, and one to Marvin Greenway about the golf tournament next month then he'd called to get some furniture delivered for the nursery. He intended to have his dad help him and Viv set it up as Viv had suggested, figuring that perhaps it would give his father something to look forward to. And finally, he'd called his assistant, asking that he contact the marina and have them fuel up his boat and have it ready to go by noon the next day. He planned to take his father fishing on Ray Roberts Lake and make up for the time he'd been gone. Viv would understand. Maybe she could spend some time with Nat and Dallie while she was home for the weekend.

By then, it had been after nine thirty, and Buck had stretched his weary bones, shut the light off and headed upstairs to bed, seeing as all the lights downstairs were off at that point, save for the lamp in the foyer. He'd headed up and into his bedroom to see Viv propped up, sound asleep with the baby book across her belly. He'd removed it, making sure to mark her page, and sat it on the nightstand before undressing and crawling into bed with her. He'd kissed her cheek and pulled her into his arms where she'd cuddled into him which literally made his heart melt.

He'd slept soundlessly in the arms of the woman he loved.

Now, Buck stretched, threw some shorts on over his boxers, and padded barefoot downstairs. He could hear his father laugh and Vivian talking as he came through the foyer. He entered the kitchen to see Viv standing at the stove, flipping the pancakes that she'd promised to make his father last night. His father sat at the island bar, newspaper in his hands, reading a section to her.

"Man, these *are* amazing, Vivian. You were right. I think they might be my new favorite pancakes." His dad bit into one of the fluffy brown pancakes on his plate as syrup dripped from his lips, and Buck grinned knowingly to himself; he wouldn't mention the fact that they were made with organic coconut flour and vanilla protein powder or his old man might change his mind.

"Mornin'," Buck stated to them both and headed to the coffee pot.

"Good morning, sleepyhead," Viv said with a giggle and turned to cock an eyebrow at him. His eyes roved over her sexy frame clad in a hot pink tank top and shorts, hair all mussed on top of her head, and cheeks pink. He wanted to pull her enticing body against the erection her presence was always inducing.

Buck poured his coffee and approached her, giving her a sound kiss on her perfect lips, lingering to inhale her heavenly scent. His father cleared his throat then and they turned to look at him.

"So...y'all are engaged now?" his father assessed, looking at the giant ring on Viv's dainty little finger. Why did she have it on so early this morning? Did she not take it off before bedtime?

Viv blushed, turning back to the pancakes, and Buck just nodded, giving nothing away.

"That was a pretty quick move, huh?" Bill asked.

Buck tried to stymie his surprise at the question but caught Viv's forlorn look as he moved forward to talk to his dad.

"We needed to get the heat off of Viv is all. But...well..." Buck fumbled and turned to look at Viv whose eyes burned into his. The heat was so stifling, Buck felt as if he couldn't breathe.

"Well?" His dad's brows went up, waiting.

"It's only temporary, Bill," Viv stated, not looking at either of them, and Buck felt he'd missed a big opportunity.

His eyes moved to his father, who frowned back at him. Buck cleared his throat, trying to loosen some of the tension of the moment. "Uh, Dad...wanna go fishing today?"

"Can't," his father stated simply. "I got lunch with Blair and dinner with Ed, and I done told Miss Alexander here that I'd help her with the nursery." He gave Viv a bright smile.

Vivian blushed ten shades of red before she turned her head to look at Buck.

"Yeah, I got the furniture coming at two," Buck stated, not understanding why Viv was acting so aloof today. "That's fine. I mean, we can go another day. I just thought it was a nice day to be out on the lake."

His words hit his gut hard as he remembered that fated day on the lake when Abby drowned. He tried to hide it as Viv grabbed his bicep and handed him a plate of pancakes, but she'd seen the ghastly look on his face. He thanked her and smiled as he moved to sit in the stool next to his father, who'd dropped the paper by then to watch them interacting.

"Well, I'm gonna take a shower. You guys enjoy," Viv stated, pulling the hand towel off her shoulder and setting the spatula down. She turned away, not looking at either of them as she headed off into the foyer.

Buck wanted to go after her, to ask her what was up, but he didn't. He looked down at his plate of fluffy, thick pancakes and although his belly growled, he suddenly wasn't hungry.

"What the hell is the matter with you?" his father said and shoved at his arm.

"What do you mean?"

"You know very well what I mean! That woman is in love with you, and I bet you haven't even had the balls to tell her that you love her back. Have you?"

Hell no, he wanted to scream but held his ground.

His father sighed heavily and squeezed the bridge of his nose with his thumb and index finger. "Have you not seen how damn short life can be, Bobby?" His father shook his head. "What are you waiting for?"

Buck wasn't entirely sure *what* he was waiting for. The time just hadn't seemed right was all.

"Listen to me. That woman is carrying your child…apparently. Not that I've heard it come out of either of *your* mouths," his father scolded.

Buck nodded. "She is, Dad. She's 11 weeks along."

"Then make an honest woman out of her. Tell her how you feel. Women like that don't come around every day. You know that as well as I do." He patted Buck's back a bit harder than necessary and looked him straight in the eye. "If you knew what I know, you'd snatch her up in a heartbeat and spend as much time confessing your undying love for her as you possibly could...while you still have time." With that, his father walked away, leaving Buck alone to his thoughts.

He didn't need his father—or anyone else for that matter—telling him how short life was and how precious. He'd lost his niece, his mother, *almost* lost his best friend in the entire world, and as he'd gotten older, he'd started to realize how important his friends and his family were to him. He wasn't sure what he was waiting on, but as he covered his pancakes with plastic wrap, stuck them in the fridge, then headed down to the basement to bust his ass in the weight room, he made up his mind.

He was going to tell Vivian Alexander that he was head over heels in love with her...and he was going to do it today.

✦✶✦

*V*ivian smiled as she put the plum-colored microfleece blanket over the rail of the gorgeous mahogany sleigh baby bed and stepped back.

The room had been painted a lovely deep grey two days ago, and as they waited for it to dry, she and Buck had picked out the rest of the furniture, accessories, and some toys and books to fill it.

"I really hope this baby turns out to be a girl," Bill said and patted her back.

"Oh now, Gramps, if it's a boy then we'll just donate the stuff to a good cause," Buck teased and winked over at his father, stilling Viv's heart.

God, he looked ruggedly sexy as hell dressed in his workout gear, his bulging arms swollen from his workout. She groaned internally as he lifted the box with little effort, his biceps flexing.

"Gramps, ha!" Bill scoffed, and they all laughed. "It's lovely though, either way. I'm happy for the both of you. This kid is gonna be rotten though, I can already tell." He smiled as he turned towards her. "Now, don't think I'm rude, but I promised to be at my brother Ed's at seven and I gotta run. Can't keep the man waiting, not real patient, that one."

"Wonder where he gets that from?" Buck mumbled. "Doesn't run in the family or anything."

"I heard that," Bill retorted and took Viv's hands. "Now, tomorrow night, you and I will dig out some old movies and make a pizza on that Big Green Egg my son never uses." Bill smiled warmly into her eyes, and she nodded.

"It's a date," Viv confirmed, eager to know more about Bill Jenkins, her baby's grandfather.

"Any room for me on this date," Buck whined and crossed his big arms over his chest.

Bill waved him off, and Viv laughed as Bill saw himself out of the room.

Vivian looked around the nursery then, admiring their work and felt Buck step up behind her.

"We really are kinda screwed if it's a boy, you know?" he noted, and Viv shrugged. It was too beautiful to change now. "Although, I guess purple *is* a royal color and with his father being a lion and all…"

Vivian laughed as she turned to face him. Buck's hands came to her waist, his eyes softer than she'd ever seen them before. Time stood still and nothing mattered but the two of them, in this room, the room they'd fashioned for the life they'd created growing inside her.

His big palm cupped her cheek, and she gulped. He was going to say it. She knew that he felt the love she felt too. He had to. He simply had to.

A hard banging came at the front door then and the door chime assaulted their ears as the moment broke. Buck took a deep breath in, startled. Viv blushed and bowed her head.

"I bet he forgot his keys." Buck shrugged and moved toward the door. Viv followed and propped herself on the railing as Buck descended the stairs easily and opened the door with a, "Did you for—"

The stance Buck took became defensive as his hand moved off the big front door to his side, and Vivian began robotically moving down the stairs, wondering who he could possibly be staring at that way.

"What the fuck are you doing here?" Buck asked and crossed his arms over his chest, his lips pulling into a scowl. Viv heard a muffled voice and moved to stand behind Buck, attempting to peek over his broad shoulder to see the person he was so intent on.

"Vivian!" It was Vince. Why on earth was Vince there?

"Vince?" She moved to stand beside Buck, who didn't move an inch.

"Vivian, please? I need to talk to you." His purple and black hair shimmered in the sunlight as his head moved up to Buck. "And apologize. Can I come in?"

Vivian looked up at Buck and silently pleaded with him to lighten up.

"You have some damn nerve showing up here, you son of a bitch." Buck took a menacing step forward, and Vince slunk back. "Do you realize the damage you've caused? We're in the process of suing you, right this minute, so your days are numbered. Mark my words," Buck growled.

"Buck, let's just hear what he has to say," Viv recommended and placed her hand on his bulky bicep. He turned toward her then, his clear blue eyes a torrent of emotion. She simply nodded and pulled at his arm. He moved enough so that Vince could come through the doorframe, and he did, seeming relieved, as if he'd just survived an attack.

"You've got five minutes. Starting now." Buck looked down at the Rolex on his wrist and looked expectantly back to Vince, who faltered.

Viv had never seen Buck so defensive and wasn't sure whether to be intimidated or turned on. No wonder he was defensive player of the year for four years straight, a pro Hall-of-Famer, and a legend. He was downright foreboding when he wanted to be. Internally, Viv swooned.

"Such a lovely home you have, Buck," Vince began. His well-manicured hands went up, and he moved his dark sunglasses into his wild hair. He was clad in a black silk button-down, purple plaid vest, and black slacks.

"*Four* minutes." Buck's blond eyebrows went up.

"Well, first off. I'm terribly sorry for the way I treated you, Vivian. *Both* of you," he added. "I don't know what I was thinking, I—"

"Save that shit for the lawyers. If that's all, you can go," Buck cut him off, his patience wearing thin as he approached, ready to haul Vince out the door.

"No, wait, it's not. I—Viv. I *need* you. Please! I can't do this movie without you." Vince's pleading was sorrowful, needy, pitiful as his hands came together in a steeple. "I tried to replace you. It's horrible. The girls. They—They're just not *you*. This movie is going to ruin me. I beg you—"

"Alright. Time's up, dude. Get out of here. She's fuckin' done with you."

"NO! Please? I'll do anything. *Anything*. This movie was supposed to be my masterpiece, and if you're not in it, Vivian, I'm gonna lose everything." Vince began to cry, and Vivian felt the pain rip through her. Perhaps it was her pregnancy, but her heart went out to the highly talented and overly dramatic director.

"Beggin' is so pathetic, Vince. Take your well-rehearsed speech elsewhere. I just can't." Buck rolled his eyes and herded Vince to the door.

"Vivian, I swear to God. I'll do *anything*. I need you. You're a Hollywood actress. It's where you belong. Think about it. Just think about it. One month. I just need one month. I promise." Vince's pleading was muffled as Buck literally pushed him out the door and shut it behind him, sighing heavily as he did so.

Vivian stood dejected in the echo of the foyer, head down, biting her lip and planting her hands on her hips.

"Do you *believe* the nerve of that guy? What the hell is the matter with him, huh?" Buck laughed humorlessly as he stepped in front of her. His hands came to her waist and he looked down at her. "Wait. C'mon, Viv? Don't tell me you're *actually* considering this?" The look in his eyes was incredulous. Then he frowned and Viv felt anger suddenly hit her cheeks.

"Well, he's kinda right, isn't he?" she said indignantly.

"Right? Right about what exactly?"

"Buck, I'm an actress. What am I doing here?"

Buck huffed and planted his hands on his hips. "Well…" he began.

"Exactly! I've been gone for weeks now. It's been a fun vacation, but let's be honest, that's precisely what this has been." And she realized it was true. She didn't belong here. Hollywood was her home, not nowhere Texas.

"A vacation? Viv. You left the set. Twice now. And of your own accord. Obviously, that wasn't where you wanted to be."

"I know," she scoffed. "But perhaps I should go back."

"Why on earth would you do *that*? He's insulted you, multiple times in fact. He threw your name in the dirt. He practically called you my whore! You don't owe him a damn thing."

"No, I know I don't…but Hollywood is where I belong, Buck. And I should finish the movie that I started. I am responsible for my own actions, and as bad as Vince was to me, I wasn't fair to him either. I'm the one who didn't uphold my end of the contract to begin with."

"I honestly can't believe you're saying this." Buck shook his head.

"Well, believe it because I am."

"Why?"

Why indeed? She'd had a similar conversation with Jill just the other day when Jill asked when she was coming "home". Home. To

Malibu. To California. Where she was from. Where she belonged. She'd told her she didn't know. For she'd been enjoying playing house with Buck Jenkins. But that's really all it had been—playing house. Buck had yet to tell her he loved her. He'd put a ring on her finger, but he'd not asked her to marry him. He'd talked about a wedding, but they'd not begun to plan it. Because in all honesty, they both knew that no wedding was going to take place.

They were having a baby together, but they hadn't even talked about where that baby was going to grow up. Vivian couldn't stay here in Abundance. Could she? Would she be happy here? She was an actress. She needed that spotlight, needed acting gigs, and this little town didn't have any opportunities for that. Would Buck move to California to be with her? *No!* His family and life were here. And hers was there...

Buck, as if sensing her sudden change in demeanor, moved closer. "Vivian—"

"We made a mistake, Buck." She shook her head, regretfully.

"*What?* Why?"

"I can't do this." She gestured to the house, to him. He gulped, the hurt evident in his eyes, but he needed to know the truth. "I need to go home now."

"You *are* home, Vivian. This is your home now. Here with me."

She shook her head. "Buck, you feel guilty because of what happened, and I see that all this has been your way of making it up to me. Faking our engagement. Pretending to be my fiancé. Coming to my rescue when my name and career were in jeopardy. I appreciate and respect that...but this isn't going to work. We're only kidding ourselves."

"And why the hell not? It's been *working*...every damn day."

"Lust is only gonna cut it for so long, Buck." She gave him a sassy look, and he took a step back as if she'd slapped him.

"Viv, we *both* know there's much more between us than that. Don't tell me that you don't feel it too." He stepped closer, placing her hand on his chest, where his heart was.

"We were vulnerable. Both of us. And we sought comfort in one another. It was fun. Truly. But—"

"I'm in love with you, Vivian. Please, don't do this." The tender look on his handsome face had her reeling. It looked so real. But he'd just lost his mother mere weeks ago. He was seeking love in any outlet he could. He was sacrificing his pride now, and she should feel special, but all she could feel was determination to salvage her career, her name, this movie that she'd not even given a chance, simply because she'd been so wrapped up in the implications of being middle-aged. It was time to make things right, on her own, without the help of Buck Jenkin's good name and reputation to keep her afloat.

"Oh, Buck. You've been kind, but I *need* to do this. I'm sorry. Thank you. For everything." She gave him a sweet smile and cupped his cheek.

"Did you not hear what I just said, Vivian Alexander?" His arms came back around her waist and he repeated his words even as they reverberated through her, filling her heart. "I *love* you." His forehead rested on hers.

"You love the idea of me, Buck. We made one hell of a star-studded cast, but the act is over."

"Dammit, don't tell me what I feel," he scolded without conviction as his lips fell to kiss hers.

She pushed him back and looked down, knowing his kiss would only stop her from doing what she needed to do. She pulled the ring off her finger—even as it stung to do so—and handed it up to him. He grimaced and shook his head, indicating for her to put it back on.

"Leave it on. There's been enough media coverage of our love life for one lifetime. We'll go to the media when the time is right." His dismissal gave her even more courage to flee. If he truly loved her, he wouldn't let her leave, would he?

Vivian nodded, agreeing that she wasn't ready to face the media with the pain of walking away from him. She replaced the ring, feeling it sear her heart as she did so.

She pulled out of his embrace then, as he reluctantly let her go, and she began walking upstairs to pack her bag.

He didn't follow, much to her surprise, and she quickly began throwing her clothes from his closet into her bag. It didn't take long as she didn't have a ton of stuff here, but as she moved to the nightstand to retrieve her baby book, the finality of it all hit her square in the chest, and she blinked back the scorching tears that started to come forth.

Save them, she told herself. *Use them for the movie that you have to finish.*

When she rolled her luggage out to the landing, Buck stood there, his face unreadable.

"I'll take this. I have a car waiting out front."

She only nodded, not trusting her voice. She followed him, glancing back into the nursery they'd finished just moments ago as her heart began to tear apart at the seams. She looked at his strong, muscular back not sure why it was suddenly so unbearable to think about leaving when she'd just told him it wasn't her home. She felt so completely out of sorts.

Buck opened the door, closing it behind them when they were out then moved to open the limo door. As she got in, he placed her luggage in the trunk, and stuck his head back in the door, his eyes orbs of blue fire as he looked her over. "I'm not going to beg you to stay, Vivian."

That's right...because he was a lion and lions had pride and didn't beg.

"If this is what you want to do then who am I to tell you not to go? This is *your* choice and your decision, and I won't be the one to stand in your way." He looked down quickly then back up, his eyes holding her captive as he said, "But don't think for one second that I'm ok with this because I'm *not*. When filming is over, you and our baby are coming home."

With that, he slammed the door.

CHAPTER 14

*T*hree weeks flew by as Buck Jenkins tried to distract himself as best he could, staying busy getting everything ready for his charity golf tournament and car show. He'd planned, organized, and gotten a shit ton of celebrities involved, and was genuinely pleased as the day approached, despite how much he missed his sexy blonde starlet.

His family and Natalie had been stunned to learn of Vivian's return to Hollywood to finish the movie she'd started months ago. Buck had made it seem less final than Viv had and assured them she'd be back, but Buck wasn't so sure, despite his demand that she was coming home following filming, especially since she had yet to return any of his calls and texts and messages to Jill.

He'd tried hard not to appear to be a man apart as he and his dad hung out, fished, cooked, and watched movies together, but inside, his heart was breaking into a million little pieces that only one thing —one woman—could mend.

How had he not actually told her he loved her until she was leaving him? How convenient it had seemed. And she hadn't believed him? And why would she? They'd made love dozens of times, and he'd had ample opportunities to say it. But no, he had to wait until she was walking away, making him look like he was desperate to say anything to keep her from going, when the truth of it was that he'd loved her all along.

From the minute he'd seen her in the Ponderosa Ballroom of the Austere hotel in Dallas that June evening, he'd felt his entire world shift. He'd felt his heart expand and knew he'd fallen in love with her upon making her his and planting his seed, his child, inside her. That had been it for him. So, why hadn't he bothered to say all this *before* he'd been stupid enough to let her walk out of his life?

He was sulking on this early October day and wondering if Vivian was as miserable in Seattle as he was here in Abundance. Sure, he could pretend, but he'd known it was only a matter of time before he had to inform everyone Vivian was gone—really gone. The thought turned his stomach. He'd not been able to sleep in their bed, not been able glance into that beautiful nursery they'd decorated, not been able to look at himself in the mirror even, because he was totally and completely wretched without the woman he loved.

He put on a good show that morning, acting the part of the grateful, exuberant host of his charity golf tournament, playing his best golf game yet and chatting it up with movie stars, ball players, and race car drivers alike. On the outside, nothing was amiss, but on the inside, he was broken, battered, and bruised, screaming his rage at letting the best thing that had ever happened to him walk away without a fight.

In the days that followed Vivian's departure, Buck tried to convince himself she just needed time to think, space, a chance to change her mind about what had been between them, but after a week went by without a return phone call, his heart had plummeted into his stomach and he realized the reality of the situation—Vivian wasn't coming back. He'd panicked, drank himself into a blind stupor, and pleaded with God above not to take another person he loved away from him. Then he'd gotten mad, mad at himself then mad at her for giving up so easily. Then he'd doubted himself—what if she was right? What if it had all been a façade? What if he was simply seeking love wherever he could because he *had* just lost his mother. His loss had been so great that he'd needed something, someone, to replace it. After all, Vivian had never said she loved him. And now he was starting to wonder if she ever had…

He smiled over at Jack and Natalie then as they approached. Jack gave him a firm handshake and patted his arm, thanking him for inviting them.

"Of course," Buck responded. "I mean after all, Nat is our famous journalist." He gave her a wink and pulled her into a hug.

"I'm gonna grab some water, baby," Jack said and headed off to a refreshment stand set up behind the clubhouse close to the practice range, giving Buck and Nat a minute to talk.

Natalie took Buck's face in her hands as he sat back down on the bench. "Buck, you look like shit."

"That's the second time you've said that to me recently, Nat. You're gonna hurt my feelings." He pouted, more genuine than he wanted her to know.

Natalie rolled her eyes. "Seriously? I'm only tellin' you the truth. What happened?"

"You mean you *don't* know." His brows went up sarcastically. Nat was Viv's BFF after all.

"No." Nat's hand went to her hips. "She says everything's fine, but I can hear it in her voice that it's not. And by the looks of you, I'm right. So…what did you do?" she asked.

"*Me?* I didn't do *anything*! Vince came to the house and suddenly, she was Mother Theresa as if he'd done no wrong. She did an instant 180 and had to go finish the movie. It was like pure duality—Jekyll and Hyde kinda shit." Buck grumbled, finally showing the foulness bottled up inside.

"Did you piss her off? I mean there *had* to be a reason."

"No. I mean—I don't *think* so. Fuck, Nat, I don't know. Dammit!" He covered his face with his hands, rubbing his tired eyes.

"Well, it's been three weeks and she hasn't talked to you, so you obviously did something wrong. And don't tell me you're giving up. Because I'll kick your ass, I don't care how big you are."

Buck gave her a withered look. "No, of course I'm not givin' up. I want her back. But apparently, she wants to stay in Hollywood. It's where she *belongs*," he grumbled again, mocking Vivian's tone when she's said the same thing.

Nat frowned in turn. "Yeah, well, it's no place to raise a child."

"Tell me about it."

Jack came back about that time and handed them both a bottle of water before throwing his own back. He chugged it dry before replacing the cap and tossing it into the recycle bin not far from where they stood. "Vivian loves you, Buck," Jack said with certainty, out of the blue.

"You think so?" Buck asked, hopefully, his heartrate quickening.

"I do. She was as nervous as a cat on a hot tin roof that day at the barn. I saw how she looked at you while we were on vacation and at the barbecue, like you were all that existed. I'm pretty familiar with those looks." Jack winked over at his wife, who gave him the very same look he'd just described, and Buck scowled.

"Guys, I don't know what to do, here. I mean. If this isn't where she wants to be then it doesn't matter *what* I want." He was whining now, he realized.

"Have you thought about going to her?" Nat asked.

"And say what? She won't even answer my calls…and her manager won't either."

"Vivian is—"

"Stubborn?"

Nat shook her head. "Set in her ways."

"Ok, that pretty much means the same damn thing, Nat."

Jack laughed. "Viv is not one to bow out easily. She sets her mind to something and she finishes it. Maybe she's trying to prove a point to herself."

"Well, she didn't finish *this*. She just up and left, saying it wouldn't work."

"Then Buck, prove her wrong." Nat's brows went up in a challenge.

It could work, but Buck had no idea where to even start proving Vivian wrong. He'd known how different they were in the beginning, but he hadn't let that stop him from taking her, loving her, and wanting to make her his in every way possible. The thing was—they had been so happy. How had she not seen how alive she made him, how good they felt together...and not just sexually?

Buck sighed heavily and closed his eyes, his entire body exhausted.

He heard Nat gasp in surprise and looked up, his heart hammering in his ribs, hopeful to see the one person he knew wouldn't dare show up, but wishing with everything in him that she came.

He was both surprised and disappointed when his eyes fell on someone he never expected to come back home in a million years. Buck stood and laughed out loud.

"Well, I'll be damned...Rick Singleton. You son of a bitch."

✦✱✦

*R*ick laughed as he approached Buck, Natalie, and Jack. He smiled, genuinely happy to see the friends he'd not seen in over eight years.

His eyes fell on the beautiful woman he'd worshipped for longer than he could remember. She looked utterly breathtaking in a coral silk dress that accentuated all her curves and highlighted her porcelain skin. Her sapphire blue eyes sparkled, her curly dark ribbons of hair framed her face. He beamed brightly at her and for once, his heart didn't ache as he did so. She hesitantly gazed back up at him as he took her hand. He understood her reproach and hated that he'd ever made her feel uncomfortable, although he knew he had—more times than not.

"Natalie," he said her name not as a prayer like he always had, but in relief, in finality, in closure. "Jack." His gaze moved to Natalie's tall, muscular, horse-trainer husband, who looked equally as irked to see him as Nat had. Jack shook Rick's hand dutifully, the ever-mindful gentleman he was, and tipped his hat at him. Then there was Buck, who smiled brightly at him and pulled him in for a hug.

"How the hell have you been?" Buck asked, patting his back.

"I'm great. It's good to see all of you. I want you to meet some-one." Rick turned to look at his gorgeous date, who was dressed to the nines in a flattering red dress that looked like it had been poured over her voluptuously curvy body.

"Guys, meet my date, Carmella Lopez."

All their eyebrows shot up as Rick's arm went around Carmella's waist, realizing that this stunning, light-brown skinned Spanish goddess was with him.

Buck's eyebrows were the first to furrow, as if Rick was playing a trick on him. "Wait a minute," he said and rubbed at his scruffy chin as his voice dropped. "Is she one of those ladies you *pay* to come to events with you?"

Rick's mouth literally fell open and he gaped at Buck, who shrugged. But it was Carmella who—instead of being offended—actually busted out into laughter.

"No, gringo, he didn't *have* to pay me." She gave Buck a wink, and it was Buck's turn to crack up. Rick laughed along with him, feeling both relief and elation.

"Buck Jenkins, it's a pleasure, darlin'," Buck said and took her hand, kissing the back of her knuckles—his usual charming self.

Rick watched as Carmella took Natalie's hand and gave her a big smile. "And *you* must be Natalie." Nat looked apprehensively from Carmella to Rick, and he couldn't fight the blush that hit his cheeks then. "I'm very glad to finally meet you," Mel said.

Nat just smiled back, once she'd recovered, and shook Mel's hand. "Thank you. It's nice to meet you, Carmella."

Mel then moved to Jack. "And Jack, is it? Es un vaquero muy guapo, amante," she said to Rick, indicating that Jack was a good-looking cowboy as she shook Jack's hand. As if Rick didn't already *know*. He rolled his eyes. She'd taught him a few Spanish phrases, and he'd picked them up fairly quickly.

"Ah, gracias, señorita." Jack winked, surprisingly understanding her, and Carmella just laughed and shoved at him.

Great! Now his girlfriend was flirting with his former arch nemesis. There really was no fairness in the world after all.

Jack tipped his hat at her as she gave him his hand back, and she nudged Rick as if to say she was only kidding. Nat tried to stifle a laugh too but didn't succeed, and she and Mel began giggling like two school girls.

"So, how'd you two meet?" It was Buck that asked. Rick just looked at Buck with an arched eyebrow, but Buck finally said. "Oh...*Ohhh!*" He covered his mouth as Jack, Nat and Carmella all looked at him.

"We met at work," Rick mumbled, feeling his cheeks flame.

"Well, we're glad to see you happy, Rick." Jack's eyes burned into Rick's then as his arm went around his wife's waist, and Nat nodded along with him, smiling as she looked up at her husband. Rick was sure Jack was simply glad Rick had stopped the relentless—albeit futile—pursuit of his wife.

"Thanks guys. I *am* happy," Rick stated before looking over to Carmella and giving her a genuine smile. She returned it, and for the first time since agreeing to come, Rick was pleased he had gotten the guts to do so.

It had been at Mel's insistence for him to attend the charity function. Rick had been adamant at first about avoiding his hometown and all the memories that simply speaking about the town brought with it. She said he'd needed closure—and he needed to be there for Buck—and there was only one way to find it. Now, as he looked at the woman he was no longer in love with, he finally felt free, as if his life wasn't meaningless, and he deserved the happiness he felt with the woman who'd stolen his heart that night in the darkness.

"So, Buck," Rick said and looked up at Buck. "Where's your fiancée? I'm eager to meet the famous, Vivian Alexander."

Rick was surprised to see Buck's smile plunge at the mention of her name and he frowned up at his tall, broad friend. "She, uh, she's still filming and couldn't get away," Buck said regretfully.

"Man, I hate that. Such a shame," Rick answered honestly. "What about Scottie and Luth, are they around?"

"Scottie's just over there with his new girlfriend," Nat said, pointing over to Scottie Warden and a pretty, petite, little strawberry blonde that his hands were all over. Rick smiled. Good for Scottie.

"Luth and Bells are over there." Buck pointed to the food trucks, where Luther and Bella Boyd stood in line for food.

"Wow, the whole gang's here, huh? Where's Nate and—?"

"*Rick?* Is that you?" Rick heard the familiar husky voice of his favorite redhead and turned around to see Jordan and Nathan Butler approaching. He gave a big smile as Jordan pulled him in for a hug. As he pulled away, Nate patted his back.

"It's good to see ya, Rick. How you been?" Nate asked as he bit into a corndog.

"I'm well. Guys, meet my girlfriend, Carmella."

Jordan's brows went up and she grinned like a shit-eating possum. "Well, well, Rick. You go, boy." She slugged his shoulder and extended her hand to Carmella, who shook it.

"Los señoras estan muy bonitas," Mel said to Rick.

"Spicy. I love it. Rick, she's good for you." Jordan winked. But really, Rick knew she was thinking, *It's about damn time you moved on.* For he'd thought the very same thing himself.

It *was* time. And seeing all his old high school friends, he was glad. He was glad to finally be free of unrequited love. Free from his bonds to Natalie Kinsen. He could now love her the way he should have been able to from the beginning. As his friend, and nothing more.

CHAPTER 15

*V*ivian cried herself to sleep for the third night in a row. She missed Buck with a pain that jolted her soul. She missed his big hands, his big smile, and his bigger than life personality. She missed his touch, his voice, his love-making; his hands on her baby bump, his whispers in her ear, his muscular body pressed close to hers. She missed everything about him. But she'd been the one to leave this time. Not him. She'd been the one to do it before he had the chance to break her heart in two…for a second time.

He'd told her he loved her three weeks ago, but it couldn't be true. Buck was a womanizer—he used them and discarded them—and she'd felt in her heart it would only be a matter of time before her usefulness had run its course. If he loved her then why had he only said it as she was leaving him? He was just saying it because he'd lost his mother and he was still reeling from her death.

Vivian tried to convince herself of these things, only she wasn't convinced. He'd been tender, kind, sweet, giving… He'd been amazing. He'd acted like he'd loved her. Was it possible that he actually did?

God help her. She was in love. Head over heels. Hopelessly. Truly.

Recklessly in love with Bobby "Buck" Jenkins. She wanted him with a hunger she'd never felt, with an ache that wouldn't be quieted. But as much as she loved him, she couldn't let him break her heart when he realized his "love" for her had all been forced, a play, a rouse. She couldn't stomach the thought of loving him and him not really loving her back. So, she'd fled. Back to her acting. Her outlet.

He'd faked the engagement just for show, faked being a fiancé, and she wasn't so sure he hadn't faked being excited to be a father. He wasn't a man to get himself tied down. He didn't want to get married, did he? He hadn't even asked her, he'd just purchased a ring and stuck it on her finger. And how was he going to deal with night time feedings and dirty diapers when the baby came? It was easy to play house until Vivian was unable to have sex with him for weeks on end, and a crying infant was keeping them apart both day and night. Their relationship was rocky, unstable... how on earth was it going to survive a baby?

He'd tried to call, text, and had left messages for Jill to give to her, but Viv had ignored them all. Unable to face him, his words, for fear she would run back to him in the heat of the moment. She had to be logical, rational. Everything that had happened with Buck had been spontaneous, random, and unplanned—a whirlwind of heated passion—and she'd loved every second of it. But that wasn't what people built relationships on. Trust. Stability. Support. She needed those things and she'd been afraid Buck wouldn't be able to give them to her.

Hollywood was her life. Fame and stardom were her life. Movies were her future. But that future had all been altered in the blink of an eye at seeing him that night at the ball and unequivocally giving herself to him in every way possible. In that moment, she'd given him everything she had to offer, without even realizing it. Now, she was left heartbroken and alone.

She cussed at herself as she turned in her California king bed to look at the clock, realizing it was after one AM. At least she could sleep in tomorrow. Filming was finally over, and Vince had been like a changed man. He'd been kind, giving, and doting, and Vivian had given him her very best over the last month. She'd thrown herself into filming, working long hours, days and nights, twenty-four/seven, so as to keep her mind off the man she loved and desired with everything in her.

She wiped at her tear-stricken eyes and got out of bed to grab some water.

She walked into the kitchen and poured herself a glass from the filtered jug in the fridge, chugged it down, and absent-mindedly rubbed her belly where the baby grew in her womb. She sat the glass down and sighed.

"Sweet baby, tell me what I should do. I don't know anymore. I miss him. I miss him *so* much. I don't know how much longer I can be strong." Viv whimpered and propped her back against the counter. "I'm scared. I don't know what I want anymore, only that I want *him.*"

But could she give up her career, could she give up Hollywood? And why did she *have* to choose? Why couldn't she have both? She sighed as she walked back into her bedroom and picked up her phone; she wanted to look at the last text that Buck had sent her—because she wasn't tortured enough, no, she had to torture herself further.

Buck: I'm not going to stop trying, Vivian. I love you. This lion needs his lioness.

She grinned at his words. They'd gone from pleading, to angry, to sappy over the weeks. But each one confessed his undying love in some form or fashion. And he'd sent flowers, cards, and love letters. When he'd sent baby booties last week, she'd lost it, burst into tears and almost broke down and called him, but she held her ground.

Jill wasn't very happy with her at the moment, saying Viv needed to at least call him back. She'd told Vivian that she had been too hard on him. But they were worlds apart, and no matter what, their lives were just too different. It simply couldn't work. The more time she'd spent on the set, the more she told herself that it was true…even if her heart stated otherwise.

Her phone beeped in her hands then and she gasped as a new voicemail came in from Buck. Why hadn't her phone rang? She doubled checked the time. It was right.

Buck: Hey, yeah, it's me again. It's like 1:05 in the morning. I'm here…yeah, at your house in Malibu. I know you're probably sleeping, but I can't take this distance anymore. I have to see you, Vivian. Touch you, hold you. I'm so completely miserable without you, darlin'. God, I wish you were awake. I'm so damn tempted to break in. God, if I knew I wouldn't scare you to death, I totally would. But I don't wanna hurt our little peanut. Dammit, I've missed you so much, my sweet starlet. Shit! I guess I shouldn't even ring the doorbell. I know you gotta be sleepin' at this time 'a night…Fuck, this was a bad idea. Dammit… I guess I can come back in the morning. I'll leave—

She ran toward the front door with the phone cradled to her ear, praying she hadn't missed him before he left.

As much as she wanted to see him, she couldn't believe he'd decided to come to her house at one in the morning. But then again, what had Buck Jenkins ever done that was conventional?

Her heart hammered in her chest, her breath catching, as she quickly turned the alarm off and threw the door open.

Her heart literally hurt as her eyes fell on him; his black cowboy hat, white t-shirt and jeans soaking wet from the rain that fell in buckets outside.

"Vivian," he said her name as if he'd just been given the keys to Heaven, and she couldn't hold back the tears that sprang to her eyes at the sight of him, here, on her doorstep.

"Buck?" She stepped back as he entered. "What are you doing here?" she asked as she looked down at his drenched clothes.

"I told you that once filming was done that you and my baby were coming home. Did any part of that not make sense to you?"

Vivian laughed humorlessly. "Buck." She shook her head.

"Did you *not* think I was serious?"

"This isn't the nineteen fifties. You don't own me. Besides we're not even married."

"Not yet we're not, but we're gonna be."

"Stop, Buck…just, please stop?" She turned and moved into the laundry room to grab him some towels. He was drenched and soaking her ceramic tile floors.

"Stop *what?*" he asked as he followed, and her body tingled with the closeness of his presence as he wedged himself in the doorframe.

"You *know* what." She turned to look up at him, his sky-blue eyes holding her suspended in space. "This game."

"What *game?* You think this is a game, Vivian? If this is such a game then why the hell are you still wearing my ring?" He took her left hand and pulled it up for her to look at the gorgeous piece of work on it. She did, and like always, her eyes were spellbound at the shimmering light that bounced off the diamond.

"Buck, you didn't even propose to me. You simply gave it to me."

"Is that what you want? A proposal? Will that make it real for you?"

Vivian shook her head.

"Then what? What's it gonna take for me to prove myself to you, Viv? Name it. You want the moon? Eh, I forgot my damn lasso." He was joking, but she didn't laugh, instead she sighed. "Baby, please? I want to be with you more than anything. I can't stand being away from you anymore. This month has been so damn hard. You want me to beg? I'll beg."

He dropped to one knee and began kissing her hand then he started to pull the ring off and Vivian protested. "Buck, stop it. What are you doing?"

"What I should've done a long time ago." He pulled his hat off and pressed it against his chest, cleared his throat, and slipped the ring into his back pocket. "Vivian Lisette Alexander. I, Bobby Joe 'Buck' Jenkins, haven't been the same since the night I finally got the pleasure to make your acquaintance. That night was the best night of my entire life, and the *only* regret I have is that I didn't get to wake up next to your gorgeous face the following morning." Vivian began to tear up then as that wonderful night flashed through her memory. "Losing my momma was the worst thing that's ever happened to me, darlin', but you…" Buck choked back a sob as tears began to fall from his eyes. "You, baby, were there for me. You helped bring me back to life when all I wanted was to go into the grave with her." He wiped his eyes and smiled up at her. "You and our baby gave me something to look forward to, something to hold on to, a reason to love again. And I do. I love you with all my heart and if that means I have to move in with you and live here in Hollywood then by God, that's what I'll do, darlin'. Because I ain't leavin' you ever again. Not even if you kick me out."

Vivian laughed then and wiped at her eyes. "Oh, Buck. I love you too."

"You do?" he asked, and she nodded with conviction in her eyes. "Oh, thank God. I was starting to wonder, but Nat and Jack said you did, so I had to just pray that they were right." Viv laughed again, but Buck's tone turned serious once more as he retrieved the ring from his pocket. "My sweet starlet, you see this ring?" Viv nodded in response. "I picked this out myself, you know? I chose it—"

"For the rubies?"

Buck shook his head, looking amused. "No, darlin', those aren't rubies." He pointed to the reddish/pink stones on the outside lining of the ring. "Look closer. They're garnets. For your birthstone."

Vivian's smile couldn't be contained and she giggled. "Oh, Buck."

"Now, will you do me the honor of making me the luckiest retired football player on the planet and let me take you off the market before George Clooney or Brad Pitt decide to take a stab at ya?"

Vivian laughed again and nodded her head. "Yes. I'll marry you, Buck Jenkins."

He gently took her finger and replaced the ring before shooting up and pulling her into his arms. "Thank God. I was afraid I was gonna have to do something drastic like visit a voodoo priestess or sell my soul to the Church of Scientology or something," Buck joked before planting his lips on hers. She had no response, for her body was starving for him, and his kiss was the spark to light the raging inferno engulfing her at that moment. She moaned as his tongue stroked hers, and he backed them against the washing machine, suddenly ravaging her mouth like he couldn't get enough of her.

"Oh, Buck," she gasped when he pulled back, and his mouth fell to her throat.

"Oh, God, baby, I've missed you. I've missed your kiss, your body, my baby." His hands moved to stroke her growing baby bump, and he chuckled. "Swear you'll never leave me again."

"Never," she agreed as his palms cupped her breasts. Her hands went to the hem of his shirt and she began tugging it off. "But if I do, you have to always come get me."

"Always," Buck confirmed, and sat her on the washing machine as his hands went to her face, angling it up to his as her hands sought the front of his jeans. He kissed her with an urgency he'd not had before then picked her up, and she wrapped her legs around him. Her tongue plundered his mouth, realizing just how much she'd missed the taste of him and the sound of his growl rumbling deep in his chest as she did so.

He walked them to the bedroom as his mouth tormented her back equally and when he laid her on the bed, she felt his growing need for her stiffen between them. His hands moved to her thighs and began tugging her pajama pants and undies down as she released the button on his jeans.

She moaned as his hands pulled at her shirt and ripped it over her head and her fingers unzipped his fly. She moved her hand into his boxers, and he swore as his head flew back.

Soon, they were naked, and their mouths were feasting on one another's while their hands explored all the places they'd been without for far too long.

Just as he was centering himself between her legs, Vivian felt a little bump inside her that wasn't a stimulation of her arousal.

"Buck?" she cried and took his hand, moving it to her rounded lower abdomen. "Feel."

She held his hand against her skin and searched his eyes as she waited to feel the little thump again. When it came, they both gasped.

"Oh my God. The baby just kicked. Hey, lil' darlin'. Did you miss your daddy?" Buck asked as tears came to Viv's eyes, and she grinned as the little kick came again. Buck gave a low chuckle. "That's all right, sweetheart, because Daddy ain't going anywhere, baby. Daddy's here and Daddy intends to make Mommy regret every second she's made him go without her." He growled as he lowered his body over Vivian's and he slowly slid his hardness inside her.

Viv cried out as her body took him in so easily. She savored how complete she felt having him filling her once more.

As he made love to her, looking into her eyes and feeding off her pleasure, time stood still, and nothing existed but their love. The love that had begun one magical June evening in Dallas. The love between a famous football player and his Hollywood starlet.

***

"*Y*es ma'am, my eyes are closed tight, Ms. Silver-screen."

"No peeking," Viv scolded even as she waved her hand in front of his palm-covered eyes.

"I would never," he admonished, and she almost laughed.

She drew Buck into her guest bedroom to where the suitcase was she'd had when she'd stayed in Dallas that night almost five months ago. It sat on the bed with a little souvenir on top. She'd not touched it since she'd come home all that time ago.

"Ok, so, you know how you said some things just aren't coincidence?"

"Yup, fate, darlin'. It's called fate."

She giggled. God, he was so adorable. "Well, I thought it was time I gave this back to you. I thought you might be missing it."

Buck uncovered his eyes and took in the black cowboy hat of his, centered on top of the small suitcase. He gave her a panty-melting smile that lit her whole body up in desire.

"My hat! I see you kept it." His gorgeous blue eyes gazed deeply into hers, and she felt her heart swell to bursting.

"I see you misplaced it." Her brows went up in humor.

"Nope. I didn't *misplace* it, my love. I left it exactly where it was meant to be."

"Oh?" She grinned, trying hard to hold her smile in even as his bulky arms wrapped around her.

"Yup! Ya see, baby doll, I didn't even realize it at the time, but I found a place to hang my hat that night."

"Oh, you did, huh?" her voice was sultry as her tiptoes lifted her higher into his embrace, her face angling up, her lips but a breath away from his.

"Yes, ma'am," his gruff voice was just above a whisper. "I told you once before. My hat's exactly where it belongs. Anywhere that you are, there I will be also."

EPILOGUE

"She's gorgeous, just like her momma," Buck said as he kissed the blonde head of his just-born infant daughter. She'd literally just been bathed and placed into her exhausted mother's arms. Buck had snapped pictures of his new daughter, crying like a baby as he watched them take blood, footprints, vital signs and dress her.

"And what are we naming this little doll?" Dr. Anjani asked, beaming up at them after she'd finished working on Vivian.

"Stella Rose Jenkins," Viv said proudly as she lovingly looked over at her husband beside her; Buck's heart melted at the sight of the two females he loved more than his own life.

"Such a beautiful name."

"Thank you, that was all my wife. I can't take any credit." Buck laughed.

The last five months had been utterly amazing. Viv had come back to Abundance with him after all. Following her last movie, she'd picked up a few cameo gigs on television shows in the Dallas area then decided to take a break in her third trimester seeing as air travel was discouraged. She'd also said she wanted to savor motherhood without having to balance a work schedule too. Buck had been relieved, but had taken his opinions out of the equation all together, not wanting to force her into a decision she would later regret.

They'd gotten married in early November at Bucks' house right in the garden with their families and friends surrounding them. They'd planned to have it at the Baptist church in town where Buck was a member, but that hadn't been good enough for Gwenyth, and Buck hadn't wanted to fight her on the issue, so they'd simply changed venues. He'd gotten to meet Viv's father Jacob, who seemed pleased to have him for a son-in-law and Viv's brothers and sisters. It had been a beautiful ceremony and reception, and Buck's sisters and father seemed thrilled to have Vivian join their family. They'd gone back to Linc's house in Mexico for a couple weeks on their honeymoon before returning home to get their nest ready for the baby that was coming.

They planned to head to Viv's Malibu home in a few months to show their daughter off, clean Viv's house out, and Buck and Viv had an interview with Naomi Wiley, the talk show host who'd originally put Vivian out of sorts in the first place. They were going to keep the Malibu house in the event that Viv got the itch to do more movies in the future. Buck hoped she stayed content in Abundance, but knew it would only be a matter of time before he'd have to uphold his part of the bargain and compromise. Perhaps this little bundle of joy in his wife's arms would keep her busy enough from wanting to return to her life of stardom too early, but Buck had a few tricks up his sleeve in case she got the itch. He planned to start a production company within the year, generating business for Vivian, himself, and his hometown. He'd already been talking to directors, cameramen, and producers and had looked into a script for a television series set out west, knowing his hometown would be the perfect setting.

Buck leaned down to kiss his wife and stroke the cheek of his baby girl, who looked so much like her mother.

"Wanna hold your daughter, husband?" she asked, and he grinned big.

"I don't wanna interrupt your time with her. She seems so content," Buck said, both nervous and eager to embrace his child for the first time.

"I've held her for nine months, I'm sure parting with her for a few minutes won't kill me." She winked and moved Stella into Buck's arms.

He took her gently, settling her into the crook of his left arm like she was a football.

"Hey there, lil' angel. Look at you," he murmured, his heart overflowing with love for this tiny infant who stole his breath. Stella opened her eyes and gazed up at him. He fell in love immediately.

"Buck, you look so handsome with our baby in your arms," Viv said.

He grinned big at his wife and arched an eyebrow at her, taking her hand in his.

"You're the most amazing woman in the world, you know that? You were such a trooper."

"You too. I'm so glad you didn't pass out."

"It was such an incredible experience." Buck stared down at his baby. "I'll never be able to explain to you both just how much I love you. I didn't realize what I'd been missing out on...until there was you." He looked back up at Vivian and kissed her knuckles, staring deeply into her eyes. She began to cry then and openly let the tears fall. "Darlin, I didn't mean to make you cry."

"Oh Buck, I know...it's just...I love you so much. Even more now that you've given me our sweet baby."

He just stared back at her, his love mirrored in her eyes.

A knock came at the door then, and Buck mentally prepared himself for the circus that was about to begin following his daughter's birth.

He took in a deep breath as Gwen walked through the door, trying hard to hide the constant irritation he felt in her presence.

Today was a happy day; she wasn't going to ruin it and if she started her shit, he would politely ask her to leave.

"Oh, honey, you look beautiful," she said to Vivian as she approached.

"Thank you, mother."

"Where's my little angel? Oh, look at how little and sweet. She's so blonde."

Did she expect their child *wouldn't* be blonde? Seriously? Buck gave a hard smile as she came to a stop in front of him.

"Can I hold my granddaughter?" she asked, smiling up at Buck and the look on her face surprised him.

"Of course, Gwen," he said and reluctantly gave his daughter over to his mother-in-law.

"Oh, how beautiful she is. Hey, sweet baby," Gwen cooed to Stella and moved toward Vivian.

"What did you two finally decide to name her?"

Buck grimaced, praying she wasn't going to pitch a fit once she found out the baby wasn't named after her as she'd suggested months ago.

"Stella. Stella Rose," Buck said before Viv could answer.

"Isn't that a wine?" she asked.

Buck gave her a look that if looks could kill she'd be dead at that moment.

"Yes, it is. And I love it, and I love the name," Viv said, standing her ground, and Buck looked back at Gwen, daring her to say otherwise.

"Oh! Well. It's a lovely name, dear," Gwen stated, looking back down at her granddaughter. "She looks like a Stella."

"She does," Viv agreed.

Buck looked at his child in his mother-in-law's arms and felt a twinge of pain and sadness encompass him. God, how he wished his mother could be here to see her grandbaby. Laurel Jenkins would have been straight up over the moon for sweet Stella. He flashed back to the last few things she'd said to him about finding a place to hang his hat and finding a good woman to settle down with. *Well, Mom. I did. And I've never been happier*, he thought to himself. He knew his mother would be proud of him and happy for him, happy he'd married Vivian and had a beautiful baby girl.

"I can't believe you're a mother, Vivian. Isn't it wonderful?" Gwen asked as she sat down on the end of Viv's bed. Buck came to sit down in the chair beside his wife, his arm going around her as he kissed her temple, inhaling her heavenly scent.

"I think I'm still in awe that she's actually ours," Viv said, grinning up at Buck.

"It's the best thing in the world. I can promise you that. And perhaps now that she's here, you can be done with acting." The surprise and hurt on Vivian's face angered Buck, but before he could respond, Gwen continued. "It's just not a reputable career, honey. That's all. It plunged you into a life of sin." Gwen shook her head sadly at Vivian. "Can't you see that? You were jumping from bed to bed. Drinking all the time. Doing things you wouldn't have done otherwise…God has blessed you now that you have settled down and gotten married. Now it's your duty to be a good role model to this sweet baby girl."

Vivian looked down, toying with her hands, and Buck decided it was best he stay quiet on this one. "Is that why you acted like you hated me? And disapproved of Buck in the beginning?"

"Vivian Lisette, I'm your mother. I've *never* hated you. Only your lifestyle choices. I apologize if I did a piss poor job of showing that to you, but I've always only wanted what was best for you. As for Buck here, well, when he showed up on my doorstep all cocky, no, I didn't like him. He was a womanizer before he met you and his reputation proceeded him. I expected him to break your heart and leave you to raise this child on your own, but I can see now just how much he loves you. It's very obvious." She gazed into Buck's eyes, trying to make him see her point, and suddenly, now that he was a father, he understood. He would battle Heaven and Hell to keep his daughter safe and out of harm's way, especially if he was uncertain of lurking danger near her.

Buck gave her a big smile then and tipped his hat at her. "Well said, Mrs. Stanfield."

"Nonsense, Buck Jenkins. We're family now. Call me Mom." She reached her hand out to him, and he looked down at it in astonishment for a moment before taking it in his own. "Thank you. Truly. For making my daughter so happy. I know you'll do right by her and my granddaughter here."

"Yes ma'am. I intend to do just that and so much more." He gave Gwen's hand a little squeeze then looked down into his wife's beautiful tear-streaked face and kissed her lovingly.

Yes, indeed. He was going to love his family with all his heart and cherish every moment life would allow, for Buck Jenkins knew exactly how short it could really be.

THE END

SNEAK PEEK AT BOOK 5

CHAPTER 1- ABUNDANCE LEGACY

Savannah Grace Kinsen huffed, wiping the unwanted tears that streamed down her face as she pulled her luggage—two oversized duffle bags, really—down the sidewalk. She hated that she was crying, hated that she'd given Siddharth Bhushan three years of her life that she could never get back. For him to end it all for some dumb blonde super model skank was mortifying.

As if Savannah hadn't absolutely worked her ass off the past two weeks, only to come home to the apartment they shared together and be literally kicked out, all her stuff forcibly packed and probably a mess of tangled and crushed items, into the two big suitcases she was now lugging down Texas Avenue towards the bus stop. It had been utterly humiliating to say the least.

When she'd opened the door—wishing only for an Alka-Seltzer and her bed—she'd been taken aback to see Sidd standing there, arms defiantly crossed over his chest, with a stunning blonde she recognized from commercials behind him giving her a Cheshire cat grin. Savannah had literally balked as her eyes lowered to see her two red suitcases stuffed to the max.

"Sidd, what the—?" Savannah started, only to be cut off by him.

"We're through, Savannah."

Since when? Savannah wanted to ask but before she could, Ms. Bimbo spoke. "Sidd, doesn't want you anymore. You're mousy...and boring," she'd harrumphed and added for good measure. Savannah had just gulped, unable to hide her shock. If he'd been unhappy at all, he'd not let on to it.

"O...kay...well, let me just—"

"All your stuff's in there," Sidd interrupted again. "Just give me the ring and the key."

As if that's all there was to the breakup of a three-year relationship; simply giving him the ring he'd proposed to her with back and the key to the apartment they'd rented together. Where did her heart fit in? Would she get all the pieces of it back that he'd taken in the course of thirty point seven seconds?

Savannah had only nodded, for what else could she do, and began pulling the sparkling one-karat diamond from her finger and handed it over. She hadn't been able to keep her hands from shaking as she fumbled with her keyring, trying to pull the key off of it. When she finally removed it, she handed it over as well then began pulling her bags over the lip of the door saddle, struggling with the one that probably had all her books in it—she did have a lot of those. Sidd shoved and finally the bag came over the sill. Before she could say anything else, the door was slammed in her face, and she was alone in the hallway of her apartment complex, looking around to see if anyone had heard the embarrassing encounter.

All had been silent, for it was still early on a Friday morning. Begrudgingly, Savannah had rolled her bags down the corridor, hopped back on the elevator, and thought about where she was going to go and what she was going to do. Sleep had been all she'd wanted and heartbreak had been what she'd been given.

Now, she meandered towards the bus stop with only bags to show for six years of living in Houston. She guessed she should probably go home, to Abundance. After all, it'd been a while since she'd been home to see her folks and siblings. She would go to Dallie's first. She couldn't call her mom and dad, for if she did, her dad was going to show up in Houston and beat the absolute tar out of Sidd Bhushan, she knew.

Jack Kinsen had never cared for the cocky Indian cardiologist that Savannah had brought home a few Christmases ago—not that he'd ever cared for either of the two men she'd brought home—for her dad had the demeanor of a drill sergeant when it came to his daughters. He and her mother had always been super protective of their girls and super suspicious of outsiders. Savannah knew why now, and thank goodness hadn't dated much in the span of her thirty-one years to have to deal with the intolerance of her father, but she knew beyond the shadow of a doubt, he was gonna kill Sid when he found out how she'd been treated today.

So, Dallie's it was, until Vanna was ready to face her dad and enlighten him on what had happened. She needed a break from work anyway. The last two weeks had been ridiculous, and she'd spent the better part of her days engrossed in her project for a new satellite NASA was testing out. Many nights she'd not even gone home or she'd slept on her office couch a few hours before once again hitting the computer and test facilities and going back to the drawing board. Her work was demanding and highly stressful, but as much as she loved it, a break was completely overdue. She couldn't even remember the last time she'd taken a vacation.

Savannah pulled her bags to a stop at the crosswalk, pulled out her phone, and called up her boss, Fred Yeargin. She told him she was going on leave, and he could email her the paperwork later because she had a family emergency. She didn't feel like it was much of a lie. After all, her nerves were shot and she felt sick to her stomach.

He didn't have much to say about her impromptu sabbatical as she'd been the forerunner, overseer, and head developer of their latest project and had seen it through to the end without much sleep and an overabundance of caffeine.

She replaced her phone, grabbed her luggage, and was strolling back down the sidewalk, her eyes burning as she was passing the window of an antique toy store. A gorgeous white wooden rocking horse stared back at her from inside, and she couldn't help but smile, for she knew that her niece, Lillian, would absolutely love it.

But where the hell am I gonna put it? she thought, even as she proceeded through the automatic door.

As she approached it, she was thinking that she might have it shipped and moved her bags in, setting them to the side. She reached out to touch the handle on the side of the weathered, wooden horse, seeking the white price tag tied to it when a hand dropped down on top of hers. She gasped, immediately looking up into a ruggedly handsome face shaded by a tan cowboy hat.

"Pardon me, ma'am, but I believe I saw it first," said a deep voice with a thick southern accent.

"Like hell," Savannah countered. She'd been had by enough men for one day; she wouldn't be overthrown by this one too—no matter how buff he was in his fitted white t-shirt and equally as skin tight Wrangler jeans.

The man laughed heartily and gave her a big smile. Of course he had to be drop dead gorgeous with straight white teeth and dimples that his scruffy blonde beard didn't cover. The hair beneath his hat was sandy blonde as well, thick and wavy, and his skin was golden tan; he looked like he could've been a surfer from California. What the hell did he want with an antique rocking horse?

"Sorry, sweetheart. It's mine." Eyes the color of rich amber burned into hers.

"First off, don't *call* me sweetheart," Savannah scoffed. "And second, have you bought it?"

"Well no, not yet, but—"

"But nothing! If you haven't bought it yet then it's not yours...technically."

"*Technically* not. But I intend to buy it." He crooked his head at her and gave her the once over, that damn smug-ass grin of his tugging at the corner of his sexy as Hell mouth. "Unless, of course, you can convince me why I should let you have it."

Let me have it? Boy, this guy was unbelievable.

"I don't have to convince you to do *anything*. I saw it first and I'm buying it. It's that simple."

"Well, I could say the very same thing, darlin'. As it were, *I* saw it first."

Savannah wasn't going to sit there and argue property rights with this ignorant cowpoke. He didn't own the rocking horse and therefore had no stand where it was concerned.

She tilted her chin up higher, not caring that her mascara was probably streaking her red, tear-stained cheeks, that her makeup had been applied almost twenty-four hours prior or that her clothes were disheveled and her thick, wavy hair was unruly. He wasn't going to get the best of her. Not today!

"Ladies first," she retorted.

"I'm a hard supporter of women's rights, so since y'all want equality and all, I'm gonna contend that you're being sexist with that statement- *I* saw it first."

Savannah's mouth just dropped. She saw red and the next thing that came out of her mouth shocked even her. "You're *fucking* kidding me, right?"

His brows shot up to the brim of his hat; he was taken aback.

"Listen buddy, I don't know who the hell you are, but this rocking horse is mine. You got me? *Mine!* I'm buying it, right here and right now, and I *dare* you to try and stop me." With that, she jerked the rocking horse up, despite that it was far heavier than it had originally looked. "I've *had* it with men like you today." She struggled as she tried to move the rocking horse away from the cowboy's grasp, looking up at him to drive her point home. His hands were up then, palms out and he was shaking his head, as if he didn't intend to physically fight with her over the horse. "Now, are we going to have a problem? Or do you yield?" She huffed as she set the heavy-ass rocking horse down and planted her hands on her hips.

"Why, yes ma'am. You've done gone and degraded my manhood, so what other choice do I have *but* to yield?" he smarted back, crossed his arms over his broad chest, and glowered at her. "You should be glad you're not a man."

"If you were a woman I would pull your lovely golden locks out one by one," she countered.

Whoa, Savannah, she scolded herself. Where had this angry, haughty side of her come from? *Getting humiliatingly dumped by my piece of shit ex-fiancé and running on little to no sleep for weeks now,* she reminded herself. She held her ground...waiting for him to lunge at her, fight her, protest in some way. If he got physical, although he didn't seemed inclined to do so, she was ready. She knew karate and tai chi, she'd been trained from childhood and could fight him if it came right down to it, despite that he looked to be as big as her father—six feet two inches tall and over two hundred fifty pounds; all broad and big shouldered like he was. On second thought, fighting him was the last thing she wanted to do...*Dammit!* Why did she had to meet this stud today of all days? He simply oozed sex appeal.

He just stared her down for a few more minutes, his gorgeous eyes moving over her once again before he scoffed and gave her that dimple-shining grin. "Damn, lady, you drive a hard bargain. How's about I offer you double what it's worth?"

Did this guy ever give up?

"I believe I've made my intentions clear, sir. I won't be making a deal with you- not now or ever." Savannah picked up the rocking horse and started lugging it forward toward the front of the store.

"Yeah, well, go figure, you ballbuster."

Savannah stopped, dropped the horse and turned to face him, cutting her eyes at him. "You're nothing but a hothead."

"And you're a sassy little minx who needs a good bare-assed spankin' in the worst way," he retorted.

Savannah gasped, completely taken aback, but before she could retort, he was winking, turning, and walking out of the store.

**

ABUNDANCE LEGACY, book 5, the finale in the Abundance series will release in February 2020.

AFTERWORD

I hope you've enjoyed Buck and Vivian's endearing story—and well, Rick and Carmella's, Scottie and Ginger's too.

If so, please be sure to leave a review. Reviews allows the book to be seen by other readers, so that they, too, can enjoy this series just like you have.

Thank you so much!

—Shanna

ACKNOWLEDGMENTS

To my husband—thank you for accepting me just as I am. You've embraced the long nights, being a sounding board, grocery shopping, cooking, and household chores that I've (occasionally) slacked on since being published ;-). You're my rock and my hero. I love with my whole heart.

To my Abundance fans, readers, fellow indie authors, bloggers, reviewers, family and friends—I just want to thank you for all your support, encouragement, and love for my characters.

Without **you**, this adventure wouldn't be possible.

ABOUT SHANNA SWENSON

Shanna Swenson is a cardiac sonographer by day and a weaver of various tales by night.

She's been an avid reader all her life and began writing at the age of fourteen. She finally published her first novel, *Abundance*, after it sat patiently on her laptop for well over fifteen years and hopes to have her debut series complete come Februrary 2020.

Shanna fits her zodiac sign of Cancer to a capital C and enjoys life's simplest things.

When Shanna's not supporting her fellow indies with her face buried in a book or writing her next novel/novella, she enjoys action and horror movies, pro football, hiking, Yoga, and traveling with her own "knight in shining armor".

You can find her on the following social media platforms.

Her website is www.shannaswenson.com

facebook.com/shannaswen

twitter.com/shanna_swenson

instagram.com/shannaswen_author

goodreads.com/Shannaswen

amazon.com/author/shannaswenson

pinterest.com/shannaswen

bookbub.com/profile/shanna-swenson